a different kind
of normal

Books by Cathy Lamb

Julia's Chocolates

The Last Time I Was Me

Henry's Sisters

Such a Pretty Face

The First Day of the Rest of My Life

A Different Kind of Normal

Published by Kensington Publishing Corporation

a different kind
of normal

CATHY LAMB

KENSINGTON BOOKS
www.kensingtonbooks.com

KENSINGTON BOOKS are published by

Kensington Publishing Corp.
119 West 40th Street
New York, NY 10018

All Kensington titles, imprints, and distributed lines are available at special quantity discounts for bulk purchases for sales promotion, premiums, fund-raising, educational, or institutional use.

Special book excerpts or customized printings can also be created to fit specific needs. For details, write or phone the office of the Kensington Special Sales Manager: Kensington Publishing Corp., 119 West 40th Street, New York, NY 10018. Attn. Special Sales Department. Phone: 1-800-221-2647.
Kensington and the K logo Reg. U.S. Pat. & TM Off.

ISBN-13: 978-0-7582-5939-4
ISBN-10: 0-7582-5939-5

First Kensington Trade Paperback Printing: August 2012
10 9 8 7 6 5 4 3 2

Printed in the United States of America

For Travis,

with love

1

My mother told me all about the witches in our family. She heard the stories from her mother, who heard them from her mother, and so on, all the way back to the mid-1800s, in London, where the twins, Henrietta and Elizabeth, started The Curse.

Henrietta and Elizabeth were inseparable from the time they reached across their mother's bosom for the other's hand. Their mother was considered to be the best witch of them all, whatever that silly statement means, and she taught the twins. They practiced their spells in the forest behind the fountains and statues on the manicured estate their mother's wealthy, titled family owned.

The twins eventually, reluctantly, agreed to marry wealthy, titled men. They did not feel it necessary to tell their husbands of a few wild years, sins committed and sins omitted, handsome men here and there, and their mother agreed, she of a colorful past herself. "It's our secret, dears," she told her daughters, a pinky tilted up as she drank her tea. "Husbands don't need to know much."

The twins' elegant estates, with lands adjacent to each other, soon held all the herbs they needed for their spells, plus Canterbury bells, hollyhocks, lilies, irises, sweet peas, cosmos, red poppies, peonies, and rows of roses, which is what their mother and grandmother grew, too.

Together Henrietta and Elizabeth had eight children who would later prove to be both saints and raucous sinners, especially the girls, as is often the case in witch families, or so I'm told.

Sadly, though, in their late thirties the twins' friendship fell apart because of a fight over, of all things, a tea set. At least that's what *started* it. Henrietta bought the delicate white teacups, pitcher, and creamer with the pink flowers, knowing Elizabeth loved it, *coveted* it, but Henrietta could not resist. They were elegant, from India, hand painted, and the flowers looked as if they could talk if let loose for but a moment. There was only that one set and when Elizabeth found out what Henrietta had done, so sneakily, she was overcome with anger.

Other rigid resentments and prickly problems, built over decades of twinship started to explode, as if the teapot had cracked in half and exposed the fine fissures between the two women. They stopped speaking to each other entirely, despite their children's pleas that they reconcile, until one pleasant Sunday in front of the church.

It wasn't hot that morning, which was fortunate, as the heat could spread such rancid diseases, like scarlet fever and tuberculosis, and it wasn't cold, which could cause a plain cough to become pneumonia in no time. There was a bit of wind, which carried off the natural odors of raw sewage, animals, rot, refuge, defecation, moldy vegetables, decaying meat, dead bodies, vagrant children, and people who had rarely bathed in their lives.

It was a perfect sunny day with no warning of the generational damage to come.

Henrietta and Elizabeth wore their whalebone corsets, white petticoats, beribboned hats, and elaborate, heavy dresses. They reached out white gloved hands to their proper husbands as they debarked from their horse-drawn carriages. Both couples and well-polished children were ready to show off their devoutness to the Lord, though church bored Henrietta and Elizabeth into an almost comatose state, the vicar droning on and on endlessly until both women thought they were perched on a shelf in hell.

The twins caught a glimpse of each other on the cobblestone path, each with a hand in the crook of their husbands' elbows. Their husbands had been chosen for their kindness, business success, and knuckleheadedness, which would allow the twins to carry on their usual witchery and spells with no interference from an observant male.

Henrietta thought Elizabeth made a face at her. Elizabeth thought Henrietta was haughty and, as if they'd been swept up by the devil's tail and smashed together, it all began.

They left the clueless, cultured husbands, locked elbows with each other to pretend friendship and deflect attention, and a quiet, but intense fight broke out, their fake smiles plastered hard on their furious faces.

Accusations were made about "stealing my precious tea set, I told you I wanted it . . ." But then things escalated viciously, as fights between sisters often will. "You're always flirting with men like a peacock . . . you are way too prideful about your children . . . why you should get Maria married off immediately before she sleeps with another stable lad . . . what about your son, Michael? Is there any girl he hasn't tumbled through the hay with? Your gowns are too low cut . . . you talk incessantly . . . always competing with me . . . you think your herb garden is better than mine, it never has been . . . you have to be joking, my herbs are always better than yours, stronger, that's why we use them in the spells all the time. . . ."

And then, the source of true bitterness and jealousy, "I should have been married to Oliver, not you, he was interested in me before you wore your purple dress with almost your entire bosom hanging out. . . . My bosom was not out. . . . Oliver would never have been interested in you with that nose. . . . My nose? Dear, a big nose can be hidden with powder, but big buttocks, horse buttocks, balls and tarnation, that's not hideable, is it?"

Oh dear.

Henrietta started to mutter and Elizabeth, knowing a spell was coming forth, slapped a hand over Henrietta's mouth. Henrietta grabbed Elizabeth's flowered hat and Elizabeth clutched a handful of Henrietta's heavy skirt. Soon they toppled to the ground, rolling, whispered curses tossed through the air, uncaring about the lace petticoats flying up, the tearing silks and satins. They were quiet in their fury, because they had no desire to advertise their witchliness. Neither wanted to be burned alive at the stake or flogged or drowned or have their clitorises checked for being too pointy, one irrefutable indication of a true witch.

And they didn't want it for the other, either, despite the delicate tea set with the pink painted flowers and their mutual love for Oliver.

The deadly dull vicar sprinted out of the church, black cassock flying. He was young and naïve, and hadn't a clue how to handle two women locked in a combative fight whispering to each other. My heavens, and praise the Lord, this would not do! Especially on the Lord's Day! He had an important sermon planned, too, about how women must submit to their husbands! Submit to your master!

Their husbands, chatting the pompous chat of self-satisfied, privileged men nearby, rushed over, shock pounding all the way around their lace collars and past their white underthings. What had happened to their demure, lovely wives? What on earth were they doing? This was church, and yes, it was tiresome to be told you were going straight to hell to burn as a sinner, but still! No fighting on the front lawn, surely they knew that?

Their children watched, surprised but highly amused, especially the teenage girls, who had already joyfully learned how to quietly rebel and not get caught. Look at their fighting mothers! Pulling hair and slapping, their dresses flipped over their knees!

The witches' last, frantic roll together marked the beginning of decades of tragedy that affected someone in each generation of one of the witch's families. In the ensuing struggle one witch hissed out a spiraling curse, and before the other witch could deflect it by shooting off a defensive spell, the husbands and vicar were forcibly separating them, their feet kicking, skirts whipped up.

"What has gotten into you, Elizabeth?" Philip Compton loved his family, but he was brought up around royalty and pompous, unearned titles, and this behavior was unseemly, improper! What was his wife doing on top of her twin sister? This was extraordinary!

"For God's sake, Henrietta!" Oliver Platts was handsome, but dense like cheese, and he could hardly believe what he was seeing! He was running for political office, too. Didn't Henrietta know they had appearances to keep up?

"Ladies, let's take a moment to pray," the vicar said, shaking, the women's perky hats long gone, their thick, auburn hair curling wildly over heaving bosoms. He felt himself growing hot at the sight of the bosoms, and the hair, and the red cheeks! Oh, shame to him! Those bosoms were enough to make him forget his vows and certainly his chastity. He dropped his head, his pale white hands clasped together tight. Oh, deliver us, Lord! Save us from the devil and devilish thoughts about bosoms! "Lord, we ask for your forgiveness today..." His voice trembled as bosoms frolicked through his prayer. "We are all sinners, unworthy of you...."

Henrietta and Elizabeth were having none of that droning, praying stuff. As everyone else bent their heads, they leaped at each other again with guttural cries, but their husbands, on alert, grabbed them midflight and shoved them back into their carriages, dresses askew, gloves gone.

In bed that night, the husbands, to their immense relief, had their docile, fawning wives back again. The witches pretended they had been overtaken by the stifling heat; perhaps it was the tomatoes they had both eaten the day before? Maybe the porridge had been poisoned? Could the devil had crawled inside of them? It took a few well-placed caresses, some dewy eyes, long kisses, a lifting of the nightgown, and soon their husbands, who saw only what they wished to see, rolled off to their side of the bed, mollified.

But in the pitch, thick blackness of the night, one witch shook with shame and guilt, and the other shook in complete and absolute terror. Both clutched the necklaces they always wore, the same necklaces they had given to their daughters. There were three charms: a cross, a heart, and a star. A cross for Jesus, a heart for family, and a star to represent the power of witchcraft.

Henrietta and Elizabeth were never friends again. How could they be with spells like that flying around recklessly? But they missed each other desperately and cried harsh, lonely tears, in private, often.

The Curse began immediately, afflicting the baby the witch didn't even know she was pregnant with yet. He was born with only one arm. Henrietta cried over him, cursing her twin.

Elizabeth cried, too. She had never meant for the spell to be so strong, so insidious, and within ten years, her guilt killed her. She toppled over in her summer garden, right between the thyme and mint.

Her sister witch cried for a year. Henrietta became an attentive second mother to Elizabeth's children. When she died at seventy-six years old, right before her eyes went blank, she sat straight up in bed, stared into a corner, her wrinkled face transformed with an illuminating smile. She held up a hand, as if she was reaching out to hold another's, and said, "Elizabeth, I have missed you, sister. . . ."

At least, that's the story I was told by my mother.

Her mother told her.

Her mother told her, and so on, who heard it from the daughter of one of the witches, who stood close by and listened with increasing fright as her mother and her mother's twin sister spewed out intricate, menacing spells. The daughter recognized the final spell and clasped a hand over her mouth. The other witch's daughter did the same.

Their mothers had taught them all they needed to know.

And that spell, well, that one was a doozer. On that pleasant Sunday morning, in London, in front of a church and a vicar who was fascinated by heaving bosoms, the damage was done. In each generation, The Curse reappears.

But I don't believe in witches, or curses, or spells.

No, I don't.

I really don't.

It's a legend. A story. A colorful history to laugh and chuckle about in our family line.

It is a fanciful tale. I am sure of it.

I am, at least, 90 percent sure.

I think.

2

He was born with a big head.

Not a slightly larger head than normal, but a huge head, as if another head had been added on and then shrunk down to about half the size, without the eyes/nose/mouth features, before getting stuck on the first head. One eye was higher than the other.

Most would call it a deformity, a mistake, a handicap. In the future, they would pity him, or be disgusted, uncomfortable, mean. Oh, how mean they would be.

When my baby nephew arrived from between my sister's shaking legs at the hospital, bluish in color, he wasn't breathing. His head seemed to be pulsing, his veins engorged, the fontanel swollen.

I thought he was dead. I thought he'd been dead a long time and I stifled a ragged, anguished cry.

My own mother, the baby's nana, America's most famous soap opera actress, a woman who is ambitious, focused, and rational, cried out, "Oh my God, it's The Curse again."

"No it's not—" I grabbed her arm. "Don't even say that!"

"It is, Jaden, it is." She sank against the wall, her slender legs giving out, her pink lace, couture dress, designed especially for her by Ruben, a new designer, wrinkled as she slid. "It's The Curse."

"Move, people, move!" one doctor, in blue scrubs, shouted

over my sister's piercing screams. "We've got seconds, make 'em count. *Move!*"

Immediately, the doctors—already sweating the difficult labor and delivery, berating my sister for not getting any prenatal care, for this should not have happened, this birth should not have happened, this bigheaded baby should not have happened—went to work.

"Shit," I heard one of the frantic doctors whisper. "Aw, shit."

"Baby's not breathing!" another doctor shouted.

"Mother's bleeding . . . oh my God, mother's *hemorrhaging!*"

The bluish, throbbing baby and my sister were surrounded, and I was pushed aside, but those words sent panic skittering through my body, tears blurring my vision.

Brooke collapsed back on the bed, all blood draining from her face, as she screeched one more time, her green eyes rolling back in her head, neck arched, as if it were her last breath. Her auburn hair, the same color as mine, the same as my mother's, was glued to her head from sweat.

The doctors and nurses, a wall of blue-scrubbed people, continued barking orders and shouting, some fighting to save my sister's life, the blood gushing out, spilling from the gurney to the floor, and others fighting to save the baby's life.

My mother was half-lying on the floor, as white as her daughter. She put her trembling hands up in the air, her perfectly polished red nails twitching as she whispered a chant, something to do with freeing the living spirits, jasmine, and love force, and when she was done she uttered, finally, a prayer, "Dear God, get in here right this minute and help us, damn it."

I tried to get to my sister, to hold her seizing body, to bring life back to the fading green eyes that seemed to be only half with us, but they wouldn't let me near her.

"Get out, get out!" one nurse yelled at me, pushing me toward the door as I fought.

"I want to be with my sister! Let me stay with Brooke!"

Oh no, that could not happen. No staying. "We're taking care of them! Go, go!"

"Move the family out of the way, *out of the way!*"

The baby, his head swollen, was placed in an Isolette in seconds as the doctors whipped him out of the room and raced into the corridor.

I tried to run after the baby, my mother wobbling behind me on her heels in shock, but two nurses stopped us at the swinging white doors of the ICU, grabbing our arms, holding us close, our hands outstretched toward the baby as we cried, we pleaded. They were gentle, they were firm, both men strong and immovable. We could not go. They were sorry.

The doors slammed shut, locking, as that teeny-tiny body was rolled away into the sterility of a white corridor, more doctors rushing to meet him.

"Help Brooke," my mother gasped, pushing me with weak hands back into the hospital room, as she tumbled straight down. The nurses lunged to help my mother and no one noticed me this time as I raced back into my sister's room. There was blood all over. I didn't know someone could bleed that much and still live. She was covered in doctors and nurses, an oxygen mask over her face, cloths between her legs.

"Okay," one of the doctors panted. "We're moving mother, on three." Again, for the second time in less than two minutes, a family member was whipped out of the hospital room and rushed behind those swinging, locking white doors, where my mother and I couldn't go.

We couldn't go there.

Couldn't go with my sister, couldn't go with my brand-new nephew.

Why? Because they were dying. One wasn't breathing, one was bleeding out.

A "Code This" and "Code That" were shouted over the intercom, people in blue scrubs and white jackets sprinting past me. I gathered my semi-hysterical mother up and we clutched each other on the floor, our tears a river.

My mother and I did not sleep for two full days. My brother, Caden, flew in from college. He is six foot six inches tall and has shoulders the breadth of a semitruck. As soon as he saw us, he burst into hiccupping tears, his black ponytail swaying as he hugged us close.

My mother and I traversed from the tiny crib where the baby with the big head was hooked up to all kinds of pumps and tubes, to my sister who was, initially, a ghastly white color, and not moving.

"The baby might not make it," Dr. Rebecca Black told us the first night. "He wasn't breathing at birth...."

"There's a chance your daughter won't make it," Dr. Sanjay Patel said. "She lost too much blood, we transfused her...."

"Traumatic birth... head swollen... eye placement issues..." Dr. Black said.

"There are complications because of the drugs in your daughter's body, we're having trouble getting the bleeding to stop, she is having seizures, problems breathing...." Dr. Patel said.

"The baby's heart seems to be struggling, too... distress... gasping...."

"Your daughter's blood pressure is dangerously low... we can't get it back up...."

"The baby has..." Dr. Black went off on her medical-ese, the language normal people don't understand, especially in a crisis.

"That's enough of that," my brother said, his voice sharp as he held up a hand. "We aren't doctors. Explain it in English."

The doctor explained. The baby was born with a big head. If he survived, and that was doubtful due to his critical condition at birth and the drugs, the size of his head would stay as it was. He would need a permanent shunt in his head leading to his heart because of an excessive amount of cerebrospinal fluid.

"Oh my God," my mother groaned, her face white and drained. "I told you it was The Curse. It came right down the family line...."

"It's not The Curse, unless The Curse is Brooke." My chest was a wall of thudding pain. I touched the cross, heart, and star necklace given to me by my mother, the same one she and Brooke wore.

"The curse?" Dr. Black asked, eyebrows raised.

"Never mind," I said.

She seemed baffled, but then composed herself. "The baby has the same drugs in his body as in Brooke's. Cocaine, pain-killers, alcohol, nicotine . . ."

"Why did she do this?" I said, grieving for the baby already. "Why?"

Why had been the question for years. The pain my sister had caused our family with her addictions had been endless.

And, for the baby, a baby I named Tate, the pain was only beginning.

Seventeen Years Later

He had been beaten up.

Again.

Tate's face was red, bruised on the jaw and along his blue eye on the left, cut on the eyebrow, blood was under his nose, and his auburn hair was a mess.

He had a basketball under his arm and a backpack over his shoulder.

I felt my heart squeeze and expand, then squeeze again, the pain of seeing my son beaten up stabbing me for the thousandth time. I wanted to kick the kids that did this to him. I whacked the wooden spoon on the edge of the pan where I was making an orange sauce with marmalade and chives for our chicken dinners.

"Chill out, Boss Mom. Hey, Nana Bird," Tate said, smiling, waving.

He dropped his backpack on the wood table my blue-eyed, formerly redheaded, curly-haired Grandma Violet had used for decades to heal people with her herbs and spices and "Silent Spells," as she called them.

"I don't think I'll need stitches this time, which is too bad 'cause I was gonna do it myself. You know, Tate, The Tough Guy Hero, sews himself up."

My mother put her arm around me, squeezing my shoulder, warning me not to fly into a rage. It never helped Tate to see my temper triggering after something like this happened, it only made things worse.

"I know the slinkiest of solutions to this problem, Tate," she drawled, her tone hiding her own anguish. "Have a shot of tequila. Tip your head back and I'll pour it down your throat."

"Mother!" I reprimanded, but it was halfhearted, my whole body throbbing with anger. Wind whipped up against the bay windows of my yellow kitchen nook, scooting around my old white house as if it owned the place.

"Yes, darling? Tequila soothes the nerves."

"Good idea, Nana Bird," Tate said. He calls my mother Nana Bird because when he was little he loved birds and he loved his Nana. He tried to smile, but it hurt his mouth. "Nothing better to top off a fight than a shot of tequila."

I have a *terrible* temper when it comes to Tate. Tate has named my temper Witch Mavis.

My mother squeezed my arm again, then shook her bob of hair and drawled, "Did you beat any of them up?"

"Yep." Tate was six feet three inches tall and muscled because of daily workouts with weights. That he won wasn't surprising. He'd won before, many times.

"Spectacular! Was there a lot of blood?" She wiggled her fingers excitedly.

"Yep."

"What about bruising, cuts, things that will scar?" She grinned, leaning forward, all those expensive pearly whites showing.

"I think I got 'em, Nana Bird." He grinned. Tate had perfect teeth, too.

"Did you knock any to the ground, flat on their backs? Boom, smash, clunk?" She clapped her hands, full of glee. My stylish mother has a love of violence when it comes to her grandson.

"Sent 'em flying."

"That's my boy." She chortled, wiggling her shoulders. "God gave you fists. Use them."

"I did." He put his scraped fists up in victory.

"Mark my words, if he only wanted you to use your hands for eating, he would have had your left hand formed into a fork and your right hand formed into a spoon."

"That would look odd, but culinary."

"Not if we all had a fork and spoon for hands, Tate, instead of fingers," my mother said. "Fist the fists and let 'em fly when people want to pound your soul."

"Got it." He smashed his fists together. "Fist thumping equals pounding of soul crushers."

"Right. You have it! I love your violent streak! It's so gleeful, so animalistic!"

She hugged him tight, then I hugged him, briefly pondering how gleeful and animalistic went together, my jaw tight.

"Boss Mom, I can tell that you're all mad because you're quivering, but I'm okay, okay? I know you want to blow up and go to these kids' front doors and haul them out by the hair, remember you did that one time, or scare the heck out of them or their parents or threaten to call in butt-devouring attorneys, but don't."

Tate calls me Boss Mom because I am the boss.

"I'm okay. I can fight on my own." His eyes pleaded with me to stay out of it.

"I want to know who did this—" I glared at him, then pointed the wooden spoon at him. "Tell me."

"I'm not telling you, and hello to Witch Mavis. You'll make me look like a baby. I can't take care of myself so my mommy comes flying in to beat up the bullies."

"You can, but they need to suffer a consequence for this. They need to be suspended just as I've had other kids suspended who beat you up. They need to be shoved into a wood box and have the lid of that box nailed down on their heads until they can promise to shape up and—"

"Sort of like me in upcoming shows, Tate!" my mother interjected, her green eyes giving me the look that said *shut up.* "Next year I'm going to be locked in one of those ship containers by a stalker!"

"Cool, Nana Bird. But I'm not going to be able to watch it because it'll scare me." He pushed his hair back. There was blood in his hair, too. "Watching you screaming gives me nightmares."

"Remember when I'm screaming, I'm surrounded by lights and cameras and handsome men, darling."

My mother, Rowan Bruxelle, is the star on *Foster's Village.* Her conniving, husband-stealing, scheming character's name is Elsie Blackton. She and I have the same auburn hair, only mine is longer and wavy and hangs halfway down my back while hers is bobbed. I have a string of tiny crystals tied into my hair on the left side that Tate gave me for Christmas because, "They're pretty, like you, Boss Mom." She has ski-slope cheekbones, green eyes, and I have one eye that is blue, one that is green.

Tonight she was wearing a purple silky wraparound top, black velvet leggings, and four-inch red heels. I prefer jeans, some tough, stylin' boots, hippy-ish sorts of blouses, an assortment of bangle bracelets, and dangly earrings.

I'm Earth Momma with an explosive temper meets cowgirl.

She's firecracker meets perfume.

"Give me their names, Tate."

"No, Boss Mom. I'll get teased more if you get involved."

"No, they'll be stomped into silence. What are their names?"

"You gotta relax and flow with this more."

"I don't relax and I do not flow."

My mother linked an arm around my shoulder again and poked me. "Your mother, Tate, for once, is going to try to not be quite so uptight and controlling, and so very serious but not so very fun. She has a turbulent nature that causes all sorts of storms for the people around her. It's the Bruxelle in all of us, from our royal witch line, Tate, you know that."

"Turbulent," Tate said. "That's a word for it. The other word might be interfering." He raised his eyebrows when I wanted to interrupt. "And, Mom, I won the fight. There were three of them. The other guys' lips were split open and two are going to have black eyes the size of Oklahoma tomorrow. I won."

My mother clapped, her bangle bracelets clinking. "This pleases me immensely, Tate!"

He grinned and gave my mother and me a hug, and the anger, momentarily, swooshed out of me.

"Now, laaaddddiieess, I have a new project and I'm going to work on it in the experiment room. But here's a hint: It's not an experiment."

"What is it, rebel child, oh my rebel child, what wild ride will you take us on tonight?" my mother sang, her voice low and husky.

"Can't tell you. I will say that it has nothing to do with this reaction:

$$NaHCO_3 + KHC_4H_4O_6 \longrightarrow KNaC_4H_4O_6 + H_2O + CO_2 \text{."}$$

"What about computer stuff that I can't possibly understand because it's too dreary?" She examined her manicured nails.

Tate spun the basketball on his pointed finger. "It doesn't have anything to do with computer stuff like super-computers that will soon solve problems to three times ten to the fifteenth power. That's in one second. And it doesn't have anything to do with quantum electrodynamics or my interest that never goes away: brains and more brains."

"You are so smart it makes me nauseous," my mother said. "Shouldn't you be sneaking out to peek in girls' windows or writing cheesy love songs with your guitar?"

"Ha. No, I don't peek, Nana Bird. And when I sing I sound like a raccoon being swung by its tail. Hey, Boss Mom, the guys are all getting together to practice basketball and I—"

I tensed. "No."

"I want to practice with them, for fun, no contact, I promise—"

"No." We'd been through this before. Tate could not play contact sports because he had a shunt in his head and the shunt needed to stay in place for him to live.

"I'll be careful."

"No, Tate, don't start with me."

"Please—"

"Forget it."

"Mom! Come ooonnn!"

"No."

I heard him sigh in frustration, then he turned and pounded up the stairs, his big feet thudding.

Tate was obsessed with basketball, watching it on TV and shooting by himself for hours every day, *for years,* on our court with two full imaginary teams in his head.

"He's the best damn person on the planet, Jaden," my mother said. "He has a golden heart and a sensitive soul. He's a gift."

"Yep, he is." I turned and fiddled with my spice sets. I have sixty spices. A small obsession that has genetic roots. "He's asking about Brooke lately."

The atmosphere changed and became prickly and tight.

"And?"

"And I'm heading him off, somewhat."

"He'll want to know all there is to know. He'll want to meet her. That child has too many brains stuck in his head, and they're always working overtime. He has brain machines."

"I know."

We were quiet, the silence between us edgy with anxiety.

She took another sip of wine. "You should let the gift play basketball."

"Absolutely not."

"Think about it."

"No."

TATE'S AWESOME PIGSKIN BLOG

My name is Tate Bruxelle.

I am seventeen years old and I have a big head.

I was born this way.

What's it like living with a big head, with one eye higher than the other, with a face that looks normal on one half, but odd on the other?

Not damn easy. I have been made fun of my entire life. In preschool, the other kids wouldn't play with me, except for two twins named Anthony and Milton, Milt for short. Their mother is from Jamaica, she's a doctor, their dad's an attorney, they live across the street from me, and we have always been friends.

Some of the kids in my class cried when they saw my face, I remember that. I was three. One kid said I was ugly, another kid said I was scary, like a sea monster. A girl with braids told me I had a face like a person on one side, and a face like pigskin on the other. I remember going to sit in a corner and crying almost every day.

Now you know why I call this blog, "Tate's Awesome Pigskin Blog."

Some kids are jealous of others because they have cool hair, or cool clothes, or cool parents. When I was in preschool I was envious of people's heads.

One time I went home and told my mom, "I want a small head. Can you get me one?"

She told me that God had given me a big head because I had big brains.

That sounded good to me for a while, but when I couldn't dress up as a cowboy because none of the cowboy hats were big enough, and I couldn't fit a baseball batter's helmet over my head, the brain part didn't matter anymore.

I remember listening to one mother in first grade, with this white-blond hair and a ton of makeup. She looked at me with hate, that's what I'd call it: hate. Even as a kid I could see it. I've seen hate a lot on people's faces, and disgust. Anyhow, she said to my teacher, while pointing at me, "Oh my God. He isn't contagious, is he?"

I grew up with people asking my mom, when I was standing right next to her, "What's wrong with his head? What's wrong with him? Why does he look like that? Can you cut that big part of his head off?"

That has to be the stupidest question: Can you cut that part of his head off? Sure, ma'am, I'll do it right now, I have a chainsaw in my backpack, stand back or you'll get hit with brain guts!

I've also been tripped and stuffed in trash cans. Here's what being stuffed in a trash can says: "You're nothing. You're trash." Plus, it's humiliating when you're trying to get out and you can't because your legs are almost behind your head.

I would say I'm used to it, but it still bugs me when people are jerks. It's not as if I go home and cry like a baby, man, that'd be weird, but when you just want to go down to the store and buy a Coke, it's not as if it's pleasant to be screamed at and called a retard or boggle head or for someone to throw a beer bottle at you (happened three times) or a hot dog (twice), or water bottles (can't count, too many).

I've spent a lot of time by myself because kids are sometimes embarrassed to be seen with me, or they feel weird around me, or don't know what to say because I have a big head so they think I can't have a personality or feelings. I get it. I don't like it but I get it.

But I have a lot of cool stuff going on, too. I like experiments and mixing chemicals and I have only had a few minor explosions and fires in my experiment room. Go, Albert Einstein, my main man!!

I actually like math and I have studied Fermat's Last Theorem, quantum physics, and advanced statistics, which about explodes my synapses, but what I'm most interested in is studying the brain, like the choroid plexus, sagittal sinus, arachnoid space, the ventricles, memory, the effects of drugs on the brain, and neurosurgery.

Here's a photo of a solar flare from sunspot 486. Unbelievably cool.

Here's a photo of a brain.

And here's a photo of three jumbo hot dogs I ate in one sitting with smiles made from Dijon mustard.

My name is Tate Bruxelle.

I have a big head. I call him General Noggin. I'm not putting a photo in yet, but trust me on the big head part.

This is my first blog entry.

I might write another one.

"Look at this, Mom," Tate said to me the next night after a steak and blue cheese dinner, which he has named "Heaven and

Blue Cheese." "I have my own blog and it's on the Internet. What do you think? Cool, right?"

Tate's blog had this modern beige-and-brown-checked background with four pictures at the top: a pig, a basketball, some complicated math equation, and a brain. I knew why he called it the pigskin blog and tried not to choke on my hurt. "You set this up?"

"Yep. It's easy. Free blog. I've got a voice and it's out out out out in outer space, Internet style."

"I love it. I love how you talk about General Noggin." I ruffled his curls. "Are you going to write on your blog every day?"

"Every week. Or every day. Or twice a day. Or when there is a full moon, inexplicable weather patterns, two yolks in one egg, a new scientific discovery regarding the brain, a special report on eastern Indonesia, which I want to visit one day, or when politicians take up dueling." He shook his head. "That will never happen. They're all wimpy and they might mess their hairdos. I'll write when I'm not playing basketball, the sport I love most in the world and want to play so bad I would give up an arm to do it. . . ."

"Many variables then, to your blog writing." I ignored the part about basketball.

"Sure is, Boss Mom. I have to write when the mood hits. Between school, getting beat up, playing basketball *by myself*, my experiments, and more basketball *by myself*, it sure would be fun to play with other kids, I'll write Tate's Awesome Pigskin Blog."

"Send it to The Brux Fam." That's an abbreviation for my mother and Caden and his gang.

"Yeah. And I'll send it to Milt and Anthony, too. They're rad."

"You're a busy guy. Don't do any experiments that explode again."

He laughed. "I'll try not."

He'd had fires and explosions in his experiment room several times. The last one cracked a window.

"I'm not putting a picture of General Noggin on there yet. I want people to get to know me without it."

When Tate was three years old, one of his favorite TV shows had a general on it. The word *noggin* came from my brother, Caden, who said to Tate one day, "You've got a fine-lookin' noggin, my boy."

Hence, General Noggin.

"You know, Tate, this is a really smart idea, but don't give out our address, phone number . . ."

"I know, Mom." He wriggled his hands in the air and grinned. "I fear the same thing. When I post a photo of myself online, girls are going to go crazy! I'm going to have women pounding at the door, coming after me, ripping off my clothes, trying to get me to leave the country with them, so they can do with me what their passions tell them to do. It's a risk to all of us, but"—he pounded his chest, which was quite wide and muscled—"I'm ready to take on the dangerous risk of mobs of women trying to take my virginity captive in order to get my voice out into the world."

I laughed. "You're a courageous man, Tate, exceedingly courageous."

He clasped his hands and held them in the air, just as he'd seen his uncle Caden do when he was a professional wrestler. "Bring it on. My courage is second only to how sexy I am."

I hugged him. "I love you."

"I love you, too, Boss Mom. I'm hungry again. Can I have some leftover beer cheese soup?"

I mock-gasped. "We had Heaven and Blue Cheese a couple hours ago, then you had two slices of caramel pecan pie and a half gallon of milk."

"One bowl. With bread. Then I'll be full. Please, Boss Mom? And can you make Great-Grandma's Falling in Love Lasagna with the fresh parsley for tomorrow night? *Please!*"

"Okay, Tate. Come back down to the kitchen. Let's see if we can fill your hollow leg with food."

He hopped up and gave me a hug. "Yay, Boss Mom! Yay!"

I love herbs, spices, and flowers. Herbs and spices are in my blood; they are imbedded in my DNA.

As a tribute to our family line, going back to England, we all grow, including Caden: thyme, sage, rosemary, parsley, oregano, lavender, Canterbury bells, hollyhocks, lilies, irises, sweet peas, cosmos, red poppies, peonies, and rows and rows of roses.

My mother and Grandma Violet both taught me that herbs have been used for medicinal purposes for thousands of years. Some worked, some didn't. Some healed, some killed. Some were neutral, there was no effect. Hyssop was inhaled if one had a sore or scratchy throat. Large doses were terminally bad for one's health, so one had to watch it. Horehound could soothe and calm a bite from a nasty serpent or kill worms wiggling away inside you.

Mistletoe has been used in the past to help with heart disease and with "falling sickness," gout, and a variety of nervous disorders. It is also, unfortunately, poisonous.

Monk's hood, quite poisonous, was used to kill.

The witches in my family line have always grown herbs and used them in food, for healing sicknesses and giving someone a sickness, for love, revenge, protection, and to make people die they thought should go. They've also been used for spells and chants.

It was those spells and chants that got two of my ancestors, born Iris and Rosemary, into trouble.

Iris and Rosemary, the rebellious daughters of Henrietta and Elizabeth, who started The Curse in our family, were literally chased from their estates outside London by a torch-wielding mob that wanted to flog them after they cast a few drunken spells in a bar.

"As they thundered away on horses," Grandma Violet told me, peering through her glasses, blue eyes serious, "one of the witch's petticoats caught on fire. You've heard your mother and I use the term a 'petticoats on fire' problem? There's where it came from."

I remember gasping. "She was on fire?"

"A spark from a torch hit her. Her brother and her cousin's brother ripped the petticoat off and they all hopped back on those horses and galloped down the road through the night to the port. The brothers told them to change their names from Iris Platts and Rosemary Compton, to Faith and Grace Stephenson, before they scrambled onto the ship to America."

My grandma reached up to a shelf to reorganize her endless, clear bottles of herbs and spices. "They figured that if they were named Faith and Grace, not only could they hide their identities as reputed witches, they would appear more holy, more Christian, and less likely to be accused of being witches again. Faith and Grace never forgot who they were, despite the torch wielders, and they taught their daughters everything they knew about herbs and spices, spells and chants, like I teach you, Jaden."

I do not grow herbs for spells and chants, because that is ridiculous, though my otherwise sane and deeply intellectual mother and Grandma Violet taught me a multitude of them as a child and both said often, "Once a witch, always a witch."

I grow herbs in my greenhouse to make my meals yummy. I grow herbs and flowers because then I feel connected to my mother, Grandma Violet, and all our women ancestors who grew the same herbs and flowers that I do. I grow them because I love to nurture living things, especially since I deal with death so much.

I also grow herbs for therapy. I call it Herbal Therapy.

Here is the weird part of myself that I do try to keep somewhat secret: Several times a week I plug in white strands of Christmas lights and light a handful of scented candles that match the season, for example strawberry for summer, pumpkin spice for fall, vanilla for winter.

Next I stand at my butcher-block table and I cut a handful of herbs up and inhale their scent. I have to touch them, crunch them in my fingers, rub them between my palms. I have a spice rack in there, too, and I add sprinkles of this and that.

I use crystal plates owned by Grandma Violet and silver spoons owned by Faith, and I mix herbs and spices together. I have normal spices and less known spices including: Szechuan pepper, boldo, annatto, lemongrass, wasabai, galangal, peppermint leaves, black lime, and zedoary. I mix cinnamon with nutmeg and lemon mango tea. Parsley and oregano and mint leaves. Szechuan pepper and garlic. Bay leaves and dill.

The scents wrap me up soft and tight, soothing me. There are flowers blooming and growing all around, my favorite books and journals are on a nearby bookcase, and when I leave, after a cup of tea, I feel better. I call it Herbal Meditation.

We all have our odd quirks; herb and spice obsession is mine.

But there's been a problem the last weeks. When I start my chopping and blending and mixing, I smell death. Not the death that is usual with my work as a hospice nurse, either.

Death, as in someone I know is going to die. I do not smell death when I am cooking with herbs and spices in my kitchen; it's only here, in my greenhouse, during Herbal Therapy, that the scent winds around me.

No, this does not indicate that I am a witch. No, I don't believe in witches. No, I don't believe the women in my family were witches, even though my mother says that Faith and Grace brought their "talents" to America, and I have them.

This death-smelling "talent" is not witchly; it's an inexplicable *thing* about myself. That's it. I don't get it, I don't understand it. It's there.

What I do know is that the putrid, pungent scent scares me; it makes me feel threatened, as if a black plume of doom is swirling around me.

I have smelled death a few times before.

I smelled death before that terrible night.

I smelled it before Grandma Violet died.

I smelled it before Grandpa Pete died.

As I bent over my butcher-block table I was almost shaking in my cowboy boots.

Who? Who would it be this time? I didn't want my mother to die, or Caden, or Brooke, but I especially didn't want it to be the kids.

Not Damini, please, not the triplets.

Not Tate, I prayed. *Not Tate.*

Take me, not them.

Please.

Grandma Violet used her herbs, and maybe something else, to kill a man. My mother helped her. My father knew about it.

I'm sure she learned at least part of the concoction, if not most of it, from Faith and Grace, via her own mother and grandma.

My mother knows the recipe for it, and though I love recipes, I have refused to learn that one.

I didn't ask many questions that night.

I knew she loved him.

3

Gwendolyn Parker was packed and ready to go. Mrs. Parker is seventy-seven years old. She is suffering from brain cancer and I am her hospice nurse. She is getting somewhat confused and scattered, but mostly she is peaceful and gentle. The cancer has spread, an insidious octopus inside her head, the tentacles sticking here and there, but we have watched her medication carefully and she is in no pain.

I was glad to see her, and her family, because I love them all. Mrs. Parker is African American and looks fifteen years younger than she is. Her modern glass and wood-beamed home was designed by her son, an architect.

"I'm pleased you're here, Jaden, what a wonderful surprise," Mrs. Parker told me. She was sitting on her leather couch. Two of her sons were there and six grandchildren. She was wearing a fancy pink silk dress and her best jewelry. "Might as well dress up in my best clothes," she'd told me when she was put on hospice care. "Don't have much longer to wear them."

She looked lovely, cheerful. People expect relatives and friends on hospice to look deathly, but that isn't always the case. I've had patients on hospice for five months, and it's only in their last few days they start to go downhill.

"I've packed my suitcases and I'm ready to go." She smiled at me, serene and calm.

Her sons looked at me, worried.

"Did you pack a sweater?" I asked.

"Yes."

"Slacks?"

"Yes."

"A coat?"

"Yes. No. Taylor, go and get my coat and pack it in my brown suitcase."

Taylor, the oldest son and an ex-pro-football player, dutifully went and found her coat and tucked it into her suitcase.

"Then you're ready," I told Mrs. Parker.

She nodded at me. "I'm ready. I'm going on a trip soon."

"Where are you going?"

"I'm going away to somewhere nice. I think it's on a train. I think I'm going up some stairs. I'm not sure. I think this will be an exciting trip." She leaned toward me and whispered, though her family heard, "I don't think I'm coming back."

Packing up a suitcase is not unusual in hospice care. Talking about an upcoming trip is also not unusual. Through the fog of disease and effects of treatments, the patients often know they're going somewhere else.

"I'm ready to go," Mrs. Parker told me. "I've done everything here I wanted to do. The kids are fine. The grandkids are fine, too. The house is clean. I've done a lot of loving and living and I'm ready for my trip and I've said I love you I love you I love you."

"I think you'll have a magnificent time."

"Oh, I will, Jaden, I know I will." She stood up and gave me a hug, her expression somewhat vacant. "You all will go on a trip one day so you always have to be ready to go. You don't know when the train is coming, when you have to climb the stairs. The invitation can arrive at any time, so make sure your house is clean and make sure you tell your family and your friends and the butcher and electrician that you love, love, love them."

"I'll do that, Mrs. Parker."

She kissed my cheeks. "You were the perfect traveling companion while I was on this trip, Jaden."

I try not to cry much over my patients.

You can see why that quest is difficult.

I spent an hour in my greenhouse that night and cried tears over my white daisies and tomatoes for Gwendolyn while I ate red cinnamon Gummi Bears.

Somehow the Gummi Bears comfort me.

Maybe it's the tiny smiles on their faces.

I enjoy eating the smiles.

"I took off my leg and I hit him with it!"

"You took off your leg?" I laughed, thinking of Damini, Caden's daughter, my daring niece, taking off her prosthesis and whacking a boy. "How did he react to the leg beating?"

"He said, 'Ow, Damini, now I'm gonna get you!' " Damini threw up her arms, as if to say, *"Whatever."*

The morning sun cast gold prisms through my nook as Caden, my mother, Tate, and I laughed. Outside the maple leaves were turning to a burgundy wine color, butter yellow, and pumpkin orange. It was nature art, in my mind.

Caden pushed his black ponytail back and passed me the coffee. I passed my mother the cream. Tate passed Damini the syrup, then he and Caden cut up the triplets' chicken pancakes. Chicken pancakes are the size, sort of, of a chicken, hence their name. There's no chicken in them.

Caden's three-year-old triplets were dressed in Halloween costumes even though it is not yet Halloween. Caden buys Halloween outfits in bulk because that's how the kids insist on dressing. If they're not an imaginary character they throw fits. He is a single father to four. He prefers fewer fits.

This morning Heloise was a vampire. She growled. Hazel was dressed as a bunny. She hopped. Harvey was an orange with a pirate hat. He yelled, "I got a bottom!" I don't know why. I love them dearly.

"Do tell us more about hitting Brett with your leg, Fire Thrower," my mother said to Damini, swirling her orange juice, careful not to let it splatter on her white, straight-lined designer dress. "After you slugged him with your leg, what happened next?"

Damini sighed, ever the dramatist. "Brett's all mad and I can tell he wants to chase me and I said, 'Brett, I gotta get my leg on and then you can come after me,' and I hit him again so he got the message."

"You hit him with your leg again, a second time?" I asked.

"This above all: to thine own self be true," Tate intoned. "That's Shakespeare, and what he's really saying is, Damini, bare all your emotions, even if it involves a leg punch or two. It's fortunate for the Bruxelle family that we didn't give you a sword to swing."

"What did he say to the second hit?" I asked.

"He said, 'You have one minute, Damini, that's it, and I'm gonna crunch you to bits.'" Damini crossed her hands back and forth in front of her. "I real quick reattached my leg and yelled, 'Slowpoke,' because Brett is slower than me and I ran off and he couldn't catch me and pretty soon he's yelling, 'I can't catch you, Damini, wait up!'"

"That's my girl!" Caden said, pounding the table, rattling the coffee mugs. "Outrun the boys!"

My mother raised up her orange juice. "Cheers to you, Damini. There is nothing so scrumptious as outrunning a male. It makes their egos seethe and croak."

Damini picked up her milk glass, Caden picked up his tomato and carrot juice, I picked up my water glass, Tate picked up the salt and pepper shakers in both hands, the triplets held up their grape juice, and we all clinked them together. "Cheers to Damini!"

Tate said, "Another lightning experience."

"Here here!" Caden said.

That's what we call Damini's *interesting* experiences. "Lightning experiences."

Damini's Hindu name means "lightning." Think of Damini as lightning and you will get an accurate picture of her. Do not get in her way. Her skin is soft, resembling light brown chocolate, her black eyes enormous. She has a tiny nose, high and striking cheekbones, and full lips.

She pulls her long, thick black hair into a ponytail. She is not interested in makeup. She wears skirts above the knee. She told me once, "I love wearing skirts. Nana taught me all about the importance of sequins, ruffles, and satin on skirts. If someone doesn't like my fake leg that's not my problem, I'm just glad I *have* a leg."

She wears T-shirts that say, HIPPIES RULE and FLOWER POWER JUNKIE and VOTE FOR EINSTEIN. She also has a shirt that says HELL'S SNOT. On the back it says, HELL'S NOT GOOD FOR YOU.

When she's older, she is going to be model-gorgeous. She's tall and thin. She has the face of an angel so when she says edgy things, for example, "You're a pain in my keester, Tate," and, "shit-ola," and, "My friend's horse has the longest penis I've ever seen. Dina and I studied it for about an hour the other day. Men's whoo whoos are not the size of horses', are they, Aunt Jaden?" it's always a bit surprising.

Damini is missing her left leg below the knee because she was bitten by a snake in the garden at her orphanage in India. Her leg was not treated correctly, if at all. It became infected and they had to cut it off.

Caden and his wife, Marla, adopted her from the orphanage eight years ago when they were still married. They were moved to tears when they saw a TV show about the kids suffering in the orphanages there. After a long process Caden flew over and came back with Damini, who had been abandoned as a baby.

Damini is blunt about life in the orphanage in India, and each time she talks about it she seems to shrink in on herself, and then her gruff, broken cries make her hiccup. "I try not to think about it but I remember cribs lined up in rows," she'd told me. "I remember that snake biting me and my leg swelling up and turning purple and green and I was really, really sick and threw up a gusher, Aunt Jaden—all over myself. A doctor came and I heard him say, 'We have to cut it off,' and when I woke up half my leg was gone and the stump was red and swollen and there was a lot of pus and blood. I remember being sick for a long time and there was a whole bunch of other sick kids lined up beside me. Four kids died when I was there. My friend, Rajani, died in the middle of the night when I was asleep holding her hand in our crib." She sniffled and cried. "And Balaji did, too."

"It was dark all the time there, even in the day, no lights, and kids were always crying and screaming and we were hungry. I remember a nurse who always yelled at the kids and sometimes slapped them. I remember being super hot sometimes and super cold. I hated it. I hated it." Her face screwed up. "I hated it. And when I get older I'm going to go back and help at the orphanages."

Damini's orphanage was shut down for the abuses there, but my mother, my brother, and I all donate to a better-run orphanage in the same city.

Damini swiped a hand across her eyes. "And then one day Daddy walked in the door and I knew, Aunt Jaden, I knew that I was going home with him. I don't know how, but I did. I rolled off my bed and I hopped over to him on my one leg, I didn't have my other leg then, and twice I fell but I got up, and I hugged him and that was that."

"Caden said he knew you were his daughter right from the start."

"Yep. I went and grabbed the two things I owned. A doll and a red T-shirt and I was ready."

"We sure love you, Damini."

"I love you, too, Aunt Jaden. I love you so much that if you ever need a leg, I'll give you mine."

She said this in all seriousness. She said this knowing that she would then have no legs at all. You want touching? That's touching. "That's enormously generous." I wiped my eyes.

"Sure is." She nodded. "I wouldn't do that for anyone, you know." She looked suddenly ticked. "I especially wouldn't do it for Brett."

"Oh no! For sure not. Yuck."

"Yeah, yuck." She drummed her fingers together and grinned. Brett is her love.

I put my fork in the chicken pancakes and dropped two more on Tate's plate, one more on Damini's.

Heloise the vampire chose that moment to roar, claws up in the air, her fake teeth pointed and scary.

"OOOOOHHHH!" We all cowered in fear.

Hazel the bunny said, "Hop hop." That's all she would say all day. Dress like a bunny, talk like a bunny.

Harvey the orange said, "More pancakes please with da chicken. I eat. I eat. I eat."

"Why were you mad at Brett, though, Damini?" I asked. "Why did you hit him with your leg?"

Her shoulders curved inward. I thought I saw a blush.

The table became quite quiet.

"Darling," my mother said, her auburn bob swinging, "if you take your leg off and hit a boy with it, there must be a reason for it. Did he flip your skirt up? Take your beer? Pull your ponytail?"

Damini closed her mouth, those dark eyes suddenly finding interest in the raspberry syrup.

"Damini," Caden said, his muscles bulging under his T-shirt. He had lost little strength since his professional wrestling days. "You can't go around busting your leg over people without reason. You have to have a reason to slam someone. At least an itty-bitty reason."

"These violent delights have violent ends," Tate said, trying to be serious. "That's also Shakespeare. What he's saying is, What would happen if we all took off our legs and hit people with them? Chaos. Uproar. Craziness. Can't have that."

"I know, Tate!" Damini said, also serious. "You know I don't hit someone every day with my leg. Only now and then! Maybe Tuesday or Wednesdays. Friday last week."

Caden's brow furrowed. He does not like violence. "Damini, I have to know why you collided your leg with Brett's body."

Damini muttered.

"Pardon?" my mother said, her rings flashing. "What was that, dear one? A love triangle? A lover's tiff?"

"Mother! She does not have a lover. She's twelve!" I said.

"The lady doth protest too much, me thinks!" Tate stuffed yet another pancake in his mouth.

Damini muttered again.

"A woman never allows herself to be silenced," Caden said. "Chin up, shoulders back. Raise your voice to be heard."

Damini sighed, so put out, as only a twelve-year-old can be. I tried not to laugh.

"I don't want to speak."

"Here's Shakespeare again: Before we proceed any further, hear me speak," Tate said. "Especially since we're working with a madwoman like yourself, Damini."

"I'm not a madwoman and he made me mad!" Damini smacked her elbows on the table. "Mad mad!"

"Why?" Caden asked.

Damini had that stubborn expression on her face that we knew well. "He said no."

"No to what?" I asked.

"No to . . ." Her face scrunched up and I thought she was going to cry. "No to a . . ."

"Yes?" Caden prodded, leaning forward, his shoulders making Damini seem even tinier.

"No to a night on the town? No to a sneak-away weekend?" my mother said. "No to a love shack?"

"Mother!" I said. "There's no love shack here!"

"No to . . ." Tate said, sending me a quick glare. "Did Brett say no to trying out for the basketball team even when you want to play more than you want your own lungs? Someone said that I can't try out for basketball and I'm still mad about that."

I rolled my eyes and flicked another pancake Tate's way.

"No," Damini said, then burst into tears. "Brett said . . ." She sniffled. "He said . . ." She wiped her eyes. "He said he didn't want to *kiss* me!"

My brother leaned back in his chair, eye-poppingly surprised, my mother smothered a laugh, and Tate said, "No one wants to kiss me, either, Damini. Join the No Kiss Club."

"I said it nice, Daddy. I said, 'Brett, I want you to give me a kiss,' and he said, 'Yuck. No, Damini, I'm not gonna kiss a girl,' and I said, 'I'm not just a girl, I'm your best friend!' and he said, 'Yeah, you are, but you're a girl and I don't want to kiss a girl,' and that's when I had a temper tantrum and I took off my leg and I hit him. He's a brat!"

My brother's mouth opened and shut. Alas, he didn't even know what to say.

My mother said, "I think I'll try that same tactic next time a man refuses to kiss me. In fact, Damini, can I borrow your leg?"

Damini didn't realize my mother was kidding and she said, "Okay, Nana," then pushed back her chair to detach her leg. She handed her leg to my mother over the syrup.

"Thank you, dear," my mother said, taking the leg.

"You're welcome, Nana." She turned to her dad. "Am I in trouble now?"

"Let me get this straight," Caden said, clearing his throat. Damini looked forlorn next to him.

"Am I to understand that you took off your leg—"

"I left my liner and my sock on my stump. . . ."

"And you hit Brett because he wouldn't kiss you?"

Damini nodded, then whispered, "And I think he's cute. I have since first grade! That's a long time to wait for a kiss!"

My brother was gobsmacked. He could say nothing further. How do you handle a daughter who chases down another twelve-year-old for a kiss?

I winked at Damini. "That's one way to get his attention, sweetie."

"Yes, I think so, too, Aunt Jaden." She was proud of her ingenuity. "Maybe next time his answer will be yes, and I can keep my leg on."

"Maybe, Damini. You can live in hope," I said. "Here. Have more pancakes."

"Hope is another way of letting life take charge," my mother said. "Hope is a drunk feather. Hope is mist on a rainy day. *You* take charge, Damini. Take charge of this love affair—"

"Mom!" Caden gasped. "It's not a love affair."

"It's the hope of a kiss!" my mother said, eyes wide, as in, *Don't you get it?*

"I live in hope that I'll get a date for Winter Formal," Tate said, tossing a piece of pancake in the air and catching it with his mouth. "It's not looking good, not looking good at all. Maybe I can take your leg as my date, Damini. Does your leg know how to dance?"

Heloise the vampire growled again and we all cringed and said, "OHHHHHH!"

Hazel the bunny said, "Hop hop!"

Harvey said, "More food, please. I eat, I eat, I eat."

Damini giggled. "Okay, Tate. After Nana uses my leg you can dance with it. I want to dance with Brett."

My brother was holding his head, unable to utter a word. He had no idea what raising a daughter was going to involve.

"I *am* going to try to kiss him again, though," Damini said, fire in her eyes. "Why did he run away?"

"He's a boy, Damini. They run." I did not miss the hurt expression behind the defiance. "Maybe don't take off your leg again if he doesn't want to kiss you. That was probably alarming."

"Not a pink-hearts-and-roses sort of romantic act," my mother said, raising perfectly arched eyebrows, her diamond bracelet sparkling off the sun. "But kinky. Some men dive into kinky stuff, dear. Chains, handcuffs, things of that nature. Perhaps later he'll grow into being beaten by a leg? Better than a leather whip."

"Mom!" Caden protested, aghast.

She rolled her eyes. "I meant a *chocolate* whip, not a leather one. An edible whip. Maybe a licorice whip."

"Mom!" Caden protesteth again, his hand to his throat.

"We cannot all be masters," Tate droned. "Again, Shakespeare. Some of us are the kissed, and others are the kissees. I think you're a kissee, Damini."

"I squish this," Harvey said.

"Hop hop," Hazel said.

"Squish and squish," Heloise said.

The triplets put their hands into their chicken pancakes and squished them.

"No chicken in da pancake," Harvey said.

"Cluck, cluck," Heloise said.

"Hop hop," Hazel the bunny said.

What a mess.

We cheered the mess, our glasses clinking.

My older brother, Caden, is about the size of a building. He has black hair, the same as our late father, Shel, and pulls it back into a short ponytail. He has the dark brown eyes of our father, too. He is fourteen months older than me. He was a star linebacker and wrestler here in Tillamina, wrestled in college, and graduated with a degree in physics. He then became a professional wrestler and made a fortune. As The Raptor, he was a beast. He won all the time.

He calls Tate, "my boy," and has treated him as a son his whole life. Fishing, wrestling, camping, guy stuff. They love each other senseless.

He also has a deep, gentle feminine side. He loves the Brontë sisters and their work, and will cry over their real-life story when he thinks about it. He loves my greenhouse, the symphony, gourmet food, cooking shows, and romantic movies. He even reads romance novels. He did not stop crying for two months when Marla left him.

He doesn't watch football anymore or wrestling shows because he doesn't want to see people getting pummeled. He does not watch horror or suspense movies because he can't sleep at night. He can sing all the songs to any Disney movie.

He is a manly man so doesn't worry about being a man. If Damini, Heloise, and Hazel are wearing a pink ribbon in their hair, he'll often wear one, too, through his ponytail. If the girls are having purple day, he'll wear a purple T-shirt with Froot Loops cereal chains around his neck.

Caden has a flower shop called Witches and Warlocks Florist, a fun nod to our witchly family history.

His shop has turned into a national business, via the Internet and some fortunate marketing exposure, for example this headline: "Pro wrestler opens a florist shop named Witches and Warlocks Florist . . . says he loves roses, pink ribbons, and romance. Love spells are extra." It does capture your attention.

Caden agrees to put together "butt-normal" bouquets in clear glass vases, but he prefers "heart-pounding bouquets with seductive beauty" in unique containers: colored glass, watering cans, African-type woven baskets, colorful boxes, and shiny pottery. He also loves to weave exotic flowers in and out of two-foot-tall twisted metal on a wood base with a vase. I can only compare it to getting a work of modern art with flowers in it.

He also adds to his bouquets ribbons, unique buttons, antique jewelry, and hand-painted plastic or glass butterflies, ladybugs, hummingbirds, and birds. He uses ivy plants and wire, chrysanthemums and daisies, to make dogs, race cars, bras, cats, wine bottles, lizards, fish, a snake for a reptile handler, and many witches on broomsticks.

How did the ex-pro-wrestler turn into a florist?

"Flowers is what I always wanted to do," he told me, thumping his chest. "It started with Grandma Violet."

When we visited Grandma Violet and Grandpa Pete during our summer vacations, she would have us go and pick flowers for neighbors who needed "some natural magic in their lives." We would add pinecones, twine, fall leaves, branches from trees, cornstalks, grape leaves, and anything else we could find outside.

We brought bouquets to the sick and grieving, and also to Wendell Petroski, who had seven personalities. We were never sure who would open the door. Sometimes we said hello to Mrs. Trina Petroski, slightly slutty lady, or Greg, uptight hippie, or Austin, sad boy in trouble.

We brought Rennie flowers a lot because she had agoraphobia and never left her home, and we took them to Mrs. Quinn, who lost her old dog.

"He was a smart dog," Grandma Violet said. "Mrs. Quinn said he could speak English when no one else was around."

People adored the bouquets.

Hence, an overgrown, tough, sensitive, ultra-masculine, ultra-feminine florist owner was born.

TATE'S AWESOME PIGSKIN BLOG

Last Wednesday three kids named Raji, Michael, and Caleb tried to beat me up after school. (Those aren't their real names, but I don't want to embarrass them, so I'm not writing them down.)

They wanted to beat me up because they don't like how I look. It's not any more difficult than that to understand. They don't like how I look, therefore, they hit me. They got in a few slugs.

They called me, "Fuck ass, retarded shit, and mongloid." I said to them, "I've heard it before, assholes," and Raji swung first.

I'm six foot three inches tall and I work out all the time with my weights. I'm not saying this to brag. I'm saying it to give you an impression of myself. I found out when I was a lot smaller than I am now that it's better to know how to beat someone up than be beaten up. My uncle Caden has taught me a lot of moves.

Raji takes a swing at my head. Remember, I have a big head, named General Noggin. It's not hard to miss, but Raji did miss because I ducked. I brought my fist up and caught him on the jaw. He flipped up like a Ping-Pong ball and landed on his back.

Michael and Caleb came at me at the same time and I had to handle Michael first, because he's stronger. Caleb is small, and he punched Ernie. That's what I call the ear on General Noggin that is the normal-looking one. The other ear I call Bert because that ear is built in a sort of rectangular shape and is the twin of Bert's head on Sesame Street.

Plus, my fists are called Billy and Bob, for Billy Bob Thornton, frickin' most awesomest actor ever.

I block Michael's punch with my arm (no names for my arm, can't name every body part, especially not THAT one, although I hear some dudes do), and then I swing my fist, Billy, into his face and off and out Michael goes. Flat on his back, too. Banged his head. Caleb hits me in the gut and I clench my stomach, then I glare at him. He's all scared, his two friends are moaning on the ground, but he swings again and that's when I deck him in the face, too. When he lands on his back he has the sense to lie there and not move. Raji and Michael charge at me together and I do go down, right on Bert's side of my head. Poor Bert.

They get me for a second because I can't catch my breath. Raji hits my Mickey Mouse, which is my normal eye and Michael hits Road Runner, which is the eye that's up at a freakin' odd angle. I thought Mickey Mouse was the best crawly animal when I was three so that's how the eye that's in the right place on my face got its name. I named the other eye Road Runner because Road Runner always gets in accidents that would kill any other animal, person, or space alien, but he still lives. That's how my eye is.

I have this amazing vision in my Road Runner eye. It's chill. I can practically see a worm squirming through grass. I can practically see China drinking tea. I can almost see Jupiter.

That's the one thing about being me. I'm a cross between a kid, Frankenstein, a creature, and a firecracker because of my red hair. But I have these cool things about me. One of them is the vision. Another is that math problems turn and twist in my head, and I can see them all strung out, plus the diagrams, shapes, and 3-D images.

I was distracted. Back to the fight.

I'm getting my breath back with Michael and Raji on me, and I'm pissed off because I really don't appreciate getting jumped, and I free Billy and Bob (my fists) and shove Michael's and Raji's heads together as hard as I can. I see this whole group of men in suits running toward us, and I know they're running to help, which is nice, but not necessary as now all three of them are spread on the ground like amoebas that have been stepped on.

These men run over, and they're sweating when they get there and one says, "You okay, Tate?" This is a small town and a whole bunch of people know me, my mom and my Nana Bird and my great-grandparents. I'll tell you another time why everyone knows my Nana Bird. You know her, too, probably.

And I said, "Sure." And I was. I stood up. I was bloody and I knew I'd have bruises on Bert and I could tell that Road Runner was getting all swollen up, and there were cuts on Billy and Bob but General Noggin wasn't too bashed up.

I was still kind of sad. Not whiny sad, just sad.

Why would I feel sad? (Warning: here comes some emotions. Watch out!)

I am not all hitched up about getting attacked for how I look and I'm angry about one thing right now (basketball, Boss Mom, basketball!) so part of me has to admit that getting in a fight made me feel better. Some anger flew out.

But I feel sad for Raji, Michael, and Caleb. I don't want to sound sanctimonious. Sanct-EEEE-Moan-Eee-Us. Get it?

But there they were, on the ground, bleeding and groaning. Three against one and they are beat to shit. I don't feel bad for them because of the blood, though, I feel bad for them because of what they don't have going in their lives. If they were happy they wouldn't be beating General Noggin and me up.

I'm not going to sound all high and mighty, but those three must have crappy lives because they go after me. What kind of person does that? What kind of person has to beat somebody else up in order to feel better? What caused all that anger in these three guys to begin with?

They gotta hate themselves. Normal dudes with normal confidence aren't going to do that.

I helped all three of them up. Raji's crying, Michael's wiping blood off and he's shaking, and Caleb can hardly stand but he leans on me to get up.

Why do people do this crap?

I don't know.

Do you?

"Hey, Boss Mom, look at this!" Tate pointed to a counter on his blog, a golden red harvest moon hanging right outside his window. "Says I had twenty-five people read my blog. Twenty-five, twenty-five! And a bunch of them answered the question about why some people are crappy. Look!"

I could tell he was tickled to death that people were actually writing to him. I read the answers. Some were touching, some thoughtful, others a rant on mean people. "This is excellent. You'll be famous in no time."

"It's starting, it's all starting." He sighed heavily, grinning at me. "I don't know how I'm going to handle all these lusty women coming after me when fame hits, I don't know how I'm going to manage my experiments and continue my study of the frontal, parietal, occipital, and temporal lobes with women fighting for my delectable body and my hand in marriage...."

"I'm sure you'll manage."

"It's going to take all I have to keep my purity." He clutched his chest, head back, the drama king. "My virginity, my innocence."

"Use restraint, my dear, control those hormones."

"I'll try, Boss Mom, but these women with their libidos, once they read my blog they'll barely be able to control their passions and seductive natures. It'll be a battle of epic proportions."

"Battle politely with the women, then. Good night, Tate." I ruffled those curls.

"Love you, Boss Mom." He turned back to the blog, then said, "I hope I'm here in the morning. There's probably women lurking outside my bedroom window right now propping a ladder against the house to sneak me away, plotting a way to get me alone and naked...."

Tate has always been incredibly funny.

It has definitely helped him through the not-so-funny stuff.

"He said you intentionally killed his father."

It felt like a dead rhino had been dropped on my heart. "You're kidding."

"No." Sydney Grants peered at me over the rim of her red-framed glasses, her elbows on the table in her office.

Sydney's parents moved here from Ghana when she was

three. She wears super-bright colors and prints, she's as tough as a redwood, and her kindness and graciousness is unending. As the manager of our hospice unit, and a hospice nurse for fifteen years before that, she knows it all.

"Why is Dirk Hassells saying I intentionally killed his father?"

"He says that not enough was done to save his father's life, he thinks we didn't try all available treatments, his father was railroaded into hospice, he had more time to live, and, my favorite ludicrous comment—you overdosed him with morphine in the weeks before he died on purpose and that's what killed him."

I felt outrage wrap tight around my body. I'd been up for much of the night with another patient, had her settled and cared for, rushed home, and sent Tate off to school. And now this. On no sleep.

"Dirk's threatening legal action." Sydney swirled a pen in her hand. "Says he's going to hire an attorney."

"Sydney, you know that Mr. Hassells, Senior, had liver cancer. It had spread over his whole body. It was as if he had a piranha inside his gut. The doctors, specifically Dr. Baharri, said there was nothing that could be done." I drummed my nails on her desk and tapped my leather boot. Today I was wearing a burgundy-colored loose blouse and jeans. "Dirk is saying I overdosed Mr. Hassells on morphine? That's ripe."

"Yes. The baboon obviously doesn't know how we use morphine. He says he was not informed of his father's true condition, that he was given hope that he would live, that had he known death was imminent, he would have visited more often, that you were neglectful in your duties not to tell him."

"Dr. Baharri told him. I told him. The sister, Beatrice, the one who's a teacher, divorced, five kids, the one caring for her dad all the time, told him, too. He told me he didn't believe his sister because she was always, and I quote, 'hormonal, emotional, whiny, the weaker sex has a hard time dealing with this kind of stuff.' He also told Beatrice, 'I'm busy, I don't have the easy career of a teacher and I can't drop my clients, my important responsibilities, and come now. He'll be fine.' "

Sydney said, "We have the son on the white horse charging in."

"We sure do."

The son on the white horse charging in is a now-and-then occurrence in hospice circles. Basically, the wife, or the daughters, or the long-term daughters-in-law, in most cases, do all the work of tending to a dying patient.

The son is "too busy." The son will not take the time out of his day to help the dying family member. The son will not take a leave from work as his sisters do. The son will not lose sleep, do housework at the parent's house, manage the medicine, the doctor visits, the treatments, the post-care, arrange for help, handle the bills, stay up all night, and arrange for hospice.

No, the women do all that.

And when the health of the patient starts to deteriorate, out the son will come, flag waving, armor on, charging in. He'll save the day! Ta-da! Bring in the hero! Bring in the genius! He'll insist on care that is ridiculous to insist on.

Dirk was, *sort of,* the son on a white horse charging in. He was a short man with a permanent smirk who had a vengeful, personal agenda behind all of this.

Sydney read my mind. "I think, though, this is mostly about you, Jaden."

"Yep. It is."

Why? Because designer suit–clad Dirk, he of the slicked-back hair, hit on me each time he was at his father's house, and I rejected him. At first, Beatrice told me, he rarely came to visit his father. But one time, a few months before Mr. Hassells died, he met me.

He was not married, no kids, but he dated women a lot. I know, because he told me. "I have a high sex drive." He asked me out, asked me to go upstairs alone with him, asked me to his home and tried to have sexually charged conversations with me, as in, "I gotta have sex every day . . . let's tell each other the best time we ever did it . . . this one time, in San Francisco, I met this woman in a bar and I. . . ."

I put up a hand and said, "I don't want to hear it, Dirk."

He smirked. "You don't?"

"No."

"Jealous, Jaden? Don't be. We can make our own memories. It's a hot story, though. You're hot." His eyes wandered down my body, as if this would be a turn-on. "One bright blue eye, one bright green eye. Red hair. You're two women in one, we could have a three-way."

"No, we could never do that," I told him. "That would disgust me."

And it began. When he knew I was coming, he'd show up.

One time he stood in front of me, blocking my way to his father's bedroom. "I think you and I would be good together, Jaden. Don't play hard to get, it's a waste of time."

I said, "I'm not playing hard to get, but I see that you are the kind of man who will insist on believing it because you won't be able to accept that I'm not the slightest bit interested in you. This is the time for you to take with your father."

"Want to take a ride in my Porsche? You can feel my engine."

"That's the stupidest pickup line I've ever heard, and no. No, I don't want to go for a ride in your car that is a reflection of your tiny penis, with fancy wheels that are obviously a reflection of your balls. Now get in there and pay attention to your dad."

He was furious with me. He was a sick, controlling man who did not take rejection well. In the four weeks before Mr. Hassells died, Dirk visited once.

Sydney sighed as we talked about Dirk. She had been well aware of what I was dealing with. She had offered to replace me, but Mr. Hassells senior, Beatrice, her kids, and I were already bonded and I couldn't abandon them.

"We have a man who is ticked off you wouldn't sleep with him so he accuses us of poor medical care and you of killing his father. What a shark."

I held my head in my hands. I was infuriated, the anger that always bobs close to the surface of my life exploding like a firecracker. I didn't sleep with Dirk—he accuses me of murder.

"We'll meet with Dirk as a group here. If he calls in the attorneys, we'll meet again . . . blah blah blah. You know how it goes."

"Yes, I know." I was exhausted thinking about it.

"Jaden, I will stand behind you, a soldier with a loaded gun, only my loaded gun will be my mouth, you know that." She reached across her desk and patted my hand. "Don't worry."

"I'll worry."

It's always a bad day when you're accused of murder.

4

I live outside Tillamina, Oregon, in a white, two-story house with a wraparound front porch, built in the late 1800s by Faith and her husband, Jack. They built the home as their country home . . . and as a place for Faith and Grace to hide, if need be, from two dangerous men, who they thought might hunt them down later.

Faith named the home and surrounding land London Gardens because she missed her family in London and knew, because of the witch hunt, that she could never return. She and Jack planted the maples that line the driveway up to the house. Faith also planted thyme, sage, rosemary, parsley, oregano, lavender, Canterbury bells, hollyhocks, lilies, irises, sweet peas, cosmos, red poppies, peonies, and rows and rows of roses, as her mother and grandmother had in England.

She later gave London Gardens to their oldest daughter. It's been handed down to the oldest daughter ever since, which is how Grandma Violet came to own it.

Tillamina is in the middle of Oregon wine country with a view of the purplish coastal mountain range in the distance. We have ten acres with the same flowers and herbs Faith planted, a huge field filled with red poppies, an old apple orchard, pine and fir trees.

My mother was raised in this country house until she hopped on a Greyhound bus for Hollywood at eighteen to become an actress, her sights on bright lights, her dreams on the stage.

I was born in Los Angeles, but we visited Grandma Violet and Grandpa Pete each summer. We moved to London Gardens permanently when Brooke, Caden, and I were teenagers after many terrible nights, and one horrendously terrible night, but before the terrible night to end all terrible nights.

My mother's father, my grandpa Pete, was a police officer and a farmer who had moved to Oregon from Arkansas, wanting to get out of the heat and humidity and the poverty his family was stuck in.

He met his wife, Violet, my grandma, when she was dancing topless in a forest near here, her auburn curls flying in the wind. Unfortunately a bunch of kids saw my half-naked grandma and the kids' mothers called the police. She was dancing topless because that's what her witchly spell required for romance.

Grandpa Pete was the arresting officer called out to investigate the topless lady.

"He was a handsome fellow. I was happy to have my shirt off, Jaden. I wanted him to see the full package. And him standing there in his uniform with his gun." Grandma Violet chuckled, her blue eyes sparkling. "I thought it was magical. My spell for a man worked! I used a bit of lavender, the thimble and needle, a pinch of thyme and rosemary, and the love chant the women of our family have always used, back down to our royal lineage. It was prophetic, spiritual, the wind blowing right by, ruffling his hair. He blushed, that man with the handcuffs blushed, and he was polite about my heavenly nudity. . . ." She sighed. "I knew I would marry him."

There was a bit of a scandal with their relationship, because of the nudity part, and some hushed rumors about the witch stuff, but it was Oregon, liberal even then, and no one paid too much mind, especially because Grandma Violet had several brothers, loggers, who threatened to "log some heads together if you peoples don't shut up." Plus, Grandma Violet, even as a young woman, was "the healer," whom people went to for help with their aches, pains, and "diseases and demons of the emotional mind."

London Gardens was medium-sized when it was built, grand

for the time, but my mother added a second family room, with a woodstove, and almost wall-to-wall windows and French doors about twenty years ago. We also gutted the kitchen ten years ago, since it had been twenty years, and pushed it out fifteen feet to create a nook for eating.

My country-style kitchen is white, blue, and yellow. White cabinets line the walls, as does open shelving. A huge butcher-block island stretches down the middle of the kitchen with two red lights in the shape of roses centered above it. The counters are granite and the tiles on the backsplash have been painted with pictures of oregano, thyme, rosemary, parsley, chives, and red poppies by an artist friend of mine.

Our home has high ceilings, wood floors, three fireplaces, and wide white trim. The walls are painted light blue, light green, and light yellow, the colors flowing into each other. We have a creaky staircase, an attic with a pitched ceiling, and a secret room.

Upstairs, there are four large bedrooms, three of which have four poster beds, two of which have grand fireplaces. The fourth bedroom is called Tate's Experiment Room.

I love that my family has lived here for well over a hundred years.

I have kept my ancestors' antiques, including armoires, a roll-top desk, and a hutch in the kitchen to display four generations of pretty, flowered plates and teacups. I also have a hundred-year-old rocking chair in my living room that I was sitting on when he said, "It's time," and not long after that she killed him.

On the walls I have hung a collection of quilts made by the women of the family. A painting of our barn by Grandpa Pete hangs in a hallway, near framed photographs by Grandma Violet of red poppies and Canterbury bells. I have repainted an old white picket fence and hung it across one wall of the dining room. I've used old doors for tables, and a weather vane with a horse that fell off the roof is now hanging in a corner.

I like thinking of Faith's or Grace's hand on the same stair rail as me, or their faces, their auburn hair, like mine I'm told, reflected in a window I look out of today. Faith had blue eyes, and Grace had green. In an odd coincidence, I have one of each.

I like wondering what my ancestors were daydreaming about as they lay on the steel daybed. I like thinking about what treasures they stored in the nine-drawer dressers. I like reading through the collection of old books we have and wondering which were their favorites. I like that I have used the old sink in the kitchen to plant daffodil bulbs and that the old brick chimney that fell down was used to create a brick walkway to the house. I like looking at the same scenes of our property out my windows, hung with white, wispy lace curtains, that they did.

But what caught your eye in all that description? It was the secret room part, right?

There's an area between Tate's Experiment Room and the stairwell. It's walled-off space. It's odd, a quirk in the house. I asked my grandparents about it about a year before Grandpa Pete died and they laughed, their eyes crinkling, their weathered hands flying up in merriment.

"It's where we keep our ancestors." Grandpa Pete laughed, always loving a good joke. "Maybe I'll end up in there, too!"

"The family secrets are all written down in there!" Grandma Violet whispered. "It's where we keep the magic wands and the skeletons!"

"And the thimble," my mother sang out.

"The original lace handkerchief is there, too." Grandma Violet giggled.

"Don't forget the needle and the gold timepiece," my mother said.

"Maybe even Faith's necklace with the cross, heart, and star charm." Grandpa Pete wiggled his eyebrows. His own wife wore cross, heart, and star charms on a necklace, the same as my mother, Brooke, and I, the same as all our women ancestors.

"I'm hoping that the knife with the *P* on it from Faith's brother that she used for the killing is there, too. Now there's a piece of history!" Grandma Violet gushed. "And the book with the black cover."

When the laughter settled down, Grandma Violet explained that the secret room was a "family story, family lore," and I took it to mean it was a joke. There were *definitely* no skeletons in the secret room she told me. "Only the beginning of our witchly history . . . at least that's what my grandma told me and her grandma told her!"

"Basketball tryouts are coming up, Boss Mom."

"No."

"Pleeeasssee—"

"Tate, stop. We've had this discussion." I was making Mighty Taco Soup for dinner and dumping the whole thing in the Crock-Pot. Mighty Taco Soup has many ingredients including green onions, sour cream, regular onions, avocado slices, cheddar cheese, tortilla chips, chili beans, etc. I serve it in giant blue mugs with a hunk of bread and butter.

"Let's have the discussion again, Boss Mom. I crave the discussion, I live for it. If you discuss basketball with me, I'll discuss the history of herbs and spices in India with you. One of your most boring topics." He muttered that last part, then spun two basketballs, one in each hand. He was still sweating from practicing outside for two hours. He'd shot, he'd dodged imaginary opponents, and he'd run lines, back and forth, back and forth. I'd heard him announcing his own fictional game. "Folks, Tate Bruxelle has the ball, three seconds left, he's at half court, is he going to shoot? He is! Can he make it? Tate Bruxelle, three points! Wins the gaaaammmee! The crowd goes wild! It's insane in here!"

Tate practices basketball daily, for hours. And hours. For years he's done this.

"We don't need to discuss basketball because my answer, miraculously, is the same." I put down the cheddar cheese I was grating, my impatience rising. Outside the maple leaves, many bold colors blending in one leaf, were swirling around, a fall wind churning the tree branches.

"You're afraid I'm going to get hurt. Like this." He slammed the basketballs together as if they were two heads. I cringed.

"I know you'll get hurt. It's basketball. There are huge, rough kids out there—"

"Hello, Mom? Have you looked at me? I'm huge. I ate twelve tacos yesterday, six chocolate chip cookies, and a pop the size of my butt. I'll be careful."

"Well done, I've always wanted a kid who could eat twelve tacos, and do not compare pop to your butt. Do not say butt. Say buttocks." I minced an onion. Onions and butter and garlic. Where would we all be without those three ingredients? "You can't be careful in sports. Those guys are all-out for blood. They want to win."

"I want to win, too. I can shoot, you've seen me. It's my Road Runner eye, it's bionic! Three-pointers. All the time. I've graphed it all, I've studied my own hands, studied NBA players' hands, the arch, where the fingers are—"

He had. He had slowed down the shots on TV of NBA players and studied them down to the minutia, he had done some complicated graph, funneled a whole bunch of numbers into a computer program he designed, then applied it to himself across various spots on our outdoor basketball court. "I want to try out for the team—"

The onions made my eyes tear up. "My job as your mother is to love you and keep you safe as much as I can. You are not playing basketball because that ball could smash you in the head, or you could fall and hit your head, or run into a wall or the announcers' table headfirst, or you could be hit so hard you smash your brain on the floor and then you'd have a problem with your shunt."

"I can't ever play basketball on the off chance that something might go wrong because I have a shunt? How is that living my life?"

"It's *living* your life, carefully, that's what it is."

"That's not the way I'm going to do it." He bounced both basketballs hard on the floor, one time, his temper rising, too. "I don't want to live carefully. That sounds boring, it sounds like a waste, it sounds like something someone old and scared would do. You have always done this, Mom, you hang over me. You're Lurch."

"Who is Lurch?"

"Lurch. You know, the cartoon character I used to draw who was green and always paying attention to everybody's business and telling people to be careful? He worried about a thousand things and predicted bad things that would never, ever happen."

"I always had a fondness for Lurch."

"Mom, you're a black cape over me and I can't breathe."

I knew he was miserable about my decision. I was miserable for him and I was miserable about being accused of killing someone. "I like capes. You can breathe. You're breathing now. I can see it."

"Mom. I have to be able to breathe on my own." Tate slammed both basketballs together again. "Even if I die early, I have to live. It's not just about basketball, it's about taking the time I have and doing what I want, being what I want, and what I want to be is a basketball player."

"Do not talk about dying early." I shuddered.

"It's my life. *Mine.*"

"It's mine, too. You're my son and I love you." I was well aware that I smelled death in my greenhouse the other night when I crushed a few mint leaves in my hand. "Go to your experiment room and combine chemicals or build another giant model of the human brain with all the parts labeled. I have to make a couple of calls while I'm making your favorite soup."

"I don't want to do my experiments tonight. I want to talk about basketball—"

"Tate!" I yelled, slamming a wooden spoon on the butcher-block island. "No, no, no, a thousand times no." I bent my head. "I'm sorry I yelled. I had a tough day."

"Me, too, Mom. I keep having tough days because I'm being suffocated and can't hang out with the other guys and be part of a team—"

"Off you go, son."

"Mom—"

"Now!"

"Man!" He slammed the balls down again and stomped up the stairs while I fought against myself. I am not deaf to his reasoning or his pleadings. I turned back to my Mighty Taco Soup and added a pinch of parsley.

Tate and I had the Mighty Taco Soup later that night, chunks of hot bread, and lemon meringue pie. It was such a quiet dinner the silence echoed in my ears.

Before he went to bed he hugged me tight. "I love you, Boss Mom."

"I love you, too."

"You're my best friend."

I could not reply because I was all choked up. "Go to sleep, you Godzilla."

" 'Night, Boss Mom, you red-haired witch."

"There are no witches in this family."

"Sure, Mom. That's why you've got a blue eye from Faith and a green eye from Grace." He thudded up the stairs. "I still wanna play on the basketball team!"

There are many medical reasons why Tate shouldn't still be with us. But he is. He's here. And I will not let anything cut his time short, especially not *basketball*.

Tate shouldn't have lived at all as a baby. The birth was fraught with problems because of the size of his head. He wasn't breathing when he was born and he stopped breathing later in the neonatal unit. He had Brooke's drugs rampaging through his body. He had to have an operation to have a shunt implanted in his head that ran to his heart. He had an infection at six months at the site of the shunt that almost killed him and he was in the hospital for three weeks.

There were other infections, and a blockage when he was two. At three the shunt shifted, more critical health issues. The tube going to his heart also became blocked by the clotting of blood, and he's had problems with inflammation.

He's had numerous operations, all, of course, under anesthesia, with the treacherous recovery one would expect when doctors cut your head open.

He still needs ongoing checkups.

I watch him carefully for anything that might indicate an issue: flu symptoms or a headache, sickness and nausea, or if he has trouble concentrating or seems scattered. If he vomits or can't see right or is having trouble staying awake when he should be awake, I don't mess around. I drive him straight to the hospital. I have headed off several emergencies by acting quick, but not all of them. Some complications happened too fast, Tate's life was on the brink, and I felt myself falling into an abyss of free-flowing panic.

There is nothing comparable to the panic a parent feels when a child's life is in danger.

Nothing.

It's a special part of hell. It is almost impossible not to be overprotective, fearful. I know that my years of free-flowing panic have shaped me into someone I was not before. I am overly serious, and a bit controlling, okay, maybe more than a bit controlling, and I overprotect too much, and I struggle with pervasive worry over Tate, which comes out as anger and a mouth that won't quit when I feel cornered.

I am grateful for every minute of Tate's life, and I have been on-my-knees grateful when he has lived through one medical disaster or another. I am also grateful for his doctor, Ethan Robbins. He is a gift. He is a gift in more ways than one. Oh yes, indeedy, he is.

Dr. Ethan Robbins makes me quiver in special places.

I saw Maggie Granelli on a windy Tuesday, the sky blue and clear, still warm. She was in her beloved, pampered rose garden. She had pink, red, and yellow blooms in her hand and threw her arms out wide for a hug when I arrived. "It's a pleasure to see you, Jaden."

Maggie had lived in her bungalow-style home in the country, with a creek out back, for twenty years and had been adamant that she be allowed to die there. Her bedroom used to be the dining room and was transformed when Maggie could no longer walk comfortably upstairs without us worrying she would fall.

Her four-poster bed with a gold and burgundy bedspread faced open French doors so she could be as close to her rose garden as possible.

She is ninety-two years old. She was born in New York City and lived through the Great Depression. Her father was one of the men who jumped out of the skyscrapers when he lost his life's savings and her mother went to work in a factory. Maggie put herself through school and became a secretary. She worked her way up and became the executive of a famous shoe company. She quit when she was eighty. Her retirement party held 800 people.

She had four husbands and four daughters. Her greatest regret, "I didn't have enough sex. I was brought up in the wrong era. Praise be to Gloria Steinem."

She is selflessly interested in my life and she asked to meet Tate a couple months ago because I'd told her he was an expert at chess. This was against the rules, but I brought him anyhow. Tate ate a third of the pineapple meringue cake on her counter, at her invitation, and they became fast friends. Maggie has been playing chess her whole life. Her father taught her before he jumped out the window.

She does not have much time. Late this summer I asked her what she wanted to do with the time she had. "I want to be with my daughters, their families, and my roses. I want to beat your son in chess. It would mean the world to me to checkmate him, fair and square, no pity wins. That's what would make me happy, dear."

Tate calls her, "Maggie Shoes." She calls him, "Bishop Tate," because of Tate's love of the bishop on the chessboard, and he has agreed to not let her win a "pity win."

She is living out her days as she wishes.

"I'm getting all geared up to lose again next year," my mother drawled, tipping back her martini. She'd flown up from Hollywood for the weekend to visit.

"Maybe you won't lose," I said. I was making crab cakes with dill, lemon juice, Worcestershire sauce, and mint leaves for dinner. Yum. Tate called them Crabby Yum Cakes. It was Grandma Violet's recipe from her mother.

"I will lose," my mother sang out. "No Emmy for me, give me another mar-tee-knee."

"I'd vote for you if I could, Mom." I stirred the Yum as a blast of wind and rain hit my windows. Today I had seen pink leaves, *pink,* on the ground.

"Thank you, darling, but I'll lose. I'll get new Botox shot into my face so that I'll appear young and youthful when I smile for the cameras but secretly I'll wish that the vagina of the winner would fall out from between her legs while she is giving her *thank you for recognizing that I am immensely talented* speech." My mother gasped in a mocking way, clutched her chest, and pretended to be flabbergasted. "Oh, thank you, thank you to my agent with his greasy hands, my co-stars whom I secretly hate, and the producer who is bipolar and screams at me on Wednesdays."

My mother has been nominated for an Emmy eight times and she never wins. I've gone with her to the awards ceremonies. She buys me a dress, we have our makeup and hair done, and she struts down the red carpet, cameras flashing. I hold my breath as her name is called and when she doesn't win, after the camera pans away, I mouth out, "Underneath that slinky dress the winner is a man. You can almost see the penis."

And she whispers, still smiling, pretending she doesn't want to tackle the winner to the floor, "I think her left breast is overly large."

And I say, "A third nipple. It's on her left buttock. She was born with a *third nipple.*"

And she says, "Did you see the horn out the back of her? She's part devil."

This goes on and on until we are laughing so hard we are crying.

My mother comes back up to Oregon and we putter in my greenhouse amidst the basil and lavender and "heal up."

I flicked through another recipe book. I wanted to bake and

gobble molasses cookies. "A vagina falling out on stage would cause quite a stir, Mother."

"Yes, it would. Hollywood types are all bizarre, but a falling vagina would definitely bring the house down. What should she do? Pick it up? Walk away and get a new vagina? Say it belongs to the male host?"

"It's a tricky situation, but you are outstanding this season, as usual." A striped sunset glinted off my greenhouse, beyond the maple trees lining the drive. I love my greenhouse. It is peace with glass. "Elsie Blackton is positively throbbing with evil and sexual tension. She is mean and manipulative and somehow oddly lovable."

"That's because Elsie does what she wants and all women wish they could be an Elsie sometimes with her men, her designer heels, and her couture!"

"I don't want to be an Elsie."

"Yes, you do, Jaden." She ate three olives after sticking her fingers into the holes. "Behind the control freak, overly serious, frazzled, somewhat explosive Mary Poppins exterior, you have a thriving witch itching to cast a few spells."

"Elsie is not a witch. She's a temptress. She's a slink."

"A slink?"

"Yes, she's a slink. She slinks around morals and values because she has none. She preys on men, and if she wants them, even if they're attached to another female, she pounces."

"Ah. But only if they are handsome and/or wealthy, dear daughter. Elsie is particular about who she hops into bed with. And I am, too. I didn't want to be on the set, in bed, with an ugly fart. I told the director that, too. Rich, don't put me in bed with an ugly fart. Don't put me in bed with a man who has a penis in his head. Don't put me in bed with a man who will try to touch me under the covers or he will lose a ball and you'll be sued. Keep it clean, Rich, I told him, keep it clean."

I laughed. For all the seductiveness in her character, my mother is the most moral person I have ever met. She has a hard moral line about motherhood, family, honesty, kindness, and friendship, and she sticks to it.

"Did you know that I'm going to get stuck in an elevator next season, the electricity off, the elevator hanging by a tiny wire next season? You know I have claustrophobia. I think I'll do that scene after shots of whiskey."

"You can be a slightly inebriated Elsie then."

"Sounds much more relaxing than being sober in an elevator." She tapped her manicured nails together. "Speaking of that, I want to talk to you about your love life."

"I don't. Please remember that you are my mother." I could almost taste the molasses cookies.

"That's why we're discussing this. Socially proper mothers address barren, dull love lives with their children to get them zinging again." She rolled rather heavily made up eyes at me, her auburn bangs fringed to the tops of her eyebrows. "Surely you've heard of a love life?"

"I've heard of it and what is a socially proper mother?" I pulled my curls up into a ponytail, the crystals that Tate gave me hanging to my shoulder.

"It's me, and you need one," she drawled.

"Need what?"

"Need a love life."

I thought of Dr. Ethan Robbins, the only person I could have a love life with.

My eyes misted over.

My mother shook my shoulders. "You have to snatch the stethoscope off his neck, rip open his white coat, yank down those pants of his, and roll him onto an operating table! Do it, Jaden, or your own vagina might fall out from lack of use. The same thing that will happen to the winner of the next Emmy!"

Argh.

I do not want my vagina to fall out from lack of use, but the only man I want near it is Ethan.

To tell the truth, I long for moments of quiet. I crave the peace of my greenhouse so I can think amidst my herbs, teacup in hand, all by myself, and dive into a soft heaven of lusty daydreaming.

I have full daydreams of how life would be lived if I was married to Ethan. I envision passionate dating, and a few blow-up fights that result in a deeper relationship with him proclaiming his undying love for me. I envision the most mind-blowing sex on a regular basis because I cannot help myself and spend hours wondering what he would think of me naked. I am not thin, and I have, as one boyfriend told me years ago before taking off for a "short vacation" to Spain that lasted three years, "an incredible boob rack and hips that will bear a dozen children with no problem."

Basically: I curve. Heavy on the boobs, not small hips.

And the dozen kids?

With Ethan, that appeals.

He is six foot four. He has a friendly smile, a gravelly, calm voice, and a reassuring manner. I think of how he looks at me through his glasses, with tenderness and indulgence, as if he cares about me. He reminds me of a hike through the Columbia Gorge when the leaves are on fire with color, hot cocoa in winter in an outdoor hot tub with snow all around, a day at the beach in spring, and kayaking on a river in summer. He reminds me of life and in any other situation, I would throw myself at that man, I would try to be gracious and elegant while throwing myself, but I'd still take a dare and do it.

But I *can't.*

Ethan is Tate's neurosurgeon. He is the best on the West Coast. He knows Tate's history and he has operated on him three times. If we were to be involved, he could not be Tate's doctor. He has cried with me several times over Tate.

He might, *possibly,* be interested in me. Maybe I'm reading the signs wrong. I am desperate. Desperate people will see signs that are, in reality, not there.

But sometimes when we're in his office, we stare at each other. Even Tate has noticed and one time said, "Okay, you two, quit staring at each other or your eyes will pop out of your heads and roll on the floor and I'm not pickin' 'em up."

Another time Tate said, "Should I leave and go find a scalpel to play with? Maybe I can open one of your patients' brains. Do you mind, Dr. Robbins?"

And finally, "I think I'll go and flirt with Leena. I think she wants my body, physically speaking."

Leena is a nurse and sixty-five years old.

One time Tate said to Ethan, "Doesn't my mom look great today?"

And, before he could think it through, Ethan said, "Gorgeous, as always. She's sunshine." Then he coughed, and *blushed,* and tore those brown eyes away, brown with a touch of cinnamon in them, and I felt myself heat up like a bonfire.

Leena said to me one day, peering over her glasses, "You know, Ethan is single, Jaden. Funny thing, but your appointments are always scheduled for a full hour, dear. We call it Happy Ethan Hour around here because he's always happy when you're coming in."

See? There's a possibility there. My normal, aggressive personality is all softened out around him. I don't have a streak of temper or testiness in me. No black thoughts. Love and lust is floating around, turning me into a bumbling, cotton candy-ish, amiable ... klutz.

Three times now, I have actually stumbled getting up *from my chair* in front of him. Twice he had to catch me.

I've run into an open door and into a closed door right in front of him. I've tripped and landed on my face. *On my face.* Repeatedly I've been talking and had to stop mid-sentence, flummoxed and flustered, because I looked into those soft, sexy eyes and couldn't figure out what on earth I'd been talking about.

And Ethan waits me out, nodding encouragingly, or he picks me up off the floor.

Ethan is kind and funny with Tate during his appointment, fielding all of his questions about brains, neurosurgery, etc., and then we talk. When I finally relax into him our conversation runs all over the place. Sometimes Tate says, "I'm going to leave you two alone, keep it G-rated," or, "Off I go, leaving for Tanzania, but you two won't notice," and he leaves and goes to chat with the nurses, and we ride that roller coaster of our conversation.

We discuss current political messes, his brothers, my herb garden, my greenhouse, funny jokes, delicious bread at a bakery down the street, our favorite pies, where we want to visit in the world, the most bare and raw feelings and fears that I have, his grief over his mother's death, the grief his father still feels for her, mountain biking, and my exotic tea collection.

But we go no further, and we won't.

I can't.

I am in love with Ethan, but I will not jeopardize Tate's medical care. If I am involved with Ethan, he cannot be involved with Tate.

Tate must have the best. His condition has been too delicate, absolutely life-threatening several times, and I will not risk it.

Ethan is the best.

If I spend an hour getting ready for Tate's appointments, and call my mother about what to wear, and change outfits multiple times after showing her, and whichever soap opera star she is in bed with on set, via Skype to get their opinion, too, so be it. And who cares if a couple of times I whipped off my shirt and skirt and put on another outfit in front of the assistant director, the lighting guy, and my mother's sister on the show? They didn't. They voted for outfit number eight, by the way, it was unanimous.

My heart aches, I want to leap on Ethan, but I can't.

Tate cannot lose Ethan.

No way.

I puttered in my greenhouse that night.

It's actually not a typical greenhouse, it's more of a long room attached to our barn with lots of windows that I'd had built years ago. There's a woodstove for heat, electricity so I can listen to symphonies and rock music, a small refrigerator and stove, a table and chairs, and colorful pots full of herbs and flowers.

I have a patio outside where for most of the year I set up a red and white flowered umbrella, a glass-topped table, and chairs and chaise lounges.

My white twinkling lights are wrapped around the main wood posts and looped above in the rafters. Down the center aisle is an old wood table where I work on my plants, seedlings, flowers, and herbs. On top of the table is a long bench, where I have purple, blue, green, red, and yellow tin buckets for gardening supplies and other paraphernalia. Hanging from the rafters are five bright, Chinese paper lanterns I bought in San Francisco beside wicker baskets and upside-down dried roses and lavender.

I have a wicker table with a glass top overlaid with a yellow and red flowered tablecloth and wicker chairs with red cushions. I have stacks of gardening books and magazines, journals to write in, and sketchbooks to draw in on white shelves. I have a collection of scented candles in cinnamon, pumpkin, strawberry, mocha, gingerbread, and vanilla. I keep a jar of red cinnamon Gummi Bears on a shelf.

I love my tea collection and I love drinking tea in delicate teacups or ceramic mugs: Arabian herbal tea, Mature Woman's estrogen tea, Animalistic green tea, Stars and Suns blue tea, River Water Magic white tea, Spirits and Witches magnetic tea, and the usual, chamomile, black tea, and mint teas.

I have a collection of fun birdhouses nailed up to a wall, three African voodoo dolls from my mother, and a collection of spotted ceramic frogs that I've attached to a wood beam so it looks as if the frogs are hopping up the beam.

Besides herbs and a bunch of the flowers the women in my family line grow, I also have, at one time or another during the year, oriental lilies, sunflowers, daisies, and tomatoes.

With symphonies floating through, my hands in dirt, or drawing and writing, or cutting and combining herbs and spices on Grandma Violet's crystal plates, or inhaling their scents, I can be quiet in my head. Some of the anger, anxiety, and seriousness in my life settles down into something pretty. I don't have to try to control anything, or protect Tate, I can just *be*.

Usually.

I rinsed off my hands in the sink after planting twenty daffodil bulbs—I have an unusual fondness for their yellow flower faces—then made myself a cup of lemon tea.

I cut up sage and marjoram with a knife and added a sprinkle of sea salt with shaking hands, fear making me feel sick. I used Faith's silver spoon to create tiny piles.

I lowered my face to the crystal plates and inhaled, hoping against hope, not wanting to smell that putrid, threatening, ominous scent.

Yes, it was there. I smelled death.

It was coming.

Once again.

Faith's silver spoon clattered to the floor.

I told my mother the next night over the phone about the death stench. I told Caden.

Now we were all worried. What was the purpose of my telling them? I don't know. I wanted them to be extra-careful, to watch the kids with eagle eyes, but we all knew there wasn't a darn thing we could do about it.

Nothing.

Maybe I was wrong about the death.

I knew I wasn't.

Tate and I used to live in the city. Initially we lived in an apartment near the medical school on top of the hill, when I was studying to become a nurse. When Tate was about two I saw the future in brutal TechniColor.

There were too many people in the city, too many people shocked at Tate's head, too many brutal comments. For example, "What the fuck is wrong with that kid's head . . . did you see that . . . God, that is a dee-formity . . . he could be on a freak show . . ." Tate didn't understand it all, but I did, and he would soon.

I cried over the phone to my mother one day about taking Tate downtown to a park and how people pointed and stared and two kids started throwing sand at him in the sandbox. Tate had no idea why the kids were doing that. He sat and cried. It kept happening with other kids. They called him names, ran away from him when he wanted to play, hit his head, called him "big head."

My mom cried over the phone from her set in Hollywood. She had been in the middle of a hot love scene with a husband, it was Damien Rothschild, aka Tom Werner, at that time, but they had to adjust the lighting so she and Tom had time to talk to me from bed. "I curse them. I wish for vermin and snakes to invade their homes," she sobbed. "I wish for warts to grow in strange places. Oh honey, I am sorry."

Tom yelled out, "Move here, sweets. We're all weird in Hollywood. What about this crazy Botox faze? Lips out two inches. Cow lips! Monkey lips! Faces that do not move, as if they're under lock and key. No one will look twice. You should see Joan Totts's latest face-lift. Soon her boobs are gonna be on her cheeks. And what about the game show hosts? Tanned to a yellow-orange color, *yellow-orange!*"

As soon as I was an RN, we moved back to Grandma Violet's/ Faith's/Mother's home, where I lived during most of high school and everyone knew my family. Here, Tate was somewhat more protected. It was a small town, they would have seen him many times, and at least the shock would wear off. Plus, out of respect to my family, I had hoped that some of the most vicious teasing would at least be mitigated. We would only be thirty minutes from Dr. Cainley, his doctor until he was thirteen.

"I'm glad you're going to live here, Jaden," my mother drawled, putting her designer glasses on top of her head as we stood on the lawn in front of London Gardens, the maple trees bordering the drive swaying, whispers of wind swirling through the fir trees. "The least I can do is make sure you're not living in a hovel."

"My apartment is not a hovel."

My mother waved her manicured hand. "Any apartment without a view of the city is a hovel."

I laughed. My mother does an impressive impression of being

a snob but she is so far from being a snob, it makes me laugh harder.

"Any apartment without a doorman is a slum. . . ."

I laughed again. I loved being with my mother.

"Any apartment without limo service, a concierge, and maids is a disgrace."

"Hey!" Tate said, all of three years old and as darling as one can be. "Nana Bird! Let's sing your favorite song from *The Best Little Whorehouse in Texas*."

I put my hands on my hips. "Mother! You taught him a song from *The Best Little Whorehouse in Texas*?"

"It *is* my favorite show." She brought a hand to her chest, cleared her throat, and sang, "I like fancy, frilly things, high-heeled shoes and diamond rings—"

And then my son, *my three-year-old son,* chimed in, "Well, I like beer and rodeos, detective books and dominoes, football games and Cheerios, and sneakin' around with you."

My mother grabbed Tate's hands and they swirled around the grass and sang the whole song together as I envisioned Dolly Parton in her whorehouse, wig on, rack up.

When they were done, I hissed, "You have to be kidding, Mother, he'll be singing about a whorehouse in his preschool class. I don't think the teacher would want to hear about 'rag-time bands, goin' a round or two, dirty jokes, or laying down the law.' "

"That would be fabulous!" She clapped her hands. "Who wants to sing that silly 'Twinkle, Twinkle, Little Star' or that old, downtrodden song about the drunken farmer and Bingo the dog? Come along and I'll make you a mai tai, Tate."

"Mother!"

She huffed at me. "I meant a *virgin* mai tai." She ruffled Tate's hair. He was resinging the *Whorehouse* song, this time shaking his hips and putting particular emphasis on the words, "Sneakin' around with *you!*"

"Do you know what 'virgin' means, Tate honey?" my mother asked.

"It means untouched, Nana Bird!"

"That's my boy!" She high-fived him.

"For God's sake, Mom!"

The next afternoon I reminded Tate of that day.

He laughed, then snapped his fingers and said, "General Noggin and I have an idea. That's gonna be my next blog post."

TATE'S AWESOME PIGSKIN BLOG

When I was little my Nana Bird taught me all the words to "It's A Little Bitty Pissant Country Place," which is a song from *The Best Little Whorehouse in Texas* with Dolly Parton.

For Show-and-Share in kindergarten I put my hand straight up and said that I had something to share. That day I wore a cowboy vest and cowboy chaps my Nana Bird bought me, and I had a cowboy hat perched up on General Noggin that a real movie star had signed.

So, to get you in the mood of this, think of Dolly Parton in a sexy red dress and that white hair piled on her head, shimmying down the stairs to see all her cowboy customers in her whorehouse.

I sang the whole song: "It's just a little bitty pissant country place, ain't nothing much to see . . ."

I sang really loud when the words, "no drinking allowed," came up and when I called it a "piddly squatin'" place, I got on my knees. When the words, "one small thrill," came up, I put my thumbs up and waved them around and shook my hips like my Nana Bird taught me. She also told me to shout,

"There's nothing dirty going," as loud as I could, so I did.

I am not kidding when I say that all the kids in the class clapped and hooted when I was done and I took off my cowboy hat and bowed and then I took out my silver toy cap gun and shot it in the air. That made all the kids scream and laugh and Carlton wet his pants.

I could not understand why my teacher, Mrs. Pizchel, had this pinched expression, her mouth hanging open to her chest. She insisted on talking to Boss Mom after class, and I could tell she was all flustered up. All Boss Mom said when Mrs. Pizchel was done shaking her tail feathers was, "How did the song sound? Did Tate sing it on key?"

Here's a photo of a graph of thermodynamics.

Here's a photo of Dolly Parton.

Here's a photo of a three-story house I made from graham crackers, marshmallows, and toothpicks.

When I returned home from work, the triplets were in my front yard skipping and scampering about. Caden, his own home down our country road a ways, was nowhere to be seen. I bent to give them all a hug and kiss.

Hazel was dressed as a dragon, complete with a green tail and dragon head with a pink tongue.

Heloise was dressed as a "cat mouse elephant." She wore a cat tail, a mouse hat, and an elephant trunk.

Harvey was wearing a banana outfit.

"Hewwo, Aunt Jaden," Heloise said, her voice muffled through the elephant trunk. "I want to eat, eat some cookies of yours."

"Aunt Jaden," Hazel said, swirling her dragon tail. "I gotta poop."

"I a banana," Harvey said, wiggling. "Want a bite of me?"

"I can see that you're a banana, Harvey. No, I don't want a bite of you."

"*V* is bad," Hazel said, her face scrunched in dismay.

"She don't like the letter *V* anymore," Heloise said, helpfully pointing at Hazel.

"*V* is bad?" I asked Hazel.

"Because *V* rhymes with pee," Hazel said. "*V* pee."

"Yeah." Harvey giggled. "*V* pee. I don't like *V* pee. I like bananas."

"Pee pee," Heloise said, patting her mouse ears and hopping. "Mouse pee."

"Does your daddy know you're down here?" I tried not to laugh. Of course he didn't know. The triplets are not allowed off Caden's property to journey forth into the wild blue yonder alone.

The three of them studied the ground, scuffed their feet. Hazel pulled on her pink dragon tongue, Heloise swung her cat tail. The banana picked a dandelion and held it up for me.

I took the dandelion. I love the triplets. They cried for their mother, Marla, when she left them when they were two years old for weeks. They burst into tears and kept saying, "Mommy home? Mommy home?"

Mommy Marla had had a breakdown. It was after the triplets had been sick, one right after the other, and she hadn't been outside for three weeks.

Marla cried often since the triplets were born and I couldn't blame her. She had Damini and three babies, two of whom were colicky and would not stop crying for hours. I would help, in four-hour shifts. I had my job, too, and Tate, and I was ripped to the bone after leaving there. Parenting triplets is insane, that's the only way to describe it. It's *insane*.

Caden found Marla crying one night, her head on the washing machine as it ran. She said, "Caden, I can't stop crying," and indeed she couldn't. She was exhausted down to nothing.

Then one of the triplets started crying, the second one chimed in . . . and that was it. Marla walked upstairs, still crying because she couldn't stop, packed two suitcases, climbed in her car, and left.

He pleaded, he begged, and she turned her cell phone off, and no one could get in touch with her for two weeks. She finally called her parents, who were frantic with worry. She had driven to a tiny town in Montana, stopped at a hotel, and slept for a week. She was going to be a waitress. She would send child support. She was not returning.

Marla snapped. She absolutely lost it. The exhaustion and the relentlessness of taking care of three babies and Damini blew her apart. She couldn't do it. My brother is still not over losing her. He blames himself. He had his business to run but feels he did not help enough, even though I know he was up most of the night, too.

The triplets and Damini have no mother, so I have stepped in, as has my mother, to form two mothers for them. Caden has stepped in, from day one, to be a dad to Tate. That pathetic irony is not lost on us.

"Can we see Slinky?" Harvey said. Slinky is Tate's lizard. "He called us. He wants to play."

"Slinky the lizard called you on the phone?" I asked.

Harvey nodded. "I think. I think it him."

"I didn't know that Slinky knew how to dial a phone." I shook my head in wonder.

"He smart lizard," Heloise said. "Smart like a cat!"

"He call me on the phone!" Hazel said. "Meow meow meow!"

"Slinky want banana," Harvey said, pointing at himself.

"A genius lizard, obviously," I said. "Does your daddy know you're here?"

They wriggled. I tried not to laugh.

"You told your daddy you were coming to visit Slinky, right?"

They squiggled.

"We want to see Slinky the lizard," Harvey the banana said. "And Tate. Tate home?"

"Tate is home. What's your daddy doing?"

They shuffled and twisted.

"He tired."

"Sleepy."

"He taking nap. Night night."

"Nap time for Daddy," Hazel whispered through the dragon teeth. "We quiet."

"Yeah, we tiptoe tiptoe out da door." Heloise squeaked like a mouse. "See Slinky now?"

"And Tate. Where Tate? I play goblins with him." Harvey smiled.

"I love Tate!" Hazel grabbed the pink tongue of her dragon outfit.

"Me, too," Heloise said. She swung her cat tail.

"But not the letter *V*," Harvey said. "That bad letter. *H*. We like *H*."

"*H* for Heloise and Harvey and Hazel," Hazel said, pointing at each triplet. "*H*. Good letter."

"You three didn't tell your daddy you were coming down here." They were naughty, darling kids.

Heloise pulled on her elephant trunk. "He sleep. Have dreams. Sweet dreams, night night. We go tiptoe tiptoe and we be back soon. Meow meow!"

"Come on." I stuck out my hands.

"Where we going?" Hazel said.

"Where do you think, Hazel?"

Her dragon hat slid down her face. I pulled it back up.

I took their little hands and we strolled through the maple trees, the leaves fluttering, down the road to Caden's house. We stopped a few times to stare at bugs and birds. Caden's house is a sprawling, craftsman-style home. His property is the same as mine—fields, an old orchard, fir and pine trees, and the flowers we all grow as a family.

When we walked through the front door, I saw Caden crashed on the sofa, as I'd suspected. He and his employees had had a wedding for four hundred this weekend in the city and each table had a dog or cat made of flowers because the bride and groom were vets.

"Come on, guys. Let's go outside." We went to their back-yard. Caden has ten acres, too. He's fenced about an acre for the triplets. There's a full playground out there with a slide, swings, professionally built tree house, and a pirate ship. For the next three hours I watched the triplets. At the end of three hours, Caden came racing out, panicked, his hair plastered to his face, that hysterical expression in his eyes that parents get when they can't instantly find their children.

"It's okay, Caden, I have the miniature troublemakers."

Caden bent over, tried to catch his breath, and swore quietly, his huge chest heaving in and out.

I heard them giggle. They were running around playing Red Monster. It's a game they made up. It means take off your clothes and run and roar like a monster.

I laughed.

Caden dropped his head in his hands. "Good Lord. I cringe thinking what the teenage years are going to be like."

I watched the triplets run naked, in circles, roaring like monsters.

"You're gonna have a hell of a time."

"*V* pee!" Hazel screamed. "*V* pee!"

5

"Mom, I gotta talk to you."

Tate grabbed a white wicker chair and pulled it close to mine on the porch.

Ahead of us, the sun was going down. Somehow it appeared that we had two suns headed to the horizon separated by blue, gray, and pink streaks across the sky. I pulled my blue fuzzy blanket closer around my shoulders.

"Take a second for the sunset, Tate."

"Yeah, it's nice. Okay, uh, Mom."

"Three stripes of pink."

"Cool. Hey—"

"It's like watching natural, outdoorsy magic. New scene. New colors. New design."

"Yeah, awesome. Uh. New topic." He poked my arm.

"You poked me." I poked him back.

"I know. I did. By the way, I'm still hungry."

"You have to be kidding. You had two huge bowls of roasted clam chowder, half a loaf of garlic bread, two oranges, and chocolate cake."

"I know, but that was an hour ago. I'm hungry again. Can you make me Nothing Fancy Spaghetti From The Old Days with Parmesan?"

"Argh."

"Thanks, Boss Mom. Tastes better when you make it. Yeah. You know, I've been practicing basketball."

"No, again."

"And, Mom, also, in PE the teacher has seen me shooting in gym and, uh, he had the basketball coach come in and watch. You know, Mr. Boynton."

"No again, Tate."

"And the coach, he's, uh . . . he's gonna call you."

"And I'll tell him you can't try out."

He leaned toward me, those bright blue eyes eager. "I want you to tell him I can try out."

"I've heard that loud and clear," I snapped.

"Mom!"

"Don't yell at me."

"I'm not yelling, but I want you to listen to me, please, Mom, just listen."

"I have listened. The answer is still no."

He stood up, said, "Damn it," and his chair fell over.

My mouth dropped. Tate rarely gets mad. I think he's had too many people say too many mean things to him from an early age and the anger burned right on out of him. Plus, he's an easygoing guy.

"I want to try out! Don't you get it, Mom?" He threw out his hands. "I love basketball. I love it. I love shooting the ball and passing it, or at least pretending I'm passing it when I'm playing by myself. I love pretending I'm a defender, I love pretending someone is defending me, and I love watching it."

"Then watch it, you're not playing on a team."

"I want to—"

"You could hurt yourself, the shunt—"

"Even Dr. Robbins said I could play. He said there's no guarantee, but it would probably be fine, and I'm not going to get hurt!" he shouted.

"You don't know you won't get hurt, Dr. Robbins doesn't know that—"

"Mom, if I'm on the basketball team, then I might . . ."

"You might what?"

He brushed his auburn curls off his head in frustration with both hands. "I might—"

"Yes?"

"I might, in some small way"—his face tightened up and he wiped away tears—"I might belong."

I closed my eyes. Oh, how it hurts a mother's heart to have their child feel that they don't belong.

"Mom, think about it. I could wear a uniform. I could be on a team. I could get to know more people. I could play in front of other kids, and it would make me seem more normal. Maybe I could even be good at it. I could make a basket or two in a game."

"Tate, it's not a huge school. All the kids know you."

"They know me as the bigheaded kid. A lot of kids can't even look at me. Or they look at me and they think I'm ugly, don't deny it, Mom. They've got these looks of disgust on their faces, or they stare. Some kids are past it, but not many. They can't get past General Noggin, they don't know how to handle me, what to say. I'm not a person yet to them. You know, a human with feelings and emotions. I'm a thing."

The pain in my chest was so piercing I had to force myself to take a breath. "Tate, you can't measure yourself by basketball—"

"Why not, Mom? Why not?" His voice cracked. "Everyone measures themselves, values themselves for something. Being a neurosurgeon. Having a family. Relationships. Why not basketball? I'm not saying I want to go and drink beer or smoke pot, I want to be on the basketball team."

"Tate, I'd love you to be able to, but no—"

The phone rang.

"That's the coach, Mom, please please please!" He grabbed my arm, then hugged me, his arms wrapping me up. "Please! Come on, Mom!"

I stalked into the house and picked up the phone. It was, indeed, Coach Boynton. I listened. I talked. He listened. He talked.

"No, he can't. I'm sorry . . . I understand he has some talent . . . okay, a lot of talent. . . . I know he wants to. . . . There are medical concerns. . . . Hey, Robert, my answer is no. . . . I'm not arguing with you on this. . . . I know you didn't mean to be pushy, and I know you want Tate on the team. . . . You can win a championship without him. . . . I know you feel it in your bones that Tate will help you win, Robert, and it's too bad for your old bones. . . . Yes, I'll tell my mother hello. You tell your patient wife who puts up with so much crap from you hello, too."

"Mom!" Tate wailed when I hung up the phone. "Mom! Come on, Mom!"

"Tate!" I slammed a mug on the counter and it shattered. "Don't ask me again, we're not talking about this again, we're done. Done!"

"No, we are *not* done, Witch Mavis, you are overprotective and you're . . . you're mean, and you're not letting me live my life and you're making me feel like nothing. *Like nothing!* All I want to do is be normal."

"You're not normal!" My voice went up an octave, and I took a breath to calm myself down. "You're not. Not only because of your head but because of how smart you are. You could be in college by now. You're a genius and you want to risk losing that, risk losing that brilliant mind because you get hurt on a basketball court? For a ball? For a basket? No."

"My real mom would let me play basketball."

I had to force air in as ragged, harsh emotions threatened to swamp me like a sneaker wave. His *real* mom? Did he mean the mom who abandoned him at birth? The one who walked out? The one whom we hadn't heard from in so long, I couldn't remember exactly when we'd last talked? "That's a low blow, Tate."

"But she would, I know she would." His face was red.

I grabbed a sponge and scrubbed the counter furiously.

"She would be a lot nicer about it. The people I talked to about the Other Mother said she was nice when she wasn't messed up with drugs."

I scrubbed more furiously.

"She would get it, you don't, because you're not trying to see what I'm saying. I'm always on the outside, Boss Mom, and only one time, this time, I want to be on the inside. I want to be part of something. I want to have somewhere to go after school.

I want to have somewhere to be on a Friday night instead of alone. I want to get all sweaty and play basketball and try to win games! I want to be in high school, a normal high school kid, and be called up front during assemblies when they introduce the basketball team. . . ."

I scrubbed until my arm ached.

"I bet Brooke would be a better mother, Boss Mom, and I'd be playing basketball!"

Now that did it. I threw the sponge across the room. Witch Mavis was flaming. "Tate, your Other Mother would not be a better mother. Your Other Mother is on *drugs*. She is selfish and irresponsible and weak. If she was raising you, you would probably hardly ever see her and be living in some hovel amidst drug paraphernalia and creepy men. Don't you ever, *ever* tell me that Brooke would be a better mother to you when you're trying to get your way, don't you ever do that again."

He slapped his hands to his face.

"I am your *real* mother, Tate. I will always be your *real* mother." I was semi-shouting. "Your Other Mother is my sister and she's a lousy sister and she's a lousy daughter and she's a lousy mother. I am the one who has happily taken care of you your whole life—"

"And you're a good mom but not about this! About this you're a bad mother!"

"I am not a bad mother—"

"Yes, you are, yes, you are!" His blue eyes became brighter with tears. "God, Mom, it's the only thing I want, the only thing!" He turned around, ran to the front door, and took off.

"Tate! Tate! Where are you going?"

I yelled at him to stop, but didn't stop. He ran down the street full blast.

I leaned against the doorjamb.

He did not come back until one o'clock in the morning. When he came back, he shot hoops for two hours and ignored me.

"I want to play basketball, Mom." He walked past me, calmly, and went upstairs to bed.

*   *   *

"He's beyond brilliant."

I nodded my head at the teachers seated in a circle. "Tate's pretty sharp."

My comment was an understatement. Tate is brilliant, but I do not brag about his academic accomplishments. Frankly, parents who brag about their children are obnoxious. I think they're using their own kid to show off their prowess as parents. *Come on.* The kid's a person, not a commodity to throw around for cheap praise.

"Tate is much more than pretty sharp," Ike Shimolo, his science teacher, said to me, running a hand over his bald head. "He's a genius. I gave him a practice SAT test yesterday in class, told him to have fun with it. I checked it today. He didn't miss any. I gave him a practice AP Calculus and AP Chem test, too, and he aced both."

"He thinks tests are fun. He always has. He's been taking practice SAT tests for years." I did not say that he started taking SAT subject tests in sixth grade for "amusement challenges," Tate's words, not mine.

My mother crossed her thin legs. She did not have to be in Hollywood until tomorrow. She was wearing a short blue dress and matching blue four-inch heels, her cleavage peeking out. She called it her Conference with the Teachers Conservative Outfit.

"When he was four we used to study the dictionary together." My mother opened her eyes, as in, *Isn't that strange?* "I wanted to take him out for a beer, but no. He wanted to sit for hours studying words and having me quiz him. He's a bizarrely odd child, freakishly smart. What to do, what to do?"

The teachers appeared a bit baffled at my mother's comments, not to mention her star status, so I hurried on in. The teachers had not been expecting a soap opera star this afternoon. "He likes the academic part of school," I said. "He likes to study. He actually reads the textbooks."

"I've seen him do it." My mother said this in an accusatory tone, as if a crime had been committed. "I gave him a book about cars one time when he was eight. He memorized the whole damn thing, then went down the street and worked for the mechanic for weeks so he could learn about repairing cars. I had my favorite designer make him a mechanic's outfit. He was precious. I thought he'd take a quick gander at the book and he and I could go to car shows and he'd get a kick out of gaping at the skimpily dressed models and Corvettes, but no. He was not interested in boobs. He was interested in the consistency of motor oil and carburetors."

"And all aspects of science, brains, numbers, and equations are of interest to him," I added, to distract the teachers from my mother's boob comment.

"Shouldn't a boy be sneaking girly magazines or something?" She leaned forward, her bob swinging. "That would be much more normal."

I kicked her with my toe.

The teachers were stunned with the famous movie star and strange things flowing from her mouth.

Mary Cho, his AP History teacher, cleared her throat. "He's in four AP classes and has As in all of them. Since he's had different AP teachers the last couple of years, he has had *somewhat* of a different learning experience. Different essay topics, books, pacing. The research papers I get from him are the best I've seen. Ever. I've taught twenty-five years."

"He writes at a graduate level for his English essays, too." His English teacher, Evelyn Pops, fiddled with her long fingers. She was obsessed with Jane Austen, even belonged to a fan club. "His analysis, his comparisons . . ."

"Last night he compared a whole bunch of chemicals to each other." My mother sighed, but I knew she was pleased on the inside. "I had to sit and listen for *two hours*. I had three glasses of wine. Things started to swim at the end, rhodium, tungsten, gallium, actinium . . . it's all dry and dreary."

"He gets teased some," Mr. Shimolo said.

"But kids seem to like him."

"And he's a tall kid, that helps. . . ."

"The other day, a kid told him he had a head like smashed

Play-Doh, and another kid, a girl, a girl in the most popular group, you know there's always that group, she tripped the kid straight-up." Mrs. Pops grinned. "He landed on his face. And then"—her face was now perplexed—"Tate helped the kid up who had teased him."

"I wish all the kids who teased my grandson would be expelled forever and sent to schools in Yemen without plumbing where they would be forced to squat and poop outside," my mother said in a singsong, pleasant voice. "Or maybe Somalia, where there's a drought and terrorist men running around with ferocious guns and the education of snails. Then they could see what a bad day truly involves."

"Okay, Mother."

"It's the truth. The punks who tease my grandson should—"

"Okay, Mother." I patted her knee. She was worse than me sometimes. She sighed heavily, tossed her auburn bob back, wrinkled that sculpted nose. She was nonchalant, but it was an act. The woman loved Tate to distraction. She had shed even more tears than me, and my tears have been endless. (True disclosure: If she could, she would have sent the bullies to Yemen or Somalia to be with snail-educated people.)

"Ms. Bruxelle and Mrs. Bruxelle, we have to figure out what to do to keep him challenged—"

"He could graduate early," Mrs. Pops said. "He's ready for college."

"In college he could get laid," my mother mused. "Have love affairs."

Two of the teachers actually sucked in their breath.

"Really, Mother?"

She drew two fingers across her red-lipsticked lips as if zipping them, then said, "Sex makes your complexion younger. Look at my face."

"That's Botox."

"A bit. And a face-lift. Or more. But the glow is there from sex. Or at least the desire for it." She gazed meaningfully at me. There had been no other serious relationships in her life since my father, but in the last couple of years she had *finally* started to be open to it. "You have it, too, Jaden, the desire for it, don't deny it."

"I don't think we need to discuss sex or desire at this exact moment, do you, Mother?"

"They brought college up!"

"That doesn't mean—" I stopped, turned back to the teachers. "I'm going to keep him here. As you know, his best friends, Anthony and Milt, are here, too. He knows all these kids. They're used to him. I still need you all to help with the bullying."

The teachers nodded vigorously. The attorneys had already been here and they all knew it.

"I understand," Mr. Shimolo said. "He's a genius. We wanted to tell you about his options."

"His brain boils with brilliance, vodka on hot rocks," my mother said.

I turned to her. "Have you ever dumped vodka on hot rocks, Mother?"

"Yes, I have, and that's Tate's brain."

"Let's not talk about vodka right now. We'll do it later, after some tea. Can you tell us about those options, Mr. Shimolo?"

I could tell Mr. Shimolo and the other teachers were still stuck on the vodka and hot rocks comments.

"And the options would be?" I prodded.

"Maybe he could study at the medical center?" Miss Cho said, a bit dazed by my mother, she does that to people. "An internship where we could release him from school? A private study?"

"College classes half the day, here half the day?" Mr. Shimolo suggested.

"Perhaps a local laboratory would have a mentor program?" Mrs. Pops said.

"Tate knows how to start fires and explosions in the laboratory of his Experiment Room," my mother said, clearly impressed with Tate's abilities. "He's careful with the dynamite, though. He knows he has to use that outside only, back in the poppy field."

"Tate uses dynamite?" Mrs. Pops asked.

"No, no . . ." I lied. I knew my mother had bought some for him.

"Only on Tuesdays," my mother drawled. "He gets a thrill out of big bangs. And don't ask him about the big bang theory or he will go off on that discussion for *hours,* you'll be stone-cold drunk by the time he's done. Don't get him going on the complexities of the human brain, either, or you'll start wishing you were a vodka bottle, you know what I mean?" She mocked drinking out of a bottle.

I glowered at her. "As teachers," I redirected the group, "let's discuss what we should do, academically speaking, for Tate. . . ."

Tate talked fluently before he was two. He was doing basic math at three. He read then, too, not a few words, but hundreds of words. He studied books all the time. We used to read together on the rocking chair. He studied thesauruses and dictionaries, and as the years went on, science and technology, quantitative physics, nuclear science, and micro- and macro-economics. He received an A in calculus in eighth grade at the local university.

He has studied the brain since he was three because he was curious about his own head. I bought him books with photos and detailed information about the human brain. He wrote letters to different high-level neurosurgeons, with his questions about brains, and included a photo of himself. He even wrote to Ethan when Ethan was still in New York because he had read an article about him. They all wrote back, and he is still in contact with a number of them via e-mail.

Tate remembers things that happened to him before he was three years old in TechniColor. For example, he remembers emergencies at the hospital, including the exact order of the medical care he received. He could repeat, and he understood, what the doctors said to him, even if they spoke nine or ten sentences. He memorized a hundred words in Spanish in two days and still knows them, and he remembers a day I cried when I was wearing a gray coat and a purple hat by a duck pond. He has a photographic memory. He grasps the sciences and technology as easy as he would grasp how to light a match. Advanced math is enjoyable for him.

Tate's utter brilliance did not take the pain away from having a deformed head, but it did help to balance out the unfairness a little bit.

TATE'S AWESOME PIGSKIN BLOG

My uncle Caden, who owns Witches and Warlocks Florist in town and recently made a four-foot-tall purple elephant in a bikini out of flowers for the manager of the zoo, reads romance novels.

Here's a photo of the purple elephant in a bikini. Here's a photo of him reading a romance novel.

Yep, he told me I could put this photo in. Why? Because he's cool. Because he's cool with himself and doesn't care what anyone thinks.

Here's a photo of my friends, Milt and Anthony, with bows and ribbons in their hair that my cousins Heloise and Hazel put in. They're cool with this, too.

Here's a photo of my Boss Mom with a bandanna around her head after she finished gutting fish for a food bank. No, she doesn't care if she's photographed with fish guts on her overalls.

Being on the outside of everyone else, that would be moi, you get a pretty good look on the inside and the inside isn't always pretty.

But what's pretty is when people are who they are and don't hide it.

That would not be me. I'm still hiding from my own blog. Maybe I'll post a photo soon of General Noggin and me.

But here's more about me: I like to experiment. I have my own Experiment Room. I love science and studying anything to do with the brain. I'm interested in DNA, genetics and Bernoulli's equations. I love basketball. Man, that is my favorite. I love to read, not romance novels—sorry, Uncle Caden—and I don't sleep much because I have a lot of thinkin' to do, and I love to eat.

I like thinking about the future, you know, what it's going to look like, especially technology with brain surgery. I like gadgets. My handwriting is craggy, that's all I have to say about that. I don't like poetry unless it's about farts or burps or something like that. I like geography, but I don't like a lot of the classics. You know, I can't get into them, they're slooooowww sometimes with that fancy language. I don't like cleaning bathrooms, but for some reason I like vacuuming. I like driving cars. I like driving them fast so Boss Mom takes me out to the track so I can race fast and not get a ticket.

I get lonely sometimes. I feel alone other times. I look different and that's always been a struggle, not so much for me, but for other people, which makes it a struggle for me.

I love my family. Man, I cannot imagine life without my family. Without my Boss Mom I probably would have constructed a spaceship and flown to Uranus (Your Anus).

Now write to me and tell me about you. I really, really want to know. I won't put it on my blog unless you tell me I can. Don't tell me your hair color and height, that stuff isn't freaking important, right? Tell me about YOU. The inside stuff. What you dream of or are scared of, what makes you cry. Here are my answers: I dream of playing basketball, I'm scared I won't get to do what I want to do because of my head, and I cry about all kinds of stuff, especially when I hear about something bad happening to a kid.

Include photos of things you think are cool, or people you think are cool, or yourself if you want.

Here's a photo of my nieces and nephews dressed as pink pigs carrying pitchforks as you can see. They are who they are and they are happy. What they think inside is on the outside. I hope they always feel free to dress as pink pigs with pitchforks.

Here's a photo of the inside of an atom. (Pretty)

Here's a photo of the inside of a colon. (Not pretty)

Here's a photo of a six-scoop caramel sundae. I ate the whole thing. Six scoops of ice cream and I was still hungry.

"Mom Mom Mom Mom!" Tate thundered down the stairs with his laptop to the kitchen. "Look at this! Look!"

I peered at the screen. He had thirty-five messages from people of all ages, including a couple of people who worked with my mother on her soap opera, to whom she'd sent the link for Tate's blog.

"They answered my question on my blog about themselves! Read 'em!"

I read them. Some of the letters made me tear up.

"I know, Boss Mom! They made me cry, too!"

I laughed at a couple.

"I *know*, Boss Mom, I laughed, too!"

This is what came out: Honesty. Sheer, raw honesty about people's lives, hopes, dreams, fears, their successes and failures, embarrassing moments, hobbies, and interests. They enclosed photos of "cool" people from around the world, quotes, and news articles about inspiring people.

"Boss Mom," Tate said, running an excited hand through his curls. "I finally think I'm relating to people, you know? I'm having conversations. I could be, maybe, a person that people want to talk to and get to know and share stuff and stuff. I'm writing back to whoever writes to me." He grabbed six double-chocolate cookies. "This blog is frickin' awesome."

The stories kept pouring in to Tate's blog. He posted, with permission, a lot of them.

His daily blog counter shot up into the hundreds.

I went to see my client, George Bonaparte, the next morning. Eight o'clock, on the dot. He insisted on promptness.

George is in his early eighties. He lives in a huge mansion with views of the city, bought with the money he made at the trucking company he owns. He was a poor young man, bought a truck, worked hard, bought another truck, and another. Bonaparte Trucking was born, and it's now a nationwide company.

The mansion is on the historic register. Inside it is filled with expensive furniture, heavy brocade curtains, ugly art, half-modern, half-old, all mixed together in a truly garish way, plus framed photos of him with Important People, heads of animals he shot during guided tours in Africa where they practically parade the animal out for you to shoot, trophies, and other yuck. It makes me feel claustrophobic and the animal heads are freaky.

George Bonaparte is obnoxious. Think of a boar and cross it with a hissing possum and moonshine. That's who he is.

His daughter, Kendra, was at the mansion that morning. She's tall, blond, forty-one years old, and wears animal-print heels. Kendra is a CEO of a major corporation. Young, famous, and competent. I've seen her pictured in different magazines, in tailored suits, impeccably groomed.

She was drunk as a skunk.

"Hello, Kendra," I said. "How are you?"

She raised a shot glass toward me and wobbled on over. "Sleeping Beauty and elephant's knees, I say cheers to you, Jaden. I am here with my father all day today. All day! All day! You know, that man in the bed who still tells me I'm a disappointment. This is what I've heard all my life." She scrunched up her face, tried to stand still, and barked out, "You are a disappointment. With a *D*, Kendra!" She waved her hand in the air, as if dismissing me. "Disappointment! You always have been! You could never get it together. Everything is hard for you to understand!"

Kendra took another drink and yelled, "To victory! To mice! To butterflies that do not get drunk!"

"I see you're practicing self-relaxing techniques."

She burped. "Glorious burp! I'm in the Disappointment House. It was Shaina's turn yesterday, and Tony's before her, and they left me liquor." She tried to stand nice and tall, then intoned, "Liquor Picker Poker Rum, I've got room for my big fat bum!" She burped again. "Ha! I'll bet Daddy would not click a dick with that one. How about this one? Scotch Potch Hopscotch One, I've got a dad that's just about done!"

I walked over to her father's bedroom door and shut it before Kendra trip-tropped into another rhyme. Too late.

"I've got tequila, I've got pie, I've got a dad who's about to die!"

"Okay, Kendra, nice rhymes. Perhaps we should keep it down? Can it for the moment?"

"Nope," she declared. "Not now. He already hates me, what's a teeny more hate? Hey! I've got another one." She snapped her fingers. "He's been mean, he's been sly, I won't shout, but I won't lie. He's rung my bell, and he's going to hell!"

"Did you study poetry in college?"

"No! No poetry. I went to Yale and I studied economics and finance and business and I was a Rhodes scholar and I married the right guy, the guy that Daddy picked, and he ended up being a gay guy, and the gay guy was cutthroat and nasty and ambitious, a younger him, and now we're getting divorced and I did what Daddy told me to do in the futile hope he would approve of me and I am"—she tipped her head up toward the ceiling and started plucking through the air with her hand, as if she was trying to find words—"I am pissy wissy! And screwy wrewy! And not happy!"

"You're not screwy wrewy, Kendra," I said softly. I had spent a lot of time with her, her sister, and brother, all who were struggling with their father's death. Not because they would miss him, but because he was miserable as a father emotionally, and physically abusive when they were young, with a fondness for spanking them with his belt. Sometimes, in my experience, the people whose grief is the worst are the ones who lose someone with whom they have unfinished business, or with whom the relationship has disintegrated.

When the relative dies they're left with broken glass, emotionally speaking. It cannot be resolved. The ones with the strong relationships, there's nothing there but clean grief, as I call it. Clean grief. Tears, but no regrets, resentments, or fury.

That was not the case here. The disappointed daddy was dying and there was no resolution, no needed apologies, no forgiveness.

"See here, Jaden. I believe the circus has come to town and there is a lion in the pantry." Kendra took another swig, then clicked her teeth together. "Also, there is a mean monkey in that bedroom. Don't go in unless you want the monkey to bite you. Don't get bit. The monkey's name is Dad. Dad is bad. Dad bad. Bad Dad."

"Kendra, how about if I make you a sandwich?"

"A sandwich! Ha and ha. That would be dee-lish-us. I'll have a sandwich with popcorn and tequila with a side of a Mona Lisa and Les Misérables, because I'm miserable. You want a bite?"

"No, thank you. Come on, Kendra. Bring yourself to the kitchen. I'll check on your dad and then make you your tequila and popcorn sandwich." I would not be making her a tequila and popcorn sandwich. Turkey and ham would do. Maybe mayo if we wanted to live on the edge.

"Yum!" she said, rubbing her stomach. Her hand stopped abruptly and she said, ever so clearly, "I believe I am now going to puke." She stumbled to the bathroom, crashed into a wall, then hit the toilet, possibly with her head.

"See ya in a minute," I called to her.

"Yuck duck!" she said. "Ew yucky!"

I entered the bedroom.

The bad monkey was in a bad mood. He threw a pillow at me.

"Good morning, Mr. Bonaparte."

"Not a good morning, Jaden. I'm dying," he wheezed out. "How can it be good?"

"Hello, Mrs. Bonaparte."

Mrs. Bonaparte looked worse than her daughter, but she was not drunk as a skunk. She was only sixty-two. She married him at twenty, had Kendra at twenty-one. For an inexplicable reason, she allowed herself to be stuck. The woman didn't leave. Verbal abuse scrambled her brain, smashed her self-esteem, and locked her up as if she were in prison with a bloodsucking gargoyle standing guard.

"Hello, Jaden." Her platinum-blond hair was all over her head, her mascara smeared, her lipstick smudged. She'd lost about ten pounds in the last month off her skinny frame. Mr. Bonaparte despised fat women and hammered the mother and daughters with that degrading fact.

"Don't hello Mrs. Bonaparte," Mr. Bonaparte snapped from the bed. "It's me you need to be talking to, missy. Me. She can't do anything. This medication isn't doing shit. The doctors know nothing. Now you get me something that works, or I'm going to get your ass fired."

"Some days I think that would be a fine, freeing event."

Mr. Bonaparte was shrunken and wrinkled. He said, "Maybe you deserve it."

"Maybe I do, Mr. Bonaparte. Balls and tarnation, maybe I should wish for it."

"You still have those fake diamonds in your hair. Fake! Fake! diamonds! I buy my wife real diamonds!"

"I wear my fake diamonds to annoy you." I loved my crystals from Tate, so my temper was now piqued.

"They do annoy me. They're annoying!"

"I know, but it gets your heart rate up, which is helpful. Want to sit up so you can shout at full throttle?"

"I don't want to sit up and I don't want help, and where did you get all that red hair?"

"Rumor has it there's some Irish blood in the line."

"Irish blood! Bloody Irish, not for me. In my company, I hired men. Didn't need women driving my rigs with all those hormones. Women can't drive at the same level as men. They get distracted easily, can't take corners, emotional! Weaker sex. My daughter, she deserted me! She works for another company, not mine. Said I didn't respect her. My wife never worked. She knew to stay home, do what she was told, and take care of me."

"That must have been a hellaciously hard job for her."

Out in the living room, Kendra started singing a beer-drinking song. She went on about stalking the town criminal and stuffing him into a trunk and pushing the car into a lagoon. "And he sang with the fishes, he sang with the fishes, oh how he sang with the fishes for the rest of his life. Kaboom and boom and there he loomed."

"Bah! It wasn't hard for her! I worked all the time. She stayed home on her fanny. Didn't do anything." Mr. Bonaparte still had a shock of white hair. "I want to get up now, I want to get up."

He swung his legs over the bed.

"Sir, please don't. You've had a hip replacement that didn't work, remember, and you have cancer all over your body. You need to stay in bed. I can't support you."

"I don't need support! I'm getting up, damn it, and I'm going to tell Kendra to *shut up*."

Kendra chortled out a new song. This one was about a woman who decided that she was going to explore the world without a man, carefree, and drinking whiskey. "Whisky this, whiskey that, I ain't going to get caught in the corporate trap! Whiskey this, whiskey that, I'm going to Paris, you can kiss my ass!"

"Shut up, Kendra!" her father bellowed.

"Shut up, Dad, you old fart!" she bellowed back, then sang a song called, "My Little Titty, My Little Kitty . . ."

Her father's jaw dropped, his face turning purple. "Kendra, shut up!"

"No, Dad, you *disappointer,* you shut up and soon you'll be shut up forever!" Kendra came to the door and burped. "I'm a disappointment. I didn't do it right. But you know what, Dad? I don't care!"

Kendra couldn't see it, but I could. Mr. Bonaparte's face fell.

"My little titty, my little kitty . . ." she chirped.

Mr. Bonaparte leaned back in bed, stared at his wife, and bit out, "Why is she talking like that to me, Joyce? I've been a good husband, a good father. She's ungrateful. Her and her siblings. Ungrateful, miserable, spoiled. Disappointments! Capital *D!*"

Joyce did not respond. She was a sticky white color and one of the most run-down people I've ever seen.

"Joyce!" Mr. Bonaparte shouted.

"What?" she clipped, short and impatient.

His dark eyes opened wide. "Joyce?"

"What?" She crossed her legs, and I noticed she was trembling. She was a skeleton. Anorexia happens at all ages. I had talked with her about this, but she denied there was a problem. Perhaps the problem would end in about a month. I eyed Mr. Bonaparte. Maybe less than that.

"Don't use that tone with me, Joyce. What's gotten into you?" Mr. Bonaparte jabbed a gnarled finger at his wife. "What? You having one of your moods again? I won't tolerate it, Joyce!"

"Nothing has gotten into me. Lie back and relax." Mrs. Bonaparte swayed in her chair.

"Don't tell me what to do, I won't be bossed around by you or any other stupid woman, you two together, you and Jaden, you do nothing for me, nothing! Standing there, staring at me, what am I, a snake in an aquarium?"

"If you were a snake in an aquarium, you'd drown or the other snakes would eat you so you'd stop biting them," I said.

"Mr. Bonaparte, I'm going to take your vitals, talk about how you're feeling, then later you can have lunch."

"Lunch, I don't want lunch. Joyce can't cook at all. Did you order out, Joyce? Did you? What did you get this time? I don't want that Chinese crap from the other day! Dumb choice! Dumb!"

Joyce stood up, pale, white, shaking.

"All these years, you never had to work a day in your life and I ask that you get my meals on time, too hard for you, too hard, Joyce. And I gave you servants and cars and clothes, you damn near spent all my money."

"I never did that, George, never." Mrs. Bonaparte put her shoulders back.

"Sit down, Joyce, no one needs you standing up. Don't you stare down at me, woman!" He pounded a fist into the pillow. "Damn it, where ya goin'?"

Joyce put her hand out to mine. "Thank you, Jaden. You're a saint."

I shook it, gently. She was a tiny slip of a woman. "No, not a saint. Dealing with irascible people is sometimes part of my job."

"He makes it miserable." She turned to her husband, flailing around in the bed. "Good-bye, George."

"What? What the hell do you mean, good-bye? Get the lunch and bring it in here, woman. I need my socks changed, I'm gonna get another disease on my feet if you don't take care of me better. This is your fault, Joyce!"

"I'm done, George."

"What do you mean? Speak up. I can never understand you. It's her background. Poor family. Dad never made much of himself. Uneducated. Never went to college."

"I can't take this anymore." Mrs. Bonaparte swayed on her feet, and I moved pretty quick, thinking she was going to fall. "I'm sorry you're dying, but you're mean. Belittling and condescending and rude. To me, to the kids."

"No, I'm not! You're too sensitive. You make me say the things I do. You don't know when to shut up. You do things to make me mad. The kids are Mommy's boys and girls. You did that to me, you did that. That's why they cringe when I'm around. They never come home to see me. I have to die before I see my kids!" He leaned over and coughed, a messy, harsh cough.

"It's you, George. You're at fault. It's always been you. I should have left years ago."

Kendra sang out in the living room, top volume, "A one, two, three . . . down down down into the earth he'll go, a coffin here, a coffin there, grass growing 'round his knees. . . ."

Mr. Bonaparte gasped.

Mrs. Bonaparte stood taller, but a couple of tears fell.

"You're crying, Joyce!" George blustered. "Close off the waterworks, you know I can't stand a weak woman! I don't need to see you being a baby!"

"I'm crying because I can't believe how many years I've lost, how many years I've cried myself to sleep, cowered from you, been scared, and I didn't leave. And now, you're dying, and you're still trying to control me, and I still stand around and take it, and I can't take it anymore." She burst into tears. "I can't take it. I'm supposed to be here until you die, but if I have to sit here one more day and listen to you—"

"Listen to me!" he shouted. "Listen to me, what do you mean? You've never been smart. I've had to take care of everything, you get confused and upset, you can't even think, and you need me to think for you! *I'm sick!* This ain't about you, Joyce!"

"Yes, yes, it is." She blinked back the tears. "It's about me. You ranting and raving and taking out your anger on me. Decades of meanness . . ."

She turned and gave me a hug. "I'm sorry, Jaden. Call whoever you need to, please. He needs nurses around the clock. I'm up most of the time getting him things he needs, and I haven't slept hardly at all in two weeks."

"I understand, Joyce. I know what to do." I hugged her back. It is not my job to be a marriage counselor. It is my job to care for the patient and be a help to the family, not repair a severely broken marriage that should have ended decades ago.

"Good-bye, George." Joyce wobbled out of the bedroom.

"You gold digger, you stupid bitch, get back in here, get back right this minute! Shit, Joyce, I ain't kidding. I will write you out of my will so fast your head will fly off. I'll give it all away, the whole lot of it, the money, the homes, the stocks, it's all going to a gorilla organization, better monkeys than you, Joyce, better monkeys than you!"

He turned beet red and kicked a foot, his healthy foot. He wheezed and coughed.

In the other room I heard Kendra, the CEO, stop singing for a moment, Joyce's low voice cutting across Mr. Bonaparte's ranting.

"I'll show her who's still the boss of the house. That woman has always needed a firm hand to keep her in line, a slap or two to wake her up, and I'm going to show it to her—"

I tried to keep Mr. Bonaparte calm, and to tamp down my own intense dislike of the man. "Please take a breath with me. . . . Let me help you, settle down. . . . I understand you want to get up. . . . No, I cannot let you strike your wife, or your daughter. . . ."

"Get her back in here now, Jaden! Now! Get your ass back in here, stupid bitch, Joyce!"

"I will not make them come back in here, Mr. Bonaparte. Especially because you're being abusive, horrible to both your wife and your daughter."

Kendra burst into a new, high-pitched drunken song. "We are free, fluffy hairy birds, no more turds in our lives . . . free to fly, free to laugh, free to sleep with men we don't bring home to Daddy . . . free because I'm not married to the gay guy that Daddy picked out. . . . Do la la la la la . . . My daddy cannot mock me, don't mess with me, you cock. . . ."

Mr. Bonaparte turned about purple, struggled to get up, and pushed me out of the way with truly shocking strength, as I pleaded, "Please stay in bed, I'll get your walker, you're going to fall. . . ." He stood up, shouted, "Kendra, I'm coming for you, you drunk, disappointing brat. . . ."

And he fell. Splat. Right on down. I tried to catch him, but his weight was too much. He crashed to the floor and broke his other hip.

We all have visions of dying with our loved ones around us, soft music playing on a harp in the background, receiving some last words of wisdom on how to live a love-filled life.

That happens often, but often it doesn't.

For the people who have been truly maniacal to their loved ones, well, they end up like Mr. Bonaparte, still a vicious rat, still unloved. The families may or may not come to be with him or her near the end.

People are often criticized for not being there when their parents die, not providing care. Now it could be that the child is a selfish frog, a self-centered and narcissistic coward when it comes to death, unsure of what to say or do because of immaturity or a lack of generosity, so they stay away. It could also be, however, that the person dying was a porcupine needle–stabbing whack job who hurt his family and anyone within twenty feet of his razor-sharp tongue.

Those people die alone.

Even if there are family members emotionally blackmailed into coming, even if they're sitting around the porcupine as death creeps up, they still die alone because no one cares when they're gone.

I ate nine red cinnamon Gummi Bears that night.

6

The next night, as a family, we celebrated our annual Captain and First Mate Rescue Day.

Captain and First Mate Rescue Day refers to the time when Faith fell off the ship into the Atlantic Ocean on their journey to America, Grace jumped in after her cousin to save her, and the captain and first mate jumped in to save both women, who were quickly sinking because of the weight of their dresses.

We celebrate the captain, who was rumored to have dolphin blood running through his veins, and the first mate, brave soul.

My mother flew up, Caden and his kids came over, and we all drove together to Portland to go on a dinner cruise on the Willamette River. My mother wore a burgundy-colored designer dress and a blond wig. Tate and Caden wore suits. I wore a red dress with a cross bodice. The triplets wore matching sailor out-fits with Mardi Gras masks. Damini wore a short gold dress and gold sparkly heels my mom bought for her from a famous de-signer. "Aunt Jaden, look! My dress shines off my leg!"

I love how Damini does not hide her prosthetic leg. As she said, "I still remember what it felt like in the orphanage to hop on one leg and how it hurt when I kept falling. Now, because of all this metal, I walk normal, I run fast, I don't crash into the ground onto my face, and I'm joining track and I'm going to run and jump and kick some butt-ola!"

Tate said to Damini, "You're in gold and silver. You look like a treasure chest. Maybe you should put a lid on it."

She slapped his arm, grinned, then put her arm through his. "You're a pain in my keester, Tate. A pain in my keester!"

"I think a pirate is going to kidnap you, Damini," he said. "Watch out! He'll probably have sharp, pointy teeth, a hook for a hand, bad breath, warts. . . ."

I knew my mother was thinking of Brooke and my dad that night as we cruised down the river, missing both of them as we nibbled on fancy-schmancy appetizers, but we still had a heck of a time, and none of us fell over into the river as poor Faith and Grace had tumbled into the waves of the Atlantic.

One must celebrate that if one's ancestor died years ago, you would not be here today.

At least, that was our excuse for the champagne.

This is how my mother summed up my love life at one point, when we were sitting on my white porch one sunny afternoon drinking peppermint tea: *You are testicle-free by choice.*

"Mother, I don't want to talk about this. I only want one man's testicles, and I can't have them."

"I know you feel that Ethan's testicles have a male chastity belt on them, so let's move to another man with the same plumbing. In fact, let's pretend there are a whole bunch of testicles out there."

I groaned and buried my head in my hands. "Let's not, Mom."

"Yes, let's." She swung her foot, clad, as usual, in a four-inch-high heel. She was wearing a purple silk wrap and leather belt. By contrast, I was in my jeans, cowboy boots, and a blousy blue shirt with embroidery across the front.

"No."

"There are testicles flying around and about." She pretended to try to catch tiny balls. "There are some at the university and at the hospital where you had all those nursing classes, some in our town, some in the city, some on online dating sites, and they're all whizzing about."

"I do not want to envision whizzing testicles. Thank you."

"I do," my mother said. She stared into the air, envisioning those whizzing testicles, and smiled. "You could reach up and grab those testicles, but you don't because you think you're too busy for testicle grabbing."

"I am busy, Mother."

She waved her hand. "I am here on many weekends and all holidays. You could date when I'm with Tate, but you don't. Instead, we stay home and play Scrabble or have movie nights or family parties."

"I live for Scrabble, movie nights, and family parties."

"Me, too. But you need testicles."

"Scrabble is better than testicles."

"Ha. See. That's because you don't grab the right ones. Firm and full of action . . ."

"Mother, must you be that graphic?"

"You work with people who are sliding into heaven, you hover over Tate as if you're a special agent stalking her prey, you spend masses of time being overly serious and thinking overly serious thoughts, and you have your gourmet recipe and herb obsessions and your greenhouse. You hide. You don't even try love."

"I do try love." I cleared my throat and ate my fifth cookie. "I did."

Josh, my high school boyfriend, and I dated through my father's death. He was kind and sweet. He had no clue how to handle a girl grieving over her father, but he tried. But Tate, and my becoming Tate's mother, that he couldn't handle.

At the time it sent me into a tailspin of sadness when he broke up with me. I missed him; he broke my heart. We both cried. But I don't blame him. We were nineteen. He did not want to become a dad.

I tried love in nursing school. There was a doctor I was interested in, he was going to be a cardiologist. We dated, and I told him about adopting my sister's son. We were friends. I thought he had character.

I showed him a photo of Tate on our fourth date. His face paled.

Now, you would think that a medical doctor wouldn't be put off by Tate.

He was.

It wasn't long before I received a telephone call. In fact, it was the next morning, though he knew I had a huge final in a class in an hour. "I don't think this is . . . uh . . . this is not . . . I don't want to be a . . . not ready to be a father. . . . I have a friend who can figure out if there's something he can do for that kid's head. . . ."

I told him to go screw himself backward with a fire poker.

There was another man, Dr. Rogey Hicks. I told him about Tate right off. He said he was fine with my being a mother. I did not introduce Tate to Rogey because I made a rule long ago that I wouldn't introduce Tate to any man unless I was going to marry him.

Dr. Rogey Hicks zipped off to this medical convention, and that doctors' symposium, and spoke here and there. Our relationship was passionate and intense, he listened, he was attentive, engaged. Lots of admirable qualities.

On a hot summer day in August he was arrested for selling prescription painkillers out of his home.

"I didn't do it, Jaden!" he protested. "I'm an innocent man. It was a setup!"

The drug enforcement agents who poured out of his garage with garbage bags full of evidence, computers, customer lists, and bags of painkillers, begged to differ.

He admitted his guilt with his two attorneys present, who took the rest of his money, and he spent five years in jail. I believe he is now in apartment management in Toronto.

And there was a man named Mason. He did not mention an ex-wife for six months. He did not mention any wife. He did not mention their children. He did not mention that he was months behind in child support and alimony. I found out when his wife arrived at our table in a fancy steak house restaurant one night. Apparently her best friend had been sitting behind us and called her. Mason's wife had not been able to get a hold of her husband for the money. She flipped our table over to make sure her point was made about the missing money. Our steaks went flying.

I helped her dump water over Mason. She gave me a ride home. I do not date men who cheat their ex-wives and children.

"You grabbed testicles infrequently," my mother said, "and the testicles you chose were poor choices, wrinkled, slack, selfish testicles, no offense, divine daughter."

"None taken. That statement is true."

I gave up on dating, on men, for years. I was swamped in work and in Tate's needs.

Then I met Ethan.

I tried a few dates after I met him, as Ethan was off-limits, but I felt lonely, alone, and deceptive on those dates because it wasn't fair to the men I was with. I was not looking for anyone else. One man even said to me, "You're not into this, are you?"

He was right.

I quit dating altogether and sank into my daydreams of Ethan and me.

"I wish for you a real man, Jaden," my mother said. "A real man with real testicles."

"I found him, but I can't have him."

My mother became quiet and contemplative, her face still, then she sniffled. "I know I've said this before, honey, but I recognize, we all recognize, that your sacrifices have been enormous."

I blew that off, waving my hand in the air. "I have Tate, Mom, it's all worth it."

"I know, sweetheart. But you gave up your twenties, dating, a husband, and you've dealt with all of Tate's medical emergencies...."

"Let's not talk about it, Mom. You help me all the time. You offered to raise Tate in Hollywood with you, and I refused to let you take him and I refused to go and live with you. We've raised him together."

"You're an outstanding mother." She sniffled again.

"Thanks, Mom. You're an outstanding Nana Bird."

She used a tissue on her nose and tried to pull herself together. "I'm going to put a spell out there for some testicles for you."

"You do that. I don't believe in your spells."

"Yes, you do," said the woman who is rational in all else.

My mother did not chase testicles, either, despite her flirty, outrageous ways, which were mostly an act. One time she told me, late at night, something I'd always known by her actions: "I live my life for you, Brooke, Caden, and the grandkids. Our family, and honoring your father's life, is what's important to me."

I reached a hand out for my mother that afternoon on the porch with our peppermint tea. She held it and said, in all seriousness, nothing about flying testicles at all, "You have blessed my life, Jaden, as you blessed your father's life. Don't ever forget that we love you."

"I love you, too, Mom."

Our hands stayed together for a long time.

"Dr. Robbins, what exactly is your opinion on participating in medical trials, not only from a doctor's perspective, but from a moral and ethical perspective, too?" Tate asked Ethan. "Especially since most trials don't work, the doctors are only *trying* something new . . ."

"My opinion is that . . ."

And those two were off and running in Ethan's office. I tried extremely hard not to stare at Ethan and pant with lust.

When they were done and I was trying to erase a graphic sex scene in my greenhouse with Ethan from my mind, Tate said, "What are you going to do this weekend, study the newest research on Alzheimer's in a medical magazine or count the taste buds on your tongue? I'm going to opt for the taste buds."

"Counting the taste buds sounds intriguing, Tate, thank you for the idea, but I'm going river rafting this weekend."

"Oh, that sounds fun," I blurted. "I'd been river rafting twice and I loved it."

"What rapid class?" Tate asked.

"III and IV."

"Man. I would love to do that."

"Come then," Ethan said, pushing his glasses to the top of his head and leaning toward us.

Those two words dropped into the room like a bomb...a bomb filled with flowers and chocolate candy and kisses in a river. I quivered.

"Really?" Tate bopped in his chair. "We can come?"

"No, no, Tate, I'm sure that we can't. Dr. Robbins has plans, probably with other people, with rafts and...and...plans with paddles and rows, the river—"

Tate crossed his eyes at me as in, *Get it together, Mom.*

"Actually, it's only one other person—" Ethan said.

Instantly I could feel the green and jealous devil in me surface. Was the one other person a *woman?* A female? With a female's anatomy?

"And..." Ethan's gaze traveled from me to Tate, a surprised, but *delighted* expression on his face, as if he couldn't believe he'd invited us, but he was glad that he did. "I would love it if you two came."

"Man, we're there, right, Boss Mom? Whoeee!" Tate jumped onto his chair, then pretended to row the raft. "I'm gonna be a younger Meriwether Lewis and William Clark except"—he fisted his hand—"my mom's gonna make the best club sandwiches you ever had. She puts on the smoked turkey, honeyed ham, roast beef, tomatoes, onions, and lettuce and vinegar and oil, but then she makes up this special warmed-up sauce with crumbled blue cheese, and she'll make cinnamon rolls with extra white sugar frosting, that are so bang-up amazing you'll cry, same as I do when I eat 'em, right, Boss Mom?"

"No, I'm sure we can't go..." But then, Ethan, tasty Ethan, I glanced at him, and he smiled at me, hopeful, and I couldn't break away. Another graphic image: Ethan in a raft naked. Me on top. I blushed.

"Here we go again. The staring contest between Boss Mom and Dr. Robbins." Tate groaned. "This'll take awhile, I can tell...."

"It's not a staring contest," Ethan said. "I...uh...I was simply waiting...waiting for your mom's...for your mom to smile . . . I mean"—he shook his head, flustered—"I was waiting for your mom to say yes to rowing. . . ."

I smiled at Ethan. Ethan smiled back. We smiled and smiled. Making love on a raft floating down a river . . . my butt could get sunburned . . . I blushed.

"Okay, I can see where this is going," Tate said, sighing dramatically, and jumping off the chair. "I'm going out to hit on Leena. She wants me, flesh and bone, I can tell. And we'll see you rafting on Saturday, Dr. Robbins. Who-hoo? Can you hear me, Dr. Robbins?" He leaned down to speak straight into Ethan's ear. "We'll see you Saturday. Thanks, dude." Ethan jumped, then Tate turned to me. "When you two are out of your staring contest, make sure you ask him where we're supposed to meet."

He turned to go. "Nurse Leena," Tate shouted. "You sexy thing, you! Watch out, I'm comin' for ya!" I heard the other nurses laugh and Tate growled, "Don't say no to me, Leena, you seductive enchantress woman, I know you've been dreaming about me for years. . . ."

I could hear Leena's response—please remember she is sixty-five years old—"Don't tempt me, Tate Bruxelle, it's always been hard for me to say no to a looker!"

"Wowza!" Tate yodeled. "Bring it on, Leena, fair lady! General Noggin and I won't take no for an answer."

The door shut and I focused on the pen in my hand. I fiddled with it, then in my fiddling it popped out of my hand and skidded across the floor. Ethan picked it up and handed it to me. Our fingers touched, I dropped the pen again, and we went through the whole thing again.

"How about it, Jaden?"

"Are you sure?" I sucked in my breath and tried to hide my primal joy panting.

"Absolutely."

I smiled at him.

He smiled back.

"I would love you . . ." He coughed, blushed. "I meant, I would love for you to come with us."

"I would love to come, too."

"Me, too."

"Yes, I'd love to come."

"Good."

"Good."

We stared at each other again, smiling, and I felt passion swirling in and around my insides. . . .

"Beautiful," he said, then blushed again.

I thought of him and me naked in the raft. Would we need life jackets?

I blushed back. "Yes. Beautiful."

I stood up and knocked over my chair.

Tate would not speak to me at breakfast after yet another argument about basketball the night before.

Tryouts were coming up, kids were practicing all the time after school. He was missing out, he couldn't improve, this was his last chance. . . .

He slammed out of the house and walked to school in the rain, the fall leaves from Faith's maple trees swirling around him, paprika red, mustard yellow, bay leaf green.

I opened the door and yelled, "I'll drive you! Tate, wait!"

He sprinted down the street.

"Tate!"

He ignored me.

I couldn't let him play.

It is not fun being a parent all the time. But sometimes you have to say no.

No, that was my answer. I was not being overprotective.

No.

He could get hurt.

No.

It had to be no.

I had not forgotten that Dirk was coming after me for "murdering" his father.

On a cold Thursday, the leaves dropping off the trees in the skittering wind, the rain incessant and heavy, I received a call from Sydney.

"I've set up a meeting. You and I, the doctors who saw Mr. Hassells, Senior, administrators, Dirk Hassells, etc. We'll come in with the information we have, the diagnosis, prognosis, treatments, the spread of his disease, the scans, blood tests, blah blah blah, and present it to Dirk. It's the usual threats of a lawsuit, cold nights in jail, banishment to medical Siberia, baloney baloney baloney, and years of hellacious torture. He's a charmer."

"He's a greedy, narcissistic fool."

"And a man who believes he's a jilted lover. You and your rejection of him pissed him off. The other day he said he thought you were 'sexually cold,' and 'unaccommodating,' and 'not friendly enough' to him, and 'were you gay?' "

"That's dense, dark, disturbing Dirk." I could feel my heart speed up with stress.

"I told the attorney. She'll annihilate him with it if she has to. What was his relationship with his father again?"

"They had a personality conflict because, as Mr. Hassells senior said, 'My son has a superiority complex about the size of Texas. He has an exaggerated sense of self-worth and self-confidence that is not grounded in true accomplishments, and he is a slut.' He was saddened, but not surprised, by his son's lack of care for him at the end."

"Got it." She let the silence hang between us for a moment. "What is it, Jaden?"

"I did all I could, all that medicine could do, to make Mr. Hassells comfortable, as I do for all my patients, and then Dirk, a sick, obsessed man, can ruin my reputation and put me under the stress of a lawsuit because I didn't sleep with him. It's not right, and it pisses me off." Oh Witch Mavis, relax . . .

"It pisses me off, too. You're a talented nurse, don't you forget it. Be tough here. We'll get rid of this problem soon and knock this goon off his white horse."

*   *   *

In my greenhouse late that night, when Tate was in his experiment room watching a video on a complicated brain operation,
I puttered about and thought about being accused of murder. I
was definitely in a "shipwreck time of life" with work, as Faith
and Grace would say.

Grandma Violet told Brooke and me the "shipwreck time of
life" story when we were little girls visiting her one cold winter
day, the snow filling the fields. We were sitting at the wooden
table that Faith's husband, Jack, built, and she told us that Faith
and Grace's ship hit a number of storms in the Atlantic Ocean
from England to America.

"Their boat flopped around as if it were no more than a bottle of rum passed back and forth in Satan's hands. The girls
thought their passage was punishment from God himself, complete with the devil cackling and wreaking havoc, throwing
lightning strikes and pelting thunderbolts from a churning, turbulent black sky. They thought the ship would be wrecked and
they would drown."

Grandma Violet was an excellent storyteller. She shook her
curly hair, auburn mixed with white, her fingers busy with her
herbs. "There wasn't enough food, what there was was soon
putrid, and there were bugs, lice, rats, diseases galore, and no
sanitation for months. These girls had come from wealth, title,
and privilege. They were silly, naughty, and they snuck out all
the time at night. They liked the men. They liked their fancy
dresses, flowered hats, whiskey in their tea, and fashionable
shoes.

"They had no idea how to deal with the suffering they found
on board, but finally they bucked up. They started taking care
of the sick and dying, and they used their spells to heal, even
though they thought the seasickness was going to kill them.
They used their cross, heart, and star charms, like you two and
your mother and I wear, and their thimble, white lace handkerchief, needle, the gold timepiece, and the book with the black
cover, although they never used them when other people were
around. They didn't need to be accused of being witches on a
ship. They might have been thrown over."

She poured paprika and cloves, one layer upon another, into a clear bottle. "These were all things that Rosemary's (who became Grace)'s frantic mother hurriedly packed for the girls in a velvet satchel before throwing them up on horses with their brothers to gallop to the dock and away from that torch-wielding, witch-hunting mob. Grace's father threw in money that the girls later used to set up their ladies' shop in South Carolina."

Grandma Violet started sorting other herbs and spices into bottles, mixing them now and then. "Some of the ill people Faith and Grace spelled on that ship died, but a number lived and said that in their delusions, in the midst of their fevers, they had seen Faith and Grace blocking the doors of heaven. One man said it was the blue-eyed and green-eyed twins who saved him, he thought they were sisters, not cousins, which was what Faith and Grace told everyone."

"But they made it?" I asked Grandma Violet.

She nodded, said a quick chant, then started putting corks on the bottles of spices she'd been working with. "They made it to South Carolina, but whenever Faith and Grace had a bad time in their lives, they said it was a 'shipwreck time of life,' and that's what all we women call the bad times, too."

I nodded solemnly.

Brooke said, "It's our saying, then."

"That's right. Don't you forget the stories about Faith and Grace now, Jaden and Brooke. When you have children, you pass it down to them."

"Okay, Grandma Violet. I'll do it," I said. "The stories are stuck like glue up in my head now."

"Me, too, Grandma Violet. I'll tell all my twelve kids," Brooke said. "We won't forget."

She gave us a hug, then we baked banana nut muffins together as the snow piled up.

I looked out the greenhouse windows at Faith's home, Grandma Violet's home, my mother's home, my home, and ate six red cinnamon Gummi Bears, four lemon drops, blasted the J.Geils Band song, "My Angel Is a Centerfold," and tried not to throw things.

This was definitely a shipwreck time of life, and though Faith and Grace's shipwreck time was far, far worse than mine, I still had my own rat-infested murder-ship with Dirk's accusations swirling around.

I kept puttering between my paper whites and my beefsteak and brandy wine heirloom tomatoes in my greenhouse, my anger simmering, as I thought about being a hospice nurse.

Maybe I needed to do something different.

Perhaps I needed fewer tears in my life.

What would I do if I wasn't a hospice nurse?

What did I *want* to do?

I thought of Ethan. Yep. Wouldn't mind doing things with him for the next sixty years. I paused to think out a love scene with him involving a log cabin in the woods with a kitchen stocked with gourmet food, goddess fruit teas, and herbs and spices for extra tastiness. He told me he loved me in front of a roaring fire, we fed each other red cinnamon Gummi Bears, etc., etc.

When I was done, I thought about who and what I loved. I loved Tate, my mom, Caden and his kids, Brooke, despite it all, and Ethan. I loved my nurse friends.

I loved herbs and spices.

I loved cooking and baking because of the hours and hours I cooked with Grandma Violet, using family recipes so old we had to laminate the crinkly paper in order to save them.

I loved tea and books.

Tate was getting older, he would be in college soon. I could do something else.

Could I start all over? Did I want to?

Why not? Why could I *not* start over?

Maybe I needed to start thinking about a new dream for my life.

One where I would never be accused of being a murderer.

Before I left that night, I mixed up parsley, paprika, and rosemary. I passed the flakes of parsley back and forth in my hands. I rubbed the paprika between my fingers and chopped up rosemary leaves. I used Faith's silver spoon to add a bit of that and a touch of this to a pile of spices.

I gritted my teeth, my heart palpitating, then lowered my face to the crystal plate and inhaled.

Death.

I quickly mixed up mint, bay leaves, and cumin.

Same scent.

The death scent. The same scent I'd smelled three times before in my life.

It was clingy, scary, life-sucking, and black.

Please, God, not Damini, not the triplets.

Please, God, not Tate.

Not Tate.

"Tell me more about my Other Mother."

I flinched, deep in my gut. Tate and I were on stools at the butcher-block island counter. I'd lit the apple cider candle. I'd made us chocolate-cinnamon hot chocolate and So Delicious Sugar Cookies, Tate's name for them, for dipping. It was raining, cool and light, creating a cozy environment to talk about the drug-filled needles my sister had consistently stuck up her arm.

I have not hidden information from Tate about Brooke's drug usage, but neither have I been graphic or boldly forthcoming. It's a small town. Had I not told him, someone else would have, precisely in this way: *"Your real mother is a drug addict."* In fact, he'd already heard it, several times.

I bit down on my simmering anger at the very thought of what Brooke had done. "We grew up in the Hollywood Hills with Nana Bird and your grandpa until we moved here as teenagers for the rest of high school."

"But tell me more about her. Tell me something new about her."

"She was, for years, a ton of fun. She was curious about life, books, traveling, animals. She was funny, bright. We were best friends. We experimented with herbs and spices and made all these weird recipes. We collected shells and rocks, which I have in the greenhouse in a blue cardboard box. We talked about boys. We helped take care of your great-grandma's gardens here and memorized all the plants we had to plant in our own gardens because we descend from a long line of witches, as Grandma Violet used to say. Don't believe the part about the witches, Tate."

"I know. You've told me a million times. But what happened? Why did Other Mother get into drugs?"

Why why why? "She hit her teen years. She started hanging out with the wrong kids." The avalanche of pain, terror, fear, and anger began for our family at that moment. "She had mood swings. Looking back, I think she might have suffered from depression and was trying to self-medicate, but Brooke also wanted to belong, and we lost her to partying and drugs."

"I know what it's like to not belong."

"I know you do." We sat quietly in that loneliness.

"Why else did she do drugs?"

"She had been bullied at school in the Hollywood Hills. We both had. It's a fast culture down there, and with Nana being a soap opera star, the other kids would say many hurtful things. 'How come your mom is so pretty and you're . . . not?' Or, 'Your mom is tall and elegant . . . but you're, well, you're kind of fat. . . .' I had other friends, I shrugged it off, and I had a temper even then and my impatience for stupid girls was legendary. Brooke, sweet and sensitive, took it to heart."

"I've been bullied, too. I've been told that I'm never gonna get laid or married. One girl told me my face gave her a nightmare."

I swear a rock of pain lodged in my neck.

"I get asked why I'm ugly." Tate dipped another cookie in milk. "I get asked why I'm a creeper. When they ask if I'm retarded, I usually say yes then start in on explaining Einstein's Theory of Relativity."

"You're a handsome man, Tate, don't you forget it." Gall. The unkindness of children. "Brooke wanted to be invited to parties, to events, dances, places. . . ."

"I'm hardly ever invited anywhere by other kids."

"Her backpack was stolen several times."

"Mine, too, in middle school. I didn't let it off my back from then on. Last time two kids tried to take it, I karate-chopped their noses."

"I remember. One of their dads called because you broke the kid's nose."

"Yeah." Tate laughed. "I heard Witch Mavis screaming at him over the phone. You scared even me. You made mincemeat of that father. You made mincemeat of the mother who called, too, and both kids apologized the next day. They haven't bothered me since."

I humphed. "Brooke's pencil case ended up in the toilet, her books, her calculator. I wanted to cry for my poor sister all over again. I had protected her many, many times. Even had a few fistfights."

"My jacket ended up in the toilet. One of the cool beige ones Nana Bird bought me."

"Brooke's hair was pulled. She was tripped."

"I can relate. My head has been hit by milk cartons, pencils, baloney sandwiches, pens, and, one time, cheesecake. Road Runner has been hit by a grape and Mickey Mouse has been hit by a baseball. Last time Chris Kochito tripped me for the third time, I was so pissed, I ran back up the stairs and banged his head into a door."

"I remember. I had to go in and argue with the principal about why you shouldn't be suspended."

"You didn't argue long, Boss Mom. I remember. Witch Mavis was out that afternoon and flying. You were shouting. We were in and out of the principal's office in ten minutes, and Chris was suspended. In fact, you've had a whole bunch of kids suspended over the years."

I humphed again. That was true. I would never stop fighting for my son to be free of harassment and flying fists at school, and I had the attorneys come in to prove it. "My sister wanted to be accepted."

"Me, too. That's one of the reasons I want to play basketball. She and I have a lot in common."

I did not want him to have anything in common with my sister. I did not want him to relate to her or build false sympathy or unearned affection for her.

"Nana Bird must have been upset with Brooke banging up drugs."

"She was hysterical. As was my dad."

"Were you?"

"I cried and worried all the time. My worry made me sick. Brooke was about fourteen when she started using drugs. I was fifteen. She did what you would expect a brain-fried drug user to do. She lied about the drugs, she came home stoned, tripping, shaking. She'd have insomnia, then she'd sleep forever, she'd be aggressive, then fall into jack crying, she'd lose her appetite, then she would eat as if her stomach would never be full. She fought vociferously with our mom and dad, and they ended up crying or yelling while she slammed out the door, stealing money if she could. Our whole house was in total upheaval all the time. She later on would leave for days or weeks at a time to get high."

"That's a long time."

"It was. One time Brooke was gone for over a year, and when she came back she was pregnant with you." I shuddered. She was eight months' pregnant when she showed up here. It was summer and I had finished my first year of college. My mother and I were outside in the garden. The cosmos were in full pink and white bloom. The summer herb garden was growing, the lettuce, corn, tomatoes, carrots . . .

"Oh my God," my mother whispered as a tiny, broken figure hobbled through the red poppy field. My mother darted past rows of roses, wrapped her arms around my sister, and sobbed into her shoulder.

I followed my mother but not for the same compassionate, relieved reasons. I wanted to kick Brooke for the fragile wreck she'd turned my mother into. But when I saw Brooke, pale, crumbling, scared, I couldn't hit her.

Brooke had tracks on her arm. Her clothes were torn. There was blood near her crotch. Her hair was matted to her head, and there was dirt smeared across her face. She smelled like rot and pot and a body that had not been washed in months.

I felt my anger dissolve in that crashing moment. She was too pathetic to be angry at, too destroyed with those huge, purple circles under her exhausted, now *old,* eyes.

"Hi, Jaden," she whispered. "How are you?"

She passed out in my arms, a puff of wind blowing the poppies around us. I held Brooke in my lap under that golden sun while my mother flew off to call an ambulance.

"We didn't know, Tate, that she was pregnant until she arrived here."

"And you said you never knew who my father was."

"That's right. We asked her."

"What did she say?"

"She said that she didn't know. I'm sorry, Tate." Oh, the pain my sister has inflicted . . .

His face was grave, troubled. "The drugs are probably what caused my head to be like this, isn't it?"

"This happens with parents who don't use drugs. But it could be, Tate. Drugs eat up a healthy person's body as if the drugs are starving."

"Maybe it was because of The Curse?" He wiggled his eyebrows. "The Henrietta and Elizabeth curse?"

"There isn't a curse." I handed him another So Delicious Sugar Cookie. "Silly. No curses. No witches. No warlocks."

That Grandma Violet had a younger sister who had a cleft palate was normal, statistically speaking. That she also had twin cousins with extraordinarily large ears was also normal, statistically speaking. That my mother's cousin, Beth, had a sixth toe could also be explained, somehow. . . . That Grandma Violet's mother had one leg shorter than the other and a niece had a missing arm . . . and her grandma's sister's son had two rows of teeth . . . this stuff happens. . . .

"I feel sorry for her."

"You do?" For years I felt sorry for Brooke, too, when she'd stumble home. She looked so pathetic, her hair matted and greasy, way too skinny, her arms spotted and scarred, her teeth chipped and yellow. But my mother was always in semi-Brooke hysteria, and my father, my sweet and funny father, who adored all of us, would go into his den and work on his TV scripts, his movie scripts, whatever he had going at the time, to bury his relentless grief. He told my mother one night, when he didn't know I was listening, "I didn't know you could worry this much and not have a heart attack. . . . I didn't know my imagination could take me to such dark places. . . . I miss her. I miss her all the time, Rowan."

My dad held my mother a lot, and about twice a week, at night, he would take Caden and me to get chocolate mint or peppermint ice cream. We'd climb in his Jeep, listen to rock music, and come back and talk.

Brooke ruined our family. All the attention went to Brooke; Caden and I often felt we were far seconds behind Brooke and her problems. We felt that our parents loved her more, cared for her more. Of course they didn't, but try explaining that to teenagers. My parents would repeatedly pay for rehab, I would watch both of them visibly relax when she was locked up, but out she'd come and it would be back to the drugs. On and on.

"Yeah, I feel sorry for her, Boss Mom. Think about it. What rules her life is drugs. Every day. She probably feels sick and always tired. She probably doesn't have any money, so she has to steal or do bad things to get it. Sometimes I think of her out there, maybe living outside, maybe homeless, under a bridge or something, and I feel bad for her. I know she gave me up, I know she walked out of the hospital. I get it. She's not a good mother at all, but then I think of her alone, when she could be here, with us, making chicken pancakes, having movie night and Oregon Trail Turkey Dinner Night in honor of Faith and Grace, but instead she's alone. She has nothing."

Tate's face scrunched up and he put his fists to his eyes, the tears seeping down. I hugged him close. Brooke did not deserve his compassion, but I had a compassionate son.

"Can we find out where she is and check on her?" His voice crackled.

I didn't want to. I didn't want Brooke and her massive problems back in my life again. I didn't want her upsetting Tate, or my mother, or Caden. "Tate, I appreciate and understand your concern about your mom. But don't romanticize this, don't romanticize her. She's a drug addict."

"I'm not romanticizing her. I am not even into romance. I can't even get a girlfriend because of General Noggin."

I thought about what my mom, Caden, and I had heard about Brooke in past years. She was found in an alley with a needle in her arm and carted off to the hospital (two years ago). In the hospital for overdosing (multiple times). She was arrested for drug possession (also multiple times). She was arrested for stealing (three times).

Brooke had been arrested for prostitution when we were teenagers, which was the last of the terrible nights before my parents gave up and we all moved to Oregon when we were in high school. I remember them crying, their bodies heaving over their prone, beat-up, and unconscious daughter in a hospital bed. Brooke had been working as a hooker. Her pimp had been unhappy with her and had bashed her to pieces. Want bad? That's soul-curdling bad.

"She's my Other Mother, and I want to know how she is."

I felt anger bubbling inside me. "Your Other Mother? She's never been a mother to you. Ever. Not even an Other Mother."

"But I still care about her!"

"That's nice, Tate, but she doesn't care about anyone." The expression on his face hurt, but coddling him would not be helpful. "I'll see what I can find out about her, okay? I'll see."

His anger simmered down as quick as it had come. "Okay. Thanks, Boss Mom. I need to know if she's still alive. And I really, really want to try out for the basketball team!"

She was still alive, I knew it.

Damn.

Not damn that she was alive, not at all. In my secret heart I hoped that Brooke would one day return to the craft-loving, garden-planting, outdoor girl she had been.

I did not want to find *this* Brooke, the addict Brooke. Not one bit.

Later that night I turned off all the lights in our house, lit a jasmine-scented candle, curled up with one of my great-grandma's quilts under a photograph Grandma Violet took of her peonies, and thought about Brooke.

7

Three days after Tate was born and whisked out of the hospital room, amidst Brooke's echoing screams and a rush of blood I have tried to forget my whole life, I sat down next to her on the bed. She was still weak and had been pumped full of donated blood. She was also detoxing, the nurses were helping her through it, but it was tortuous to watch. Brooke was sweating and her breathing was troubled. She took deep breaths, then panted, then back to the deep breaths. She'd thrown up many times and was clearly anxious, jittery, and emotional.

I cradled Tate in my arms. He was wrapped in a yellow blanket, sleeping peacefully, his coloring perfect, the blue color he'd been born with gone. I looked into those tiny, uneven eyes in the middle of that big head and I knew, as I had known that first day, that I loved him.

"Good luck, Jaden," my sister panted, her arms tracked with vicious lines from her soul-sucking addiction. "I can't do it."

"What?" What did she mean, she couldn't do it? I felt ill.

She pulled an IV out, then swung her bony legs out of bed, moving slowly, her emaciated arms barely able to hold her up.

"Get back in bed, Brooke. You can't get up!" She was sick and frail, deathly.

"Yes, I can and I am."

"You're not supposed to, the doctors said you're still sick and you're still bleeding. You've had stitches, you have to finish getting the drugs out. Please lie down. Mom went home for a couple of hours to rest, she's coming right back—"

"This is a hospital, not a jail, sweet Jaden. I've been to jail, I know what it's all about."

I swallowed hard. "What . . . what did you go to jail for?"

"For bad stuff I did. I'm not going to tell you. It's over and done, and that's it." She climbed into her jeans, bending carefully, while I pleaded with her to stay. The jeans were too large for her, a far cry from the stylish jeans she used to wear, with her colorful tops, and pretty jewelry, some of which she made herself. She was as skinny as a wisp of wind. Frightfully skinny. She pulled a rope, not a belt, but a *rope,* through the loopholes and knotted it tight so the jeans wouldn't come off. The daughter of a woman who wore couture was wearing a rope.

"Did you even eat today, Brooke?" What had happened to my gentle and kind sister? The one I made daisy rings with for our hair? The one I cut out paper dolls with and explored Mom's garden in Hollywood and Grandma Violet's garden in Oregon?

"I wasn't hungry."

"How can you not be hungry?"

"I'm not." She was jittery, hyped up. She'd come in to the hospital with unexplained bruises, and they were now turning purple, green, and blue. "I'm leaving, Jaden, I'm sorry."

"Please, no, Brooke. Stay." I hugged Tate close.

"I can't." Her green eyes were bleak holes in her face, her skin pale and lined. The drug use had aged her ten years. It was making her shake.

"I want you to stay—"

She muffled a sob, hand to her mouth.

"We can help you, Brooke!" I loved her. I wanted her with me, with us. There is little worse than knowing that the person you love will probably kill themselves with drug use, and I wanted her healthy again. I wanted my sister back.

"I don't want help, I don't need help."

She pulled on a black sweater, even though she didn't need it, the day sunny and hot. She added a black sweatshirt and flipped out her red hair. Her hair looked so much better than it had when we'd first arrived at the hospital. Then, it was matted and dirty and stringy. It smelled of smoke, dust, and mildew. The nurses had cleaned her up, as had my mother, who had cried while she brushed her daughter's hair, then used scissors to cut the knots out, and chopped six inches of fried tangles off the ends.

"But Tate needs you, Brooke—"

"No, he doesn't. He doesn't need a drug addict for a mother." Her eyes filled. "I'm leaving him with you, Jaden. I'm done."

She was done? The mother of the baby was *done?* "What . . . What do you mean?"

"I mean that I can't be a mom to him." She put both hands to her head. I knew it was throbbing. "I can't bring Tate into my life. Tate won't . . ." She gasped, then put a hand to her mouth. "He won't survive." The phone next to her bed rang and she picked it up, so irritated. "Austin, shit, quit yelling, I'm coming downstairs now. Yes, by myself, what did you think? No, I'm not bringing the baby. I don't care if you don't want kids around. Yeah, I'm still fat. I had a baby, you ignorant shit." Her voice cracked and splintered, and I heard her take a huge, shuddering breath, her body quaking. "Did you call Darrin? He's waiting? Stop talking, I'm sick of it."

My sister was abandoning her son. I was sickened, but I knew I was talking to the drugs, not Brooke, and the drugs were nasty and cruel and dishonest. You might as well be talking to the devil himself.

"Yeah, I have some cash, Austin. Do you? Why the hell don't you have any money? Why is it that I always have to get the money? You're getting it from who? When? Yeah, I'll go. Then we're outta here. Arizona is fine. I need some sun." She hung up.

I held Tate closer to me and planted a kiss on his forehead. He couldn't understand what she was saying, but I wanted to protect him anyhow. I swear he smiled. They say it is impossible for a baby that young to smile. They are wrong. I know he smiled. It was my first inkling of his shiny brilliance.

"I'm sorry, Jaden." She leaned over Tate.

"God, Brooke—" She had been beautiful once, but she was battered to bits now.

For a second the veil lifted and I saw sheer, raw pain in her eyes. Two of her tears landed on Tate's cheeks, and slid down, as if Tate was crying, as if he was mourning the loss of his mother, the one person who should have protected and loved him above everyone else.

"Bye, Jaden. Bye, Tate. I love you."

The phone rang again, she swore, picked it up, and shouted, "What the fuck is it now, Austin?"

It was the drugs. A sober Brooke never would have spoken to anyone like that. It was only a few years ago that I would have told you that Brooke was the kindest person I had ever met in my whole life.

Brooke wobbled on out as her tears slid down Tate's face.

"I love you," I whispered to him, broken. My sister was on drugs and would probably end up dead. She had left her son, who was born with a big head. He was mine now, and I loved him. "I love you, Tate."

He smiled again, yes, he did, don't you doubt it, then he slept.

I walked to the windows. In a minute, I could see my sister's auburn hair, the exact color as mine, floating in the wind. She stopped and looked up at the windows and waved. She couldn't see in, but I knew she was waving at me, at Tate. A car pulled up alongside her and she climbed in. The car sped away. She was gone. Gone again. Pain rippled through my body.

I could not predict Tate's future then. I knew it would be hard. I had no idea how crushingly hard, but what I did know was this: I was Tate's mother. My sister gave birth to him, but he was my son.

I was nineteen.

Would my sister have allowed Tate to play basketball even with his medical issue? Sure. Why the hell not? The kid would have been running loose and taking care of himself from the moment she left the hospital with him. He would often have been hungry, cold, scared, neglected, abused, and completely alone because his mother would have been high or chasing down her next fix—if he had even lived through his first year with his medical issues, which was highly improbable.

That's how drug addicts "parent."

In fact the words *drug addicts* and *parent,* together, at best, are an oxymoron.

I am Tate's mother. I will do what I believe is right.

That means no basketball.

TATE'S AWESOME PIGSKIN BLOG

I am going to post a picture of myself soon. Real soon.

I want to hide longer because then you can get to know me without my head in the way. But keep sending me your stories about yourselves! I'm posting all the ones that people want posted, and there's tons to look at, dudes and dudettes. We have people being real—so read 'em!

Did you know that Africa has 11.7 million square miles? How many lions does that work out to be? I wonder.

Did you also know that an adult's intestines are about twenty-five feet long? Man, if I could take my intestines out, I could use them as ropes. Maybe I could rope cattle with them, or I could use them to swing from one tall building to the next in a city, or to make ladders. You know, an intestinal ladder.

Did you also know that Trang's farts smell like the devil burning his tail? He has the worst farts. I think something died in him.

Did you know I really, really want to try out for the basketball team, but my mom said no? I know!! Insane!!

Also I am listening to Max of Grunge Punge. He is so chill it's sick.

I think part of the reason I'm writing this blog is because I'm trying to get enough courage to get out there, you know, "out there in the world," because I live in a small town now, and I figure if I get my face floating into the universe now, and I don't freak that many people out, then it'll give me some courage to leave here.

It's not that I want to leave here, Tillamina's cool. We're close to the beach and skiing, we're out in the country, but I know I have to leave someday. I mean, I can't hide because of my head, right? How am I going to go to college and study cellular neurophysiology, cognitive information processing, the Renaissance, Italian art? How am I going to study my favorite subject: the brain? How am I going to figure out how to bottle up cow's farts for energy? How will I see Venezuela or Machu Picchu or study how Venice was built on water? Can't do that if I hide, right?

And I want to do all that. I can't let my head get in the way.

So I'm writing the blog.

Who's out there today? What do you want to do with your life?

"Guess what, Boss Mom?"
"What?"
"Look at this. I wrote: Who's out there today? And a whole

bunch of people are. Some of them are kids at school, one is Nana Bird, four are people from *Foster's Village,* including the current bad boy villain that she lusts after, and Uncle Caden wrote, 'I love your head, don't knock it, my boy.' Damini wrote that she is 'out there' and would I quit bugging her, I am a pain in her keester. A couple of my teachers wrote, too, and a bunch of people I don't know. They're all talking about what they want to do with their lives, where they want to go, who they want to be, what's holding them back, their worries."

"This is amazing." I read the comments. I was impressed with the frankness, the dialogue, the sharing, the encouragement.

"This is chill." Tate laughed.

The blog was giving him a voice. A voice without people reacting first to his head. A voice that could show his personality, his humor, and his character, which then allowed him to talk with others honestly and with respect. I reached down and hugged him. "I love you with my whole heart, son."

"Me, too, Boss Mom. And I know you'll change your mind about basketball. You know, the guys are practicing, getting together. I can do that, too. Carefully. I'll be careful."

"No."

"You're gonna give in, Boss Mom." He rubbed his neck. "Hey! Maybe the Other Mother might see my blog. Then she can get to know me."

It felt as if I'd been hit in the gut with a car. "I already know you, Tate, so does Nana Bird and Caden and his kids and we love you in a monster-sized way." That was the way I told him I loved him when he was a kid and he loved monsters.

"Yeah, me, too, Boss Mom."

"This is a bad idea," I told my mother the morning of the raft outing with Ethan, scurrying around the kitchen getting the club sandwiches slammed together with the warmed-up crumbled blue cheese dressings and adding extra powdered-sugar frosting to the cinnamon rolls I'd slaved over.

"Here's a list of adverbs to explain how I'm feeling. Ready? Stupendously, colossally, jarringly awkward."

"Awkward is an adjective and this is a spleeennnndid idea." My mother was wearing what she thought was fashionable gear for river rafting: pink, all pink, including a shiny pink jacket with gold buckles, and her gold bangles and dangly diamond earrings. Initially, she was wearing pink stilettos with a shiny white heel.

"Mother, really?" I pulled my hair into a ponytail, the crystals from Tate hanging to my shoulders. "Pink heels?"

"Nana Bird, you're gonna puncture the raft," Tate said. He was eating his fourth bowl of cereal in the nook.

"I'll keep my heels up or I'll take them off." She brought her leg up to hip height and twisted her ankle. She had flown in last night, after telling me, there was "no way in the world I would miss out on your first official date with Ethan!"

She had then called my brother, Caden, and told him, Damini, and the triplets to get ready for "Jaden's Raft Date with the Sex Doctor, Ethan." I'd had to call the raft company to add another raft. My brother's family had all arrived early at my doorstep.

"Lucky me to be here on your first date with Ethan," Caden said, winking at me. "I'm a witness to love. That's why I'm wearing my red T-shirt. For love."

"Yeah, a date, date, date," Damini said, then giggled. "Jaden's Raft Date with the Sex Doctor, Ethan."

"Did you need to say that to Damini, Mother? She's a young innocent."

"Yep. Young and innocent," Damini said. "I'm corrupted now."

"It's all titillating, if you ask me," my mother said, twirling a diamond earring. "I'm hopeful for you."

"What's a tit-a-lating?" Damini asked.

"Is there nothing that you think that doesn't come out of your mouth, Mother?" I hoped Ethan found my cinnamon rolls mouthwatering.

My mother winked a perfectly made-up eye at me. "No, sugar, there isn't."

"Sex doctor!" Hazel yelled, brandishing her sword.

"See what you've done," I protested. "Hazel, don't say that!"

"Sex doctor!" Heloise giggled and Harvey said, "Ha ha ex!"

I put my hands to my ears and groaned.

The triplets were in their best river-rafting gear: Heloise was dressed as a ninja. Hazel was a pirate with a purple tutu and a sword, and Harvey was a princess in a sparkly white dress with an army helmet on.

"Hazel is wearing the tutu because she had a fight with Heloise, who wanted to wear it with her ninja outfit." Caden sighed. "Harvey is a princess because he saw a princess on TV last night who was magic."

"I magic now, Aunt Jaden," Harvey said. He waved a star wand.

"I fight!" Heloise said, karate-chopping in the air.

"I a dance pirate," Hazel said. "Dance pirate! I got a patch on my eye. You wanna patch, Aunt Jaden?"

I hugged all three of them before they ran off to "hug" Slinky the lizard.

"Mom, those heels are pretty," Caden said, "but you can't wear them or you'll sink the raft. Wear your pink tennis shoes with the white stripes. They'll still match with your outfit."

Caden is always helpful with clothes.

My mother tapped her heels, prickly impatient with our silly fashion advice. "I won't poke the raft, and changing will ruin the flow and pinkness of my outfit."

"But remember, Nana Bird," Tate said, Damini sitting next to him. "Nothing can ruin your shining beauty."

That brought a smile to her face, and she kissed Tate and Damini, then scooted off to find her pink tennis shoes to match her pink pants, pink T-shirt, and shiny pink jacket with gold buckles.

Damini said, "I can't wait to hang out with your boyfriend."

I scowled at Caden. Caden coughed into his hand. "Now, Damini . . ."

"What? Aunt Jaden has dreamed about marrying Dr. Robbins for years. But she can't even date him because he's Tate's doctor, but she doesn't know if he's interested, anyhow. . . ." She eyed me. "You're in lovey-dovey kiss kiss kiss with him, aren't you? I can tell by the way you're dressed."

"What about the way I'm dressed? He's Tate's doctor, Damini. I'm in jeans and a green T-shirt."

"Tight jeans," she observed. "Tight T-shirt. You have big boobs, Aunt Jaden. Do you think I'll have big boobs?"

"I don't think you'll have any boobs," Tate said. "I think you're a sea monster. They don't have boobs."

"Shut up, Tate," Damini said, wrapping an arm around him.

"I can't shut up. I am destined to be a truth-speaker and you're gonna be a no-boobed sea monster. Maybe you're a boy. A boy Martian."

"I am not a boy Martian!"

"I see that you didn't deny being a sea monster, did you?" He scooted out of the nook to avoid Damini's wrath.

"You're a pain in my keester, Tate!" She ran after him, both of them laughing.

"You told her I wanted to marry him?" I hissed to Caden, who squirmed and pulled on his ponytail, which, today, was in a braid with a red ribbon as was Heloise's, Hazel's, and Damini's hair. "Tell her not to say a thing to Ethan, not a word. I'd be so embarrassed."

Caden yelled to Damini, "Damini, don't say a word to the doctor about how Aunt Jaden wants to marry him, you got that?"

"Got it! I won't say that Aunt Jaden wants to marry the sex doctor!"

"If you do, Damini, I'm going to . . ." Caden paused, brow furrowed. "Your punishment will be . . ." His face scrunched up in concentration. "It'll be something bad, Damini! Zip it, okay?"

"Zip it!" She laughed. "I'm zipped."

"She's zipped," Tate yelled. "A zippered sea monster."

The triplets came thundering back in.

Hazel raised Slinky the lizard in the air. "I hug Slinky!"

Heloise jumped. "I ninja."

Harvey grabbed a spatula and yelled, "I a damn princess!"

My mouth dropped. Caden groaned. "I said damn once and now he won't quit saying it! Stop it, Harvey. Don't say damn."

"But I a damn princess!"

With much to-do and confusion, the lunch hauled out in bags, we finally clambered into Caden's truck and my car and headed out to the river, the sun peeking over the horizon. When we were down the block, we realized we didn't have Harvey and had to drive back to get him. He was waiting on the porch with Slinky the lizard. "Slinky lonely," he told me.

Driving to the river, I was so excited I could hardly sit still and I could not stop smiling.

A whole day with Ethan!

"Remember, dear family, I'm threatening you," I yelled before we all left the second time. "Don't embarrass me or I won't cook for you again."

I heard Tate take a quick inhale.

Damini turned to me, eyes bugging out of her head. "Are you serious, Aunt Jaden?"

"Totally serious."

"That be bad!" Heloise the ninja said.

"Bad!" Hazel echoed.

"Damn bad," Harvey said.

"That's a petticoats-on-fire problem," Damini said.

I heard my mother laugh. "Burn those petticoats!"

"Okay, Aunt Jaden," Damini said. "I'll behave and keep my mouth in my control. I will. And your shirt *is* tight, but you look pretty and I hope I have knockers like that one day."

"Thank you. And whatever you do, Damini, don't hit Dr. Robbins with your leg."

She grinned. "I probably won't."

I have always treasured Damini's grin. When she joined our family when she was four, she had one leg, huge, sad eyes, and seemed to be semi-checked out of this world, as if she wasn't sure she wanted to rejoin it. She was scared of loud noises, crying, the dark, boxes, closets, being alone, anyone angry, and, oddly, men in hats. She had a habit of huddling in corners.

She wouldn't go to bed without an extra sack lunch she would eat in the middle of the night. She would sneak into Caden's and Marla's bedroom to sleep on the floor. Her favorite person next to Caden and Marla was Tate. She clung to him.

She still clings to him.

Damini didn't smile for six months. Her first smile? Tate picked her up and showed her a butterfly. She didn't speak for six months, either. When she did speak, she spoke English in short, but full sentences. Her first sentence? I love you.

I have always, and will always, treasure Damini's grin.

"Dr. Robbins," Tate yelled. "Dr. Robbins!"

Ethan turned. Instantly, he smiled.

I about melted. I love that smile.

Tate barreled into him and hugged him as usual, while all I could do was gape at Ethan, how tall he was, how broad, how the autumn sun glowed around him as if he were sporting a gold cloak. He was comfortable but sexy. Friendly but sexy. Smart but sexy. And he was happy to see me! He was! I saw it in that split second.

Then I saw *her*.

A *woman*. A woman with my Ethan.

An evil, spidery, donkey woman.

My mother's red-lipsticked mouth twitched. "His face lit up like a drunken sailor's when he saw you, witch daughter, but it appears he has a Barbie beside him."

I felt a green jealousy monster with fangs swell in my chest. He had brought his girlfriend! I didn't even know he had a girlfriend. But of course he had a girlfriend. I had been daydreaming about our relationship for so long I was deluded. I had imagined he cared for me. He didn't. He was Tate's doctor, that's it. He was kind.

I fought off a flood of emotional doom as I studied Barbie. All done up. Wearing tight white jeans, white T-shirt, white coat. Lots of makeup. Lots of platinum hair. I would bet her oversized watermelon boobs were false. She was skinny in a way that said she did not believe in eating.

Ethan introduced Tate to the woman and, as so often happens with people who do not make up "normal" in our society, who are different in one way or another, the woman reacted to Tate and to General Noggin with her most basic emotions: Disgust. Fear. Mortification.

Disgust toward my boy, Tate.

Fear of my son.

Mortified that someone had an oversized head and uneven eyes.

I hated her on sight.

"I don't like that bitch," my mother said, in her normal voice, as if she was saying, "Pass the sugar, please, for my tea."

"I don't, either," Caden growled.

Damini, no stranger to discrimination, said, "I think she's a blond zombie in a horror movie."

Tate saw, immediately, the woman's disgusted expression. We all saw his face fall, a fall I'd seen a thousand times. The rejection always, *always* hurts, no matter how many times it's received.

"I think I can head-lock her with no one noticing," Caden said, quite loudly. "Put her out for a few hours. She'll wake up later feeling fairly refreshed."

"These things can be done quietly," my mother said, fiddling with the large designer glasses she wore. "No one needs to know."

"Now can I hit her with my leg?" Damini said.

"I think that would be appropriate," I said. "Forget what I said at the house."

"Balls and tarnation, we're going rafting," my mother said, zipping her shiny pink jacket with the gold buckles. "Why is she dressed up in that . . . *white* outfit?"

I almost laughed. My mother, all in pink, disdainful of the Barbie's white outfit.

"We're going rafting with Barbie," Caden mused.

"Barbie!" Heloise said. "I no like Barbie."

"I put my Barbie's head in dirt," Hazel said.

"I a damn Barbie," Harvey said.

I strode up to say hello and to *hit* that woman if she did anything else rude to my sweet son, Caden and my mother following. I saw Tate yanking himself back together. "Yanking myself back together" was a catch phrase Tate used for rebooting after dealing with one ignorant, insensitive, rude member of the public after another. Tate shook the woman's hand, and she dropped hers almost immediately, as if he were grossly contaminated.

Between bites from the green jealousy monster, I realized I was surprised. I would not have imagined Ethan choosing a mean, shallow Barbie doll. Not at all.

"This is gonna be cool, Dr. Robbins," Tate said, turning to Ethan.

"It is, buddy. You're in my raft, that's for sure." I saw Ethan glare at the Barbie.

"Oh, I don't think—" the Barbie protested.

"You don't think what?" Ethan said, his voice sharp.

"I'm sure . . . I'm sure he wants to be with his family."

Ethan glanced at me, my mongo-sized brother with the red ribbon in his hair, the triplets in their costumes, Damini, and my mother. I had left a message that the gang was coming. He'd called back and said he was delighted. He had actually sounded delighted. He knew who my mother was. He had met her and my brother, too, many times.

"Hello to the Bruxelles!" He ambled over and shook hands, hugged my mom. Heloise kick-boxed as a greeting, Hazel said, "Argh! Hello, matie!" and Harvey, in his princess dress, said, "I damn magic."

Damini said, in all seriousness, dark eyes honest, "I have to keep my mouth closed around you because I'm not supposed to say anything or Jaden won't cook for us again."

Ethan appeared a mite confused and I shot Damini "the

look" to get her to clam up. Caden put his hand over her mouth.

"Aren't you sexy as usual," my mother said to Ethan, mockingly blinking her eyes at him, to quickly take the attention off Damini.

"And you are even more lovely than the last time, Rowan. Hi, Jaden."

"Hi, Ethan."

And then he hugged me. I hugged him back, soft and warm and happy.

It was a rather long hug under a happy sun and Tate said, "Here they go again. We should load up the rafts and get ready, this ogling could take awhile. Take the children away first, that includes me. I can't be corrupted by this lovey-dovey stuff, this romance, this blatant lust."

Ethan cleared his throat, pulled out of the hug, then put a hand out toward the Barbie and said, "I'd like to introduce Terri Torkleson." He told Terri our first names.

"Aren't you Elsie on *Foster's Village?*" the Barbie asked my mother, awe in her voice.

"Yes, I am." My mother flashed her a toothy smile. "Did you know"—she leaned in close—"in an upcoming season we're going to kill a woman who looks exactly like Barbie? Platinum hair. Lots of makeup. Wears white. Too thin. Extra large boobies. Rather mean, she is, and cold!" She wrinkled her sculpted nose. "She's going to be roped up, first, then she's going in a dark hole, then we're dumping scorpions all around her, and if she moves"—my mother clapped her hands together with glee — "she'll be bitten to death."

"Oh!" Terri said, shivering. "That . . . that sounds *scary.*"

"We only do it to characters that the audience hates." My mother fluttered her manicured nails.

Tate came up close to Terri. She pulled back, a tiny, repulsed sound escaping from her throat. I took a step toward her to let her have it, but Caden pulled me back. "Let Tate handle it," he whispered. "Let him be a man."

"I have a big head," Tate said to her, quite cheerfully. "But I don't bite. Except on Tuesdays."

The Barbie's mouth dropped open.

"Bite!" Harvey said, hopping in his sparkly dress. "Bite me! I a damn princess!"

"What's happened is that my head has grown and grown and grown since last year." Tate spread his arms out wide. "The doctors, for example, Dr. Robbins here, they don't know what's going on." Tate stepped in real close to Terri, who actually leaned away from him. Caden tightened his grip on my slugging arm.

"Watch this and mark my words"—my mother giggled—"I love his ingenuity, his creativity, most of all, his zingers."

"Hold on to your panties," Caden muttered. "This is my boy."

"Hold your panties!" Hazel yelled. "I don't got panties. I got Superman underwear!"

"I got pink panties!" Heloise shouted.

"I got princess panties!" Harvey said. "Damn!"

"My head used to be a normal size, the same as everyone else. A normal human's." Tate threw his hands straight up in the air, as if baffled by his growing head. "I woke up one morning and it was bigger. The next day bigger still, and now, I mean, I have one eye higher than the other and one and a half heads. General Noggin, that's what I call the other part of my head. Dr. Robbins thinks I have a virus."

Terri's expression moved from disgust to abject fear. She actually gasped.

"It's this head-growing virus. You get it, and your head expands."

Ethan laughed, covered it up with a cough, and studied the ground.

"All that fat in the squiggles of your brain, it expands and pushes the bones out, pushes the skull out, the stuff moves and shifts around, including that blue jelly-like substance in your brain, and all the prickly points that move messages across your mind, and all the squares and triangles in the center of your head, boom boom, it all swells."

"Oh my God!" Terri spit out. *"Oh my God!"*

"Somehow my thinking brain became infected and my head keeps getting bigger."

"Oh my God!" Hazel shouted, her tutu bopping.

"Oh my God!" Heloise and Harvey shouted, too. Harvey spun in his white princess dress. "Damn!"

I caught Ethan's eyes and muffled my own laugh.

"This virus that I have, it's called bigorollautilliomousous type B virus number one-two-four."

Terri sucked in a terrified breath with a squeak and took two steps back, willy-nilly frightened.

"My head has grown in the last month, too," Caden said, picking up Harvey, the princess. "It's been tough and double rough on me."

"What? Your head has grown, too?" Terri said to my brother. She mini-screamed, hand to mouth.

"Yes," Caden said solemnly. Caden did have a large head, but it was the large head of a muscled, giant-sized, He-man.

"It's contagious, then?"

"I'm afraid that's the truth," Tate said. "I'm afraid so. Contagious. Highly."

"I can feel my head expanding." Caden bent over to show Terri his head. "You can see a straight crack at the top where things are starting to split and spread."

Terri's mouth opened wide as she leaned in and examined Caden's crack. "You have a crack?"

"Yes, I have a crack," Caden said, not smiling, standing up again, Harvey clinging to him. "My crack is cracking."

"I have a crack, too," Tate said, holding his arms way out. "A wide crack and it's getting crackier overnight. It keeps spreading. Crack crack."

My mother patted her bobbed hair. "My head is still small. I haven't caught the Big virus three-two-one yet, thank heavens, unless it's in my bust. It could be." She stared at her chest. "They are blooming."

"I..." Terri said. "I... don't think I want to raft today, Ethan...."

Ethan smiled at me. I grinned back. We kept staring at each other. The man softens me out to mush.

"Ethan!" she whined.

Tate said, "Oh no no no. Chill out. The bigorollautilliomousous type B virus number one-two-four is only contagious through my spittle. Do you know what spittle is?"

"No," Terri whimpered, wringing her hands. "No."

"It's spit! Spit! Spittle is spit!" Tate pointed both fingers at his wide-open mouth and took another step closer to the cringing Terri. "From my mouth."

Ethan's muffled laugh traveled up into the blue sky.

"He wouldn't," Caden whispered, about to bust his sides open from trying to keep his laughs in.

"He's no spitter," my mother said. "He's a polite young man, with a deep knowledge and appreciation of Emily Post. He read her when he was six, you know, but one must take revenge when one can."

"*Spittle,*" Tate said. He touched his tongue, then studied the spittle.

"Shit!" the Barbie shrieked, taking steps backward.

"Not shit," Tate said. "It's spit!"

"Get away, step back, step back."

"You won't catch it unless I spittle on you, Terri!" Tate shouted.

My mother giggled. "He is priceless, priceless!"

My brother wheezed out between choked laughter, "Prepare for the comedy show."

Terri's face was scrunched up tight.

Then Damini brought the house down.

"It's nothing to worry about." Damini took off her leg and held it up. "The Big virus number six-four-one-twelve works differently on all Americans. For me, I lost my leg. But it's okay.

I don't need a bat for softball anymore because I have this. I have a weapon attached to my knee. And I can use my leg like a javelin, too. The bad part is that I always get pulled out of line at the airport for extra screening. You'll get used to it, Terri. Your head may not grow. An arm might drop off, though, or your butt. It could happen to your front privates, too."

Damini swung her leg through the air, circling it over her head like a gladiator.

"What? What?" Terri shrieked.

"Remember, you can only catch the Big six-four-one virus with spittle," Tate reminded her, leaning in close.

"Stay back, stay back," Terri of the fake boobs screamed, then whipped away and ran.

Tate turned to smile at all of us, his eyes, those sweet blue eyes, mischievous and full of humor.

"Get her," Caden whispered.

"Your humor is luscious," my mother said, wriggling her fingers. "Luscious."

"I'm proud of you, son," I told him. "Very proud."

Tate did a wee hop and hurtled after Terri.

"Oh, Tate!" I yelled, but I was laughing too hard to make much noise.

"Run, Tate, run!" Caden called.

Damini strapped on her leg. "I'm gonna catch her!"

Heloise yelled, "I fight ninja!" and whooped.

Hazel held up her sword, tutu bopping. "I a sword fighter!"

Harvey yelled, "I magic! Damn!"

Damini took off, and the triplets joined the chase, too.

I glanced at Ethan. He was bent over, cracking up.

I thought my mother had sprung a leak in her eyes she was laughing so hard. Caden's laugh was booming, *booming*, and I had to cross my legs because I thought I was going to pee.

It was my mother who did it. She yelled, "I'm going to wet my panttttieeess!" and made a wiggle-run for the bushes, knees tight together. That made me laugh harder, and not even thinking about what Ethan thought, I scuttled off after her, trying to hold my legs together, but also trying to hustle my butt before I had an accident.

Behind me I could hear Tate yell, one more time, close on Barbie's heels, "Unless I spittle on you, you're safe!"

Damini said, "It probably won't be your leg that falls off! It might be your boobs!"

"Da boobs!" Harvey said.

"Da boobs!" Heloise and Hazel echoed.

8

Dixie bolted straight up in bed, blank eyes staring into the corner, her mouth open in awe. "Oh my goodness!"

"Momma," her daughter said, stricken at this sudden movement from a woman who had hardly moved in three days. Lynnie reached for her mom. "Are you okay?"

Dixie stared at the corner, her eyes open wide, joyous.

This was not the first time I had seen this happen. In fact, as a hospice nurse, I've seen this same scenario with dying people many times.

Usually this abrupt and surprise movement, where the person who is dying suddenly sits straight up in bed, even if they've been in a deep, semiconscious sleep, takes place within seventy-two hours of when they die. Now, they may not have moved much, if at all, for many days. They may not be talking much, if at all. Their eyes, to us, are not focusing, or focusing less and less often.

"Momma," Lynnie said, rubbing her mother's back.

"Oh my goodness," Dixie breathed, still staring. She smiled into space.

We were gone to Dixie, she was not aware of us at all, and she would not be again.

Tears streamed down Lynnie's face. "Oh, Momma."

"It's okay, Lynnie," I soothed. "Let her be."

"But what, what is she doing?"

"She's taking a peek into heaven."

"What do you mean?"

"She's seeing where she's going next."

Dixie made another gasping sound, then whispered, "Oh my goodness! Wow!"

As quick as she was up, Dixie lay straight back down again, her eyes blank, staring, the light completely extinguished, as if someone had blown out the lit match inside of her. Seconds later, her eyelids closed, her chest rising and falling gently.

I patted Lynnie's back.

In the last months, I'd spent a lot of time holding Lynnie as she cried.

That's what I do.

I spend a lot of time holding people. Sometimes it's the person who is dying. Often it is the people who love the person who is dying.

Dixie died peacefully the next day. She had not been with us since before the "Oh my goodness" moment. Her soul was gone, her body was shutting down. I was there with her, as was Lynnie and Lynnie's daughter, Sarah, who was sixteen.

"You know she used to be a Rockette?" Sarah said, through a fountain of tears.

I thought of the many times that Dixie's legs would kick, of their own volition, these last weeks. "Yes, I knew that. She told me. I bet she was talented."

"Yeah. She was. I can't even imagine Grandma as a Rockette."

"When you're old, you won't be able to believe that you're old." I grinned at the kid. She was dressed in black with black makeup. She told me later that she pierced her nose with a bullring to piss off her father, who took off with a coworker. "You'll peer in the mirror and think, *That can't be me. I'm not that old. I still feel twenty-five, only I'm not such a loose cannon anymore and my knees don't work.*"

She snickered. Sarah couldn't imagine a time when she'd be old.

None of us can. But if we're lucky, four-leaf clover kind of lucky, we become old.

And hopefully we have the same type of Rockette adventures and experiences that Dixie did.

When Lynnie and Sarah left the room, weeping, I whispered to Dixie, "Well done, Dixie. You kicked up an amazing life. I shall miss you."

When I returned home, I headed straight to my greenhouse, cranked up Mozart, ate ten cinnamon red Gummi Bears and cried my eyes out in front of my tea collection.

Dixie had been one of my favorites.

Sometimes it is remarkably difficult to be a hospice nurse.

On my drive home from Caden's florist shop several days later, after I'd helped Caden make a white Corvette out of chrysanthemums for a man having a midlife crisis, I went over each minute of the raft trip from heaven with Ethan.

Terri had sprinted back to Ethan, with Tate and his spittle, the triplets, and Damini in hot pursuit. She wrapped her arms around Ethan, standing behind his back and whimpering, as if she needed protection from my son and his bigorollautillio-mousous type B virus number one-two-four.

"He's kidding, Terri," Ethan said, stifling, unsuccessfully, his laughter.

"He's kidding?" She was red and blotchy, her white-blond hair all over her face.

"Yep, he's kidding. And he wants to say he's sorry," I said. I frowned at Tate, but then I laughed, and it spoiled the disciplinary moment.

"Do apologize to me, too, Tate," my mother drawled. "I almost wet my pink designer slacks! Then what would I do?"

"Me, too, son," Caden said. "My stomach hurts I laughed so hard. I need a beer."

"I need a beer, too!" Heloise said.

"Ear!" Hazel said.

"He's not contagious?" Terri's voice shrilled. "That head, that big head, it's not contagious?"

"No, ma'am," Tate said. "I was born with this powerhouse. I have extra space because of my brains. I have a lot of them."

Terri's face creased, once again, into lines of confusion. Could someone need extra space for more brains? I could see her grinding that idea through her fluffy mind.

"Three sets of brains." Tate tapped his head.

"You have three sets of brains!"

My mother actually squealed.

Damini said, matter-of-factly, "She is dumb."

"Yep. Three sets of brains. That's why I have this head."

"Then don't joke about it!" Terri huffed. "You can't joke about getting a head like that!"

I sucked in my breath as something carnal popped to mind when Terri said, "getting a head." I tried extremely hard not to sneak a peek at Ethan and think anything naughty.

My mother said, her gold bracelets jangling, "Tate has already gotten a head? Remember, mad passion equals safe protection!"

"I won't joke about getting a head again," Tate deadpanned.

He's a teenager. He was not naïve. The slang for that particular sex act was not lost on him.

"You made me think you were going to give me a head like yours!" Terri put her hands on her skinny hips.

"Yes, ma'am, I did. I am guilty about pretending I was going to give you a head. It was bad."

"I can't even think about getting a head like that!" Terri's angry face tightened up. "I sure don't want one!"

"I don't want you to give me a head, either." Tate wrinkled his nose.

"Oh Tate, you are wonderful," my mother breathed.

"Quick on his feet," Caden said, crossing his arms, those muscles bulging.

"Sharp as a tack," I said.

"I wasn't going to give *you* a head," Terri protested, too flustered and riled up to understand the undercurrents. "You were trying to give me a head!"

"I can't give you a head," Tate said again. "Technically that's not correct."

"I love his sharp, incisive intellect," my mother said.

"It's General Noggin," I said.

We all nodded. "General Noggin."

Ethan stepped in. "How about if we start the raft trip? I think we're all acquainted and ready to go."

"I a damn princess," Harvey said. "I go in da boat."

"I want a beer!" Heloise said. "Daddy beer."

"Boo boo!" Hazel said.

The guides were standing nearby, they had not bothered to cover their laughter.

Terri's face scrunched up tight. "I hope the rest of my day is not going to be rotten!"

"I think it's going to get worse for you, dear," my mother said. "We're going to be on water. You might get your hair wet."

"It's only the beginning," Caden said. "You've told her about the Class Seven rapids?"

Terri's mouth dropped. "Class Seven?"

"Come along," my mother said cheerily. "That man over there is waving at us. Must be our guide. I believe it's our time to hit the river. I hope we don't drown. No heads, Tate!"

"Yes, don't give her a head!" Caden said. "That's just not right."

"Fine. We'll forget about the spitting," Damini said, that jokester. "But Tate's germs did cause my leg to fall off. I'm never going to forgive you for that, Tate. I miss my leg. Never stop missing it, not for one minute."

"I know, I'm sorry, Damini. I should have kept my germs to myself."

Terri's eyes almost popped out.

"He's kidding," we all said to her. "He's kidding."

We had a most excellent time on the river.

I hadn't been that happy in a long time. Probably years.

Ethan sat by me on the raft. He was attentive and protective. He was funny. He told me early on, whispering, that Terri was his brother's wife's sister and Terri was driving the sister-in-law crazy with her meanness, so much that the sister-in-law had begged Ethan to take her for the day.

"Trix is pregnant," he told me, "and she's a great sister-in-law, but she has a two-year-old, too, and she's wiped out and still has morning sickness and her head is over a toilet and Terri is giving her lectures about not becoming fat and frumpy and why isn't the house cleaner? My brother's in Japan on business, and Trix called, crying, then my brother called, pissed off at Terri for upsetting his wife and begging, so I had to."

"Ah. I thought she was your girlfriend," I whispered back.

His face froze. "No, Jaden. She is not my girlfriend. I don't have a girlfriend."

"I'll be—"

Oh dear. I snapped my mouth shut. I had been about to say, "I'll be your girlfriend."

"I'll be . . ." I cleared my throat. "I'll be gosh darned surprised at that."

"Gosh darn surprised?"

I put my paddle back in the water. Gosh darn surprised. "Yes. Darn surprised, doctor."

"Ethan."

"Ethan Doctor."

"Just Ethan."

I stole a glance at him, not too long, because the longer I stared, the hotter I became for that man. "Ethan."

"Stroke."

"Stroke?" Like stroke my body with his hands?

"Yes, stroke."

His voice was gentle and pure and low.

"Okay. Stroke."

He nodded at my paddle.

"Oh! Stroke. Stroke that. The paddle. I'll stroke the water," I told Ethan.

"Yes. The water needs a stroke."

An awesome image of me stroking Ethan popped into my mind and I couldn't help but slide him a glance.

He knew.

I knew he knew what I was thinking about.

He smiled.

It was an exhilarating, sexy rafting trip down the river. Not only because all of us, except for Terri, jumped off the raft and floated down part of the river with life jackets, splashing each other, and not only because the picnic lunch was delicious, despite Terri's complaints about it being "too fattening for her figure," and not only because my mother led us in raunchy songs, to which we all (except Terri, but including the guides) joined, and not only because my mother pushed Terri in the river and she did, indeed, get her hair wet and came up swearing, and not only because there were incredible rapids and animals to enjoy and a yellow sun all friendly overhead, but because I was with Ethan.

Ethan and I.

On a raft, in a river, together.

Together.

At the end Damini announced, "I am double and triple glad we were all invited on Jaden's Raft Date with the Sex Doctor."

Hazel said, "Hex doctor!"

Heloise said, "Ex doctor!"

But Harvey had it right, twirling in his princess dress. "Sex doctor! Damn!"

Terri seared me with a mean gaze.

I could not have turned more red.

My mother positively cackled.

Ethan smiled at me. I smiled back. What else could I do?

A couple of days later, after planting purple and yellow mums in pots in my greenhouse for our front porch, I mixed up coriander, sea salt, fennel, and sage, running them all through my fingers, comparing the textures, using Faith's silver spoons to blend a tad here and there.

I didn't want to do this, but it pulled me. I was compelled. Compelled to do what I didn't want to do over Grandma Violet's crystal plates and Faith's silver spoons though I didn't want to know the answer.

I smelled what I didn't want to smell: death.

My hands froze over the herbs and spices, panicked, sick. Anguished.

Please, not Damini, not the triplets.

Not Tate.

Please, God, not Tate.

On a rainy afternoon Tate played basketball on our court for three hours. He came in for dinner. He would not acknowledge me.

My sweet, kind boy had turned into a cauldron of anger.

He worked in his Experiment Room that night for two hours. When I tried to give him a hug, he pulled away.

"Not even a hug, Tate?"

"No. My brain waves are not feeling it."

"Tate, you're hurting me and you're being vindictive."

"I don't have a vindictive bone in my body, Mom. I'm not feeling it for hugging you. I love you, though. It's almost too late. All the guys are already practicing after school. The coaches are watching. I know they're picking teams in their minds. I'm a junior, Mom. Two years. That's all I have left of high school."

"You—"

"Me, what, Mom? You are always interfering, always hovering over me, always overprotective as if I'm a baby, as if you think I can't handle anything on my own. You won't let me do what I want, what I need to do. I can hardly breathe I'm so mad. You say you're keeping me safe, but I am hating this, Mom. I am hating my life."

I was miserable.

He was miserable.

I called my mother at one in the morning. She was up. She always is. She sleeps about five hours a night. I tell her it's because she's hungry, being that slender. She says it's because she's still enjoying the cocktail she had before bed.

"Throw him out in the world," my mother said.

"Throw him out in the world? Are you kidding me? No."

"Throw him out into the wide, wide, wonderful world of high school basketball then."

"No."

"My darling daughter, you're suffocating your son and you need to stop it."

"I am not suffocating him."

"You are. You absolutely are."

"Mom, you know he is not a normal kid. He is a kid with a shunt in his head. Do you get that if he's hit hard enough on the head, he could have serious problems? He could die?"

"I know. But it's unlikely." For once all flighty and raunchy comments, that dry humor, was gone. "Even Ethan said so."

"Unlikely isn't good enough."

"It's all we all have. We all take risks. Getting in a car is a risk. Scuba diving is a risk. Skiing is a risk. It's improbable he'll be hurt, even with the problems he's had."

"What about the kids on the other teams? What about the fans? You've heard it almost every time we're in public: Retard. Martian head. Two heads. Cockeyes. Frankenstein. Bobble-head." I felt tears spurt up. "Freakoid. I'll sit there and I'll watch his face shutting down, closing up like he does when he's humiliated or attacked, and that excitement will ebb away. We're playing other kids in other communities. They'll make fun of him. They'll be rude, they'll yell mean stuff from the stands, they'll chant. They'll yell, 'Crooked eyes.' Maybe they'll come after him after the game. . . ."

"Jaden—"

"He's tough, and he uses humor to deflect a lot, but he's sensitive, too. I can picture him running onto the court, excited that he's being allowed to play, and the audience getting quiet and staring and laughing and snickering. . . ." I put a hand to my tears, thinking about people attacking my son.

"Is that why you're really not letting him play? That you don't want him to be hurt by the fans?"

I couldn't even speak for a moment, my throat constricting so tight. "No, I am worried that he'll become critically hurt, but do I want Tate to endure more teasing than he has to? No. Of course I don't."

"Your wanting to protect him is hurting him more than hearing ignorant, pubescent, zitty, awkward teenagers with elf ears saying cutting things to him."

"That's not true." My shaky hand could hardly hold the phone.

"It is true."

"You're wrong. My job is to protect him."

"That's my job, too. I'm his Nana Bird. But he is furious with you, Jaden, and your relationship will go downhill for the next two years unless you let him play. He may grow to hate you and anything that happens on that court—even if it is self-esteem smashing—will pale to how he'll feel about you the rest of his life for not letting him at least try out."

"He wouldn't do that to me." Right?

"He doesn't want to. But he loves basketball, Jaden. Loves it. Could something bad happen? Yes. But sometimes you have to risk the bad happening to let the rainbows in. This is his rainbow. Let him dance with the rainbow."

"I hate dancing," I muttered. I jiggled my legs to rid myself of stress.

"That's because you never learned how. You haven't danced for years, Jaden. The dancing was beaten out of you when you were young. I understand how it happened, but you need to dance, you need to let him dance."

"I don't want to dance."

"You're still young. Dancing should be in your life. Tate's young. He needs to dance his own dance."

Sometimes my mother can be darn poetic.

"Let him play," she said. "Let him play."

Later I made hazelnut chai tea and stared out my window at the moon. It was getting dark much earlier, the skies heavier, cool winds blowing. Soon all the maple trees lining the drive would be bare, their branches intertwined sticks outlined against a white or gray sky. There would be rain, probably snow, definitely icy mornings.

How many times had Faith stared out this window and watched the weather, the snowflakes, windstorms, rain, a quilt wrapped around her shoulders, troubled, anxious, worried?

Miserable?

TATE'S AWESOME PIGSKIN BLOG

Here's another photo of my uncle Caden. His arms are the size of tree trunks. He's six foot six and yeah, the dude has a ponytail and he looks as if he could rip apart Halley's Comet with his own hands. He was a professional wrestler, now he's a single dad of four kids and owns Witches and Warlocks Florist.

Here are photos of his flowers. Yep, he made a zebra out of black and white carnations, and that tequila bottle flower arrangement is six feet high. The boobs in this photo were made out of pink flowers for a woman who beat breast cancer. He made them three feet across and a foot tall with red rosebuds for the you-know-whats, and the lady loved them. "She's gotta celebrate," he told me. "She's gotta celebrate in a huge way, too."

Here's a photo of my cousin Damini, dancing.

She was adopted by my uncle Caden when she was four from an orphanage in India.

She is wearing a silver sparkly dress made by the designer, Cattrell Five, which my Nana Bird bought for her.

See that prosthesis? She lost her leg in the orphanage when it was infected after a snake bit her.

Sometimes she takes it off and chases a particular boy with it. I'm not going to say anymore or she'll call me a "farting fruitcake," and come after me.

BUT HERE ARE DAMINISMS, DAMINI'S RULES FOR LIFE:

1. Sometimes you have to swing a leg to make a point.
2. Every time you eat, be grateful you're eating.
3. If you are a stupid person, please shut up.
4. Be nice to animals. In your next life you might come back as a slug, remember that.
5. Plant the same flowers as your ancestors did, then you have a true family garden. We Bruxelles each have one; the tradition started a long time ago by my great, great, etc. super duper brave grandma, Faith Stephenson.
6. Learn how to make Taco Soup because it is delicious, and read a lot of books because they are delicious, and if you don't read how do you learn anything?
7. Watch the seasons change, that's what my aunt Jaden says, and I think she's right.
8. I wear short skirts with ruffles, sequins, and fluff because I love them. I'm not gonna hide my leg. Don't hide anything about yourself.
9. I know what it's like to sit in a dark room in a crib alone and feel as if no one loves you. Love a lot of people for a happy life.
10. Tate is a pain in my keester.

When Damini and I hang out together in public, we receive a lot of odd looks, and sometimes mean comments. I'm bigheaded. She has only 1.5 legs.

We don't care.

So that's Damini.

Here's a photo of her on a skateboard. Here's a photo of her skiing. Here's a photo of her bicycling. Here's a photo of her chasing me with her mouth open wide enough to catch a goose.

Here's a photo of your brain's neural pathways. Damini, I don't know if you have any neural pathways. Could be all you have up there is a green Cyclops monster telling you what to do. . . .

Everybody, send me your list of ten Daminisms. You know, the stuff you know about life, the rules you live by, what you know in your own noggin, that kind of thing.

Tate and I spent almost two hours reading the entries.
His blog received 400 hits that day.

I took Tate to play chess with Maggie Granelli on Saturday.
"Hello, Maggie Shoes," Tate said. "I've come to beat you. I will give you no quarter, I will be merciless, I will be thorough in my attack, and then I'm going to have some of that lemon cake on your counter, okay?"
"Greetings, Bishop Tate. Today I am feeling lucky. Your demise on this chessboard will please me greatly. And have all the lemon cake you want."
They began. Tate won both matches. There would be no pity wins.
Maggie's roses still have a few blooms. Pinks, reds, yellows . . .
Her time is shortening.

There are many reasons I became a hospice nurse.
One was because of Grandma Violet. Violet was a healer, as was her mother before her. People all over our town, for miles out, came to see her, from the time she was seventeen years old.

She used herbs, massage, meditation, a little sterilized acupuncture to "release the evils," and she used her Silent Spells.

She used "talk healing," too, where she sat and listened, her red curls bopping around, her hands holding her client's.

Every summer Brooke, Caden, and I came up from Hollywood and watched Grandma Violet work. Her patients cried, they talked as if no one had listened to them before, they told her their aches and pains, in both body and heart. She listened, she soothed, she healed.

She did not hesitate to send them to a doctor when needed. For example, when Davis Castille crawled to her on his knees because his appendix had burst, she called an ambulance. "I want you to take it out, Violet," he pleaded, pale white. "You do it. I don't trust them damn doctors. Stealing my money, that's what it's about, all for a bad stomachache."

When Lizzie Hasten's son's arm had split to the bone from a tractor accident, same thing. "Get out your sewing kit and sew him up, Violet!" Lizzie said. "He wants you to use red thread to make him seem manly, isn't that right, Reggie?"

When Ruby Black had shingles, she came to Grandma Violet for the "magic herbal tea." Grandma Violet made her a cup before driving her to the doctors. "It wasn't the medicine that cured me," she told anyone who would listen. "It was Violet's magic herbal tea."

The magic herbal tea was soon in great demand.

"What I do, dears," she told Brooke, Caden, and me one summer, her blue eyes huge behind her glasses, "is help to heal the heart and the head, the passions, the pain, loss, grief, frustration, disappointment, and anger. All of those emotions will cause your body to fail in one way or another. Joy lifts the spirit and sorrow weighs it down. Joy gives health, sorrow brings illness." She held our hands in hers. She smelled like a blend of nutmeg and vanilla. "And I do a few Silent Spells, to help things along, spells I learned from my mother and her mother, all the way back to Faith and Grace, and their mothers, the twins Henrietta and Elizabeth, immensely talented witches."

We nodded, still in blind awe as children at the thought of our magic, chanting, spell-throwing witch-ancestors.

I wanted to be a healer, too.

I became an emergency room nurse first and worked to heal people who were sometimes on the brink of death. Most of the time we saved them, sometimes we didn't. That job certainly gave me nerves of steel and a deep background in trauma. But I also understood grief. I lost Grandpa Pete before Grandma Violet; my father, Shel, on that terrible night; and Brooke to drugs. Your own grief helps you understand others' grief, therefore you're in a unique position to help.

So I became a hospice nurse. My job isn't to heal my patients physically, they're past that point, but to make sure they're comfortable and getting as much quality time out of the rest of their lives as possible. I offer medicines for various symptoms and problems that come up with the terminally ill, and pain and anxiety management. I listen, comfort, help, and explain various aspects of the patient's health and what will happen in the future.

Another reason I became a hospice nurse was because I crave raw, honest relationships and have zero patience for superficiality.

When you are working with people who are dying, all pretenses are off. There is no shallowness, no silliness. I don't have the patience for relationships that float and skim across the top of human existence, relationships that have no depth or that are based on shopping, manicures, gossip, men, clubbing, etc. I want *real* relationships.

I had found, after Tate was born, and after his critical medical emergencies, that many people annoyed me. I could not relate to their problems: bad hair days, a fight with a husband, a jealous sister, a kid who didn't get into the college she wanted, an extra twenty pounds to lose, an irritating cold that produced endless whining, a PTC president who is an obsessive control freak, a fender bender, etc. These were not *problems* to me. They were vague irritants. They were everyday life.

A kid who has medical issues is a *problem*. Someone critically ill is a *problem*. Someone dying is a *problem*. A kid on drugs is a *problem*. I could no longer relate to many people. I found myself rolling my eyes, sometimes in front of people, when they would complain about one ridiculous thing or another, as if they had a *problem*.

I snapped at people, too. One day I said, "You know, Randi, no one wants to hear about your mother-in-law anymore. Stop obsessing about her. For God's sake, is that all you have to worry about, you lucky whiner?"

Another time a gal named Deborah was gossiping, and I said, "Come on, Deborah. Is that all you have going on in your life? You have all this spare time and the only way you can think to fill it is to judge other people?"

When I was an emergency room nurse, an administrator who sat on her ass all day was complaining about how hard she worked. "It's a job, Cheryl, you get that? It's a job. There are a whole bunch of people who have no job and therefore no health insurance. You think you have problems? Go and talk to the lady in room 489. Then you'll hear problems."

Many people, all of a sudden, seemed to me to feel *entitled* to have an easy life, as if it were a guarantee, as if they had done something to deserve it. If something went slightly wrong, it was an affront, shocking, horrible. They came off seeming spoiled, sheltered, and petty to me.

I had lost family to long-term illness and tragedy. I had a sister on drugs and a kid with severe medical problems. Nothing in my life was light and frilly. It was all serious. I was, I am, a serious and rather impatient person.

Hospice patients, hospice nurses, they are right in the thick of that seriousness, they are in the thick of what is important in life. I think that's another reason that I relate to Ethan. He gets it, too. He gets what's important and what's not. He gets life and death.

I have loved being a hospice nurse. It is not an easy job, but it is an honor. It is a privilege. It's a calling.

That said, I don't know how much longer I can do it. This last year, it's been wearing on me in a way I can't explain. I won't say that it's killing me, that's an unfunny pun, but I have taken to eating red cinnamon Gummi Bears for comfort and my heart sometimes beats too fast. It's stress. Stress from the dying.

I have watched many people die and I remember all of them.

Sometimes I think I need more life in my life.

"Hello, darling!" My mother's cheery, modulated voice rang through the phone.

"Toodle, toodle, Jaden!" Sammy Zieker called out. My mother had put me on speakerphone on her end. Sammy Zieker is Mrs. Evelyn Carrodine on *Foster's Village*. She is the grand dame with all the money, and my mother is slowly poisoning her to get her money. Mrs. Carrodine has a son, Alistair Carrodine, with whom my mother is having a tempestuous affair. When Mrs. Carrodine dies, my mother will ditch her husband and marry Alistair and be rich!

"Jaden, my dear!" Mickel O'Dierno called out, aka Alistair Carrodine.

"Hello, Mom, hello, Sammy, hello, Mickel! How are you all?"

"Splendid, my dear! We're in the middle of the poisoning but the lighting is off, so we've a few moments to tittle-tattle," Sammy said. "Your mother brought the Naughty Brownies you baked to the set, and now I know nirvana exists in a heavenly sphere."

"They were nirvana?" I needed another compliment.

"We love them! Life is now grand," Mickel called out. In his real life Mickel has been married for twenty-two years and has six kids. "I've had four. It makes for a better day since your mother is plotting to kill Sammy."

"Murder and brownies, don't they go well together?" I asked.

"Oh yes!" my mother agreed, cackling evilly. "It's a sweet murder! Chocolate and poisoning!"

"I couldn't agree more, honey nut, and I'm the one being slowly murdered," Sammy said. Sammy is on her third husband in real life. She is seventy-five. "Third time was the charm!" Her current husband is eleven years younger than herself and still "frisky as a colt! I ride him, the bucking bronco."

"You must send us cinnamon rolls, though, dear," Mickel said. "I have to have another one. They're the best! The best!"

"It was like having a cinnamon roll orgasm," Sammy drawled. "With melted powdered sugar."

"Hey! I need one for my wife," Mickel said. "With six kids she could use a cinnamon roll orgasm."

We chatted and laughed.

"I love the violence on *Foster's Village,* it pulls it all out of my system," my mother told me later. "Witches have that streak, as you know."

I laughed. I don't believe in any of that.

No, I don't.

I don't think so.

9

I received Tate's PSAT scores. He did not miss one question. Not one.

I showed him his scores in his experiment room. He pushed back the goggles he was wearing, a row of glass tubes with liquids in front of him. "Superb work, Einstein, and please don't blow up the house."

He glanced at his PSAT scores. "I would never blow up the house because I know what I'm doing."

Tate's Experiment Room had loads of science stuff. Books, beakers, and experiment tables with all sorts of goo, liquids, and models. There were also graphs, charts, and posters, almost all of them about the human brain, plus life-sized models of brains. He had a collection of DVDs featuring brain surgeons and brain operations. He had been on robotics teams so that paraphernalia was around, too, plus an engine, old radios, computers, routers, electric gizmos, and stuff I could not name, plus his weight set.

"I'd rather have flunked the PSAT if it meant I could play basketball."

"I'd rather be in the Bahamas." I tossed my hair back, the tiny crystals brushing my ear. "Life's tough. Want to play chess?"

"No, you green- and blue-eyed mean mother."

"Come on, Tate."

He snapped the goggles back on. Because of the size of his

head, he'd had to re-engineer them. He'd done an excellent job using an elastic strip. "Mom, I love you, but I don't want to talk to you right now unless it's about my trying out for the basketball team."

"I know you don't want to talk to me, Tate. I get it. Do you think I haven't noticed the silence the last few days?" I had missed him. I had missed his interesting conversation, his laughter, his jokes, his hugs . . .

"There are hardly any more weeks until tryouts, and I want to practice with the guys."

"I'm not discussing this with you again."

"Okay, fine. But I'm not going to discuss chess with you, either."

"You don't have to discuss it. Come play it with me."

"No, Mom. I'm going to stay up here experimenting with chemicals because I want to learn how they react, and later I want to read some scientific papers on why the universe keeps expanding when gravity is pulling us in. You can go back downstairs and cut up all your herbs by yourself."

"I'd rather talk to you."

"Then let me play."

I watched him for a few more seconds. "I love you, Tate."

"I love you, too. Me being mad at you doesn't mean I don't love you. I do. But I need space because I'm so mad at you I want to cry."

"You want to cry?" Sadness settled even heavier on me.

"Yeah, Mom, I do. I want to cry. I want to be on a team. I don't want to spend all my time playing imaginary basketball outside and hanging around in my experiment room by myself. I want to make friends if I can, shoot baskets, wear a uniform, and be a regular kid. Can you leave now?"

"Okay, Tate."

"And I still want you to find my Other Mother so I can meet her. She can get to know me through my blog, too."

I glanced outside his window. It was a chilly night. It had hailed earlier. It would be a cold winter.

*   *   *

The next day, I received the same cold attitude from Tate.

He played basketball on our court. He would not talk to me, except to say that he loved me and wanted to play basketball.

The day after that we repeated the whole scene yet again. I felt like I'd dropped into a pit of sadness. I loved that kid, loved him a million times over, and I do not do silence well.

Over the weekend, the silent treatment continued. I even offered to set up a weekend trip to the mountains.

"I don't want to go."

"Please, Tate."

"No. I want to play basketball."

"Go outside and play on our court."

"That's not what I mean, Mom, and you know it. I want to try out. I'll probably get cut, but I want to try."

"Let's go to the mountains. It's snowing—"

"No. I'm going to my experiment room to see if I can concoct a potion to alter your brain and make you reasonable, and then I'm going to take apart a radio piece by piece and put it together again. When I turn it back on, it will play songs about mean moms."

He stomped up the steps.

On Tuesday I arrived home late from work.

Tate was not on the stools at our butcher-block island eating his second lunch. He was not in the nook doing homework for his online advanced statistics class or listening to a lecture about brains on TV. He was not at the long, wooden table that Grandma Violet used for her herbs and that Faith's husband, Jack, built.

He was not practicing basketball with his imaginary team on our court or working on his blog.

I knew where he was.

"Darn that kid." I grabbed my keys and headed out to the high school.

*   *   *

From my parked car I watched Tate leave the high school gym with a bunch of boisterous, laughing boys, including his best friends, Anthony and Milt.

I was steamin', boilin' mad. I had said no and there he was, completely disobeying me.

I was trying to *protect* him. He was being a stupid teenager who would not acknowledge the unique, personal threats to his life and health. He didn't get it because he didn't want to get it.

I opened my car door and started to scramble out. I would let him have it. A millisecond before shrieky recriminations left my throat, I stopped . . . and watched.

The boys were patting Tate on the back, laughing, talking. I heard one of them say, "You're frickin' bionic, Tate. Man!"

And another one said, "Dude, you're sick and awesome."

"You're on Varsity, for sure. Where you been all these years?"

"You made all your friggin' shots, every friggin' one! How you doin' that, man? You're trippin'."

Another guy shot out of the gym doors and grabbed Tate from behind. Tate hoisted him up on his back.

And Tate, my dear Tate, Tate of the big head and slanted eyes, had an expression on his face that I'd never seen before.

Unadulterated, free-flowing joy.

It lit up his face like a star.

Anthony and Milt grabbed him, pushing him good-naturedly. He was part of the group. Part of the gang. Part of a bunch of boys who had just finished practicing basketball.

That was what he'd wanted.

I watched him smile, the happiest, most glorious smile I'd ever seen in my life.

Until he saw me.

Then the smile rapidly disappeared and he froze, a stalked animal who knows they're being watched and probably about to be eaten.

The other boys stopped the roughhousing and stared, probably frightened by the stormy expression on my face.

"Get in the car, Tate. Now." I was still furious.

* * *

"Mom, I was tight, please, Mom, you should have seen me!"

"I don't need to see you. I know what I would see." I slammed the front door of the house. Our trip home from the high school had been in total silence on my end. Tate had tried to talk, but I'd held a hand up so he wouldn't speak and I could rein in Witch Mavis. "You are not going to tryouts again tomorrow, Tate. You are not to go. Do you hear me?"

"But, Mom—"

I slammed cabinets in the kitchen, looking for ingredients for dinner. He followed me. I couldn't even meet those bright blue eyes of his. I knew he was devastated. It didn't mean his disobedience was okay. I put the scene with the other boys out of my head. "My job isn't to keep you safe until you play your next basketball game, Tate, my job is to keep you safe for years. Your life is not worth a basketball game."

"It's more than that, Mom. Don't you get it?" He shoved his backpack on the butcher-block island as I popped three red cinnamon Gummi Bears into my mouth. "I can hang out with the other guys. I can be more than a weird-looking, bigheaded genius. I'm an outcast."

"You are not. I hear that the kids like you—"

"Some of them are nice to me, but that's because they've known me since kindergarten, and also because Milt and Anthony are really cool and popular, and that helps, and some are nice because they feel sorry for me, which makes me want to blow, and others are nice because they're trying to pat themselves on the back about being nice to a pathetic deformed kid, and some are nice because they're nice, but a lot of them aren't nice to me, Mom, or they avoid me because they think I look freakish. I know that, they know that, and they can't get past General Noggin enough to see me as a person. But this way, maybe . . ." He bit down on his lip, and I knew he was trying not to cry.

I tried not to cry, too. *Be strong, Jaden. Be strong!*

"Maybe they can forget, or try to forget, about my head, my crooked eyes, if I can shoot baskets, Mom. It makes me less gargolylish weird to them. I'm doing something that they get. They understand basketball. It's like I'm—"

He ran both hands over his face.

"Like what, Tate?" I slammed a pan to the counter.

"It makes me, I mean, it makes me more . . ."

"More what?" My heart was breaking for this kid. High school is tough, cliquish, and exclusive. Try it with a big head. I reached for my spices.

"*Normal*. Mom, I want to fit in for a few minutes, maybe an hour, during a game. I want to pretend that I'm the same as the other kids . . ."

"Tate—"

"Don't tell me that I fit in. I don't. I never have. I never will. I accept it. But right now, if I play basketball, if I'm good . . . maybe it'll be different for me. Maybe." He brushed his hands across teary eyes.

"And you want to risk your life for a maybe?" I grabbed my measuring cups and sent them tumbling to the counter. "You have to be kidding me, Tate."

"I'm not kidding, Mom. I'm not as aggressive yet as the other kids, but I'm fast and I make points. I created and studied that computer model about shooting—"

"I know you studied it and it doesn't mean anything. Stop studying it."

"Mom, you don't know what it's like. I'm lonely. I'm alone. It's always going to be that way for me. I know it."

I'm lonely. I'm alone. It's always going to be that way for me. I know it. Crushing words that sank straight into my heart. I stopped banging my way around the kitchen. "You have friends, Tate, and Milt and Anthony, and you have me, your Nana Bird, Caden and his kids . . ."

"I know, but I want to . . ." A loud sob burst from him, his face red.

"Tate." I swallowed hard, my anger gone, my heart splitting.

"I want to be a part of this, of basketball. The team always loses and I can help them. I know I can. Coach Boynton wants me to play, I can tell."

I thought of Coach Robert Boynton. Rangy, tough, had a face

like a hardened Mafia leader. I'd known him in high school where he was a star athlete. He was married to my friend, Letty.

He cried over opera. He cried when kids made baskets who never made them. He cried when he had Letty's annual birthday bash, calling her, "The best wife a guy could have. I love you, Letty!"

Letty could not have kids, so they had a round of foster kids living with them at all times. He cried over them, too.

"All these people were there watching practice today and I made a three-pointer, I shot it with my Road Runner eye, it was my fourth one, and Coach shouted so everybody in that gym heard, 'Outstanding, Tate, you're *outstanding*.' He yelled it, Mom. And people patted me on the back and Rick Santorini said, 'That was fuckin' hot, man.' He said that. Sorry about the F word, Mom." He bit his lip, trying to control himself.

"You are outstanding, and I don't need a game to prove it. It's a game, Tate." I pulled out my mixing bowls. I had no idea what to cook. "Basketball is a game."

"It's more than that to me, Mom. Take your work with dying people. It's not only a job for you, you're not only a nurse, it's who you are. You help people die. You said before that it's an honor and a privilege, that you love your job even though it makes you cry."

"My job is not going to possibly cause me an injury or death, do you get that?"

"It's only a slight chance, Mom. Slight. So slight." He brushed tears off his cheeks, his hands shaking.

"It's there." I did not like to see my son crying or his hands shaking.

"Mom, what would you do if I took away your greenhouse, your herbs? You wouldn't be happy, would you? What if I took away your job and helping people? You'd feel lost, you know you would. You'd feel alone, lonely. That's how I feel, *all the time*. I've wanted to play basketball my whole life, and you've always said no."

I didn't tell him that my work was making me feel lost lately or that aloneness and loneliness had stalked me for years, that not having Ethan in my life was a constant sadness. This conversation was not about me.

"Mom, I'm a junior in high school. These are my last two years. I have to play now or I'll never get to play. I have to."

"No." My whole body hurt for him as he took a shuddery, pathetic breath.

"Mom, please."

"No. And don't go to practice tomorrow or you will be grounded and I'll take your computer and your phone."

"Aw, Mom." He burst into another round of tears and dropped his head on the butcher-block island.

After a minute I walked around and put my arm around him but he swatted it away, his huge shoulders shaking.

I tried again and he turned, grabbed his backpack, and stomped up the stairs to his bedroom. He blocked his bedroom door with his dresser so I couldn't hug him good night.

Tate was not the only one crying into his pillow that night.

The next day I drove home after work and Tate was not home.

Once again, furious, I drove to the high school.

I slammed the door to my car, my black leather boots thudding on the wet pavement, my long hair soon wet from the rain. I yanked open the door to the school and strode to the gym. As I had attended high school here, many memories assailed me, one in which my friend Bryan Wernerson exploded a toilet and laughed so hard he fell off his chair.

I tossed the toilet memory aside, though, whipped around the corner, and glared into the gym just in time to see Tate take a three-point jumper in a scrimmage. The ball swooshed, all net. My breath caught.

I saw him shuffle back to play defense as two teammates gave him a high five. I saw him steal the ball from his opponent and charge back down the court. I saw him come close to dunking the ball, the ball slipping through the net. I saw him pass the ball off to Anthony, who made a basket. I saw Anthony point at him in thanks. Tate passed it twice more to teammates, all who credited him with a laugh or a hoot.

I saw him, pass, steal, shoot—and he made almost all his shots.

There were about twenty other boys and girls watching practice, and for each three-pointer that Tate, or anyone else made, they cheered. The thing was, Tate was making almost all the three-pointers.

I wanted to charge onto the court, grab him by the ear, and haul his butt out for blatantly disobeying me, but something stopped me and I hovered by the door so Tate couldn't see me.

The scrimmage continued, the kids cheered, Tate played the whole time.

At the end of practice, I saw Coach Boynton joke with the whole team, "Okay, my peeps, gather 'round. Come to me, come to me, behold your miraculous coach."

A bunch of sweating high school boys laughed and gathered 'round.

"Now we're going to play a game here with our newbie, Tate." He clapped a hand around my kid's shoulders. "Ole, Tate, here, who should have been playing basketball for years. We could have used him last season, couldn't we?"

"Oh yeah ... yeah, man ... yep," the boys said. Milt grabbed Tate and started shaking his shoulders. "Dude! Dude!"

I watched Tate beam, his smile lighting up that gym like a strobe.

"Peeps, I'm going to let Tate here take a shot," Coach Boynton said. "If he makes it, I'm takin' the whole team to pizza, my treat."

Oh, they cheered and yelled, they wrestled around, they banged Tate on the back, oh those boys, they do love to eat. My stomach twisted.

"Okay, my peep, Tate, not to put too much pressure on you, man, right?" Coach Boynton jokingly put Tate in a headlock and messed up his red curls. "No pressure, man, but ..."

Tate was laughing, the team was laughing.

"Gentlemen!" Coach Boynton yelled, arms thrown out. "I am going to ask Sir Tate to shoot from . . ." He walked toward the free throw line. "Not here." He kept walking across the court, to the three-point line. "Not here, either." He grinned at Tate as the boys made those manly groaning-man sounds.

"Here!" He pointed at a place about two feet outside the three-point line. "Tate, baby, you make this shot, and we're going to pizza."

Oh, the boys hooted, they linked their arms around Tate's back. One gangly kid, Charlie, who had braces and tight brown curls, kneeled in front of him and pleaded, "Tate, make it, buddy, I'm starving, starving! I haven't eaten in days!"

Another kid, tall and skinny Kendrick, who reminded me of a gecko, said, "Tate, please don't mess up my pizza night," then jumped on his back so Tate was forced to hold on to him piggyback.

I felt sick. All that on Tate's shoulders? That hard of a shot? I felt myself getting angry. Did Coach Boynton have to set Tate up for failure in front of all these kids on his team and also the kids up in the bleachers?

Coach Boynton tossed the basketball to Tate.

Tate kept smiling.

"Good luck, man." He clasped Tate on the shoulder, man to man. "Remember: The impossible is possible. A shot can be made on a wing and a prayer. Wish upon a star, you know . . ."

Tate bounced the ball in front of him, all nonchalant and cool. "Okay, Coach, I'll take that bet." He kept bouncing the ball, real slow, as if he was deeply pondering the bet. "You're gonna buy us all pizza if I make this shot?"

"Yep, I am, Tate. Pizza for all, even though you guys are garbage disposals with teeth."

"What about drinks?" Tate said.

"Ha. How about some beer!" Milt said.

"No beer," the coach said, pumping his chest out jokingly. "But I'll buy pop, too. Don't think I'll have to, though. Nope, nope, nope."

"Whoaaa . . . oh man," the boys groaned.

I was nervous and getting more nervous by the second.

"Hmmm . . ." Tate tossed the ball up in the air, up and down. He pondered some more. "The pizza parlor also has ice cream, too. I like chocolate."

"Yeah, Coach! Pizza, beer, and ice cream, if Tate makes it!" Charlie yelled.

"Sure. If Tate makes this shot I'll buy pizza, pop, no beer, and ice cream. Somehow, though"—Coach Boynton rocked back on his heels—"I don't think I'm going to have to buy anything. I think I'm gonna go home with a full wallet, money flowing over the top. I'll take my wife out instead. A date night."

"Hmmmm . . ." Tate tapped his temple. "I don't want to ruin your and Mrs. Boynton's date night. You need some time to have deep conversation, you know, plunge the depths of life, get all philosophical. Women want that stuff, I hear."

"Hey, ruin it," Coach Boynton said. "Ruin it. I dare ya, buddy."

"Come on, Tate!" his teammates yelled.

"You need a date night, Coach," Tate said. "It'll help you get in touch with your feminine side."

The kids howled. I had to laugh at that. I put my hand over my mouth.

"My feminine side!" Coach Boynton shouted, his Mafia face fierce. "I'm already in touch with my feminine side. Can't you tell?"

Oh, how those boys fell all over each other.

The coach pointed to his bald head. "I am a feminine thinker, Tate. I am a sensitive and loving husband!"

Too, too funny, those boys thought.

But I knew Coach Boynton. He was sensitive. He was a loving husband.

"A date with your wife would add romance to her life and to yours," Tate teased. "Champagne, caviar . . ."

"Romance? I'm a regular Renaissance man. I'm a romantic knight! A rescue-the-fair-maiden sort of knight!"

Ho ho ho.

In the stands, a bunch of kids started yelling, "Tate, Tate, Tate!"

His teammates joined them, "Tate, Tate, Tate."

Tate's smile was huge. I couldn't believe it. I would have thought he would be nervous, with his whole team hoping he would make an impossible shot for pizza. Wasn't he worried his teammates would be disappointed in him? I was. I was so nervous my knees were about knocking. Tate didn't need this, didn't need the failure.

Tate threw the ball up and down a few more *pondering* times as the kids yelled, "Tate, Tate, Tate."

"I'll make it easy on you, Tate," Coach Boynton said, expansive, funny. "If you make one out of three shots, I'll still take you all out to pizza, the whole works. You up for it? That fair?"

Tate stopped bouncing the ball and stared up at the ceiling, as if contemplating the deal. "At the risk of you missing a romantic and productive date night with Mrs. Boynton, I'll take it."

The team cheered and the kids in the stands raced down to stand on the edge of the court.

"But I'm not going to need three shots, Coach."

"Whooo!" the boys hooted.

The team cleared back as Tate took his place in Coach Boynton's designated spot. I cringed, my stomach flipped. I didn't want my son to fail in front of all these kids. I didn't want him to miss. I didn't want to see his face, to see all those kids' faces fall when he didn't make it. He'd made it before, but now they were all staring at him, depending on him for pizza.

I knew it was in fun, I knew Coach Boynton would take the team out to pizza anyhow, but my son did not need any more pain or disillusionment or embarrassment in his life. Damn. Double damn.

Tate positioned himself, bending his knees.

He didn't need to fail in front of all these kids.

I felt nauseous.

Tate stared at the hoop.

He didn't need kids to groan at him, to moan, to act as if he'd let them down.

I thought I was going to be sick. Why? Why was this happening?

Tate brought his arm back. He was going to pelt it at the hoop.

Why did Coach Boynton do this? Did he want Tate to feel stupid?

The kids kept chanting, *"Tate, Tate, Tate."*

It was an almost impossible shot.

"Remember, you get three shots, Sir Tate," Coach Boynton called out.

For a second I saw Tate close his eyes. He does this when he's lost in his thinking, whether it's about a math problem, physics, or organic chemistry. He'll close his eyes, dig down deep, and think think think.

I glanced at Coach Boynton, and I saw that underneath the humorous bravado, the showmanship, he was tense. Tense and tight. He wanted this for Tate. He wanted Tate to make it.

That's the kind of coach he is, the kind of man he is.

"Tate, Tate, Tate!"

Tate opened his eyes and I wanted to cower into a corner and cover my head. He took a few steps back to power himself forward.

I could not stand this. I could not stand the self-recriminations he'd belt himself with later, the harsh judgment.

"Tate, Tate, Tate!"

Tate drew his arm all the way back, his muscles strong and tight.

Oh dear God. I put my hands over my eyes, then slit my fingers so I could peek.

His arm lashed through the air, quick, like a wink.

I felt my throat constrict, my heart palpitate. . . .

That ball arched, arched, arched, spinning, spinning, spinning. . . .

I could not breathe.

Closer and closer and closer . . .

Oh please, oh please, oh please.

Whoosh.

A clean shot, all the way through, nothing but net.
Pandemonium.

Later that night I made a cup of lemon mango tea and puttered in my greenhouse.

I hung up another strand of white Christmas lights, threading them through the rafters, then checked my bulbs, picked off dead leaves . . . and thought about Tate.

After the ball slipped through the net, his teammates whooped into happy hysteria and tackled him to the floor, the kids on the edge of the court streaming toward him like stampeding buffalo. Coach Boynton leaped into the air, arms raised high in victory, and shouted, "I knew it! I knew he'd make it! I felt it in my bones!"

He pulled Tate out of the pile of kids and hugged him, hugged him off his feet.

Tate caught my eye, seeing me because I had thrown my hands up in the air and cheered a truly high-pitched screech of triumph.

We stared at each other, me hooting, he shocked to see me, more shocked to hear me hooting, and then a smile, this huge amazing smile spread across his handsome face, his teammates and the other kids jumping up and down and yelling.

"Tate, Tate, Tate!"

Tate, Tate, Tate.

They lifted him up on their shoulders and ran around the gym. I saw Coach Boynton discreetly wipe tears from his eyes.

Later they all went to pizza, pop, and ice cream. I was told that Mrs. Boynton joined them there, sort of a romantic date night, and they toasted Tate with root beer.

Overcome, I slipped into a wicker chair, held the cross, heart, and star charms in my hand, and cried. I cried like I hadn't cried in years.

Cried and cried.

I remembered that Grandma Violet told Brooke, Caden, and me that Faith and Grace often cried, too, although they tried to do it privately without, as she said, "Too much self-pity. Everyone has their burdens to bear, but I'm told they understood the power of a strong cup of tea with a shot of whiskey, herbs, and a pretty parasol."

Faith and Grace lived through that wretched journey across the Atlantic and when they arrived in South Carolina, filthy, bug infested, emaciated, nauseous, and exhausted to the bone, they were half-dead.

"They itched," Grandma Violet told us one summer day as she kneaded a loaf of bread. "Their hair was matted to their heads with grease, grime, and probably vomit, their own and from others on the ship they tended to. Their long dresses had swept the decks of the ship and were caked with defecation, rancid water, rat droppings, body fluids, seawater, and rotted food. There was something wrong with their stomachs. They had another petticoats-on-fire sort of problem, indeed they did.

"Anyhow, Charleston was bustling. Men in top hats and suits and women in swishing hoop dresses and flowered hats, their hair in ringlets, stood right next to sailors and merchants, laborers, con men, pompous business owners and beggars. There were carriages and dogs, slaves with their masters, horses and livestock, and a cacophony of languages from the French, Scottish, Caribbean, Jewish, Bermudan, and German people who all lived there together.

"Faith and Grace were attacked by two men that first day off the dock who ran off with their raggedy bags and the velvet satchel, which held their witchly items and all their money." Grandma Violet pounded the bread with her fist, as if even thinking about it made her mad.

"The women followed those scoundrels into an alley and fought both men with the knives their brothers had given them." She dropped the dough in a pan with a heavy thud. "They were so weak but they were desperate for that satchel. The men tried to attack their womanhood and they ripped their dresses. Faith and Grace used our family's most potent and fiery witch spells, stabbed them, twisted the knives, grabbed their tattered bags and satchel, and left them crumpled in the alley."

We gasped, as Grandma Violet swished her hands together to get rid of excess flour. "They were no longer silly girls but strong women." She locked her blue gaze onto my blue and green one, then to Brooke's and Caden's, for emphasis. "That's what you'll grow up and be, too, dears. Not women and men who fight in alleys, necessarily, but women and men who know their minds and can speak them clearly. Anyhow, Faith and Grace skittered on out of that sleazy alley, looking behind them to make sure no one saw, then found a boardinghouse to stay in and collapsed. They had survived a treacherous journey. They were ill and itchy, and they had lost everything: their families, their homes, their friends, their country. They cried, oh, how they cried."

She shook her head, her own blue eyes filling, then told us the rest of the story.

When Faith and Grace finally ventured out, they found Charleston to be hot, humid, and chaotic. The slave trade disgusted and appalled them. When they saw how slaves were treated, they cried again.

"But they decided to turn their tears into action," Grandma Violet said, her chin tipped proudly. "Those women loved fashion and they started a business called Faith and Grace's where they sold dresses, petticoats, corsets, lacy undergarments, parasols, jewelry, handkerchiefs, pretty shoes, bonnets, fabrics for clothing or curtains and pillows ... and naughty things."

"What naughty things?" I asked.

"Precious, lacy, seductive naughty things that women wore at night. They rented a tiny corner shop with large windows. They lived above it in a teeny-tiny room with a window, one bed, a washbasin, a battered dresser, and a slanted roof."

Grandma Violet put the bread under a red and white cloth, her hands gentle now. "They planted a tiny garden out back, all the flowers and herbs we have now, but they tried to hide the herbs a bit, no use getting anyone suspicious again of them being witches, the screaming mob who had wanted to flog them hadn't left their minds. The point is, dears, they took adversity, they did cry, but then they put up a fight—not only for themselves, but for the slaves. I'll tell you the story of the slaves another time. That's a scary one." She shook her finger at us. "But remember this: Tears and toughness go together."

I smiled in memory of Grandma Violet, of the stories of Faith and Grace.

I thought of all the tears I'd shed in my years as a hospice nurse, and the tears I'd shed over my grandparents, Tate, Brooke, and my father as I stared through the windows of my green-house, through the inky night, at my home, the home that Faith and Jack built. The home Faith lived in and loved in and cried in.

I figured I should turn my tears into action, too.

Just like Faith and Grace.

TATE'S AWESOME PIGSKIN BLOG

I have been given permission to try out for the basketball team.

Boss Mom said yes.

I don't know if I'll make it, but man, I'm going to try.

See, I have a shunt in my head that goes from my brain to my heart that gets rid of excess fluids called cerebrospinal fluid. This is the stuff that acts like a liquid pillow in your skull. It swishes through the four ventricles, like the rooms, of your brain. You need this liquid stuff to nourish yourself and for the ol' nervous system. It goes all over the brain and your special, slinky spinal cord, and then it heads for the hot red stuff, yes, my favorite, BLOOD! The shunt in my head, I know, I know, it's seductive to you young ladies out there to know I have a shunt, but it regulates the fluids as they flow as smooth as syrup.

If something hits my head too hard, there is a sliver of a slim and narrow chance I will need another operation or pass out or do something weird like start waltzing around a gym with an invisible partner while yodeling or taking off my clothes and then the women would faint with ecstasy, seeing my naked-ness and muscles and masculinity and all.

There's also a teeny-weeny chance I could die.

I know this.

But I could also die because a helicopter goes down and lands on my ears, Bert and Ernie.

I could also die if we're attacked by space aliens. Even my cyber-blasting, fire-shooting, alien destruc-tion gun operated by Billy and Bob can't cream all the aliens.

I could die if I swallowed an entire orange at one time and it stuck in my esophagus.

These things maybe could happen. It's the same risk as playing ball. Sort of.

But I can't say no to life because of the maybes.

I can't say yes to fear.

I have ancestors named Faith and Grace. They were part of the Underground Railroad in South Car-olina and they got caught hiding slaves under-neath their house. Now, that's scary. But they didn't say yes to fear even though they knew all along they could have been jailed, hung, or shot for hid-ing slaves.

I'm seventeen years old. Saying yes to fear is not really in my vocabulary.

People say this is the best time of your life. I hope not. I hope it isn't. Because a lot of being a teen-ager is hard. It's awkward, it's lonely, you feel alone, no one wants you around, and you're close to having all your friends reject you. You'll never have a girlfriend. You're different.

Try doing all that with a head named General Noggin.

I'll always be different.

But what I want, this one time in my life, is to be a part of a team and not so different.

I want to be part of a whole group of guys playing ball. I want to be as normal as I can be. For once.

I wanted to play basketball.

Boss Mom said no.

Then she said yes.

Now I'm in tryouts.

I hope I make the team.

Here's a photo of Faith and Grace, Underground Railroad conductors and women who said no to fear. Faith had blue eyes, Grace had green eyes, and my mom got one of each. That is so radical.

Here's the question for today: What are you afraid of? Why?

The night before, a kid sitting in the bleachers when Tate made his long shot for pizza downloaded it to YouTube. He included Tate's blog address. The video showed Tate pretending to think about the deal, asking for ice cream and pop, all the kids laughing, Tate's concentration, the ball careening up, up, up through the air and swishing through the hoop. It showed all the kids leaping up and down in excitement, and Coach Boynton grabbing Tate and hugging him off his feet.

Friends sent it to friends who sent it to friends.

"Mom, look at this." Tate pointed to the stats on his blog, awed. "Man. Unbelievable. I could almost call myself a real blogger."

5,200 hits.

And hundreds of responses from people about what they were afraid of, as Tate had asked. Their responses ran from cryptic and funny, to tragic and rawly honest, the words almost burning up the screen with their searing pain.

"I guess people are reading my blog." He was absolutely thrilled, almost giddy.

"Yes, son, I believe that you're right." I put an arm around his shoulders.

"I think I'm getting to know some people finally, without General Noggin in the way." He patted his head. "No offense, General Noggin. You're cool."

"You are definitely getting to know people, and they're being honest in what they write."

"Yep. I'm talkin', they're talkin'." He pumped his fists together. "I'm not invisible anymore or someone that others wish was invisible. Somebody's listening to me and I'm listening to them. I have something to say and people are actually reading it. We have a miracle in this old, creaky house, a miracle! Hey! Boss Mom! Can I have some cinnamon spice cookies? Please? I'm double and triple bashed hungry for them."

10

From then on out, when I picked up Tate from basketball practice at night, he came out of the gym grinning, spinning a basketball on his finger, other players jostling around him.

"How did it go?"

"Good. I think. I let a guy go past me today and I should have been a better defender, but he wasn't looking fast out there and I was afraid he was going to get cut if he didn't get one drive in, at least."

"You let him go by you?"

He squirmed. "Yeah. It's Zeke. I don't think he's going to make it but at least he had a try."

"Did he make a basket?"

"No, he air-balled it."

The next day: "How did practice go?"

"Okay. I moved out of the way to let Ronnie shoot, and the coach yelled at me to 'Defend, Tate, defend, you know what that is, do it.' "

Oh boy.

"Did you make your shots?"

"Yeah, I did. Road Runner was on fire." He wriggled his eyebrows at me. "Mickey Mouse helped, too. Except for one shot. Patel was guarding me, and I shot but I missed so the coaches would think he was a fast defender. I don't think Patel has a grip on his feet yet, Mom. I mean, in school he'll trip when he's walking down the hallway."

The next night: "Maybe tomorrow you should play as best you can and let the other kids play the best they can. . . . The try-outs are coming up soon, as you know."

"Yeah. I should." His face brightened. "Man, Mom, it's much funner to play basketball when there's other guys on the court and not me all by myself imagining that I'm playing against a full team."

"I'm sure."

"I mean, when I'm out on our sport court I've got both teams all around me in my head doing different stuff, but now I know where all the other real life nine dudes are and what they're doing. This is cool, Mom, it's radical!"

I listened to him, excited, but my worry knocked up another hundred notches. I hadn't wanted him to make the team, I didn't want him hurt, but he wanted it, he wanted to make the team more than anything, he was off-the-charts hopeful, so I started to crack and I wanted him to make it, too.

It would devastate him not to make it, and yet, even though I had seen him shoot, though I thought he had a solid chance, I had no idea how he was doing compared to all the other kids, many of whom had been playing since kindergarten, and how he was doing with the other skills he needed to play basketball.

"I love you, Boss Mom, thanks again." He sighed, grateful, relieved.

"I love you, too, Tate. And you're welcome."

"I called Dirk Hassells a couple of days ago to reconfirm our meeting, ostensibly, but basically to see if he had changed his mind or if I could change it for him."

"And?" I asked.

Sydney Grants leaned back in her chair in her office, then flicked her black braids back and sighed. She was wearing an African-styled silk blouse in browns, beiges, and greens and a matching headband. "The conversation went poorly."

I was in jeans, leather boots to my knees, a white T-shirt, and a skinny leather jacket. I tapped my fingertips together. I could strangle Dirk. How's that for a hospice nurse?

"Dirk is still proclaiming that the care you provided his father caused his father to die much earlier than he would have, including all that morphine, and I quote, that you 'poured down his throat.' He was mad that you wouldn't return his e-mails, calls, and texts. Mad that you were avoiding him when you were caring for his father. He even said you didn't want to go out to lunch with him, refused to have conversations with him that weren't directly about his father, and did not seem interested in who he was, and I quote again, 'as a man. Jaden Bruxelle blew me off.' "

I laughed, but it was a bitter laugh. The whole thing was a mess and causing more stress in my life. This incident didn't make me appear poorly to the other hospice nurses and doctors, I knew that. I had worked with them for years. Hospice nurses, because of the terminal nature of our business, will, like any other medical profession, sometimes get caught up in something that is not our fault at all. You are dealing with dying people. Family members are emotional, they want to blame someone. This kind of thing happens.

But it was hard all the same and contributed to the exhaustion I felt with my profession.

"He said you denied him personal time and physical comfort, hugs and such, even though you talked to his sister, Beatrice, all the time and her kids and hugged all of them. He said he was excluded from hugs. He said that twice."

"He is disgusting."

"He is. He says he's going to bring in lawyers, blah blah blah. He insists on seeing you at the table. Another quote, 'Make sure Jaden has her butt at the meeting, I want to talk to her, she's avoiding me, she's going to talk to me or else. Does she understand who I am? Does she know I'm rich, that I own a business?' "

"He is a scary, odd, controlling duck." My heart sped up again and I wanted to eat the smile off a cinnamon Gummi Bear. Stress!

"Definitely creepy. I'm sorry that you have to be there at the meeting, hospital regulations. We should go to trial. I think the jury would be entertained."

"I would prefer it if he choked on his tongue."

Sydney nodded. "That's a special image I think I'll hold on to."

"I've paid Ernest Rodriquez to search for Brooke," my mother said that night over the phone. She'd had a busy day on *Foster's Village*. She had arranged for evidence to be planted so it would appear that her younger stepsister had stolen millions of dollars and would go to jail for years.

"I still don't know if I'm doing the right thing, Mom." I rocked back and forth on our old rocking chair, a rainbow arching over our fields through a light rain. "Tate wants to meet her, but I don't think I want him to meet her. It'll be upsetting, at the very least, and I can't let him meet her if she's all drugged up, which she probably is."

"I know. Let's see what Ernest finds out about her, then we can wrestle this lion to the ground and declaw it." She paused and sniffled. "I must show you the new dress that Cooley designed for me...."

My mother is not as into designer clothes as she appears. She clings to that type of thing for distraction because the pain of losing Brooke to drugs threatened to kill her for years.

When Brooke was out from one of her rehab jaunts, my dad, Caden, Brooke, and I moved up here to London Gardens so we could all be in a different environment, different school. My mother flew up every weekend.

My father stayed home and wrote his scripts. "I had no idea a man could feel this much pain and still breathe," I'd heard him say to my mother about Brooke. "I had no idea a man could feel this much fear and not scream. I had no idea this level of desperation existed."

I loved living full-time in Tillamina. I loved my new friends who wanted to run around outside and ride horses more than go shopping. I loved that people wore jeans and sweatshirts to school instead of the latest couture fashions, and no makeup.

I loved that everyone went to the football and basketball games at the high school and how downtown was a fifteen-minute walk and my dad let me go by myself. Though my grandparents were no longer alive, I loved their house with all the history, the stories, the antiques, ancient books and quilts, and the maple trees that lined the driveway that Faith and Jack had planted. I wondered if Faith loved watching the leaves change color as much as I did, if she watched the hawks, blue jays, and robins, too.

I loved Grandma Violet's garden, the herbs and flowers our family had planted and tended for generations, in honor of the "witches in our family line."

We thought London Gardens would be a new start for Brooke.

It wasn't. It was simply a new place.

Anyone can find drugs at any time, in any town, in this country, and she found them.

She found a kid named Corey who had dropped out of high school. His parents were addicts. They lived in a trailer park. They did coke together. One night Corey almost died. He later told us he saw Jesus in his dream and that's what got him off coke.

Corey eventually became the senior pastor of a megachurch. He personally apologized to my mother several years later, the tears unending.

Brooke kept using. She had not seen Jesus in her dreams.

We all loved Brooke dearly. Even when she was on drugs, she was kind to me. Brushing my hair, styling it, making me special gifts with whatever was in our art box—sequins, shells, beads, flowers from outside, shiny rocks. Her hands would shake, her eyes would be funny, she would giggle inappropriately, and make odd comments about seeing stars, snakes, and sugar, but she'd always hug me.

She made things for my parents, too, and Caden, and wrote, "I love you," on the gifts.

I mourn for my sister and that "I love you," to this day. I

have never stopped missing her, though her drug addiction caused ceaseless pain in our family and devastated all of us.

I rocked harder in our old rocking chair, my mother and I talked a few more minutes, then hung up.

The rain was now a deluge, as if the clouds had been poked, the water streaming out, the rainbow gone.

"How are you doing, Tate?"

"Atom based radically. How are you, Dr. Robbins?"

Ethan smiled at me. "Fine, more than fine."

While they chatted I took the time to surreptitiously, without drooling, stare at Ethan with barely concealed lust. He drums up my engines, I will not deny that.

I wanted to take off his glasses, his white doctor's coat, and the blue shirt he wore beneath it. I wanted to rip off that belt, yank down his underwear, and I wanted to—

"Mom!"

I startled, pulling my eyes from Ethan to Tate. Tate opened his eyes super-wide at me as in, *Mom! Hello? Quit staring!* "Did you hear what I said?"

"Uh . . . oh . . . uh . . ." I could feel a steamin' red flush flying up my cheeks.

"What I said was I wanted to go with Dr. Robbins to the research lab again at the hospital this Saturday, and can you drive me up there?"

"Yes, yes, of course." I tried to stamp out my graphic sexual thoughts. "Thank you."

"It's my pleasure," Ethan said.

I swallowed what felt like a giant boulder in my throat. Can your throat create boulders that you choke on when utterly transfixed by the sexiness of a doctor not three feet away?

"Good," I said. I closed my mouth, embarrassed. Why had "good" flown out of my mouth?

"Good." Ethan smiled at me, then he dropped his head to study his chart and coughed.

"Good," I said.

"Good," he said.

"And a goody-goody-two-shoes to both of you," Tate sang out. "I'm gonna go say hi to Dr. Sheila and Dr. Craig, and my favorite, Nurse Leena, the object of my rampant desires." Tate wriggled his eyebrows at us, then ambled out. "Hey, Nurse Leena! Watch out, seductress, I am coming to prove to you that my love is enduring, passionate, bold, and . . . *peppery.*"

I heard people in the office laugh before the door shut. Someone called out, "And there he is, Tate Bruxelle, resident Romeo."

"Peppery love?" Leena laughed. She has a booming laugh. "I love it. Add some salt and we have salt and pepper. . . ."

I stood up. "I should go, too, I know you're busy."

Ethan stood up. We were then about two feet away from each other. Two feet. I could take two steps and be eye to nipple with him. His nipple. That's about where my eyes come to. If I touched those nipples, what would happen?

"Oh no, not busy, Jaden. Please sit down. Thank you. How's your greenhouse?"

Ha. One of my favorite topics. We talked on that.

Then I said, "Tell me about your last kayak ride."

And boom. Off and sailing.

He said, "How's your work going?"

As usual. I was helping people die peacefully. Some cases harder than others.

I promised to bring him some herbs.

He brightened up and said, "I'd appreciate that."

And all the while I wanted to kiss him. I fought an overwhelming impulse to leap up and hug him around the waist with my legs.

I finally stood up to leave, not wanting to overstay a welcome. I turned to open the door, he moved to open it for me, and he ran into me. We both paused.

My back was to his front, not touching, but so close I could feel the heat between us as if my body embers were on fire. I heard him take a deep inhale of breath. I exhaled and closed my eyes.

"Jaden . . ."

"Ethan . . ."

"I . . ."

"I . . ."

And another pause.

"Yes?" I said, nervous and pained.

"You're the mother of my patient. And I could not be his doctor if you and I were . . . together." I felt him take a deep breath. "It's unethical. . . ."

"I know." My voice cracked. It went along with my heart. "I would never want to lose you as Tate's doctor. I can't. We can't."

Silence. And there it was. Out in the open.

"But, Jaden . . ."

There were no "buts." "I have to do what's best for Tate."

"There are other highly skilled doctors."

I understood what he was saying. My whole body became stiff, and I clenched my teeth. I envisioned what could be. What could be between Ethan and me realistically, not just in my rambling imagination. I could be with him. Date. Sleep with him. Jump that tall and lanky body. Talk honestly way into the night as we ate popcorn. We could grow herbs in my greenhouse, fish in my drift boat, and play cards when we were old together. We could hobble around on canes, grandchildren frolicking around and about, a hundred of them.

"I could call one of those highly skilled doctors," Ethan said.

"No." My voice sharpened up, mother bear beginning to growl. "It has to be you." It had to be. Ethan was the best pediatric neurosurgeon on the West Coast. He had even been written up in the paper and it was noted how other hospitals, larger and more prestigious hospitals, constantly tried to lure him away from Oregon.

"I want you to be his doctor, Ethan." I put my hands to my face to still the tears. Maybe to keep the sheer loneliness that had stalked me for so many years from spilling out, too. "At any time Tate could have an emergency, a problem, and I can't give you up. You're the best doctor."

"I could introduce you to a talented, reputable doctor. You could grow to trust someone else—"

"No. I couldn't. I'm sorry."

Heavy, sad, breaking silence. I felt my eyes flood with tears as I stood there. I leaned back, or he leaned forward, I don't know which. His arms went around my waist, and I dropped my hands around his arms and tilted my head back, my temple to his cheek. The heat had been growing and growing, but now it broke apart, to be replaced by iron-heavy hopelessness and sheer longing. Our tears mixed together. I felt his chest heave, my red hair a curtain.

I wanted to be with Ethan. I daydreamed of him constantly, the daydreams bringing me both peace and anguish. I had done it for years. It wasn't healthy, don't daydream for what you can never have, but I hadn't been able to help myself.

"I'll look forward to you bringing me some of your herbs again, Jaden." His voice was tight, cracked, and he pulled me closer.

I answered, my voice strangled. "I'll bring them straight from my herb garden."

I turned and hugged him and he pulled me in, tight and warm, and I heard him sniffle and I knew he was dragging a hand over his eyes. I shuddered and I used my sleeve to wipe my eyes. I heard him sigh and I sighed, too. We held each other close, knowing that more closeness was not coming, then I pulled away and yanked myself together. I made sure the tears were gone, I put my shoulders back, my chin up, and a false smile on my face, as so many of us do.

He held the door open.

I walked through it.

I did not look back.

I lost a patient later that day after I dropped Tate off at school. I cried with the family. They ended up comforting me.

That was unprofessional, but when I left, they hugged me again, thanking me profusely. I heard one of the aunts say, "Jaden Bruxelle is an angel." And the other aunt said, "She cared about Tish. I could see that so clearly."

I did care about Tish. She was a great woman with a naughty sense of humor.

But I was crying for Ethan, too.

Would the loneliness of him not being in my life ever, ever go away? Would I always feel hollow? Would I always feel alone? What if he married someone else?

I shut down on those thoughts as I had a hundred times. It didn't do to think about them. What was the point?

Tate needed him, that was all I needed to know.

And I love Tate.

He's my son.

My beautiful, funny, perfect son.

TATE'S AWESOME PIGSKIN BLOG

Here's a photo of Milt. Nice Mohawk, Milt!

Milt hates snakes.

Here's a photo of a copperhead and an Indian king cobra. As you can see, I Photoshopped the photo and added a pink bow and bra to the copperhead and a baseball hat and cigarette to the king cobra.

Anyhow, I went to about five stores and bought a whole bunch of different-colored plastic snakes, different sizes, too, and then Anthony, his twin brother, and I stuffed them in Milt's locker at school.

We tell everybody what we've done so they're all waiting and Milt opens up his locker and all these snakes fall out and he screamed!!! He sounded like a car when the fan belt's all dried up. Anyhow, he jumps back, drops his books, turns, screams this creepy scream again, and runs and actually bashes himself face-first into a door.

He gets all twisted up, falls on the ground, and yells, "Shit! What the hell?!" and scrambles away again.

It was freaking funny. I thought we were all gonna die laughing.

When he knows I'm the snake worshipper Milt starts running after me around the school, but he can't catch up.

We gave all the snakes away and all day long dudes and dudettes were wearing snakes. Patty put one through her ponytail and Devon attached his snake to his baseball hat, and another girl, Marnie, put the snake in her cleavage. She said that now she had "snakey boobs." Even the teachers wore their snakes.

Here are some photos.

Here's a photo of Milt and Anthony after the snake attack at the locker. Milt won't wear a snake. That's Anthony next to him with a whole bunch of snakes all over his body. Duh. They're twins.

Here's a question: What's the funniest thing that ever happened to you?

One more note: Don't ever try to mess with nitro-glycerin. It is way unstable and it can cause an explosion. It's melting point is 13.5 degrees Celsius and it decomposes at 50 to 60 degrees Celsius. This is the formula $C_3H_5N_3O_9$ and its explosive velocity is 7700 m/s. That's bad and I learned it the hard way.

That evening Tate and I made toasted cheese, basil, honey, and tomato sandwiches and watched my mother's soap opera, *Foster's Village,* off the DVR. We watched her nightly, together. If we missed a couple, we waited until the weekend and watched it with her.

This last show was absolutely gripping. She'd told us about it weeks ago. "It's goose bump scary. This actor who's playing the psychopath lights my fear on fire. I told him, 'Joshi, you frighten my soul to pieces!' and he grabbed me and threw me over his shoulder and I thought I was going to have a heart attack! It was sensual!"

The show was actually a white-knuckler, though I know that may be hard to believe about a soap opera. I kept fiddling with my cross, heart, and star charms. My mother had been kidnapped out of her home, in the middle of the night, and was locked in a windowless room, a bunker underground, the walls dripping with leaking water, held there by Joshi, the psychopath.

She was right about Joshi, too. Tall, blond, light eyes. Controlling. Freaky. The man radiated danger. I found myself clutching Tate's hand.

Honestly, she gave the performance of her life, as did Joshi.

On the show, she woke up, dazed, and for once she was not made up much. She tried to find a door, and couldn't because there wasn't one. No windows, either. There was a dirt floor, it was pitch-black, and she started panting, sweating, hysterically trying to scrape her way through with her nails. She whimpered in fear when she hit the walls and could find no opening. In the end she collapsed in a corner, huddled up, destroyed.

I actually found myself forgetting to breathe and feeling teary-eyed for my mother's calamitous state. Tate watched it and burst into tears.

"It's okay, it's okay, Tate," I said, hugging him. "We know it's not real life. . . ."

"I know, I know, I can't help it! That's Nana Bird!"

Even the critics were impressed with her performance.

I called her at her home in the Hollywood Hills after the show and put Tate and myself on speaker.

"Mom, I'm still trembling! You scared me to death!"

"Nana Bird," Tate said. "I can't watch it again until this part is over. It's gonna give me freakin' nightmares. I'm not gonna be able to sleep. I might even have to drag out Pansy." Pansy was a huge purple rhino that my mom had given him when he was three. He used to sleep on top of it.

"I wasn't completely acting. Joshi has a criminal record from years past, but his sexual energy was overpowering. Overpowering! He was mouthwatering."

Because of that overpowering sexual energy my mother probably flirted with him, but it meant nothing. Her flirting always means nothing. I don't believe there has been a man in her life since my father died. I am not sure there ever will be again.

As usual, she slides over her own tragedies with wry humor, ribald jokes, and brassy confidence.

She will never get over losing my dad. It isn't going to happen.

I don't think I'll ever get over not having Ethan. It isn't going to happen. He was it for me. I know it and we will not be together. I am not being melodramatic, I am being honest. He was the one. It's not like I'm going to whine or give in to depression or curl up in a ball or not move forward in my life, but it will be without him.

I try not to let that breath-sucking truth overtake me until late at night, when I can jam my head into a pillow and muffle my sad sounds.

"Boss Mom. This week is my Olympic week. Four nights of tryouts," Tate told me early the next morning. I handed him his two lunch sacks. He eats an enormous amount of food because, he says, he has to feed "my second set of brains." He peered in to make sure I'd included La La Lemon Meringue Cookies with vanilla frosting that he inhales by the dozen.

"I know, buddy. Strip that basketball away from your oppo-

nent, play defense so hard the other players know they're coming up against a steel robot, and shoot the heck out of the ball."
I smiled tightly, my nerves clanging, and pushed my hair out of
my eyes. My fingers brushed the crystals he'd given me. "There.
Do I sound like a supportive mother now? I'm doing my best."

"Yeah, you do." He tossed a handful of Cheerios up and caught
three of them, then picked the ones off the floor he missed and
ate them. "I really want to make it. I don't want to spend the rest
of the year by myself imagining another nine basketball players
out on our sport coat."

"I think it's hopeful, Tate." More than hopeful. He was making three-pointers all the time. Surely he would make it?

"I dunno. Lots of kids are trying out. I don't have the defense
thing down because I've only been playing with invisible people
in my head and they mostly get out of my way. I have to work
on my passing, too, and sometimes the other players steal the
ball from me."

"But you can shoot, Tate, you can shoot."

"Yeah, yeah. I can shoot." He nodded. He again threw a
handful of Cheerios back up and caught a couple. The rest fell
to the floor and he picked them up and ate them, too. "I might
not make it. I might not be good enough."

"And I might decide to turn myself into an elephant."

He grinned. "And I might decide to turn myself into com-
bustible chemicals, a super computer, or nuclear fusion."

"And I might decide to leave for Tanzania."

"And I might turn into an invisible wisp of gas, capable of
slinking inside people's brains and making a quick research
study around the corpus collosum, cingulate sulcus, and temporal lobe."

"Out you and your brain go, Tate."

"Yep." He put his dishes in the dishwasher, threw two more
Cheerios up in the air, caught them, and turned to lope on out
with his lunch sacks in his back pack. Whenever Tate left the
house I felt a pang because I didn't know how bad things might
get for him out there. I could not predict what hurts people
would fling at him, nor could I lock him in my home.

"Tate."

He turned.

"Good luck."

He loped back to me. "Yeah. Okay, Boss Mom. Thanks." He gave me a hug, then flicked the crystals in my hair.

I loved that kid.

I was so scared he'd make the team.

Arty Mossovsky is ninety-three years old.

He has a giant-sized Saint Bernard named Boat. The Saint Bernard is ten years old, creaky and limping, and is always in Arty's bedroom with him and his wife, Margaret, usually on the king-sized bed with them.

Boat believes he is a human. He wears a pink collar and a tiny gold bell even though Boat is a boy dog.

"I brought home a red collar and he refused to put it on. Bah!" Arty told me one day as he lay in bed, heart failure chasing him down. "I go back out and get him a green collar. Wouldn't wear it, dumb dog. Bah."

"Stubborn dog," Mrs. Mossovsky said. She was knitting a pink sweater for a three-year-old great-great-granddaughter named Margaret. Her fingers didn't move nimbly anymore but the love was there.

"That bad dog gives the word *stubborn* a new definition. What is he, a fashion model dog?" Mr. Mossovsky rasped out, struggling a bit for breath. "I go back out to the pet store again and I get him a pink collar with the jangly bell, that's all they have left in his size. His neck is the size of a tree trunk. Tree trunk dog. I should have named him Tree Trunk!" He slapped a hand on the sheet.

"Why did you name him Boat?" I asked.

"Because his feet are so floppy they remind me of boats! Boating! And I got a hankering for boats. Had to go boating on Saturdays to get a break from the Mrs." He pointed to his wife, next to him in bed, whom he adored.

Mrs. Mossovsky leaned over slowly, her bones not working so quick anymore, and kissed Mr. Mossovsky on the cheek, her white curls soft. She is also on hospice care because she is also suffering from heart failure. No, it is not odd that they have the same thing. They are ninety-three. Hearts go.

"The Mrs. has lush lips," Arty told me. "See them? Always has. That's why I married her when we were eighteen. I saw those lips and I said, 'Margaret, I can't live without those lush lips. Will you marry me?'"

Mrs. Mossovsky chuckled. She'd heard the joke thousands of times, but they still found it funny together. She poked a knitting needle at him. "Stop that, Arty. Don't get fresh."

"Fresh?" he wheezed. "Fresh? Don't let me get started on your Tillie and Tabby."

Tillie and Tabby are Mrs. Mossovsky's *breasts,* yes, they are. Tillie and Tabby reminded me of Tate's General Noggin, Bert and Ernie, Billy and Bob. . . .

"Arty!" she admonished, a tiny voice from a tiny woman whose tiny heart was slowing. "Now, stop! Stop!"

But it was routine, she knew it, I knew it.

Arty winked at me. "Best breasts in the nation, right there." He pointed at his wife's breasts as if I would not be able to locate them on my own. "Always thought that, too. She nursed all seven of our kids and she still has a rack that gets me going, can't help myself. I love the Mrs."

"That's wonderful news, Arty," I said. "Precious."

"Yeah. That woman has made me a lucky man. Lucky almost every night, that right, Margaret?"

"Arty! That's enough! Stop!" Mrs. Mossovsky continued to knit. I saw the smile. She wasn't embarrassed. She was ninety-three years old and there was no such time for that foolishness anymore.

"And Boat?" I prodded Arty.

"The bad dog, Boat. What a bizarre, frisky dog. I think he's gay. Gay as gay can be! Gay! One of our sons is gay. The nicest one, I will say. I like his husband, too. Brian. Nice guy. Right, Margaret?"

"Right," she answered. "We love Brian. Carpenter. He made us a dining room table. Sits the whole family!"

"Sits the whole family, that's right! It's a finely crafted table! He's a wood artist! So the gay dog, that—Boat." He pointed at the dog lying on his king-sized bed at their feet as if I couldn't locate the dog, either. "He doesn't like the red collar, doesn't like the green collar, and I come home and I show him the pink collar with that clingy-clangy bell on it. As soon as Boat sees it, he starts barking, jumpin' around like he's a kangaroo or something, twirling around, and I put it on his neck and he loves it! Loves it! Don't you?" He raised a weakened hand to Boat's head and petted it. "You gay dog, you. Bah!"

"How old is Boat?"

"Old! He's damn old. We spend hundreds every month on his medical care, don't we, Margaret?"

"Hundreds!" she agreed.

"He has special food. Special vitamins. He has bad hips, a bad heart, can't see so good, partly deaf, or maybe he's faking that part, I don't know. He's old and sick. Same as me and Margaret here. Poor Margaret," he whispered, but he wasn't skilled at whispering. "She's got a bad heart, too. I'm not going until after Margaret. I gotta be around to fight off all the men, you know."

"That's a fine idea, Arty. I'd stick around, too."

"The Mrs. is sexy as hell."

"Sexy!" Margaret mocked. She was still stunning. Perfect bone structure doesn't quit. Neither does peace. Peace makes a face lovely.

"The gay dog, Boat, likes a pink collar. What does he expect me to do? Paint his fingernails pink? Give him a pink bow? You'd want all that, wouldn't you?" He petted the Saint Bernard. "Pink all over. I'm a man. I don't wear pink. Blue. Gray. Brown. Those are my colors. Margaret wears pink. She's got three pink negligees. I know, 'cause I bought them for her. She wears them to bed all the time, isn't that right, boobs?"

"Arty, please! Stop! Jaden is here."

"I don't care, sweets. I like to see you naked. I want to see you naked now."

"I will be soon, Arty. Take a nap first."

"Nap schnapps. Naps are boring. When I'm dead I'll be able to take all the naps I want."

Whenever Arty or Margaret left the bed, Boat the Saint Bernard would get gingerly off, so carefully, and wobble around to keep an eye on them. He was old. He didn't have long.

The night that Arty started to die, Margaret called me over to their house.

"Dear, I can't do this alone. All the kids are coming, but I want you here in case. Please, Jaden?"

The large bedroom held the whole family that night. I knew all of them because they were constantly visiting, helping around the house, mowing the lawn. They were an emotionally healthy family, cheerful, polite, and grieving, but accepting of their father's illness, and their mother's illness, and what that meant. Their oldest son was seventy-one. The youngest member of the family was a one-year-old.

Arty left this world peacefully, with some medication from me to keep him comfortable, Margaret in bed with him, with her knitting, Boat in there, too, the kids and grandkids all around.

Right before he died, though, his eyes opened and he found Margaret.

"Hello, Margaret, my Margaret," he rasped out. "I love you. I have always loved you."

"Oh, Arty, I love you, too." Margaret's tears dropped on Arty's face.

"I'm sorry, my love. I wanted to see you out first, but it doesn't seem it will work out that way. I will wait for you, Margaret. We'll go into heaven together."

He took in his loving, crying family and smiled; then Boat wobbled up the bed and licked Arty's face and he petted his bad dog. Boat put his head on Arty's chest.

With his eyes on Margaret, Arty's lids slowly closed. Within two hours he was dead.

When his heart stopped, Boat lifted that huge head off Arty's chest and licked his face. He licked Margaret's face, then gingerly left the bed with the help of two great-granddaughters and creaked over to a corner and stood staring up at it, the bell on his pink collar ringing. He didn't move for thirty minutes; he stood and stared at that corner. He barked a few times.

I knew what he was doing. I'd seen it before with animals and their owners.

Arty was up in the corner. He was waiting. He was watching. He was saying his good-byes to the sobbing family members in his bedroom.

Within one week Margaret was dead, too, Boat beside her, his head on her chest. I was there, as were the kids and generations of grandkids. Boat licked Margaret's face, then gingerly left the bed again, so painfully, the bell on his pink collar ringing. He stared at the same corner and barked a few times.

The next morning Boat died.

Now this could be seen as a tragic story, but it's not. Margaret and Arty were in their nineties. Their lives had been long and blessed, with both fortune and trouble, but they had each other through it all and they had their children and grandchildren. Boat was ten years old. He was an adored dog.

They had had it all.

I want to have an Arty and Margaret kind of love.

I want to have a Grace and Russ and a Faith and Jack kind of love. Grandma Violet told me both couples were "mad for each other." I think we all want that love madness. We all want someone we will be *in love* with forever. Not a rather vague love, the kind you have for a spouse who's been pretty good over the years, and you're used to each other, and you're friends, and you have kids together and you've built a life. That's a valuable love, too. It's a gift. To have someone you love walk through life with you, that you really like, is a blessing.

But what we all crave, I think, is the *in love* relationship.

Where the passion for each other is still burning when you are old and dying, your hands wrinkled, your face showing decades well lived, in bed together, holding hands, a bad dog like Boat at your feet.

I wanted to have a Boat at my feet with Ethan.

I smashed down the utter loss I felt and buried it in my loneliness.

On the last night of tryouts I picked up Tate at the gym.

I waited and waited, outside in my car, in the dark, the cold
rain streaming down.

They were five minutes late, ten minutes, fifteen. I saw one
kid after another come out of the gym and climb into cars.

Charlie with the braces came ambling out. Milt and Anthony
climbed into their mom's car. Kendrick who resembled a gecko
came out.

No Tate.

I envisioned him in the locker room, hiding, head down.

I envisioned him up on the bleachers. Maybe he'd run there
to cry?

I envisioned him walking home through the rain, too dis-
traught to face me.

I closed my eyes and tried to get a hold of my quaking emotions. All these years he hadn't played basketball on a team. If I
had let him play, he'd have done better in tryouts. I slapped a
hand to my forehead. Had I been too paranoid about his safety?
Was I making the right decision even now? What if he made it?
What if he didn't? How would he feel? What were the repercus-
sions either way?

I heard a pounding on my window and sat straight up.

It was Tate.

He wasn't smiling.

I climbed out of the car and stood in the drenching rain, facing him. "Tate?"

He didn't move for long seconds, then slowly, dramatically
slowly, a grin spread across his face.

"Oh my gosh," I breathed. "Oh my gosh! Did you make it?"

His arms flew up into the air. "I made it, Boss Mom, I made it!"

He picked me up, swung me around, then stood back and did
a jig in the rain.

A jig. Exactly like the jig my mother had taught him to do when singing a song from *The Best Little Whorehouse in Texas*.

I did the jig with him, then he hugged me again, lifting me off my feet.

"Thanks Mom thanks Mom thanks Mom!"

I had never, truly, seen that kid so happy.

He had made the basketball team.

It was miraculous. It was exciting.

I was thrilled for him.

I was scared to death.

I called Coach Boynton that night.

There was nothing he could do about my medical concerns and I knew that. So I went to concern number two.

"I am concerned that Tate will be made fun of by the other teams."

"I know all the coaches. I'll tell them about Tate, and they'll talk to their teams. Hopefully the message will get out that they are to be respectful toward Tate as are the students at their school. I can't guarantee you anything in that area, and they can't either, Jaden, but we'll try our best." He sniffled. He's sensitive. "I worry about that with Tate, too."

"I've worried for seventeen years."

"I know."

"I didn't want him to play."

"I know that, too, but, Jaden, how do you stop this?"

"What do you mean?"

"The kid has a dream and you know teenagers. When they dream, they dream wide and far, whether it's realistic or not, and anyone who stands in their way becomes the enemy."

"I have been that enemy."

"I'm sorry, I am."

"Okay, Robert. He can play."

He whooped. "This is gonna be a hell of a year, Jaden, hell of a year."

"Keep him safe or you'll lose the family jewels."

"Letty would come after you for that. The family jewels belong to her, after all."

"Then watch out for my kid or I'm comin' after you."

He laughed, then hollered, "Whooeee! Tate Bruxelle, you are gonna bring a championship into my life! Yes sirree! We're goin' to state, I can feel it *in my bones.*"

11

"Ifound her." I heard the catch in my mother's voice over the phone. "I found Brooke."

I slammed the lid on my Crock-Pot. I was making cowboy soup with garlic, marjoram, oregano, beef, and several different types of beans and onions. I had only shed two tears into the pot for Ethan, then bucked up and moved on with the recipe.

"Where is she?"

"She says she's at a women's shelter in Los Angeles. I'm going to pick her up."

"She's letting you come get her?" Brooke often refused to see us. My mother would hire a detective, as she had this time, to make sure her daughter wasn't dead, in a hospital, or in jail. He'd find her, my mother would contact her, and Brooke would say, "No, I can't see you. I'm sorry. I'm a mess. I don't want you to see me right now. Mom, you'll cry. When I'm better, when I'm better."

Her refusal would break my mother down. She'd have to go to bed for two days and pull the covers over her head, then she'd get back up and go to work.

"At least she's alive, Jaden, we know she's alive, there's still hope. Damn that girl. It would have been easier to raise a loose python."

"How does she sound?" I instinctively braced myself. That's how it is dealing with people on drugs. You are always bracing yourself. Always in some state of grief, unresolved anger, absolute emotional chaos, or determined detachment.

"She says"—my mother paused, and I knew she was yanking herself together—"that her ex-boyfriend beat her up recently, but that she's been sober."

"Heard that before."

"I know, sugar, I know."

My mother sounded exhausted, but utterly relieved. It is obliterating and wrenching and a slip of hell dealing with addicts.

"I have never given up hope on Brooke," my mother said. "She's made me down whiskey by the gallon, and now and then I've snuck a cigarette, and I have cried so much there should be no drought here in California, but I have always hoped."

I hoped there was hope.

A couple of days later I told Tate I was going to fly down and spent the night with my mom. Tate was spending the night at Anthony and Milt's with the basketball team so I didn't have to worry about him. He was so excited to go. Being part of the team had meant a lot more social activities for Tate, which I tried not to feel guilty about, but did anyhow.

"Tell Nana Bird that I saw her in that love scene in the hotel. She needs to know that I know what she's doing when my back is turned." He shook his finger. "Tell her I'm watching her cheat with Alistair, that it will bring her nothing but pain, mark my words!"

He loves to say "mark my words," because my mother says it. "I'll tell her."

"Tell her, too, that protection is important." Both pointer fingers were now pointing up while he intoned, his voice deep, "Condoms should always be used. No one is safe anymore. There's nothing to be embarrassed about."

I groaned. "Your Nana Bird does not need a condom. She's acting, Tate, there are cameramen, directors, other actors, all on set watching and eating doughnuts."

He opened his eyes wide, mocking innocence. "I know about these private things because of the piles of women pounding at the door at night seeking my purity, Mom, wanting to take that special part of Tate Bruxelle! They can't get a lid on their passion, I'm just sayin'."

I shook my head. "It's been hard to keep the women from your body, Tate."

"No kidding! I'm a chick magnet. Also, tell her that she needs to cover up. It's weird for me to see my Nana Bird in black lingerie." He shuddered. "Yeah. Tell her to put a robe on or, better yet, a parka. Yeah. A parka."

With dawn breaking over the horizon, I drove to the airport through the column of our bare maple trees, their branches a stick maze in the sky, waiting for winter to be over.

My mother lives in a hacienda-style house that sprawls on top of a hill in the Hollywood Hills.

There's the expected high wall, a gate, security, etc. But once past that, her property is filled with palm trees, jacarandas, magnolias, lemon and orange trees, and a swath of manicured lawn. It's a slice of hacienda tranquility.

Her home has a breezeway that guides visitors to the front door, past a huge fountain in the shape of Aphrodite, goddess of love, in the center of a circular patio. The house has white stucco walls, and the air flows through it as if there are no walls at all. Wood shutters close things up, a red tile roof keeps things cool, and my mother's Mexican pottery, ceramics, colorful art, embroidered pillows, and plush, red, blue, and yellow furniture set the whole place off. She also has a few voodoo dolls, which she says honor our "witchly past, the witches in our line were related to royalty, you know."

There are three bedrooms upstairs. Brooke and I had always shared a corner room with doors that opened to an upstairs porch. We all had views of the patio, pool, and the city beyond that.

The family room opens to a kitchen filled with bright, hand-painted colored tiles bought from Mexico on the counters, island, and backsplash. Off to the side is my father's den, where he used to write his scripts. It hasn't changed a bit since he died. My mother simply shut the door on that room, and that was that. She couldn't bear to do anything else. She goes in there now and then to talk to him.

"I give your father an update on our lives in there. I open the doors and watch the butterflies, like we used to do. I eat oranges; we used to eat oranges together. I watch the sunset, we loved sunsets, and I have strawberry daiquiris while I watch it, because that's what we used to do together. I feel closer to him there. When I leave, I feel the loss, but it's dimmed somewhat over the years and I know he loves to hear how things are going. He always wanted to know everything about you kids. He loved you crazy-mazie."

I think of her sitting in that den, alone, talking to my dad, and it hurts. The whole thing still hurts.

Anyhow, out back, a pool with a cascading waterfall and a hot tub with its own waterfall shine in the sun. She has her own vegetable and herb gardens that she lovingly tends and has also planted her "hereditary witch flowers," as she calls them, Canterbury bells, hollyhocks, lilies, irises, sweet peas, cosmos, red poppies, peonies, and rows of roses.

My mother does work a lot, but she has free time. "I miss you and Caden, but I want to be here in case Brooke ever pulls her red head out of her buttocks and accepts help. I have to see things grow, I have to make pretty out of this hot and dried-out land, I have to be completely absorbed in my garden, or I will go straight out of my head with worry about that kid, plant myself in a jacaranda tree like a nesting peacock, and refuse to come down and face life."

Her garden, with its pathways, separate rooms, trellises, and patios, has been featured in numerous magazines. She has two trellises full of honeysuckle, and the reason behind it makes me sad.

Her home is a piece of utter peace.

Peace in the Hollywood Hills.

It was endlessly sad that Brooke wrecked that peace. She was glass smashing through glass.

I hadn't seen Brooke in years.

I didn't expect it to be peaceful.

Brooke cried when she opened my mother's front door and saw me, the fountain trickling behind us, the trellis overhead dripping with pink bougainvillea.

I tried to harden my heart to her, there on my mother's doorstep, to toughen up, so I wouldn't be hurt again, sucked back into her miserable life, her troubles, her drug addiction, her lies, because I knew I would collapse under the weight of it if I did.

I tried to see her dispassionately, or at least with the anger I felt toward her for breaking up our family, for leaving Tate, for not being a sister to me.

I tried to summon up some of that righteous, roaring anger and piercing resentment as the wind whistled through the jacaranda trees.

I could not.

Her face was swollen on one side, one green eye almost shut. She'd had stitches. Her body was thin, her hair was thin, her clothes were thin. Her life was thin, paper thin, as if it hung by a feather of a dying bird. It was she who had lost out. She had lost out on Tate, our family, a family of her own. All those years of her life, ruined.

I threw out my arms and she hugged me close, her body shaking, her tears a steady stream pouring from her eyes.

"I have missed you so much, Brooke."

She said, "I missed you, too," but I could hardly understand it through her sobs.

Brooke appeared to be completely sober, but she looked half-dead, a tired skeleton with skin and dried, dead-looking auburn hair.

"It has not been a pleasant time," Brooke said, a wry under-statement. "It's a shipwreck time of life."

I put my teacup down on my mother's kitchen table. The table had been a gift from one of her co-stars, Blake Montorio. She had chosen him out of three other hopefuls to be on *Foster's Village*. He'd made his mark on the show before the manipulative Elsie had him locked away in an insane asylum for five years. In real life he'd gone on to a successful career in movies. He'd been grateful ever since.

Brooke traced one of the carvings in the table with her finger. The table, long enough for ten, had been made by a Santa Fe artist especially for my mother. We called it The Table of Witches. It was a blend of oranges, yellows, reds, blues, and greens.

My mother had told Blake of our witchly past, and the artist had painted pictures of women with auburn-colored hair in bold dresses with stars and hearts high up in the branches of trees, a half moon shining in one corner, a group of white stars in another. The trees looked alive, their branches twisting and turning, entwined with one another, the witches dancing across the bridges and arcs. It was magnificent.

"It's a shipwreck time of life *and* Brooke's having a bad hair day," my mother drawled. "Look at her locks."

I shook my head at my mother. "We're getting into that now? She's had a shipwreck time. I'm not worried about her tangles." I was horrified, sickened by Brooke's appearance, though I'd seen her in this state before. You don't get "used to" seeing your sister beat up. I reached for Brooke's hand, chilly cold to the touch, and squeezed it.

"Um . . ." Brooke said, her voice hoarse as she pushed a trembling hand through her lank hair. "I left my . . . uh . . . my ex-boyfriend before rehab and he disagreed with my leaving, so when I was released from rehab, and he was later paroled out of jail, he came and found me and rearranged part of my face. I then went to the women's shelter."

"I took her to the doctor." My mother's face was ashen, but she was trying hard to regain her sassiness. "We went to see a handsome doctor and all Brooke wanted to do was talk about the bruises on her face, the cracked ribs, the stitches she needed in two places, and the red line she had growing up the side of her leg toward her heart that could have killed her."

"Brooke—" I felt faint. I gripped my teacup. We were all having orange herbal tea and spinach mushroom omelets, but no one was eating.

"Brooke's conversation wasn't engaging, it wasn't . . . *inviting,* if you know what I mean," my mother reprimanded, her coiffed bob swinging. "It was a poor choice of topic. The doctor was very handsome. No wedding ring. I asked him if he was married, he said no, and I said to him, 'I know of a girl for you.' "

I leaned toward my mother, aghast. "You didn't!"

"She did," Brooke said. "Mom, what else did you want me to talk about with him?"

My mother sighed, impatiently, but I knew it was an act. She was flattened by the semi-deathly state of her daughter and was using wry humor and false bravado to handle her own emotions. It was the way she'd gotten through this mess and through the varied tragedies in her life. My mother plucked at her white silk shirt and white pencil skirt, designer wear, for sure, her feet clad in Manolo Blahnik. "You could have asked him out."

My jaw dropped, and my eyes connected with Brooke's one unbeaten eye. Brooke was all squished down, a broken bird whose wings had been ripped out.

"You have to be kidding, Mom. You wanted me to get a *date?* I'm a former drug addict. We don't usually"—she put her fingers up for quotes—"date."

"A proper date." She waved a finger at Brooke. "One who will treat you nice, take you to the symphony or tea on Sunday afternoons or to Maui for a luau, and not bash your face up and ruin your ribs and cut you with a knife."

Ugh.

"Mom, I was in the doctor's office, on a hard, padded, brown table wearing a blue sheath thing that opened up for the world to see my butt and my bruises, and I was supposed to turn on the charm? Flirt? Be suggestive, seductive? Gee. I could have batted my eyelashes out of my one good eye."

Ah. There was Brooke, the funny one. She winked at me with the one unbeaten eye, it was a weak wink, but it was there.

"You should not have shown him your ass, you are right there, daughter. There's nothing to it anymore, no curves, and men like curves. Take a gander at your sister. See her boobs and butt. She flows. Men want that flow. You need to put on weight and get some flow. I have an amazing cook and she'll have you all fattened up in no time, then you can go back and ask him out."

"Gee, Mom. I wasn't thinking of dating, or hitting on the doctor while he was loading me up with massive doses of antibiotics and his nurse was sticking an IV up my arm, after stitching my face up. I don't know why."

My mom wagged a perfectly manicured nail and arched a perfect eyebrow. "Never pass on an opportunity to bring a gentleman into your life with whom you can picnic, receive bouquets and jewelry, and play in the waves."

Her comments were so ludicrous, as she meant them to be, that I finally laughed. My sister and a picnic, a symphony, playing in the waves? Clearly there had been none of that, and there she was, in my mother's home at The Table of Witches, the first time I'd seen her in years, a complete and total mess, and my mother was lecturing her about getting a date.

Brooke tapped her fingers on the table. "Maybe I could have invited him on our first date to a Narcotics Anonymous meeting. He would have been impressed. Or Alcoholics Anonymous. Or to see my counselor, where I could reveal my colorful past."

"Her hair is a mess, as you can see, Jaden," my mother went on. "It needs highlighting and cutting and good Lord, Brooke, you could not clean your hair? When she first arrived, I washed it for her, Jaden. I think spiders and webs and frogs were in it."

"I don't think frogs," Brooke said calmly, through split, swollen lips.

"There were!" My mother pointed in the air. "And you need to do your raggedy nails and you need a facial to smooth things up and out, too."

"A facial is not going to cover up the bruises, Mom, which I think are now electrifying puce, magenta, and violet colored."

"You do have a rainbow face," I observed.

"Yes, a rainbow."

"You need new teeth," my mother said.

I peeked at my sister's teeth. Beige, missing one, chipped. "New teeth."

She said, "I did a number on those, didn't I?"

"It's not exactly a Farrah Fawcett smile, dear," my mother said. "It would have been hard to attract the doctor with those viperous brown things, or even an insect repellent tradesman, but if you're truly through with drugs, my gift to you will be new teeth."

"It's okay, Mom—"

"It is not okay! No one needs viper teeth, and let's get you some new clothes," my mother drawled, using her only personal weapon against this tidal wave of horror. "Rodeo Drive, here we come!"

Brooke bent her head and cried, her tears tracking straight on down her pale, bony face, and not because of an offered shopping trip on Rodeo Drive. "Thank you, Jaden, for coming, and thanks, Mom. It's nice to be here."

"And thank *you*," my mother said, her diamond earrings swinging, "for never wearing that outfit again in your life. It does nothing for your figure. Nothing."

I caught Brooke's eye.

"Please, darling, I've taught you better. Sloppy jeans, stained shirt, no figure, no jewelry, a non-modern haircut, if you've had a haircut in years it doesn't show, and no makeup. No lipstick. It's a sin, a cardinal sin!"

"You're right, Mom. I've sinned. I've got a petticoats-on-fire sort of problem with my personal image."

"You're a Bruxelle. We *dress*," my mother insisted. "You are simply not fashionable, not vogue, or even hip in a drudge sort of way."

There we were, in my mother's home, the fountains trickling, the California wind puffing through, a pile of herbs, oranges, and lemons on my mother's counter, and she was criticizing my beat-up, drug-addicted sister's outfit and calling her *not fashionable.*

"Some wear couture better than others. Some neglect their manicures and pedicures." My mother stared pointedly at Brooke and we all laughed. "Some don't understand the value of a bit of Botox." She patted her cheekbones.

I could tell Broke hadn't laughed in a long time. Maybe years.

"I do have one thing of value, though." Brooke pulled her necklace out of her shirt. "I still have the three charms. These are the only things I haven't lost or sold over the years."

I could tell my mother was overcome with a brick of emotion but trying hard not to show it. She pulled out her charm necklace, so I did, too. For a moment, we three sat there, the scent of lemons and oranges in a bowl on the counter swirling around us.

"Enough talk," my mother declared, sniffling. "We're going to the spa! Brooke's makeover begins today, and none too soon, if I do say so myself! Lord above, she needs one!"

My mother is a millionaire but I have rarely accepted any of her wealth. I do have an inheritance from my father that initially went to my mother, which she generously passed on to Caden and me. She has never given Brooke money. I have not used the inheritance.

I have accepted from her, obviously, her invitation to live in Faith's/Grandma Violet's/her house. That was an enormous gift and meant that I didn't have a mortgage. She also insisted on pouring Tate the basketball court and she insisted, when Tate was young, on paying for a nanny when I was at work or in school, and all medical bills that weren't picked up by insurance.

"He's my grandson, Jaden. Allow me to help." I did, and I was grateful. We were raising Tate together.

But my mother's money has padded our lives, I can't deny it.

We all go on splendid vacations a couple of times a year. We are always welcome in her home in the Hollywood Hills. And she knows the best spa in Los Angeles and can pay for it.

We were there for hours. Hot rock massages, facials, steam rooms, manicures and pedicures, haircuts and highlights. Champagne, tiny layered sandwiches, and chocolate mousse.

I tried to lock out all thoughts of Ethan and his brown cinnamon eyes and my sister's beaten-up eye and relax.

It was glorious.

Two nights after I returned home, still reeling from another alarming, frightening conversation I'd had with Brooke on the patio of my mother's home, there was a winter windstorm. It knocked down trees all over our area, even some old ones that had withstood many storms in the past, including several on our ten acres.

I would miss those trees. I imagined all the women in my family who have lived here and watched those same trees change with the seasons, the green leaves turning to burnished oranges, burgundy reds, butterscotch yellows, then dropping off, snow and ice covering the branches. The trees would bud again in the spring, green leaves, pink and white flowers. I imagined all the times that Faith had walked among them, with Grace, talking, remembering. . . .

It was under a tree whose branches seemed to stretch a hundred feet out that my mother told Brooke and me, on a hot summer's day, how Faith and Grace became involved in the Underground Railroad.

"It started with the whipping of a slave. Faith and Grace were at a mansion owned by a hoity-toity woman who was ordering dresses from them." My mother held her charms in her fingers, as if even thinking about the whipping hurt her.

I pulled my arms around my skinned knees, my tennis shoes muddy from running through the poppy field, while Brooke put her head in our mother's lap and shut her eyes against the rays of the sun.

"His arms were tied above his head by a rope to a tree branch, his back arching in and out, head thrown back, screaming, his screams racing around the plantation, the white-columned mansion, and the magnolia and oak trees. The overseer, a skinny, short man with a leather hat, brought the whip snaking through the air again and again."

My mother sighed, so sad, all these years later. "Faith and Grace ran out to stop it, but they knew they were only stopping one particular incident. They heard about other brutal plantation owners, how the slave women were used and abused, how children were sold away from their parents, how plantation owners even sold their own half-black children on the auction block.

"These two women, women who had been coddled and spoiled their whole lives until escaping onto that ship to come to America, decided they would not stand by and watch. They couldn't. Both knew slavery was a sin, and to do nothing was participating in the sin. They joined the Underground Railroad, hiding frantic, starved, desperate slaves beneath the floor of their shop."

"Wow. They were like Wonder Women," Brooke said.

"That was really brave," I said, awed.

"It was. Women need to be brave, don't you forget that, Jaden and Brooke. And sometimes you have to fake being brave, until the bravery is real. Faith and Grace did their spells, they prayed, they sold their naughty, sweet nothings in their shop, and it went well for a while." My mother's fingers were tight around those charms again. "Until those two got caught."

Tate's first pre-season scrimmage against another school did not go well.

He did not start, which was a given.

He played two minutes of the first quarter. I say this with love, but he looked gawky and confused out there in his orange and black uniform. He was outrun by his opponent. His defense was . . . not so good. He basically ended up following his opposing player, instead of trying to get the ball. He missed a shot, missed a pass.

Now, he'd been in practice, but a true game, with fans, noise, the other kids, this was a whole new environment.

But the worst was what I knew, and feared, would happen. Tate endured catcalls from the kids in the audience rooting for our opponents. "Alien Head . . . Monster . . . Dumb ass . . . what's wrong with your head, buddy?"

A group of kids about twenty feet away from me in the bleachers was particularly nasty. One yelled out, "Shoot again, elephant man!" when Tate air-balled a shot. The last of many heckling comments, "Hey! Goon! Are you a person?" did it for me, I marched across the bleachers, stood in front of those boys, and said, in a polite tone, "Look here, pencil dicks. That's my son out there. Clam it up. No one wants to hear what you have to say."

Most of them were cowed and they dropped their heads, but not one of them. There's always a wisecracker. "I want to hear what I have to say, lady. Your kid has two heads." He smirked at me. Smirked. I hate smirks.

I leaned in close. "Yeah, he has a big head. That doesn't mean you should be making fun of him." And then I skated into meanness, as I can do, quick as a lick, when Tate is being attacked. "But you have purple acne, a nose like a toilet plunger, and a wimpy voice. We all have things to work on now, don't we?" I leaned in close. "Now you can close that gaping buck-toothed mouth of yours, or I can stand in front of you all night and stare down your toilet-plunger nose, which is it?"

He gulped.

"Lovely. I see we have an agreement."

I went back to my seat.

Caden had come up the bleachers behind me. He asked, "What happened there?"

I told him. I pointed at the obnoxious kids. He dropped Hazel in my arms who was wearing an M&M costume, as were Harvey and Heloise. He stomped over to the boys, the bleachers shaking, and they ran out, Damini stomping behind Caden. She yelled, "Assholes!"

The game continued. Caden, Damini, and I all cheered for

Tate and his team. The M&M's jumped around. Tate played in the third quarter with the same results, except he had two passes intercepted and seemed utterly flustered about how to get around the guy pressing him on defense. Tate was pulled out after he tossed, and that would be the word, *tossed* not *passed,* the ball away again. The other team took off with it, and scored.

I was relieved when the bell rang and so was Caden, who exhaled. "I'm going to do something to help. I am. I gotta do something."

Tate left the game, head down, feeling all those eyes on him, staring at him and his big head.

When he left the court, I heard one boy yell, "Good night, Deformity!" As if deformity was his name.

I followed the kid out and said to him, "Good night, Deformity, you peculiar short child."

He was shocked. "What?"

"If you close your mouth, the world will be a better place. We need no more idiots here."

"I'm not an idiot!"

"Yes," I told him, in all seriousness. "You are. Trust me."

I headed out to the car and laid my head on the steering wheel. I could not go around verbally smashing all the kids who made fun of Tate. No, that wouldn't do.

That night, I cried into my pillow. I cried because all of those taunting, selfish, stupid kids had made fun of my son. I cried because they tried to hurt him. I cried because he was trying so hard out there, he had finally gotten his dream to play basketball, and there they were: cutting him down. I cried because when he missed his shots, I heard, "Get your head out of the way and maybe you'll make the shot, creep!" When he passed poorly, I heard, "Do those eyes see?" I cried because he had tried as hard as he could and felt he failed.

But what did Tate do that night after the game when he returned home after I bought him a triple-decker ice cream cone?

He shot hoops for two hours, he feigned this way and that, and I could see that he was imagining himself in a game, against opponents. He watched a professional basketball game that he'd recorded.

Every day, after practice, he practiced more.

And more, and more.

He shot, he feigned, he practiced passing the ball against a cement wall of our garden and demolished a vine I had growing up it.

I didn't say a word.

I can always plant another vine.

TATE'S AWESOME PIGSKIN BLOG

Here's how my first scrimmage went: like crap.

Here's a picture of a horse taking a crap.

Here's a picture of a dog taking a pee.

Here's a picture of a slice of brain. I need my brain to play basketball better.

I tried to ignore the scent of death in my greenhouse when I cut and blended herbs and spices during Herbal Therapy on a freezing cold evening.

I had made my decision. Tate could play ball. I did not think the death scent was for him anyhow. I thought that because I didn't want to think it was about him and because there were many other people the death scent could be for, including myself or Brooke. After our visit, and how poor, physically, Brooke appeared, it could easily be her.

Maybe the herbs were wrong, too. Maybe.

I knew they weren't.

They hadn't been wrong ever, even when it was one person killing another.

My mother says this particular skill of mine is because of the witch in me. "Once a witch, always a witch," she sings at me.

"Faith built this house, her spells are all around. Plus, you have the red hair, Faith's blue eye, and Grace's green eye."

The very thought of witches in our family line is simply entertaining to me. But that my mother, super-smart, rational, and reasonable in all other areas, believes in a "royal witchly past," and "ancient spells," and "thimbles, charms, needles, and gold timepieces with power," makes her even more endearing to me.

Most of us have our bizarre quirks and irrational beliefs that directly contrast with our other beliefs. This is hers. I indulge it. She calls me a "pretty witch in denial." I call her a "pretty lady who erroneously believes she's a witch." We laugh together about it.

In terms of my own beliefs clashing, I know I am not a witch because there are no witches. She says that because I can smell death in spices I am denying my own truth and being a hypocrite.

Yes, I can smell death during Herbal Therapy in my greenhouse. I smelled it three times before this. I was right each time. That's not normal. It doesn't mean I'm a witch.

I swept, with shaking hands, all the herbs and spices off my cutting board and into the trash, made myself a cup of tango tea and thought about my meeting with Brooke.

Brooke was up when the sun started to rise over my mother's hacienda home. We had slept in our old bedroom the night before, our beds with the pink and yellow striped comforters five feet apart. We talked until our eyes fluttered shut.

I try not to see sunrises. Nothing against sunrises, but you're either up way too late or you're up way too early. I heard Brooke leave our bedroom. I tried to go back to sleep, but couldn't.

I wrapped the white lace robe my mother keeps for me here around myself, slipped on white slippers, and padded out to the patio, near the pool with the waterfall.

Brooke was staring at the sunrise from a wrought-iron table with a cup of coffee in her hand. She stood up when I came out and hugged me, then insisted on getting me coffee with cream and sugar, the way I'd always taken it.

"Thanks, Brooke."

"You're welcome."

"Why are you up this early?"

She didn't say anything for a minute, her nervous fingers fiddling with her cross, heart, and star charms. "I went to rehab. I went to Mom's place."

I was stunned. "Mom's place" was called "Faith and Grace Rehabilitation Center." It's associated with a local hospital that has had impressive success with drug rehabilitation. When my mother learned they were expanding, and constructing their own center, she made a massive donation. The committee offered to name it after her but she declined. She did not want to embarrass Brooke.

Brooke's struggle with drugs had already been in the newspapers and magazines many times because she was the daughter of famous parents. It had made a tragic situation more tragic for our whole family because of the publicity. "Rebel daughter of Rowan and Shel Bruxelle, Hollywood's golden couple ... enters rehab again ... accused of ... found on a park bench ... arrested for prostitution ... arrested for possession ... jailed ... inebriated and high on cocaine ..." People loved to read about our family's devastation.

"Does Mom know you were there?" The golden globe of the sun was peeping higher, pastel colors streaking over the horizon. I looked away from the two trellises full of honeysuckle. It brought back too much pain.

"She does now. I told her. They couldn't tell Mom I was there, it's confidential, so they didn't, but I stayed nine months. They wanted the daughter of their largest donor cold-stone sober and highly functioning before she left."

"Did the rehab work?"

"Yes. I've been clean for fifteen months. That's more than a year now. I still go to Faith and Grace daily for meetings and counseling. Anyhow, when I was there I watched the sun rise. I have to know that it's there."

"It's always there. It doesn't usually go on breaks to the Bahamas or the Keys."

"I have to prove to myself that it's there. I figure if the sun can come up one more time, I can get through one more day. I'm still struggling with a whole bunch of issues."

I could only imagine. "What's the worst?"

"Tate. Tate's the worst. I think of him all the time, I always have, except when I'm trying to block him out because I feel guilty down to my core for leaving him. I walked out and you walked in. You were nineteen." She reached for my hand. "I'm sorry, Jaden. I am so sorry. I'm sorry for . . . everything."

We talked about that "everything" for a long time, then moved on to additional appalling things.

"I destroyed a lot of lives to make money." She wrapped her arms around herself, her eyes dead. She had gone to a bad, bad place. "I am up nights wondering how many people I killed who took the drugs I sold them. I am up nights wondering how many pregnant women took my drugs and what that did to their babies. I am up nights wondering how many mothers' sons are now addicted to my drugs, how many fathers' daughters are drugged out and doing scary things with terrible men because they're addicts, like I did."

"That would keep me up at night, too," I snapped. I was sickened. *What had happened to her?* Had she lost all of her morals? It's one thing to take drugs, it's another to sell. You're bringing sheer hell, and possibly death, to someone else's life, and to the lives of their families and friends.

"If it had been only me that screwed up, I could live with that. But what I did has clobbered other people. I abandoned Tate. I destroyed our whole family, other people, their families, that's what I struggle with. Black, sticky, corrosive memories follow me. It's part of the reason I didn't want to get clean. Because I knew if I sobered up I'd have to deal with my reality, and I don't like my reality at all. I don't like me at all."

"Then start over, Brooke. Please. Keep going to counseling, talk to me, talk to Mom. I love you and I'm your sister and I want to help you. Move forward. Volunteer, help others, try to atone for what you did. . . ."

"I get pricked with images of me doing something awful and sometimes I feel the drugs calling me back, so I can disappear into them for a while and block it all out."

I wanted to reassure her, to comfort her, but I couldn't say, "It'll get better," I didn't know if it would. I couldn't say, "It's okay, Brooke," it wasn't. It is not okay to sell drugs and destroy families. I couldn't say, "Don't feel bad, Brooke, that's over. You won't do it again." It's not as if she stole a box of brownies. She fed drugs to vulnerable people who smashed up their lives.

That's not a simple one.

"I can't seem to shake my past at all and all that I did that was wrong, cruel, demeaning to someone. I can't get rid of it, can't put it behind me. I don't know if I ever will. Maybe I shouldn't ever put it behind me. That's an appropriate and deserved punishment." Brooke rubbed her hands over her face. "There's nothing like wanting to get a fix. Nothing. You can't see anything beyond that drug." Her voice was so ragged, glass and bricks.

We drank our coffee for a while, listening to the rushing waterfall in my mother's pool, watching hummingbirds flitter and birds land in the orange trees.

"Tate says that when problems are too much, you should deal with them the same way you eat Skittles. One by one."

"Smart boy." She sniffled, then reached for my hand. "I'm begging you, Jaden, tell me about Tate."

It took a long time. My mother joined us. Later we had Chinese food delivered and chocolate cheesecake. I showed Brooke a few photos I always kept in my purse of Tate, and my mother showed her photo albums. I showed her his blog, which she loved. I told her about his basketball team, about General Noggin, Billy and Bob, Bert and Ernie, his friends Anthony and Milt, his experiment room, and how Tate joked about women beating down the door to get to him. She was emotional the whole way through.

"I love you, Jaden, and again, I'm sorry—"

"I love you, too, Brooke. I always have."

"And I love you both," my mother announced. "We need to go shopping! We must fix Brooke's monstrous clothing faux pas. It's a disgrace! A sobering reminder of how slothful and frumpy people can get in a hurry when they don't attend to fashion-forward thinking and design detail!"

Brooke and I rolled our eyes at our mother.

"What?" She wobbled her head at us, as in, *you silly girls*. "Brooke has lost her style compass! It doesn't point true north anymore, it points to the testicles of a redneck, beer-slugging, burping convict! This will not do, not do at all! Dress like a lady or dress like a Dumpster, which is it, Brooke?"

We laughed. Our mother is quite clever, particularly when she is covering up acute distress over her youngest, beloved daughter.

I hoped Brooke would stay sober. The black stickiness that followed her alarmed me greatly. Mostly it alarmed me for Tate's sake.

I eyed the honeysuckle. One day I would sit beneath it. Not today.

12

For Tate's first official game, which was at another school's gym, complete with a band and cheerleaders and dance team, things went somewhat better.

My mother flew in and wore the team colors, orange and black, only she wore an orange designer dress and four-inch black stilettos. Caden came, huge and intimidating, carrying Hazel, who was dressed as a frog. Heloise was dressed as the sun, and Harvey was dressed as a piece of chocolate cake with a cherry hat. Damini wore a short ruffled orange skirt my mother had bought her especially for this game, a black T-shirt, and a jean jacket.

I wished Ethan was there. I pictured him beside me, then I made myself smash the image. I could not continue to do this to myself; it made me too upset.

When we were in the bleachers, about three rows up from the bench, my mother squealed, "He's so handsome! Tate! Tate! You're so handsome!"

Tate went in during the second quarter, and the coach played him for four minutes. He only gave up one pass. His defense was no longer a joke. He put full pressure on his opponent and forced the other guy to turn the ball over twice.

We cheered wildly.

He tried to shoot from about ten feet away from the basket, but didn't make it. I could tell he was flustered by the opposing team swooping down on him.

This game was not as bad as the first in terms of obnoxious young people, but not perfect. I still heard the following things: "God! What is wrong with that fucking head?" and, "Has he not evolved? That is wrong, man, wrong!" And this gem: "Hey! Creature from the blue lagoon!"

It was not my fault that I walked along the bleachers and my drink went straight down the backs of those three kids. They whipped around, startled, and I stood, towering over them. "Sorry about that. When I heard you saying such cruel things about Tate, I thought you needed cooling off."

One of them jumped to his feet and said, "Man! Shit!"

And Caden, who had come up behind me, said, "Man! Shit! I hear one more word out of your mouths about my nephew, and I will, man shit," he mocked them, "make your life unpleasant. Are we clear, man?"

Hazel, who had hopped about as she followed Caden over, yelled, "Man shit!"

Harvey said, "Damn!"

And Heloise said, "Stink!"

Damini said, "Why do boys always have to be such immature jerks?" The immature jerks were smart enough not to say another word.

I picked the frog up, Damini grabbed the sun, Caden picked up the chocolate cake, and we went back to sitting with the other parents.

"I'm going to get the parents going. Then Tate won't hear all the meanness," Caden said at a time-out. He marched down the bleachers and yelled to the parents, "We're gonna cheer for this team."

I have mentioned that Caden is huge and seems sort of scary with the black ponytail and muscles and all, but everyone knows him, likes him, and appreciates his unique flower arrangements.

He had the parents spell out the name *BEAR CATS*. He had them do the wave. He had them yelling for our team, in a chant, first at a whisper then louder and louder until they were screaming. He had them stomping on the bleachers and clapping, then doing a combination of both while calling out, "Bear Cats!"

And whenever he heard someone saying something nasty about Tate, he had the parents yell louder.

Tate played four minutes in the third quarter.

Marked improvement. He even shot the ball from inside the key, missed both times, but he tried.

Even so, I could tell he was not feeling great about his game.

Tate went back in for about two minutes at the end of the game. He made one basket. It did not alleviate the stress and disappointment in his game. I saw him turn his head and glance up at the boy who had been harassing him during the game. The boy stuck his middle finger up in the air. After the game Caden went over to the boy, the triplets dancing around him, and said, politely, "If you ever flip my nephew off again with that tiny dick of a finger of yours, I'm going to break it off."

The boy gulped, and he agreed not to do it.

Caden is gentle, true, and kind, but he loved Tate, so he lost it, a wee bit, as I did, in his quest to protect him.

I left the game aching for my son, for the courage it took to even be out on a court in front of that many people, some of whom were demeaning and rude. He had character, he was brilliant, he was trying, but they wanted to ruin it for him, to intimidate him, to tease and mock him into submission and defeat. They were so mean. It is enormously hard to see your kid ridiculed and harassed and not lose your head.

Tate's reaction to that game?

He practiced.

And practiced.

And practiced.

This went on and on.

TATE'S AWESOME PIGSKIN BLOG

I can't say that my basketball games are going good because they aren't. I have to try harder. I have to be better. I have to study the graphs I've made of the pros shooting. I have to practice out-side more. I have to practice better. This is embar-rassing. I think I would take a lot less harassment with General Noggin on my neck if I could play like a decent kid.

Here's one word to describe how I'm feeling about my game: Shitty.

Here's a photo of brain waves.

Here's a photo of the triplets at the game.

Here's a photo of a model of a brain I made from clay labeling all the different sections. I know, geeky, isn't it, that'd I'd sit around and do that. Whatever.

Tell me about a time that things went bad for you so I'll feel better.

After reading some people's responses on his blog, Tate did feel better. Then he ate six Heart to Heart Chocolate Chocolate Mush Mush Cookies.

"You don't have to play, Tate."

Tate's head jerked up from the breakfast table. It was early, he was studying an article about the latest research in brain operations, and was on his third bowl of cereal.

"What do you mean?"

"I mean . . ." I stumbled about. "The kids aren't nice to you during the games."

"So what?" His eyes were innocent, inquiring.

"So what?"

"Yeah. So what? They're not nice to me. It hurts my feelings for about a millisecond, but I have Bert and Ernie block it out and I keep playing."

"But . . ."

"But what? But for butt? But for bottoms? You could say

buttocks. Or ass. Or bum or fanny. Hmmm. Buttocks and brains. Do they have anything in common?"

"Aren't you funny, Tate? I don't want you to get hurt—"

"Mom, I live with General Noggin and we're good friends. I've got Billy and Bob to help me when kids want to knock me out. Plus, I'm huge. They say mean things because they want to scare me. I'm not going to let anybody scare me or push me off the court or get rid of me. No way. I ain't no wimp."

I was, once more, humbled by his courage. I had always been humbled by his courage. "You are one stud of a brainiac, Tate."

"I'm not a stud. Okay to the brainiac part. But this is the way I am. They can deal with it, not me. I've already dealt with it. General Noggin and I have a lot of brains, and I needed more room to put them in, right?" He smiled at me, then snuck out a Skittles bag, tossed three into the air at one time, and caught two. "Darn it. I almost have that down." He picked up the one on the floor and ate it.

"No Skittles at breakfast."

He put the bag in his pocket.

"You're going to play through the noise and I'm going to sit in the bleachers wanting to pound some of those kids into dust."

"Don't, Mom." He became serious. "You know, you've always been way more mad about this stuff than me. Always. You're ten times angrier than me about it. I let it go most of the time. I don't like getting hit, but it does give me a chance to hit back and get rid of some of my energy. I imagine smashing my fist into a molecule. I picture the molecule, then I set the molecule on fire or sandblast it and it's incinerated. You gotta do that, too."

"I'll try. But I'm your mom, so it hurts me—"

"Mom, you and I are Tate and Boss Mom. We have Nana Bird, Uncle Caden, Damini, and the triplets who dress way weird." He grinned. "I have everything I want. I even get to play basketball with real live people now. Nothing, not one thing on the surface of this continually moving, shifting, volcanically erupting, heating-up earth is going to make me quit playing."

"No, it wouldn't. You've never quit anything."

"As Nana Bird says, balls and tarnation, hell no. I don't quit and I'm not quitting now." He tossed three more Skittles up. Caught all three. "Ha! Did it! Now I have something worthwhile to put on my college résumé: Multiple Skittle Catcher."

"I am proud of your Skittle eating skills."

"Yup. Can I have scrambled eggs with cheese, green onions, and mushrooms and the Special Bruxelle Gold Sauce? I'm starving."

"Okay. I put your lunch sacks by the front door."

"Did you put in one of those cinnamon rolls from last night? How about two? I'm sooo hungry at lunch."

Sometimes seeing a family member you haven't seen for a while brings to mind another family member who is long gone.

That's how it felt when I saw Brooke. I thought of my father, Shel Bruxelle. He called me Aquamarine, because of my blue and green eyes. When I was younger, I grew interested in cooking with lots of spices, so he bought me cookbooks with lots of spices in the recipes, which I still use. When I was interested in roller-skating, he bought us all roller skates. When I was interested in tea, we went tea shopping together. He bought me a pink tea set, which I still have. I loved walking around our ten acres, watching how the seasons changed it, and he would come walking with me.

"The best way to figure out life is to walk in nature daily," he told me. "Seasons are like life. Some seasons are better than others. Some have more sun and rainbows. Others have storms and tornadoes. Some have both. You have to accept that, bring color and light to the season you're in as best you can, and always look forward to the next season."

He had not come from any money; in fact, he always struggled for the basics growing up. His parents were potato farmers in a small town in Idaho.

His father drank himself to death and his mother married four times after that, each husband worse. He had a front-row seat to all kinds of pain and barren loneliness. That pain and loneliness morphed into his scripts. Humor often comes from loss and aloneness, from not belonging, and it did for him. That's why people laughed at his shows and movies: He *got* it. He got the full spectrum of the human experience.

"I could let my childhood crush me or I could get the heck out of Idaho," he told me once. "That's what it came down to when I was eighteen. I opted for getting the heck out of Idaho. I met your mother in Hollywood the first month we were both there, and that was it. She was it for me. I loved her on sight."

My parents played the Hollywood game because they loved what they did. He loved to write stories, she loved to take part in them and transform herself.

But they never bought in to it. Never bought in to Hollywood. Their first priority was our family, and they stuck hard and high to it.

If you knew my dad you loved him. My mother, Brooke, Caden, and I loved him most of all.

It was shocking when he died that night.

I don't think I've ever gotten over the shock.

Tate's third game, initially, was another mess.

The game was at our home gym, which made me feel a bit better.

Caden had taken it upon himself to make orange T-shirts. There was a picture of our team on the front. To advertise his floral business, there was a snapdragon with a fierce face curling around the team. It was hilarious. Printed on the back were the words MID COURT MOB.

"We're the Mid Court Mob," Caden told Tate and me. "Ha! We're going to deafen the competition, deafen them, my boy!" I knew why he wanted to deafen the competition. He wanted to deafen the effects of the heckling on Tate.

He is such an excellent older brother I became a tad emotional.

My mother and I passed out hundreds of Mid Court Mob T-shirts that my mother had insisted on paying for. "We're going to support our Tate and his teammates, and if they're mean to my Tate, I might toss a snake down their throats." She smiled a toothy, pleasant smile as if she'd said, "I love tea and crumpets!"

Caden led the cheers from the floor to the parents in the bleachers. Damini was next to him, as were the triplets who were dressed, for once, the same. They were ladybugs.

Tate did not start the game. Coach Boynton told me later that he regretted that decision. "I could not have foreseen what would happen, Jaden." He wiped sweat off his brow. "No one, *no one,* could have foreseen that except the basketball gods."

The whistle blew, the band played, the cheerleaders jumped about, and we quickly fell far behind. The opponent had fifteen points within a few minutes. Our team was not together, our passes intercepted, the ball stolen, shots air-balling, and the defense was poor. The team was off.

My brother, he of a wide chest and bellowing voice, started leading the parents in a cheer.

Coach Boynton signaled Tate to go in the game. He headed out at the next buzzer. I tensed, waiting for whatever was going to be yelled down, insultingly, at Tate. I felt tearful, angry, and scared as only a parent can feel when they know their child is going to get clobbered.

I felt my mother tense, too.

It didn't take long.

"Frankenstein's son! Yeah, you! Frankenstein!"

Soon it became a chant from the opposing team's student section: "Frank-en-stein, Frank-en-stein, Frank-en-stein!"

My stomach flipped and turned over. Honestly, I hated those kids, I did. I wrapped my fingers around the crystals that Tate had given me and tried to calm down.

My mother started wiggling her fingers. I didn't stop her. "I'm spelling for a miracle to make them shut up. You wait. It'll work."

"I don't believe in spells."

"Tra la la. I do. I bet Faith and Grace used this spell to make things go their way."

Caden had made a tagboard sign that had Tate's name on it.

He flipped it over and held it up high. It said ASSHOLES on the other side. The kids from the opponents' school saw it. It probably made things worse.

"Frank-en-stein, Frank-en-stein, Frank-en-stein!"

Not all the kids were doing it, but about thirty of them were, and their voices rose as Tate dribbled the ball down the court. He lost the ball. He grabbed it a minute later, lost it again.

Tate seemed overwhelmed and awkward out there. He made another bad pass, missed a shot. He was pulled out of the game in two minutes.

"I have to work harder on my spell," my mother muttered. "Let me try again."

"Go for it, Witch Rowan." I pulled on my ponytail and tapped my cowboy boots, my nerves on fire.

Damini came up, sat close to me, and held my hand. I felt it tremble. With her other hand she fiddled with her cross, heart, and star charms. "Tate's a pain in my keester, but I love him, and next time someone makes fun of him I'm going to hit him with my leg so hard his head will come off."

My mother nodded. "I love your violent retribution. Spill some blood."

Halftime came and went, and we were down by twenty points. Tate was not put back in until the middle of the third quarter. Again, he seemed befuddled and out-played. Milt passed him the ball and he actually ran the wrong way. The student section jeered and laughed, and I saw Tate's face flush red in embarrassment. The chant "Frankenstein" started up again.

That's when the miracle happened. The opposing coach, a towering, bald, African American man, whom I later learned was named Traynor Watson, called a time-out, his voice booming. The refs stopped the game and the teams jogged to their sides. Traynor, however, stalked across the gym over to his own student section, head down, like a charging, truly pissed-off bull. The gym grew quiet.

Traynor stood in front of that group and hollered, "Shut the hell up! Trachtenberg, Braustein, Sophie Elizabeth Smith, if you don't close your trash mouths right now I will drag you out by the hair. *Shut up!* You're a disgrace to all of us! You're a disgrace to our school! You're a disgrace to yourselves!"

An Asian man, over six feet tall at least, whom I later learned was the principal of the school, stomped up into the student section, grabbed two huge, beefy boys by the arms, yanked them into the aisle, and pointed at the door. He grabbed two more boys, and two girls, and shoved them out, too. They were all red-faced with embarrassment.

A mother, round and tall, strode across the court and grabbed her son, pulling him down the bleachers *by his ear.* When they were on the gym floor, she pulled her purse back and whopped him on the butt, then started shaking her finger at him, three inches from his face. She climbed two stairs and did it to two more kids. I do not know if they were her children.

"Now you listen up!" Traynor yelled at his student section, all the kids now seated, cowering, and quiet. "I hear you making fun of Tate again, I hear one word out of your trashy mouths that shouldn't be coming out of your trashy mouths, not only will I forfeit this game, I'm coming across the court again and it's gonna get really ugly, you hear me? You hear me?"

They nodded, chastened.

"I'm embarrassed!" Traynor yelled, his words echoing off the gym walls. "You embarrass me! Do not embarrass me again! Is that clear? No embarrassment or you will regret it!"

He turned around and the entire parent section gave him a standing ovation. He put his head down, the charging bull, and stalked back to the bleachers, face stormy. He did not go to his own bench. He charged over to Tate. Tate told me later what he said as he shook his hand.

"I am sorry for the despicable treatment those kids are giving you."

"It's okay." Tate smiled at him. He told me later he couldn't believe it. Couldn't believe that their coach had gone over and hollered.

"No, son, it's not okay. They're gonna behave, those wild animals, and we're gonna have a fair game and I apologize again.

It's an embarrassment to me. Embarrassment to my school." He stomped back to his side but not before pointing at his student section and yelling, "Behave yourselves this *instant!*"

My mother said, "Now do you believe in my spells, blue- and green-eyed daughter?"

I grinned. What else could I do?

The whistles blew again.

The Mid Court Mob continued to yell and cheer.

Though we made a few baskets, none by Tate, we were still down by twenty. Coach Boynton sat down beside Tate on the bench at the end of the third quarter. Two of our team had fouled out and one was hurt when he tripped over his own feet and landed on his face. Tate's head was down, but he listened. I knew he was discouraged, deeply disappointed in his game.

Coach Boynton was trying to build Tate up, encourage him. I glanced over at his wife, Letty, three seats over. She is a strong-willed, outspoken column writer for the paper. She nodded at me, I nodded back.

The opponent scored again and Coach Boynton called a time-out. All the sweaty, dismayed players gathered around, including the one who fell on his face, their expressions defeated. The cheerleaders skipped out to the floor and did their thing. Coach Boynton, red-faced and eager, grabbed Tate's uniform and pulled him to within three inches of his face, in the center of that group of boys. He said something fast and furious, Tate nodded, eyes down, and the coach yelled at him, not in a mean way, but in a *Come on, son, get yourself together* way. Tate nodded again. Coach Boynton yanked him up even closer and yelled again from, I swear, not more than an inch away.

The whistle blew.

Tate's eyes cut up to me, his uncle Caden, the triplets in their ladybug outfits, Damini, and his Nana Bird. Caden yelled, "I believe in you, Tate!" which probably would have embarrassed any other kid, but not our Tate, and Damini yelled, "You need to use my leg!" and my mother yelled, "Fire up your balls, Tate!"

"Really, Mother?"

"What?" She opened up her eyes innocently.

"Fire up your balls?"

"He needs the heat, the burning heat!" She whistled super loud and I went back to whooping and hollering, as Tate ran out to the court with four other teammates.

The basketball was in play, one of our guards caught it, and passed it to Tate. Tate dribbled in and shot. He missed it. It was rebounded and the other team scored. Coach Boynton buried his face for a second in his hands as the other student section went wild, then stood and yelled to Tate. He pointed beyond the three-point line. "Do it, Tate. Now! Do it!"

The ball was back to us, Milt passed it to Tate, and Tate dribbled into the key and was blocked. We lost the ball.

Coach Boynton ran both hands through his hair, then bent over and screamed at Tate, *"Do it, Tate! Do it!"*

The other team had the ball, but lost it when Kendrick stole it.

"I am not kidding, Tate Bruxelle! You do this right now!" Coach Boynton's voice boomeranged around the walls of that gym.

Kendrick lobbed it to Tate, who was two feet outside of the three-point line toward half court.

Tate caught the ball. I saw the hesitation on his face, the fear.

"Now, Tate, now!"

He waited another second, looking this way and that for a teammate to pass it to.

"Shoot the ball!" Coach Boynton screamed. *"Shoot it!"*

Tate's expression changed, from insecurity to determination, and he focused in, laser-like.

He shot. The ball arched way, way up...and I held my breath.

My mother gripped my arm.

Damini gasped.

The ball swirled around the rim.

Swirl, swirl, swirl...

Slow motion...so slow and then...

It fell in.

I could hardly breathe. My mother jumped up and down. Our whole parent section flew to their feet, cheering. Coach Boynton slammed a fist through the air. Both of the referees' arms shot up, *three-pointer*. Our cheerleaders kicked. Our band blasted a victory note. Our student section about busted their spleens.

Tate had made a three-point basket!

The other team brought the ball down and, miraculously, Shandry stole the ball. Tate sprinted ahead, arm up for the pass. He parked himself outside of the three-point line. Shandry whipped the ball to him.

Tate aimed.

He arched his hands.

He shot. It was a high arc, the ball spinning . . . spinning . . .

Swoosh again.

Three-pointer, refs' arms flying up.

Coach Boynton actually jumped in the air. Our student section about busted their spleens and their livers. Caden's arms made a *V* for victory and I could tell he was crying. "Oh yeah, oh yeah, that's my boy! That's the way to do it!"

My mother was euphoric. "You're breaking their balls, Tate, keep breaking them!"

The ladybugs hopped up and down.

I will not bore you with a play-by-play. Here's what happened the rest of the third and fourth quarters: Our team was revitalized by Tate's shots. Our guards, our forward, our center, passed the ball to Tate, all shots outside of the three-point line. Tate missed only once.

"He's got a hold of his balls," my mother yelled.

Caden led more cheers. He had to wipe his eyes, those darn tears! The ladybugs flew around. Damini danced and said, "He's a pain in my keester, but he can shoot!"

It was deafening in that gym. *Deafening.* I could hardly hear my own self screaming, our band pounding it out during timeouts.

Anthony and Milt put up two two-pointers. Ten seconds left and we were down by only one point. The other team had learned to guard Tate beyond the three-point line but it didn't help. He moved lightning quick, he caught the pass, he put it up.

Nine seconds, eight, seven, six . . . Shandry passed Tate the ball outside the three-point line, Tate shot, it swished, the buzzer rang.

Game over.

Absolute, utter *chaos*.

The students streamed out of the bleachers, their feet thundering. Tate was surrounded, then lifted onto his teammates' shoulders as they paraded him around the gym. Coach Boynton sat on the bench, held his head in his hands, and sobbed. His wife laughed.

Tate, my Tate, the boy with the big head, put both arms up in victory. When he saw his Nana Bird, his uncle Caden, the ladybug triplets, Damini, and me, he yelled, "I love you, family—I love you, Boss Mom."

Caden burst into tears, his huge, muscled shoulders shaking. "I love you, too, Tate, I love you, my boy!"

Damini made the victory sign and joined the kids. Before we could stop the triplets they scampered on down and flew around with all the other kids, their arms outstretched. (Ladybugs fly, they don't run.)

His teammates started bopping him up and down, Tate wobbling on their shoulders, grinning ear to ear.

That was the photo our local paper ran with the article about the game: a bigheaded kid held high on the shoulders of his whole team, his face lighting up that whole damn gym.

The reporter interviewed Tate via his cell phone later that night.

These are Tate's quotes: "I think General Noggin finally learned how to shoot a three-pointer under pressure. . . . My teammates are radical . . . it's the best team on Planet Earth and in this galaxy, not including the black holes. . . . My coach about had a heart attack when I made that last shot. I thought I was going to have to give him CPR. I really don't want to do a lip-lock with Coach Boynton, either, but I will if I have to. . . . I can balance two apples on my head. . . . No, I don't like being called Frankenstein. The girls call me Mr. Seductive when I'm not within earshot. . . . Why? Because I am Mr. Seductive. . . . Oh no! Gotta go. One of my experiments caught on fire . . . shoot! This could cause a small explosion. . . ."

It listed his blog site.

The hits for the next day: 2,400.

Late the next night I made tea with honey in it, opened the door to my porch, and stared out at a few snowflakes mixed with rain. Tate was beyond thrilled to be on the basketball team. Maybe I should have let him play before. Guilt assailed me like a slow-moving tsunami, getting worse and worse as I swirled the thought around. I had wanted to keep him safe. Maybe I had been too overprotective.

It could be.

Damn, but I felt guilty.

Lonely and guilty.

"If my father had received better care, if she hadn't made mistakes and drowned him in morphine"—Dirk Hassells pointed a fleshy finger at me, his indignant face squished up—"he would not have died when he did."

Dirk Hassells squirmed across the long table, a storming boar. This meeting, with the hospital's attorney Sandra Torelli, Sydney, Dr. Baharri who was Mr. Hassells Senior's head doctor, and a few other medical professionals and hospital administrators, was held in a conference room in St. Clare's. We were hoping to reason with Dirk before he hauled in the chomping attorneys. It is difficult to reason with a storming boar.

I sighed. Loudly. Dirk sent me a withering stare.

"Mr. Hassells," Sandra said crisply. "Can you please tell us what you know of your father's illness?"

Dirk flushed. "I know that my dad was sick, but he shouldn't have died. I had seen him recently before he died and we had dinner on the patio of his home."

"When was that?" Sandra has long blond hair. She wears it

straight down. She has oversized, quite white teeth. I have noticed that she smiles brightly right before she goes in for the kill.

Dirk shifted his fanny. "It was a few days before he died."

I did not correct him. Neither did anyone else. We knew this was Sandra's job and Sandra had told me, "Hold on to your temper, Jaden. Chill out and let me do my job."

"Hmm," Sandra mused, riffling through the paperwork. "I believe that your statement is"—she smiled, showing a host of teeth—"false. The last time you saw your father, according to Jaden's paperwork, and according to your own sister, was about four weeks before he died. Is that true?"

Dirk shifted about on his fanny again. "I don't keep exact records. I'm a busy man with an important job. But he was healthy then." He pounded the table. "He could sit up in bed. His oxygen tank was helping him breathe. He was able to swallow milk. He could talk."

"Hmmm . . ." Sandra said again. "You do realize that in four weeks a man who is suffering from liver cancer can fade rapidly?"

"Not my dad," Dirk said. "Not *my* dad."

"Why not your dad?"

"Because he was strong."

"Ah. Okay dokay. I have Dr. Baharri here, and he is going to tell you, once again, about your father's physical condition and diagnosis."

"I already know it!" Dirk argued. "He had liver cancer—"

"How far had the cancer progressed, Mr. Hassells?" Dr. Baharri asked. He was born in India, but arrived in Florida when he was five. I have rarely met a more gentle, competent physician. He is second to Ethan only.

"It wasn't far enough to kill him!"

"How do you know?"

"Because I know! I heard the early diagnosis. Liver cancer. That's it. Nothing else."

"Do you know what the liver does?"

"Yeah, I do."

"What does it do?" Dr. Baharri asked.

"It does its function. . . ."

"Which is?"

Dirk squirmed again. "Why are we talking about this? What we need to talk about is why my father wasn't treated right."

"He was," Dr. Baharri said. "I was his doctor. From the start, there was no hope because the cancer was not only in his liver, it was in his lungs and bones." Dr. Baharri then spun off on a concise, but complete lecture on the late Mr. Hassells's health.

"But when he went to hospice he had time," Dirk said. "A lot of time!"

"Mr. Hassells, do you know what hospice is?" Sandra asked. There went those flashing teeth again!

"Yes, it means he's getting extra help."

"It means he has less than six months to live." Teeth. "You don't enter into hospice unless you're dying and the patient, along with his doctors, agrees that there is nothing more to do, there are no more treatments, no more operations. Hospice is what people enter into when all options are over for that patient."

"Not all options were over!"

"Yes, they were," Dr. Baharri said. He then detailed what treatments were given to Mr. Hassells, Senior, and the outcome of those treatments. Basically he told Dirk, once again, but in a different way, how the disease had mangled Mr. Hassells, Senior's health. "Surely you are aware that his liver cancer was not curable?"

"I didn't say curable, I said that he didn't receive competent help, especially at the end. He died because"—Dirk stuck out his chest—"he died because his hospice nurse, Jaden, gave him too much morphine those last weeks and killed him. She killed him!"

I didn't move. I tried to stay calm and not leap across the table and bash him. I knew I had not done that. It was a lie. But still, to hear the accusation thrown at me, especially in front of my colleagues, was galling and infuriating.

"That is false," Sandra said calmly. "False."

"I must disagree with you completely," Dr. Baharri said.

"Completely. You are incorrect. You could not be more incorrect. For Miss Bruxelle to have killed your father she would have had to give him large amounts of morphine, and she would not have done this. I have worked with Miss Bruxelle for years and find her to be the finest hospice nurse I have ever met. She is highly educated and trained, she is infinitely kind and compassionate to her patients, she did not do this, your comments defame her—"

"Yes, she did!"

"How do you know?" Sandra asked.

"Because when I was at the house once I saw Jaden give my dad morphine through his mouth."

"Did you expect her to give him morphine through his rectum?" Sandra asked. "Through his ear?"

"It's used for pain control," Dr. Baharri said. "Perfect drug for the cancer he had."

"It was too much. She killed him. I know it." But Dirk's words fell soft. He was starting to sweat.

"You're repulsive," I said to him.

He brought his fist onto the table.

"Do you understand the accusation you're making?" Dr. Baharri said. "Do you? You're accusing a nurse of murder."

"Yes, yes, I am." Dirk's tight mouth twisted.

"This is a deeply serious matter," Dr. Baharri said, leaning back as he steepled his fingers. "Deeply serious."

"It's called defamation of character," Sandra said.

"Then that's what I'm doing!" Dirk slapped the table. Twice. "Defamation! Jaden's wrong, she's in trouble, and that's why I'm getting my attorneys in here and we're gonna sue you." He slapped the table again and watched me with his weasel eyes.

"I did not kill your father. Go ahead and sue. I'd find it amusing."

"You would?" Now that was baffling to Dirk!

"Yes. Because in court the jurors will see the neglectful, cold, selfish son that you are, the neglectful, cold, selfish son that your father thought you were."

Sandra kicked me under the table. I kicked her back.

"That's it, Jaden!" He pointed at me and stood up. "That's what gets you into trouble! It's that mouth of yours. You were rude to me when I was at my father's, you were neglectful of me, I mean, you were neglectful of him and you didn't care about me, I mean"—sweat actually dripped off his forehead—"you didn't care about him, you would only talk to Beatrice and her bratty kids, not me, you never wanted to talk to me alone and your care was"—another drop of sweat rolled off—"reckless! That's what it was, reckless! Plus, you wouldn't keep me updated and call me when I called you."

"We kept you updated," Sydney said. "I ended up updating you regularly because you hit on Jaden so much, according to Jaden and your sister, and I cannot have my employees sexually harassed."

"Not true!"

"True," I said. "It was incessant. I told you that I did not want to go to your home and see your porn collections or sex toys or your hot tub or your naked art that you asked me to see. I don't care for you, Dirk, and I am not forced to spend time with you. Your dad was my patient. Not you. I said no. That ticked you off. That's why we're here today."

Dirk leaned over, fleshy face red. "And that sarcastic *no* of yours is going to get you into a lawsuit, Jaden. If you had smiled today and been nice to me and said you were sorry, we could have gone to my place for dinner and worked it out, but no!" He waved an arm in the air. "I'm suing you and I'm going to enjoy making your life miserable." He stomped toward the door. "For years! You will regret this, Jaden! I will not leave your life for years! I will be in your head, I will be in your mood, and in your day. You will regret how you treated me, you stuck-up witch!" He slammed the door.

Ah. A witch. How quaintly fitting.

Dr. Baharri leaned forward. "I will testify for you at any time." Sydney and the other medical professionals and the administrators all concurred. I was touched by their support.

I pushed my auburn curls back. "Thank you. He's an obnoxious, lying slug."

"I will beat him down with a stick until he's mush, that's what I'll do." Sandra smiled at us. She has such shiny teeth. I love those teeth. They are sharp. "Yes, he will be pudding when I'm through."

"I have never found pudding pleasurable to the palate," Dr. Baharri said, steepling his fingers again.

"Too soft," Sydney said.

"Me, either." I tapped a pen on the table. "I want to put that pudding man in a blender and turn it on high, though." My Witch Mavis temper had been triggered.

On my way home, through a driving rain, almost cold enough to snow, I indulged myself in my black mood. I was depressed about Dirk's accusation. My job was killing me. I loved my patients, I loved the families. But being accused of murder...

I had been working with the dying for years and I was burning out. I hate that phrase. To acknowledge it is to acknowledge a deep exhaustion and a wall to scale.

I was burned out on not having Ethan in my life, too. The burning had caught my heart on fire in a slow but deep simmer, as if even that were dying. Last time, when Tate had a checkup appointment with Ethan, I had not even gone in. I had stayed in the car, too upset.

I passed the Fischerson house, which is on the main street of our town. No one had lived in it for years. It was a two-story white house built in 1920. It leaned a bit to the right, but it had charm, too. There was a porch, columns, and some gingerbread trimming.

The first owner was a farmer. He had eight children. Rumor had it that he shot one of the daughter's boyfriends because he was sleeping with his daughter, and the boyfriend, Frank, has been haunting the house since then.

The next owners were three sisters. They were nurses, never married, and they lived there thirty years. They said they did not marry because, "Frank wouldn't approve of another man there."

The third owner was a man named Rickets, what a name,

and he loved zinnias and grew rows and rows of them. It was rumored that he chatted to Frank the ghost there, too.

It was all talk, I knew that, a fun story in town, but I loved the house. If I opened up a tea/herb/spice/sandwich/dessert shop, I would buy that house, paint it in different shades of yellow, polish up the original wood floors, knock down some walls, add plush, old-fashioned furniture in burgundy and blue, buy wood tables that would hold fresh flowers, install an old-fashioned bar, a couple of church benches, and run my business.

It appealed more than I wanted to admit.

13

~

TATE'S AWESOME PIGSKIN BLOG

The kids on the other side chanted and called me Frankenstein during our basketball game Friday night. Their coach made them shut up. That coach is now on my list of Awesome Dudes.

We played the game. I finally lost some fear. We won.

That's about it for today, peeps. I have physics homework. Thanks for all your comments on this blog and for being real. I think we're gettin' to know each other.

Here is a photo of my favorite math problem. Don't be scared, you break it apart bit by bit and it'll work.

Here's a photo of bread I made today.

Here's a photo of my cousins, the triplets. Yes, Hazel is dressed as a hummingbird, and yes, she is wearing a monster mask with it. Harvey is the one dressed as a dolphin. He also has a holster and a plastic gun. No, I don't know why. Maybe he was afraid a whale might leap out of the ocean and

240

bite him. Heloise is the devil. Not in real life. Just in the photo.

Here is a photo of my favorite neurosurgeon, Dr. Ethan Robbins.

Question of the day: If you had thirty days to live, what would you do?

Tate's blog was deluged with thoughtful, funny answers. Deluged.

I ran a finger down my computer screen on Ethan's face.

I missed him so much I could hardly breathe. I ached. I ached all over, as if vital organs had been ripped from my body. I loved him, I did. I would not sacrifice Tate's health for that love, though. I would not. I am not a martyr. Not at all.

But I love my boy.

On a chilly, rainy night, complete with earsplitting thunder and lightning off in the distance, which would sound unbelievably corny if it weren't true, I headed out to my greenhouse. I wanted to drink tea, listen to Vivaldi, hang more dried roses, and study Italian recipe books. I told myself that I would not combine herbs and spices. No, I would not.

Faith and Grace, to my knowledge, had never smelled death in herbs and spices, but it's family legend, according to Grandma Violet, that the ladies from England had another talent: They apparently killed a man using a voodoo doll. Voodoo dolls were not in their customs or culture, that black magic was taught to them in the middle of the night by a slave who had arrived in shackles from Africa only ten years prior.

When Faith and Grace were working on the Underground Railroad, helping slaves out of South Carolina, there was one dangerous, demented landowner they wanted to get rid of because he kept attacking and impregnating the women slaves, then selling off their children. He did not seem to mind seeing his own flesh and blood up on an auction block, bound for the deep South.

Mr. Taft had lynched two slaves who tried to escape. He had his wife sent to an insane asylum because she protested his treatment. There she was tied up, beaten, half-starved, and laid on a bed infected with fleas and lice. When he returned in three months, she was only half-sane. Still, Mrs. Taft was sane enough to whisper what she wanted done to her husband at an appointment with Faith and Grace to plan her spring wardrobe and two new hats.

To get rid of Mr. Taft, the slave, Emmie, made a doll out of straw that looked remarkably like Mr. Taft, began her chants, and stabbed the doll with a knife. It didn't work and she was bitterly disappointed, as her son was soon to be auctioned off, punishment because Emmie had fought off Mr. Taft's advances.

Faith and Grace used the needle from the velvet satchel, the thimble, white lace handkerchief, gold timepiece, and the charms to do what had to be done. They did not use the book with the black cover, they couldn't go that far, but they did use the spells their mothers, Henrietta and Elizabeth, taught them.

When Faith stuck the needle into the heart of the straw doll, they heard Mr. Taft's screams shooting across the plantation. When Grace stuck it in his crotch, they heard more screams. Emmie stuck the needle back in the heart.

Mr. Taft died after clutching both his heart, then his crotch, and back up again, as if he was being struck in both places.

His wife was later seen doing a jig of joy in the woods, Emmie's son was not sold, and there were no more lynchings on that plantation.

I would never use a voodoo doll—not that I believed Mr. Taft died via a voodoo doll, or that they work. They don't. But it is family lore, it is a tale handed down, and it is probably based in *some* truth. For example, maybe someone shot Mr. Taft a few times that night and the voodoo doll got the credit, or he had a simple heart attack.

When I was done reading Italian recipe books and ready to go inside, I was called to that darn cutting board, as if a rope were around my waist tugging me there. I was wishing, so hard, with everything I had, that it would tell me something different tonight.

I chopped up bay leaves, then squished them in my trembling hands.

I picked apart mint leaves.

I rolled the hard nobs of coriander between my fingers.

I mixed them together.

I smelled death. Raw, black, clinging.

Threatening. Imminent.

The scent of a life filtering away filled the room, swirling all around, rancid and rotting. Mine?

My mother's?

My brother's?

Brooke's? That was, rationally, the most probable.

Or Damini?

The triplets?

Tate?

I put my head on my cutting table, the scent of orange tea surrounding me sweetly, my candle burning off a blueberry scent, my white Christmas lights twinkling, such a cozy contrast to the putrid stench of death that had snuck into the room.

"Tate, remember how you said you wanted me to locate your mom so you could check on her, make sure she's all right?"

"Yeah, yeah! I did." He rolled away from his computer in his experiment room. It was freezing outside, but the sun was out. Earlier in the day it had rained and a rainbow had arched over the mountains.

I eyed a couple of beakers he had that were boiling. "What is that?"

"Water, Mom, water. Maybe a harmless mixture or two. Simple stuff. This and that. Nothing, it's a blend." He stood up, blue eyes eager. "Where is she?"

"And what is that?" I eyed a radio that was hooked up to several other wires, a cell phone, and foil.

"Another small experiment. Is she okay?"

"She's okay, Tate. Currently she's sober."

"Cool." His face relaxed. "I am out of this galaxy glad. Drugs are sketchy, unbalanced, and chemically destructive things with an unreliable creator and distributor, plus they can rewire and destroy your brain."

"You got that right, buddy." I put my hands in my pocket, unsure, utterly not confident this was the right way to go. "This might be painful for you to meet her. You can say no. . . ."

"I want to meet her. I do. I do, I do."

"You still do?"

"Yes! I want to meet the Other Mother. I know she screwed up, I know it. But I still want to meet her, please, Mom!"

"Okay, son. You'll meet her."

I hoped this wouldn't end in a melting-down disaster. So much of parenting is doing your best and hoping you're making the right decision with the information you have at that time without resorting to sneaking whiskey in your closet. It's darn scary.

What a mess.

I hugged him close. "I love you, Tate."

"I love you, too, Boss Mom!" He hugged me tight and lifted me up. "You're my mom, Boss Mom."

I knew what he meant: I was the *real* mom.

I rocked in the old rocking chair that night by the windows. I wondered how many women in my family line had rocked in it, their emotions rolling, their control tight, as they analyzed how to handle one crisis or another as they stared out at the red poppies in the field, the fir trees, their abundant herb gardens. Oh, what to do, what to do, what to do. . . .

I'm sure Grandma Violet spent hundreds of hours rocking in this very chair before that one night when he told her, "It's time," and she did what she did.

It did not bring me much comfort.

*   *   *

At my last appointment with Maggie Granelli she asked if Tate could come over soon and play chess.

I brought him over on a Saturday.

He was merciless. He won. He beats all his opponents.

"Ha ha!" he cackled. "Victory is mine, Maggie Shoes!"

"I fought to the bitter end," she said, holding up her lone pawn and king. "The bitter end!"

"For my prize I'm going to eat your coconut layer cake."

"Be my guest, then get yourself back in here. Next time the victory is mine, pip-squeak."

Maggie's roses are not blooming anymore. We talk about our favorite types of roses anyhow. Tate told her that she had a mouth like a rose. It wasn't flirty, the words slipped out of his mouth, genuine and sincere.

Maggie smiled and reached out her hand. "You are a gentleman, Bishop Tate, a true gentleman."

"Guess where I am now?" my mother asked.

"On the set? In your trailer?"

"Yes, I'm on the set and I'm in bed. Beck crawled into bed with me. He's tired because his nephew is sick and he was up 'til one o'clock playing him songs on the piano. He may fall asleep if the director doesn't get it together soon. Anyhow, we're shooting the scene where we secretly reunite. Say hello to Beck, Jaden, you're on speakerphone."

"Hi, Beck," I called out. Beck was a neat guy. He was tall and had white and black speckled hair. He'd been with his partner, Jason, for twenty years. Secretly, obviously. Who wanted to know that her favorite soap opera star, who was lusty and sexy with the ladies, was gay?

"My dear Jaden," he boomed out. "How are you?"

"Oh, I'm fine and dandy, Beck."

"Tell me, Jaden, about this scrumptious seafood dish your mother told me you made last weekend called Seafood Bust Up. You used snapper, lobster, shrimp, and clams, right?"

Beck and I were off and cooking—at least verbally. We discussed Seafood Bust Up, named by Tate, and the garlic, olive oil, cumin, and green onions I used. Then we discussed an okra salad I made with lime juice, green onions, tomatoes, pepper flakes, and vinegar. Tate named the okra salad, Okay Dokay Salad. Beck's a master chef.

"All righty, the cameramen are all ready now," my mother called out. "You ready to go, Maryana? And you, too, Roz? Okay, sweets. Beck and I have to have a wild love scene and then we'll call you back."

"Okay, Mom."

"Bye, honey!" Beck called out. "As a reminder: Butter is your friend. Do not skimp on it ever."

"I will carve that into my walls."

Before we disconnected I heard my mother say, "Okay, Bodacious Boy Beck, I'm ready for you, baby. Hold on. Have to arrange my boobs. Maryana, how do my boobs look . . . oh, you flatterer, you. Okay . . . move the left one up? Beck, remember when your arm is under me give 'em a lift . . . yep, you're doing it, sweets . . . all right, kiss me, Becki, you burly bear—"

I envisioned my mother and Beck rolling around in bed, their faces heated, tight with their forbidden passion. Beck did call me back not too many minutes later. He wanted my great-grandma's recipe, from her mother, for a banana cream pie.

I wish I could roll around tight with passion with Ethan. For a while I tried not to daydream about him. It didn't work and it made me depressed. The loss was more unbearable when I was done with the daydream, but I couldn't help myself. I needed to think about him. I needed him in my life, even if it wasn't him, the living, breathing, smiling Ethan.

I am pathetic. I know this. And I need to snap out of it, get a life, stop being dramatic and sappy.

How does one snap out of love, though?

*   *   *

Although he was excited at first to meet his Other Mother, the next days were an emotional roller coaster for Tate. He wanted to talk nightly after he came home from practice, then again after he practiced outside on our court. I think he finally took some time to examine the whole Brooke situation. Before she was abstract, never met her. Now, she was a reality and she was coming to our home.

He gravitated from excitement at meeting her, to anger and frustration for her being absent from his life, to relief that he knew she was safe, to hope that they could have a relationship, to disbelief that she'd abandoned him, to loss and sorrow, a bit of mourning of what could have been, to curiosity, and back to anger and excitement again.

"What kind of mother does drugs, especially when she's pregnant?" He wiped his tears. "My mom. That's the kind of woman that does it. I don't get it."

"She's an addict, honey. They don't think. The drugs have wrapped them up tight, taken their brains captive, poisoned them, stripped them of morals and ethics, taken away who they really are. Nothing gets through to them except their next hit."

He nodded, his lips trembling. "Yeah. But still. She made a choice to stay on drugs . . . I don't know. Even though she sounds so messed up and what she did to our whole family and me was wrong, I still want to see her. I don't like what she did, and I love you, Boss Mom, but I still want to meet her. Talk to her."

"I get it. She's your biological mother."

"It's this screwed-up tie I have with her. I don't even know why. I want to know who I came from. I want to see her. I want to ask her questions. I want to know why she did what she did and see if I feel anything for her. I'm living with space. Living with empty space, this weird mystery that you and Nana Bird get, but I don't, and I need to get in that space and see it better because she's the space."

I groaned inwardly, and it was a shaky, troubled groan.

This meeting wouldn't be easy. It would be emotional and unpredictable. Brooke was unpredictable.

I could be making an awful mistake by letting her in Tate's life. I could be.

I hoped I wasn't.

TATE'S AWESOME PIGSKIN BLOG

I do not have a date for Winter Formal.

It's not as if ladies are bashing down my door. Who wants to go to a dance with a kid with a head the size of a spaceship? I get it. But the formal sounds fun. You can dance. You can eat. All the food is free. There's some bubbly, sparkly stuff to drink. There's cool music.

I don't think I dance with any rhythm, no beats either, but I'm going to give it a shot. I can wiggle. Maybe that's enough. I know I'm a better dancer than Milt and Anthony. Those two look like worms on hooks when they dance.

I probably look like a half lizard/half bouncing atom when I dance. So, if anyone wants to go with me, a half lizard/half bouncing atom dancer, to Winter Formal, please let me know.

I am looking for someone with these special qualities:

1. Female.
2. Not from outer space, although I will bend this rule if there are no antennae.
3. A brain. Again, not a firm rule.
4. Dressed. No naked dates. My Boss Mom would have a fit. Hey! I'll take a naked date, but I would have to meet you at the school.

That's it! If you want to be my date, let me know!

Here's a photo of Albert Einstein's lab.

Here's a photo of Clara Barton helping people.

Here's a photo of Itzhak Perlman playing his violin.

Here's a photo of Bobby Fischer playing chess.

Here's a photo of Madame Curie.

"I want to die."

"I understand."

"No, Jaden, I don't think you do. I want to die now. Immediately. I don't want to wait this out another six months. I don't want to wait this out another month."

I held the hand of one of my favorite patients ever, General Jerry Ross. General Ross is ninety years old. He is career military, starting in WWII. He landed at Normandy. He does not talk about it.

He stayed in the military for twenty-five years, married Mrs. Ross, and had five kids. He was bored being a retired military man so he bought a failing lumber company and built it back up. His daughter runs the company now. She had five kids, too.

Perhaps this story will best explain General Ross's character.

Ten years ago, a young man with an impressively long rap sheet named Arrel Hood hit Mrs. Ross in the face with his fist, and ran off with her purse. Mrs. Ross was seventy-nine years old and had a cane. Mr. Hood later said he thought Mrs. Ross would be an "easy target," because she was old and the guy next to her was even older.

That was a bad mistake. General Ross took off running after Arrel Hood, his legs pumping. He tackled Arrel to the ground, hit him in the face three times, *boom boom boom,* flipped him over, then used his own belt to tie the guy's hands behind his back until the police arrived. Two men in their twenties told the police, "We ran over to help the old guy, but he was beating the crap out of the purse stealin' guy and didn't need help so we watched. It was awesome."

In court, the young man admitted what he'd done. General Ross stood up, straight and tall, and barked out, "I demand an apology for my wife. Stand up, hoodlum, and apologize to my wife like a man."

The judge told him to do it. Arrel stood up and mumbled something.

"Shoulders back, chin up, chest out," General Ross ordered, drill sergeant–style. "Speak articulately! Speak!"

The young man tried again, General Ross interrupted.

"This is what you say, repeat after me and you'll learn how to make an effective apology and you won't sound like a stoned baboon! Mrs. Ross, I am an idiot. Say that!"

The defendant bent his head, then lifted it up when General Ross ordered him to. "Pull your head back up on your neck and do what I tell you to do!"

"Mrs. Ross," Arrel said, embarrassed. "I am an idiot."

This is the rest of what the young hoodlum was forced to repeat: "I stole your purse because I am lazy and don't want to work, therefore I have no money of my own. I have a problem with marijuana and alcohol. I use both because I have no backbone. I am sorry that I hit you, Mrs. Ross. I am sorry I took your purse. I am sorry I scared you and gave you months of nightmares. That is no way to treat a lady. I am sorry that I am a coward. When I get out of jail, I'm going to quit being a weak, spineless, jellyfish loser. I'm going to get a job and be productive and pay taxes because I live in America and no one should be allowed to be deadweight, especially me, Arrel."

Now and then General Ross would yell, "Shoulders back, chin up, chest out! Stand up! What are you made of, glue? What are you made of, rubber?"

It made front page news.

That's General Ross. As he was quoted in the paper, "That young man needs the military! They'll shape him up! They did me!"

I held General Ross's hand as he rested in bed, wearing an adult diaper.

"Jaden, my lady, I'm ready to go and give God a hello." He smiled at me, totally at peace.

"I think we need to talk about more pain control and—"

"Jaden." His voice was raspy. "I am dying of bladder cancer, which has spread all over this ol' boy. I am in a diaper, as you know. The other day I pissed myself and it ran down my leg. I am in terrible pain, which I can only control with a massive amount of drugs that make me dizzy, exhausted, incoherent, and nauseous."

"We can try—"

"No, Jaden. You're a dear lady, but we're not *trying* anything else. We've tried it all. I can't live like this anymore, peeing on myself, my bowels a mess, hurting all over, all day. It's not a life. I need you to inject whiskey into me until I die a drunken, but happy death. Any chance you'll help me?"

"Hmmm." I tapped my forehead with a finger. "Let me think. I might. My ancestors had an innate love of whiskey. I can put it in your IV."

"On a serious note"—he patted my hand, his eyes firm, somewhat sad, but resolute—"I want an assisted death."

I was not surprised to hear this from him.

Assisted death is legal here in Oregon. It should not be called assisted suicide. Assisted suicide somehow implies that the person has a choice—to live or to die. An assisted death is radically different. The person is dying already and there is zero hope for recovery. Nada. No chance.

Assisted death helps a dying patient to leave earlier, on their own terms, with a shred of dignity still intact. Sometimes they are in torturous pain or enduring hellacious symptoms, like vomiting up fecal material or slowly suffocating. We hospice nurses and doctors do everything possible to help to alleviate this fallout.

In the end many people fear they will have no control over their withering bodies, their minds intact. There are stacks of rules and laws regulating it, doctors are involved, counselors, psychiatrists, etc. It is not as if a person who is terminal can decide one evening to cut out of life after watching their favorite cooking show and swallow something by the next commercial.

Some people hate that assisted death is legal; some staunchly defend it. And after all the outraged hoopla we've had here in Oregon, very, very few people actually do it. We control the pain and symptoms of the terminally ill, and they die naturally. The ones who do elect for an assisted death often share the same characteristics as General Ross: independent, educated, strong-willed.

"I want to cut out early and miss the rest of this," General Ross said. "I don't like good-byes. I don't want to put my family through any more of this, either, but mostly I'm being selfish. I've got a diaper on my ass and someone wiping it. Stupid. This is exactly where I didn't want to be. Yesterday two young nurses lifted my ass and gave it a cleaning, then put a diaper on and I messed it up five minutes later. God has a strange sense of humor, that's clear.

"Yesterday I was in so much pain I had to get help getting off the can. I can't walk anymore. I used to run strategy sessions, now I'm inhaling medicine like they're peppermint candies and trying not to wet fart in my diaper. I can hardly breathe and I know this is gonna get worse. Do you want to experience air being slowly sucked out of your lungs while you flop around, a human fish on land?"

"No."

"That's what is happening to me. Can you help me?"

"No. As a hospice nurse, that isn't my role. But you can talk to your doctor, your wife and kids, and they'll handle it from there. You're sure about this?"

"I'm perfectly sure. My life was my own business and my death is my own business, too. It's not anyone else's and I'll do what I think is right for me, no interference, damn it."

I squeezed General Ross's hand, he squeezed back.

"I've had a blessed life, Jaden. I want to end it blessed, too.

On my terms, not helpless and hopeless and riding out one hu-
miliation after another as I decay further, a living corpse."

"I understand." I tried not to cry.

"I knew you would. So, let's change the subject. Let's talk
about the craziest things you've ever done, Jaden...."

We chatted about the craziest things we'd ever done and
laughed and laughed. I leaned down to hug him before I left.

"I smell cinnamon on you, Jaden, as usual."

"That's because before I came to see you I ate eleven red cinnamon Gummi Bears and I smell nutmeg on you."

It was our usual parting good-bye.

It would be our last good-bye.

Assisted death is a newish sort of term.

It is not a newish sort of . . . concept.

It's been going on since man began.

Think people haven't suffocated, poisoned, or shot dying
family and friends, dying buddies on the battlefield, to put them
out of their misery over the centuries? Ha.

People sometimes suffer terribly when they die. The process
can be minutes, hours, weeks, or months long. Sometimes people are suffering greatly for years.

It is an understatement to say that it's hard to watch.

It was hard for my parents and Grandma Violet to watch. It
was hard for Caden, Brooke, and me to watch, too.

My grandpa Pete broke his back when his tractor rolled over
him one summer when I was thirteen. He was sixty-eight and in
the hospital for weeks. When he came home, he was still in
grave pain and could hardly move. He was struck with double
pneumonia, which came back again and again like repeat hurri-
canes. In the last eighteen months of his life he was diagnosed
with two malignant, untreatable, metastasizing tumors on his
back, with several shattered vertebrae. It turned each inch of his
world into an ocean of pain.

Pain management wasn't what it is today, and his suffering
was almost unspeakable. I remember as a child listening to his
raspy screaming.

Grandpa Pete was a quiet, kind man.

He and Grandma Violet were in love from the moment they met, Grandma Violet topless in that forest, until the moment she killed him. For months, my spices and herbs at our house in the Hollywood Hills had smelled threatening—rotting, molding, decaying. I didn't know what it was. I told my mother. She told me it meant death. She wrapped me in her arms and said, "I bet I know whose death it is."

"Sweetheart," Grandpa Pete groaned to Grandma Violet one night from bed, with me sitting in the hundred-year-old rocking chair nearby, his voice hoarse from agony, "it's time."

And that was it.

Two words. "It's time."

My mother, Brooke, Caden, and I were already here, and the next night my father flew in from the hacienda house in the Hollywood Hills, his handsome face miserable, tears streaming down. He had been in the midst of a movie script, but family came first and I hugged that teddy bear of a father tight. "I love you, Aquamarine. I'm sorry about Grandpa Pete."

We all sat around Grandpa Pete's bed and sang songs and laughed and talked that summer night, when the wind was soft and the sunset particularly bright, streaked with red. We had steak, sweet potatoes, and key lime pie, his favorites. He couldn't eat, but said, "I'm enjoying the meal through you."

Caden had Grandpa Pete's steak, I ate his sweet potatoes, and Brooke ate his key lime pie.

My parents cried, as did Grandma Violet.

That night when I was in bed, I heard the floor creak outside my door and I spied on my mother and Grandma Violet. They were mixing something in the kitchen, carefully, quietly. It was a liquid.

I ducked behind a door, then crept down the hallway to Grandma Violet and Grandpa Pete's bedroom.

My father was there, hugging Grandpa Pete, candles lit, Mozart in the background.

Grandma Violet climbed into their four-poster bed with him and held him close, their tears mingling.

"I love you, sweetheart," Grandpa Pete said. "Love you forever."

"And I love you. You were my greatest joy."

My mother bent to kiss his cheeks.

"I could not have had a better daughter, Rowan. Never."

And I watched, in the dim light, as Grandma Violet held the glass for Grandpa Pete with the mixture she and my mother had concocted for him. He drank most of it. He could not drink the rest because his eyes shut and he slumped down.

I sat in the hallway and cried. I knew what had happened. I knew why they did it.

I have never, even in all the years I've been a hospice nurse, seen anyone in the kind of sustained, excruciating pain Grandpa Pete had been in.

When Grandma Violet and my mother finally limped out of the room, leaning heavily on each other, they hugged me close, after exchanging a shocked look. They had not known I was there. I could hear my father crying from the old rocking chair.

"You understand, Jaden?" Grandma Violet said.

I nodded. I understood. It had been time. "Yes, Grandma Violet."

"Sometimes healing is used to help dying people into heaven. The women in our family, even Faith herself, have always known this, and used it when they had to." She kissed me. She was broken. She had lost her husband, her best friend, her life.

Do I think my mother and Grandma Violet, at that time, with the medicines they didn't have, did the right thing for my Grandpa Pete?

Yes, I do.

Absolutely. Immediately after Grandpa Pete died, the stench in my herbs and spices went away, but the grief for Grandpa Pete cut Grandma Violet in half.

In a little over a year, on a fall day when the leaves were burnt orange, sunny yellow, and rose pink, Grandma Violet was gone, passing in her sleep, a serene smile on her face. In the three months before she died, I could hardly stand my herbs and spices because they smelled rancid, nauseatingly foul and, again, *threatening*. Now I knew what it meant. I told my mom what I smelled. I told her I thought it was for Grandma Violet.

The death smell in my spices and herbs have never given me names.

Sometimes that's a blessing and sometimes it's just another curse.

14

Tate's next game was at home again and the gym was packed. We were people sardines. I was a people sardine with a heavy heart because of Ethan, but I was determined to stop thinking about him for two hours. Two hours, I told myself. Breathe, block out the throbbing pain.

The team was practicing when my mother, Caden, Damini, the triplets, and I walked in. It had snowed earlier in the day, the snowflakes light, drifting down in a snowflake dance, but it had melted by game time.

We were all wearing the team colors, orange and black, we simply wore them differently. I had on jeans, black knee-high boots with buckles, and a Mid Court Mob shirt. Caden had cut the sleeves off his Mid Court Mob shirt so his bulky shoulders and massive arms showed. Damini had French-braided his hair with an orange and black ribbon. She wore jeans and the Mid Court Mob shirt and a huge pile of ribbons around her pony-tail.

My mother wore a Mid Court Mob shirt, fashionable jeans, a black belt around her waist, and four-inch black stilettos. The triplets all wore Mid Court Mob shirts and a combination of these things: a black cape, orange wings, a Spider Man mask, bear feet, leopard claws, a unicorn horn.

The whistle blew. Tate did not start.

My guess is that Coach Boynton was giving him time to warm up—mentally speaking.

Six minutes into the first quarter, we had two points. The opponent had sixteen.

"Tate!" Coach Boynton called. Tate ran up from the end of the bench and stood by the coach.

He seemed nervous. Before the game he'd told me that he was afraid he was going to be a disappointment. "I made all those points last time, Mom, but I don't know if I can do it again."

I saw the stark fear in his eyes and some lurking sadness caused by an awareness that he could take a lot of heat tonight. "Honey, do your best, that's it."

"Mom, you don't get it. Kids at school have been coming up to me and talking to me. In one way, it ticks me off because I'm the same person I was before I scored all those points, and now I'm getting all this attention, but in another way, I'm glad I'm not being made fun of, either, and people aren't avoiding looking at me.

"Plus, my making all those points gave people something to talk about with me. You know, it started the conversation. But now I'm afraid I'm going to blow it, then they'll all hate me again, and avoid me, and I do think that's pathetic, you know, that I want to make points to make friends, but it's my reality in this galaxy. For once in my life, I want to have friends, people to say hi to in the hallways, to sit with at lunch, hang out with at PE, and be normal, you know what I mean?"

"Yeah, I know, Tate." How I had wished for, longed for, Tate to be "normal."

And yet.

The truth is, Tate would not be Tate without the insight, compassion, and sensitivity that had come to him through this hardship. That's the gift of not being normal. Let's face it, you become a deeper person amidst adversity. You become a more perceptive, strong, resilient person when life is not handed to you on a silver platter held by a butler.

"I don't want to screw up in front of all those people, Boss Mom. I don't want kids to say, 'Why didn't you do better? We lost because of you!' "

I thought about what to say. I didn't want to spurt out platitudes. I didn't want to tell him that he'd do "great." We didn't know if he would do great. I didn't want to roll over and dismiss his genuine and understandable concerns. Eventually, I said what I thought, off the tip of my tongue.

"Tate, just throw the damn ball up."

I could tell he was surprised, then his face broke into a grin, that grin I love seeing. "Okay."

"Aim, throw. That's it. Start there."

"Got it, Boss Mom."

But his nerves were still jangling, I could tell. "Come on, Tate," I whispered, as he sprinted up the court after the opposing team scored yet another basket. "Come on, Tate." *Please don't let Tate get hurt. Please don't let Tate get hurt.*

His teammate, Kendrick the gecko kid, passed him the ball, three feet out of the three-point line.

Tate aimed as a defender rushed him. He shot. It arched way, way up, then slammed into the backboard and swished.

Oh yeeeaaahh! Three-pointer.

We flew out of our seats, the players on the bench jumped up, Coach Boynton fisted both hands into the air and shouted, "Taaatttee! I felt it *in my bones!*"

The opposing coach put a hand to his face.

Caden yelled, "That's my boy, Tate!"

The triplets bopped up and down and growled. Damini hooted 'til she was hoarse.

I thought my mother and Caden were going to die of ecstasy.

"He is dancing with his rainbow!" my mother screamed. "He is dancing!"

Water ran in a steady stream out of my eyes.

Tate's game was incredible.

He made three three-pointers in the second quarter alone. The opposing team quickly started double-teaming him. That left a man on his team open. Tate passed it to that open player, that guy made the point, or passed it off.

With one minute left in the third quarter, Coach Boynton

pulled Tate out. He was way across the court, in the corner, and started running toward the bench.

And for my Tate, the kid with the big head and the uneven bright blue eyes, my endearing Tate, who has endured taunts and relentless bullying and aloneness his whole life, there was a standing ovation.

Even some of the parents and kids on the other side stood up and clapped for him.

When Tate was almost to our end of the court, Coach Boynton met him, hugged him, and lifted him up high, then pointed at the parent section and the kid section, both standing and clapping for him, along with his teammates.

Tate, sweet Tate, turned around, a three-hundred-and-sixty-degree circle, his face absolutely, positively stunned, then he broke into a huge smile, and cried. He wiped a hand across his face.

His tears made all of us clap harder, stomp harder, cheer harder.

He is his momma's boy.

"Yea, Tate! Yea, Tate!" I shouted.

"Hip boom bah! You're the crow's caw!" my brother yelled.

"You're a ball breaker, Tate," my mother boomed. "Ball breaker!"

At that time, we were ahead by fifteen.

We won, seventy-eight to fifty-four. Tate went back in in the fourth quarter and made twelve points, much to the delirium of our crowd. This was the first time, the first time, *in years* that this team has won games.

Tate was not able to come home and shoot baskets after the game. He was invited out with his team for pizza and pop.

When he came home he said, "Best night of my life, Mom. Best night. I squished pepperoni pizza, a hot dog, and chocolate pudding together with my Billy and Bob hands and ate it."

"And how did that culinary art taste?"

"Not bad, not bad at all. I took a photo of it for my blog. I also ate eight pieces of pizza. Pretty impressive, if I do say so myself."

TATE'S AWESOME PIGSKIN BLOG

Here is a photo of what pizza, a hot dog, and chocolate pudding look like together.

What's your favorite strange food?

Have a nice night.

I pulled on my red rain boots and a coat and headed outside into the dark, snowy night. I tipped my head back and caught snowflakes with my mouth, my arms straight out as I spun.

I made a snow angel.

I made a second snow angel by the first angel and had them holding hands.

I thought of Ethan until I was soaked, lying there in the snow, alone.

Alone.

"Hey! There's Dr. Robbins!"

"*What?*"

"Yup." Tate ate half a maple bar with one bite, and through the doughnut mumbled, "That's a yum yum doozer. I need another maple bar." He checked his cell phone for the time. "I knew it. He's on time. To the minute."

I dropped the wooden spoon I was using to make spice muffins with walnuts and blueberries. Tate calls them the Blue Nut Man Muffins. I had many cookbooks laid open on my kitchen table in my search for the perfect recipe, there was flour in my hair, nutmeg on my tattered college sweatshirt, and I had no makeup on. I stared out the window, past our brick path, covered in a cool winter rain, and there was Ethan coming on down in his truck.

"What . . . why is . . ." I sucked in my breath, hard and raspy, even as I felt my heart heat up at the sight of him.

Ethan smiled and waved at me through the windshield. I

backed away from the window as if a grenade had zipped through it.

"What is he doing here, Tate?" Part of me was whizzing with love and lust, the other with baffled confusion.

Tate ate the other half of the maple bar, then mumbled something else through the dough and maple icing that I didn't understand.

"Tate!"

He chewed and chewed and I could tell he was laughing at me.

"Why is he here?" I heard the door of Ethan's truck slam.

"I invited him."

"You what?"

"I invited him. It was a polite invitation. Charming. I was charming."

"You didn't."

He looked at me quizzically. "Yes, I did. There's proof. He's right there."

"But . . ." I started to sweat. "Why?"

He winked at me. "Yeah. You need to ask why? Think, think, think!"

"What are you talking about?"

"Come on, Mom. You're in love with him. He's in love with you. Let's get this show a rollin'." He did a few dance steps, jiving his shoulders, wiggling his hips. "Love is in the air and you two won't do anything about it, so General Noggin and I sat down and thought about things, and Billy and Bob made a phone call to Dr. Robbins, and Bert and Ernie listened, and now he's here on a Saturday morning. Too bad Nana Bird's not here. She would have loved to be here. I'll call her later and give her the details and she'll be cackling like a witch." He grinned at me. "You know she's a witch. You, too, Boss Mom. I need another maple bar and I think General Noggin does, too."

"You didn't tell me he was coming, you didn't tell me you were doing this, you should have asked—"

"Yes, I did tell. I told you one minute ago."

"Tate, take a peek at your mother! I was up 'til two in the morning with a patient, I haven't had a shower. I'm as gross as . . . as . . ."

"As a sick witch, out dancing under the moonlight with her coven? I like that word, *coven*. Do witches like maple bars?"

I sucked in my breath. "That bad?"

"Yup." He laughed. "Nah, Mom, I'm kidding. You're cool."

The doorbell rang. I sniffed under my arms. Oh no. I felt my hair. Yuck. I glanced at a mirror in the hall. Yikes. I knew I'd let myself go some after saying good-bye to Ethan, and now it had caught up to me. "Get the door, Tate," I whispered. "And you're grounded for . . . for . . . forever. I'll be down in a minute."

I shot up the back stairs and leaped into the shower.

How do women talk and lust at the same time? How do women coherently discuss their greenhouses, the climbing frogs on the post, the watering can collection, and an obsessive number of books on herbs and spices while thinking about making love between potting tables?

How do women explain why they enjoy having their teacups, favorite teas, and a full and complete spice rack inside that greenhouse, when staring into the brown cinnamon eyes of a man they love?

How?

I tried. I did. But my, it was burnin' hot all of a sudden with Ethan next to all my herbs. Maybe it was all the candles I'd lit at first, being jittery and nervous, and not knowing what to do with my hands. I must have lit thirty, all now flickering. I am endlessly strange.

Ethan was kind and funny and gentle. "Tate didn't tell you that he invited me out, did he, Jaden?"

"Ah, no." I picked up a group of clay pots, I don't know why, and held them in front of me.

"Ah. He invited me to lunch here. . . ."

"Yes . . . to lunch? We can have lunch soup or pancakes or Popsicles and, and, and . . ." I rushed. "I'm . . . I'm glad you're here." I put the clay pots down. I don't know why they had to be set down. I forgot to check and see if the pots were over a shelf or a table and they broke into a hundred pieces on the floor. "Darn it."

We picked up the pieces and I grabbed paper towels, a broom, and we had that pot mess cleaned up in a second.

"Would you . . . could I pour you some tea, Ethan?" I wiped my simmering brow when I thought of him strolling naked amidst my tomatoes. "I also have gingerbread cookies out here. Tate, the triplets, and I made them. We even decorated them with icing. We turned them into Cyclops, robots, and pink spiders, but they still taste tasty. He calls them the Gingerbread Brigade." *Please do shut up, Jaden.*

"Sure. Thanks. This is the most incredible greenhouse I've ever seen." He grinned. "It's not a traditional greenhouse, though, is it? The woodstove, the Chinese lanterns, your collection of teapots. It's amazing. I can see why you like being out here."

I hoped I wouldn't start to sweat profusely. "Yes, it's peaceful and romantic." *Shoot! Shut your mouth, Jaden.* "Not romantic. I didn't mean that. It's herby. Spicy. Peacefully." *Peacefully?*

We waited in the awkward, steamin' silence together. I reached for another clay pot, then withdrew my hand as I thought of straddling Ethan on my wicker chair with the red pillow. The pot toppled over and I caught it before it hit the floor. I put the pot back, then stared at a ceramic peacock I had on a shelf to distract my rampaging lust.

"Jaden." Ethan took a step closer, towering over me. He seemed taller, and broader, he was a love-tractor, without the white coat on.

"Jaden, I don't know how to say this exactly right, so you'll have to forgive me." He exhaled heavily, and I knew he was nervous. That made me nervous. I had lust and nerves, all swimming around together.

"What . . . what do you want to say? It's nothing about Tate, right?"

"No, he's fine, but yes, it is about him. It's mostly about what we talked about earlier. Last time. When you were in the office with Tate. Me. And . . . and you."

"Me . . . me and you?" Ha! A me and him! His soft brown eyes were luscious.

"Yes." He turned away for long seconds, then turned back, steel in his voice, brooking no argument. "I have found another doctor for Tate."

My lust flew out the windows of my greenhouse. "Oh no! You didn't! I thought we talked about this? You can't do that. Please say you didn't do that."

Something deep and painful flashed in his eyes. "His name is Dr. Raminsky. The hospital, on my recommendation, has hired him and he's here now. I've known him for years. We went to medical school together. He graduated second in our class, and he's an extremely talented pediatric neurosurgeon. Top-notch."

"But, but, but . . ." I swallowed hard. "I don't want Dr. Raminsky, I want you. I want you to be Tate's doctor." I felt myself growing cold now. Freezing cold.

Ethan ran a hand over his face. He was so stressed, so strained.

"You're not moving, are you?" That was my worst nightmare. Losing Tate's doctor for Tate and losing Ethan for me. "Please say you're not moving."

"No, no. I'm staying right here. But Jaden . . . you see, I . . ."

I felt Witch Mavis start to rise; it did whenever I was scared or worried about Tate or his well-being. I became snappish and rude. Was this because of our last conversation? Couldn't he ignore what was between us? Maybe he was sick of all this. I was an embarrassment to him. "I know this is awkward, maybe I'm clingy, too. I'll be better. I'll be more calm. Sweet. I can be sweet and detached. It'll be hard for me, but I'll change. Please. I don't even have to come in with Tate anymore to see you. I'll stay in the car. I'll sit there. No honking. I'll wait. Please. I want Tate to be your patient."

"I'm sorry, I don't want to make you uncomfortable, feel free to ask me to leave immediately, but I think I owe you an explanation."

"I think you do, too. Yes, you do." I crossed my arms over my pounding heart. "Give it to me."

"He doesn't need me anymore, Jaden. He's doing great. If something comes up, Dr. Raminsky can handle it."

"He does need you. I need you—" I shut my trap. *I need you.* Lord. "I mean. I need you to be the doctor for Tate. Don't hand him off, please . . ."

"Jaden, I can't be his doctor anymore because I don't have a professional relationship with you."

"What? Yes, you do. We have for years! What are you talking about? It's always been us. The three of us."

"That's it, Jaden, right there. It's always been the three of us."

I saw the anguish on his face, the unleashed emotions running below the surface.

"Always," I whispered. "I don't want that to change."

"Jaden. I like you." His jaw clenched.

"I like you, too." And I love you. *Please stay as Tate's doctor.* "But then . . . why? Why would you leave us? Why, Ethan?"

"I can't be Tate's doctor because I . . ."

He was sick of us. Oh my God. He was sick of me, my pitiful, longing eyes, my semi-obsession with him. He probably knew I daydreamed about him all the time, and wanted to get away from my daydreams . . . he felt stalked . . . "But we're all friends . . ."

"Yes, we are. But I . . . I haven't said this before because I wanted to make sure, absolutely sure, that Tate wouldn't need me anymore, but he doesn't, and, Jaden, I . . ."

I held my breath, then tipped my head back for a second to study the dried lavender hanging from the rafters between wicker baskets and tried to get my heart to slow down.

"Jaden, for years now—"

I could barely stand this.

"Jaden . . . I . . . I am in love with you."

I am in love with you. I am in love with you.

For once, I was speechless, in a spectacular sort of way. In a relieved, joyous, click-my-heels way. *I am in love with you.*

"I think I'm catching you off guard, not going about this right, but I have felt this for a long time." He pushed his glasses up. "I have not felt that I could develop a relationship with you"—he raised his hand—"and I am not presuming that you would wish a relationship with me, but I never would have told you today that I loved you if there hadn't been another doctor for Tate that I trust implicitly."

I put the love part aside for a millisecond. "You're sure about the doctor? No question on your end? I have to have an outstanding doctor for Tate . . ." Dare I hope?

"I would never let Tate be with any doctor that wasn't outstanding. Surely you know that by now?" he said. "This is why I've waited until I knew he was completely stable, had been for a long time, and I had another doctor in place."

My thirty-odd candles flickered again as I felt happiness slip on in. . . .

"I . . . Jaden, I have loved you for years, pretty much since the first day that we met. I thought I was falling, but in a good way, in a way I never have before, and I have fought with myself about how I felt about you because I didn't see a relationship working. And maybe it won't work now, but after all this time I . . ." He rubbed his face with both hands, then lowered them. "I've been alone for a long time, waiting for you, waiting for this to possibly work, and I don't want to turn eighty and always, always wonder what would have happened if I'd been honest with you."

I wrung my hands. Oh, how I loved his romantic honesty!

"I don't want to be pushy here, Jaden, but think about this, if you want to. Call me. Or e-mail if you don't want to talk. Send a smoke signal."

"Ethan." I tried to gather my thoughts. The man was a wreck. Anxious. Worried. And in his eyes . . . oh my goodness. There it was. Love.

Love. Tra la la. Love.

"I . . . Ethan." I could be coy. I could take this slow and easy.

Ha! That is not my way! "Ethan, I have loved you since I met you, too."

His eyes grew bright, and I realized there were tears in them. Tears! For us!

"You have, Jaden?"

"Yes. For me, too, it was the first day, when we shook hands."

"I remember. I didn't let go of your hand."

"I know. You didn't. Tate had to pull our hands apart. But are you sure about me, though? I'm temperamental. Moody. Too serious. Sometimes vengeful. I have a bizarre relationship with my herbs and spices that no one else appears to have. I'm picky about cooking. I'm blunt and pushy and I have not had a boyfriend in years, so that's going to make me awkward. And I am clumsy and blunt, I don't even know if I'm romantic. . . ."

"You're incisive. You're interesting. You're light and laughter and depth all in one. I love how loud you laugh, how you love Tate. I love the sound of your voice, how engaged you are in life, and the way you move. I love that you're unselfish, you gave up your life for Tate. I love your dedication and your loyalty and your whole family. I don't mind the temper or the seriousness I see in you because I understand where it comes from. It's who you are. And I have never, ever felt around anyone as I do you, Jaden. I'm happy when I'm with you. And when you walk out of our appointments I'm not happy anymore. I miss you."

"You miss me?"

"All the time." His voice caught. "I miss you. I want us to be together, as a couple. It feels as if we've been dating for years, only not the normal way."

"Then, then . . ." I paused. "Okay!" I chuckled. I didn't mean to, but I did, and he smiled and I chuckled again. I think the chuckles sounded how a chipmunk's chuckle would sound. "Okay!"

I don't know who moved first. Let's say that lust powered us forward, his arms pulling me in close, and I sank into his kiss, warm and sexy, my head tipped back, my chest pressed up tight to his and we kissed and kissed, hands running around some, and a few pants and groans and we only stopped kissing when we realized I was on fire.

Literally, truly on fire.

I smelled smoke, I felt heat, I saw the fire leaping on my shirt.

Within seconds Ethan literally ripped my shirt right off my body, then dumped a watering can, full of water, over my back and side.

"You're quick, Ethan." I stood there, soaked, no shirt on, my pink lace push-up bra on full display.

"Are you okay? You're not burned, are you?" He was worried, professional all of a sudden, touching me where the fire had been. I had apparently leaned back into one of my scented candles.

"Yes, I'm fine." I laughed. "That was an unforgettable kiss."

He grinned at me, his gaze for a millisecond slipping to that pink push-up bra. I glanced down. I am rather proud of my lush rack, and in one of those expensive push-up bras, the boobs were up and alert and bouncy. I was deeply grateful that I had worn my pink lacy one, rather than the white, stained one.

"You don't know how grateful I am that I didn't wear my white stained bra," I breathed.

Then he laughed, and I laughed and he swept me up into another kiss, chest to chest, and he took my pink push up bra off and sent it to the floor.

We were positively *on fire*.

That night, as I stared at the stars from my rocking chair in the dark, I dared to hope. I dared to believe I could be with Ethan, that I would have him holding my hand, holding me, for the rest of my life.

Finally, some of the loneliness and aloneness that had been with me for years was ebbing away. I felt myself losing some of my own hardness, my own toughness, my temper mellowing because the anger inside of me was mellowing.

It was love that was doing it. I knew it. It was love.

I rocked gently.

TATE'S AWESOME PIGSKIN BLOG

I want to thank all of you who wrote to me and said you would be my date to the Winter Formal. I now have nineteen requests from girls at our school and about forty from other places, and I am pumped up. But see, now I have a problem because, who do I take to the formal?

This is the most excellent problem I have ever had in my life. General Noggin and I are stoked and we appreciate all the ladies.

So, I have a thought.

Let's all go together. Dudes and dudettes. No one has a real date, know what I'm saying? We'll go in a group to the Winter Formal and dance our brains out.

Boss Mom said we could all come over here before it starts. We can have pizza, pop, beer. Ha! No, I'm kidding on the beer. No alcohol. Boss Mom would call the police herself if she saw anyone here with alcohol, so leave it next to your Barbie collection, or in Uranus, or under your sister's armpit, or wherever it is you keep your liquor, and come on over.

Who wants to come?

Later that night, Tate banged down the stairs with a sheepish grin.

"Hey, Boss Mom, how many kids did you say I could have here before the Winter Formal?"

"Why?"

"Uh, ugh. Hmm. You know I'm hungry."

"You're always hungry. How about another Cornish game

hen? I believe you named the first one you ate tonight Sarah Intestine. Maybe you can eat her sister, Sarah Intestine II. There's an extra one."

"Yeah, that'd be sweet. I'll eat it, but about that number."

"You invited a few people, right?"

"Yeah. Boy. Yeah, okay. Ugh."

"What's the number, Tate?"

"Dudette, you know you always say I can have people over."

"How many?"

He put an apple in his mouth and muttered something.

"What?"

He stuck a banana in there, too, and muttered something else.

"Now, Tate. What's the number?"

"One hundred and twelve kids."

Brooke had to stay in Los Angeles until her face lost the purple/blue/green colors from the bruising, that was a given. I could not have Tate traumatized by her most recent beating, but I told him he could call her at my mom's house in the Hollywood Hills if he wanted.

After basketball practice, lasagna, and a huge piece of chocolate cake with peppermint ice cream, I said, "Are you sure you want to call her?" I was sickly nervous.

"Yeah, Boss Mom, I am."

"Okay, son." It felt like I was pushing my son to the edge of a cliff and we didn't know if there was a parachute attached to his back.

"She's my Other Mother. I've never talked to her. I want to hear her voice. I want to know something about her that I don't already know. It's weird to worry about someone you've never met, and I know she doesn't deserve for me to worry over her but I do. I want to know about her, who she is, so I know more about myself and our whole family. I've heard a lot of stories about Faith and Grace, but not a lot about her. It doesn't make sense, I know, but I can't get this out of my head."

"Here's the number, sweets." I bent over as my stomach

cramped and I envisioned Tate's toes edging over the side of that cliff.

The clock ticked loud in my kitchen. The kettle whistled next to the tiles painted with red poppies. I was making black tea.

My sister knew that Tate was going to call tonight. I hoped she answered. I hoped she didn't.

"Hi," I heard Tate say. "Uh . . . this is Tate."

I waited for a minute, listening carefully, feeling my stomach sink, my hands sweat, my mind a swirling mass of emotions. I couldn't tell if Tate was going over the cliff with a parachute or in free fall.

"Oh no. You're crying, aren't you?" Tate said into the phone. "I'm sorry! No, okay, I won't be sorry. . . . I don't want to make you cry. . . . They're happy tears? . . . I know you're sorry . . . I know. . . . General Noggin and I aren't mad. . . . General Noggin is my head. . . . Mom told you that already? We've had a cool life. . . . Yeah, Boss Mom is rockin'. . . . We all make bad choices, Brooke. Is that okay to call you Brooke? . . . You've always loved me? You have?"

I drank my tea, then ate four red cinnamon Gummi Bears. Only in the future would I know if Tate had that parachute on.

15

Tate's team played Sunrise, our school's closest rival, on Friday night. They were a good team, but there was one kid on the team, TJ Hooks, who was a beast. I knew TJ Hooks because I knew his father.

Martin Hooks and I were the same year in high school. He was madly obsessed with Brooke. She turned him down, she was not attracted to beefy football players who weren't that bright and had faces scrunched up like warthogs, but he would not take no for an answer. My mother had to call the police so he would quit pestering her.

About a year later, Martin moved on to me, asking me out, calling. I refused. Again, my mother had to call the police on him because he would not quit driving by our house, coming to our door, and calling. I do not say this lightly, but the man truly does have a violent personality disorder. There is something insidious, something truly off about him.

Martin Hooks was currently a "businessman" who owned a gun shop in the city, and we all hated him. He had been married to TJ's mother, Joyce, for five years, but she left him and took custody of TJ, partly because Martin threatened her with a gun.

It turned out that Joyce Hooks, who had been a meek, homely, and intensely shy mouse of a woman when she first married Martin, was having an affair. It is the only time I have heard of someone having an affair and *no one* blamed the spouse for cheating.

"I would cheat if I was married to him, too," Caden said. "I want him to hit me one day, then I could put him in a headlock until he begged for breath."

"I wouldn't cheat. I'd poison him," my mother said. "Use the secret family combo of death-killing herbs and set that dog right down."

The man Joyce was having an affair with was a rather nerdy, but kind, college professor. Joyce had gone back to school. As soon as the class term ended, her English professor and she started meeting for coffee, then lunch, and fell in love over gourmet pizza. He told her one month into it to leave Martin or lose him, Mr. Professor.

Joyce made the right choice. She told me later it took less than one second. She went home after the pizza, packed up, took half their savings, left, rented an apartment, and started a new life.

Martin, however, had a fit. It was ugly. It was public. He rammed his car into the professor's. He started stalking both the professor and Joyce. He went to Joyce's classes at the college and sat in back of her, kicking her chair, until she called campus security and they took care of that right quick.

He parked in front of the professor's house and repeatedly tried to get Joyce to come out and talk to him, yelling, "You cheating scum whore!" until the police came. He attacked the professor once, swinging a huge fist at him, but the rather thin, nerdy professor had a black belt in karate and was also a marathon runner, and Martin ended up beat to crap and left prone and groaning on the sidewalk.

Martin had vowed to get Joyce back, "that cunt." He had been absolutely stunned when she'd left him, "that whore." I knew because he'd called here looking for her as Joyce and I are friends. "You tell that bitch to get her ass back home before I—"

"Shut up, Martin," I said.

"What?"

"Shut up. I'm not going to tell Joyce anything except, 'Why didn't you leave him sooner?' "

"What?"

"Quit harassing her. She's in love with someone else and doesn't want to be with you."

"In love?" he sputtered. "What do you mean?"

As if "in love" was a foreign concept. "As in, she's not in love with you."

"Yes, she is!"

"Why do you think that? What on earth did you do to keep your wife in love with you?"

"I . . . I . . ." he blustered. "I bought the house."

"You *both* bought the house. She put down half."

"I worked!"

"She did, too, and all you did was make her life miserable. Leave Joyce alone. She finally has her brains growing straight in her head and took off. Good-bye, Martin."

"You bitch, Jaden—"

I hung up.

There was no love lost between Martin and me. He was a tall, overweight white guy who resembled a sausage with shark eyes. He had a bulging stomach.

His son, TJ, was tall and lean, and overwhelmed by his father, who always stood on the sidelines of any game TJ was playing in. Martin would open his foul mouth, a gaping garbage disposal, and didn't shut up 'til the bell rang. He would be verbally abusive to the coaches and referees, too, and was often banned from games.

Martin Hooks is the type of arrogant, blind parent who believes, erroneously, that his son is bound for college basketball greatness. The truth is, TJ is a solid player, one of the top three scorers for his team, which, on a team of twelve, in a small town, isn't saying a ton. He is nowhere near strong enough for a college scholarship, but his father is delusional enough to think that he is.

The whistles blew the night of our game against Sunrise, the ref lowered the ball, then tossed it up for the tip-off. I could already hear Martin Hooks screaming, "Get in there, TJ, come on, move it, move your butt!"

The tip-off went straight to Tate.

"For God's sake, TJ!" Martin's voice zinged around that gym. "Don't let the Mongloid get it."

I exchanged a searing glance with my mother. Her eyelids lowered in disdain.

Martin shot me a dirty, victorious look across the gym as in, *I'll call your son whatever I want and you can't stop me.*

"I believe I'm going to beat the shit out of Martin," Caden told me, matter-of-factly. "It'll be after the game. You'll have to keep Damini and the triplets with you. Don't lose Harvey. He's dressed as an explorer tonight and he might wander off and you know Hazel always follows him. I'm going to lead a cheer now."

"Ohh! Can I watch the pummeling?" My mother clapped her hands. "I love a fist-punching fight. Will there be squirting blood? Mangled bones?"

"It will depend on my mood, Mom, and what Martin says to me, but you can watch if Jaden agrees to watch the kids."

"I'm going with you, Daddy!" Damini said. "I'm not gonna miss this."

"Ha ha! Jaden, you babysit! I'm going to the match!" My mother tapped my knee. "I will relish the moment and tell you all about it later so you can live it vicariously."

"But I want to see the pummeling—"

"Too bad! I'm older, I'm first. And"—she poked a finger in the air—"I'll have to protect Caden if he gets hurt."

It was so ludicrous to think of Martin hurting Caden it set off a giggle stint.

I will, again, not do a play-by-play of the game, but suffice it to say that Tate had four three-pointers right off the top. TJ Hooks was guarding Tate, and I could see his increasing frustration.

In a quieter moment I heard Martin shout, "It's called defense, TJ. You know what that is, right? Block the retard. . . . The space alien kid gets another basket? Hell, TJ, you can't do better? Are you even alive out there?"

"I think I will go after Martin myself," I said. "Then Caden can finish the job."

My mother cackled, then said, "Ohhh! I'll watch that, too. Caden babysits first while I watch you, then you babysit while I watch Caden!"

Martin peered with his beady eyes at my mother and me at that moment and tipped his mouth up at the corners in a creepy smirk. I did not hide the disgust on my face. My mother didn't, either. She flipped him off with both hands. She does not worry about someone taking photos of her and posting them on YouTube. She is too cool for that and too entrenched in Hollywood. Plus, many people in Tillamina grew up with her, they knew her parents and grandparents, they do not ever gush over her, and they proudly protect her privacy.

"First, though," my mother drawled, bringing her hands down, "I will finish my spell against Martin, the man who chased Brooke, who resembles boar's slobber." She wiggled her fingers. I put my hand over her hands. I don't believe in spells, but still.

She moved her hands from under mine, I grabbed them again, she moved, I grabbed. Honestly, we probably looked ridiculous. I'm trying to hold my mother's hands and she's pulling them away. I stopped when Caden yelled, "Stand up for the stomp cheer, folks!"

This one involved all of us parents standing up. We chanted, "Bobcats, bobcats, snarl and bite, don't give in, we'll fight fight fight!"

When we said "snarl," we were supposed to make scary faces. When we said "bite," we snapped our hands together. We fisted our hands in the air and stomped when we said, "Fight fight fight." At the end we yelled, "Bobcats!"

The triplets love that cheer. Damini added an extra hiss at the end.

My mother ripped her hands away from mine for about ten seconds. Ten. That was all it took. She touched the cross, heart, and star charms on her necklace as I made an "I can't believe this" sound in my throat.

I glanced over at Martin Hooks as my mother whispered a chant about stomach death. Within seconds, his mouth was shut and he was gripping that bulging stomach like he was holding a baby.

She wriggled those long fingers again. Martin bent over, then tried to straighten.

She giggled and said, "Hello, diarrhea!"

"He is diarrhea," Damini said. "Yuck."

I knew my mother did not cause his pain with her spell. The man was huge. He probably had a thousand farts wrapped up in that stomach, all dying to get out.

Martin tried to stand again. No go.

She giggled again. "Such power! I wish you were a spell believer, honey."

I rolled my eyes.

"I'm a spell believer, Nana!" Damini said. "We're witches."

Martin remained leaning half over, his garbage disposal mouth finally shut and not insulting TJ.

Meanwhile TJ was sticking to Tate like glue, and Tate the same to TJ, but Tate's defense was better. TJ could hardly shoot and he made few baskets. TJ was called for a technical for language and unsportsmanlike conduct against Tate. Tate shot the ball on the fouls and made the points.

Martin straightened up for a second and lambasted his son. "Get that creature! What the hell's wrong with you! Wake up!" A second later he hobbled off the bleachers and into the hallway.

"I love that spell." My mother sighed. "I am sooo good. I had a petticoats-on-fire problem, and I solved it."

"You did the freeing-of-the-bowel spell, didn't you?"

"Yes, I did. Freeing of the bowels is a specialty of mine, you know that."

"You know I don't believe in your spells of any sort."

"I know, darling. But he won't be back for a while, and that's what's important."

Martin Hooks wasn't back to see his son foul Tate a second and third time, but he was back to see the fourth foul.

"Are you a loser, TJ?" Martin roared at his *own son*. "You can't even win against this stupid team?"

Tate caught a pass with one hand, dribbled outside of the three-point line, turned, and shot. TJ rushed him, and Tate was knocked to the ground. The ball zipped through the net, three-pointer. I inhaled, sharp and tight, but Tate scrambled right back up.

"Nice going, TJ!" his dad hollered, but this time Martin meant it as a compliment, as in, excellent work bashing that kid. He grinned, maniacally, up at us. Caden spread his arms out wide and yelled, "You're still a dick, Martin."

Martin's face fell. There was no way he would challenge Caden. Caden would have him squirming on the ground like a pig.

Tate was called to the foul line, where he made three shots in a row.

We won by nineteen. Nineteen points. We had never beat Sunrise as far back as I could remember.

The win sent our crowd into delirium, and when the final whistle blew, kids jumped off the bleachers onto the floor. The triplets and Damini followed them down. Tate's glorious smile told me all I needed to know.

He was safe. He was happy.

I was grateful.

My mother tapped me on the back. "Now do you believe in my spells?"

"Oh, Mom."

"Once a witch, always a witch." She kissed my cheek. "Let's you, Caden, Tate, Damini, the triplets, and I go and have some wine after the pummeling."

"The kids can't drink wine, Mom."

"Darn it. You're right. I'll make them White Russians. There's cream in there, right?"

Later that night, in the parking lot, TJ Hooks leaned out the window of his team bus and yelled at Tate, "Hey, deformed, two-headed fuck, next time I will cream you into the ground and you will be a bowl of oatmeal with crooked eyes, which is what your face looks like."

To which Tate smiled, amidst all his victorious teammates, and said, "I love oatmeal! Apple cinnamon is my favorite, followed by brown sugar, third favorite is plain. You know, nothing special. Hey—you would relate to nothing special, TJ."

And Milt, such a true friend, said, "He's got a big head, that's true, but it's not a fuck. You're confused, TJ. Do you know what a fuck is? You probably don't. Never will. But you're not a bright light in the chandelier, are you? You're probably not a bright light in a flashlight, either."

"Brighter than you and brighter than the retard, blackie," TJ said.

I started to charge, but my mother and my brother held me back. "Don't humiliate him, Jaden. Let him be a man," Caden said.

"He can't say that to Milt or to Tate!"

"Let your son defend himself," Caden said, although I could tell he was barely controlling himself. "Same with Milt."

"We can always send them herbs in a coffee cake that will crush their rectums, now watch," my mother singsonged.

Damini said, "I want that coffee cake recipe, Nana."

Hazel, Heloise, and Harvey danced about until Hazel said, "Rectum." Heloise said, "I love Tate and Slinky." Harvey said, "I eat I eat I eat. I not eat Slinky."

I turned back to the scene at the bus. Tate's teammates squared off against TJ.

"You're gonna get fucked next time, Tate," TJ said.

"One day I will, I hope!" Tate said, smiling. "I hope she's gorgeous, too. Hot. Oh yeah, I'm totally into it, TJ, but I won't use the F word because I'm classier than that. I don't think it'll happen to you, but for me, yes. With a body like mine it's hard for women to think straight when they see me. It's the arousal that gets in the way, the rush of seduction."

Tate's teammates chortled like drunk hyenas.

"You got lucky, Tate—" TJ said, thumping the bus.

"Hey, temper-tantrum man, loser, you lost. You lost because we're better," Anthony said. "Be cool about it."

"I am not gonna be cool about it because I'm gonna kick

your asses next time. This is personal, Tate. Personal. It's you and me, Tate." He jabbed a finger at Tate, his face squished up and pissed off.

"I can't get personal with you, TJ." Tate put his palms up in the air. "I'm sorry but I'm not gay."

Tate's team hyena-laughed again, as did the boys on the bus.

"I love the ladies, so I can't get together with you, dude," Tate said. "But you can find someone else. Or at least someone in your imagination. You probably want a tall, dark, handsome man who kisses you gently, hugs you close, whispers sweet things, takes control. . . ."

"Fuck you, Tate!"

"Again, dude, I can't do that." Tate raised his hands higher in the air in mock frustration. "I already told you! I'm not gay! I do not want to see you naked! I don't want to do the F word with you."

TJ's teammates even laughed. Obviously TJ wasn't popular.

"I didn't say I wanted to see you naked, either!"

"You did, you said it, TJ. You're thinkin' about it, thinkin' about me, and hey. Uh. Not gonna work."

"What are you talking about, you idiot!"

"Now don't start calling me, TJ, or texting or friending me, okay? I don't want you to be a scorned lover or anything—"

"Shut up, Tate! I'm gunnin' for you, you hear that, you gooky blob? I'm comin' to get you, I am comin' to get you!"

The bus pulled away.

Harvey inhaled sharply. "Damn. He bad boy."

"Ya," Heloise said. "Mean. I kick him."

"I no like that bad boy," Hazel said.

"Martin's created an inferno of anger in his own kid," I said.

"Martin's a dangerous man. Dangerous kid, too," Caden said, eyes serious as we watched Martin Hooks lower himself and his hard gut into his car, the dark of the night not hiding how menacing he was.

"Together those two are a lethal mess," my mother said, tapping her manicured fingers together, her diamond earrings swinging. "I can feel it. Way down deep. They're bad news. Very bad news for all of us. I hate bad news."

Caden ambled over and talked to Martin.

Martin lumbered out of his car and took a lurching swing at Caden.

Caden knocked him right onto the hood of his car, where he lay like a dead pig.

"Caden is smooth as silk, isn't he?" my mother said. "How about some wine now, dears?"

"I have some swine!" Hazel said.

"Swine in Cinderella sippy cup!" Heloise insisted.

"I drink some swine, too!" Harvey said.

"Nice hit, Dad," Damini said, touching her heart. "That was rewarding to watch. Nana's going to give me a recipe that will crush rectums."

Tate had been able to defend himself, with humor, from TJ Hooks.

He had made friends.

He was excellent at basketball.

I was almost overcome by guilt. I should have let him play before this, how much easier his life would have been with these friendships, with being on a team.

I let my tears drip off my chin.

Parenting is often head-bangingly hard.

The next day I apologized to Tate, the apology simple, my emotions making a mess of me.

"It's okay, Boss Mom. If you make me chicken pancakes, we'll call it good."

I made him chicken pancakes.

We called it good.

He is a forgiving young man. I am grateful for that, too.

"Thank you for the silver watering can with the roses."

"You're welcome." Ethan's voice was deep and low over the phone. I envisioned his face, his mouth, I remembered how he did not get mad when I whizzed open his shirt and he lost a couple of buttons up in my bedroom one afternoon. It was exactly like the movies. I didn't think that buttons could fly off with such speed but, alas, they could! They did! I did it!

I felt my body heat up to the simmering level when I heard his voice. Okay, the boiling level. I had seen his body naked. I had played with that body. It was divine.

"It's beautiful." It wasn't an ordinary silver watering can. It was overly large, fun and creative, and it had herb designs on the sides.

"You're beautiful, Jaden."

Yes, that naked body of Ethan's was mine for the pleasing and I had found it pleasing many times since our delightful afternoon in the greenhouse. He seemed happy to handle the curves I have, again and again. . . .

We made plans for dinner that night, when Tate was at basketball practice.

Ethan came to the house.

You know how you see a steamin' hot love scene in the movies where the kiss goes on and on, in a totally orgasmic and out-of-control sort of way? Clothes are torn off hurriedly and dropped, shoes are kicked haphazardly away, a bra is tossed, and the hero picks the heroine up in his arms and they tumble to the bed and roll and kiss and you can tell that the sex is quiveringly, outrageously blissful?

That's what happened to me!

Me!

Jaden Bruxelle.

It was swwwweeeettt.

On Sunday I decided that I should stay in bed until twelve. I never stay in bed until twelve. I never stay in bed after seven thirty.

I don't know how to relax, enjoy, and treat myself, which is what my mother says my problem is. "You live as if every moment of your life must be accounted for and you must be doing something productive at all times, or worrying, or planning. Lord, you are boring to *yourself*. No fun! Do you not realize that life is a gift? Besides, working all the time gives a woman yeast infections."

I told her I did not have yeast infections.

She sniffed. "Working all the time also makes women shrivel."

"Shrivel, Mother?"

"Yes. Their intestines shrivel. Causing constipation and frustration."

"Thank you for that vital information."

"You're welcome. You must play, Jaden. Frolic. It'll make your liver happy."

"A happy liver?"

"And a happy . . . a happy *bottom*."

I lit a Blueberry Bobbles candle as I laughed at my mother's prediction of a happy bottom, then went downstairs in my robe and slippers and brewed a cup of orange spice tea. It was a gray, dreary afternoon, the rain pounding down. It was peaceful, calming. I climbed back into bed after checking on Tate, who was still sleeping.

My bedroom, with a four-poster bed, is in the corner. It used to be Faith and Jack's bedroom. I love the ornate fireplace and the windows, two of which were added in the last fifteen years. I also have a deck for watching the sunrise, that kaleidoscope of colors growing and stretching over the horizon, like mixed and blended paints.

When I was all snuggled in, I remembered the story that Grandma Violet told Caden, Brooke, and me, on a rainy spring day, about Faith and Grace when we were little. We were right here, in this bedroom, which had been hers and Grandpa Pete's.

"Faith and Grace hid slaves under their shop in Charleston, sometimes for hours, sometimes for days, even weeks, if the slaves had been whipped to bits or injured." She rocked in the rocking chair by the fireplace as she knitted a pink scarf, all of us at her feet, the fire dancing over her auburn and white curls.

"There were two nasty, ghastly brothers, Dwight and John

Stanfield, plantation and slave owners, whom Faith and Grace had refused to marry, though the men continued to bully them. Their refusal made those men furious, mark my words, and their fury turned them into stalkers, oh, curse them! They spied on the women one night after getting drunk in a bar and saw slaves being snuck beneath the shop through the shadows.

"The men were livid, as the slaves happened to be theirs. They rammed their way into the shop, then shot through the floor, flying bullets almost hitting the slaves. The slaves shook like dying, dry leaves in the wind as they faced their masters." Grandma Violet caught our mesmerized gazes. "Faith and Grace were lovely, elegant, red-haired ladies with fiery tempers who would have shot those two clean through if they'd had the chance and not looked back, but they were stuck. Stuck like fish in a barrel." She clicked her tongue as she told us the rest of the story, rain splattering the windows.

Dwight and John forced a compromise out of Faith and Grace that night. The women would marry them, live on their plantations, and they wouldn't turn the women in, offering them freedom from jail and/or their necks cracked in a noose. Jail didn't appeal to the women. There were dirt floors awash in vomit, body wastes, disease. There were rats, lice, putrid water. Starvation was a real possibility.

Faith and Grace didn't want to agree to the marriages, but they had to, at least for the moment, the men had guns, they were violent and dangerous, they wanted to keep their necks from cracking.

Grandma Violet's blue eyes filled with tears as she told us how Dwight and John whipped all the slaves to bloodiness that night in the woods, even one pregnant with Dwight's child, and chopped off one finger of each slave so they would remember to never run away again. They made the women watch.

Two of the slaves later died from infections. "Faith and Grace were devastated." Grandma Violet sniffled as she knit faster. "They never got over that trauma, oh, oh, those poor people! Whipped! Axed! Oh, how they cried, but Faith and Grace still hid two more slave women who arrived the next night, two babies strapped to their backs. What could they do? Where else would the women have gone? They had to help them."

Grandma Violet stood up, agitated, then peered out the windows, straight down the column of maple trees, as if she could see Faith through the raindrops. "They started casting their spells, using the thimble, the lace handkerchief, the needle, and the timepiece. They chanted a death spell, centering their witchly powers on Dwight and John drowning in a swamp or being hit by a carriage, then they prayed for divine intervention." Grandma Violet raised both hands to the heavens. "Divine intervention came on horseback."

Two men rode into town on stallions. Best friends, both Irish. One was a blond giant named Jack O'Donnell, and an equally large ex-military man named Russ McLeary. The girls flirted with them as if their lives depended on it, which they did, at a town picnic over raspberry pie.

Soon Jack was smitten with Faith and Russ was sweet on Grace. The women told the men the truth about the Underground Railroad and the threats on their lives, and on an inky black night, the moon hidden in a plume of clouds, the four of them saddled up four horses, and they galloped far, far away. They were headed toward Independence, Missouri, and the Oregon Trail.

Faith and Grace's guilt over deserting a safe haven for runaway slaves followed them for the rest of their lives, but they could not see being raped, every night, for the rest of their lives, by John and Dwight, either.

The first night the four rode long and hard, same with the next day, and the next night. Didn't take too many nights under a white, shiny moon for love to strike, it sure didn't. "Faith and Grace had the same eternal love for their husbands that I have for Grandpa Pete and your mother has for your father.

"Both men later touched the cross, heart, and star charms around the necks of Faith and Grace with reverence and love." Grandma Violet patted her heart. "One would add a clover to the mix for luck, the other would add a treasure chest, for prosperity." She gave each of us a hug, then tipped our chins up so she had our full attention. "That's what you have to wait for in your life, dear grandchildren. A spouse who loves you beyond love, a person of goodness and character, courage, and honesty. A wife, a husband, who sees you for the treasures you all are."

Thinking of that story, in my four-poster bed, orange spice tea in hand, I sighed happily, my hand to the cross, heart, and star charms on my necklace. I had found that same love with Ethan, yes indeed, I had.

I took Tate to play chess with Maggie.

They chatted and laughed. He beat her, spared her not at all.

She seemed frail, but she said, "Bishop Tate, I will now challenge you to a duel."

To which Tate grabbed two white chocolate chip cookies on her counter, intoned, "*En garde,* Maggie Shoes!" and they dueled with the cookies until they turned into crumbs.

"Yum, Maggie Shoes. These are delicious. Can I have six more?"

"Take all you want, Tate."

Her roses are sticks in her yard. The leaves are brown.

They have no more color.

"What have you learned from being on the team, Tate?"

I dipped a banana into melted chocolate. On rainy nights it is my favorite treat. I don't know why.

"I learned that I friggin' love basketball and Billy and Bob like to shoot and Road Runner can see things with his x-ray vision. Too bad I can't see girls' panties through their clothes, that'd be a gift. I want to play 'til I'm ninety."

Tate had already had two chocolate milk shakes, a plate of scrambled eggs with cheese, and a pile of grapes. He made me take a photo of him smiling, his lips holding five grapes in a row, for his blog when he was ready to post a photo of himself and General Noggin.

"Ninety-year-old men need something to do. It'll keep you young."

"And I learned about the guys on my team."

"What have you learned, buddy?"

"You know Kendrick?"

"Yes, the guard." Gecko kid.

"Yeah. His parents are divorced and his dad is in jail and won't get out for ten years because he embezzled a bunch of money and he said they were sued and now his mom and him have no money."

I had known that about the family. "I'm sorry to hear that. Kendrick's a neat kid."

"You know Jacob on my team? He has all that acne all over? He told me he thinks he's the ugliest person on the planet. I said, 'Hey, blondie,' you know, 'cause he has that white-blond hair, I said, 'Look at General Noggin, you think I'm a hot chick magnet or something? You think this body is getting jumped?' and he laughed, and I said, 'Man, I get laid all the time with this head of mine!'"

"Tate!" He laughed at my protest. I knew Jacob. The poor kid had those purplish-pink acne bumps. Being a teenager is soul-destroying sometimes.

"Baron, that tall kid with huge feet who doesn't get to play that much because he can't make baskets? He has dyslexia and thinks he's dumb. I told him, 'Man, you're radical. You're awesome at making people laugh, you're good at being a friend,' and he looked at me like I'd sprouted a third head, Mom. A *third* head. Bigger than General Noggin."

"That's because he was probably shocked at the compliment."

"Righty you are, Boss Mom. He goes, 'Really, Tate? You think that? You think I'm funny?' and I said, 'King Baron'—I called him that 'cause Baron's a fancy name—'you make me laugh all the time. You're a wily comedian. You should do stand-up or something.' And he said, 'But I can't write, the words get all mixed up, and I'm dumb,' and I go, 'You're not dumb, you have something called dyslexia, that's what you told me, so let's rename it, Dreamin' of Ecstasy, okay?' and then he laughed and goes, 'Okay, so I tell people I don't have dyslexia, I have Dreamin' of Ecstasy?' and I said, 'And make them call you

King Baron, too.' Then we joked the rest of the day about ecstasy."

"Do you know what ecstasy means, Tate?"

"Yeah. It's when I'm playing basketball, Mom. That's ecstasy."

"I see you understand. You're sure getting to know those kids."

"Yeah, I am. I think they tell me stuff they don't tell other people because I've got a big head and they think that my problems are way worse than theirs."

"And they trust you, Tate."

"They can. My mouth is a vault. I'm telling you what they said, but someone would have to have a sword to my throat and pressing hard into my esophagus"—he used a table knife to pretend someone was stabbing him—"before I told anyone else." He grabbed three more grapes, tossed them way up, caught two. Impressive. The third fell on the floor and rolled. He picked it up and ate it. "With this basketball team, they're talking to me." He picked an apple out of the fruit bowl and balanced it on his head, then balanced a second one and put four grapes between his lips. "Take a photo for my blog for when I want to introduce General Noggin."

I took the photo. "And what about the other kids at school?"

"Now other kids are sitting with me at the cafeteria, I don't have to go off and wait 'til everybody's gone through the lunch line and then go quick and hide out in the corner to have lunch after most of the kids have gone so I don't have to be a pathetic loser and sit alone. Plus, I didn't find it fun when they lobbed their milk cartons at me or their bananas. I think they actually want to talk to me now."

I couldn't talk because I was all choked up. Not because of the new friends, but because of such a sad, sad picture I had in my head of my son plotting out how to eat, when to eat, where to eat, to have the least amount of embarrassment and hurt. I'd heard it before. It always hurt.

"Now I go to the cafeteria and get out my lunch sacks. I sit down at a table where maybe somebody else is sitting all alone and I say, 'Hi, dude or dudette,' and in thirty seconds, the whole table is all filled up and all the dudes and dudettes are talking and laughing and throwing food and stuffing grapes up their noses and making sandwich pancakes and snorting noises. Want to hear my snorting noise, Mom?" He snorted at me.

"You're a very authentic snorting warthog choking on a hair ball."

"Gross, Boss Mom! Yeah, we're all snorting, and having raisin races where we see whose raisin can come closest to hitting Toby Tandem's lunch sack and it's fun." He snorted again. "Toby always wins. He's got a skill with raisins. I don't get it. He's a science nerd but he can throw raisins."

"A snort-fest."

"Yeah." He laughed. "A snort-fest. I'm hungry. I need some Alfredo Pasta Explosion." He batted those bright blue eyes at me pleadingly.

"You have to be kidding. You can't still be hungry. I fed you already."

"I am still hungry. My stomach is totally empty. I'm dying of starvation. Withering. I'll probably be dead by morning from hunger. I can hardly think. I need more and more food."

I kissed his cheek, and he raised up those long ol' arms and hugged me.

"Okay. I'll make you Alfredo Pasta Explosion."

"Yeah. That would rock. Thanks, Mom."

I cannot resist that child.

Ethan and I had many other dates. One date was for a picnic lunch with soup, salad, sandwiches, and chocolate that he brought. There is hardly anything more romantic than a man with glasses and a sweet smile carrying a picnic basket. It was winter, but it wasn't too cold that day, the sun shining, so I brought out a pile of blankets and we settled under a towering fir tree.

"I love you, Jaden." He cupped my face in his hands. "I have loved you for years, and I will love you forever. I want you to know that. I will love you forever, babe."

I nodded. My lip trembled, my face scrunched up, I'm sure my nose turned red, and I made a funny sound in my throat. The tears trembled on my lashes, then fell down my face. He did not seem to mind when I had to roll over and blow my nose like a honking turtle.

For long years now I have stuffed my emotions down, stuffed the gentle, fun, romantic part of me down, so I could deal with the many responsibilities that came with Tate's care and health and the demands of a job that were serious and complicated. I had become too toughened up, rigid in the way I lived, because I had to be, because I had to be vigilant, because I had to protect Tate, because his medical disasters were life and death. It had kicked all frivolity, all lightness, out of my life.

I didn't want to be tough or rigid with Ethan, ever. I wanted the frivolity of love, the lightness of life.

I put my hand behind Ethan's head and pulled him closer, the warmth of his body heating me from head to foot, the warmth of his love heating up a heart that had always been hopeful, but way too alone, way too lonely, for way too long. "I love you, too, Ethan."

We piled three blankets on top of us and made love.

I tried to keep it down. It was hard to keep the noise in. I do believe I startled a blue jay.

Ethan is extremely talented at carnal activities, especially when under a pile of blankets, under a fir tree, the winter sun shining.

16

~

For our next meeting, Dirk brought his attorneys, Ralph Tol-
loway and Nigel Pinkerton. They were expensive people
from a prominent firm. I was pleased at their expense.

Dirk's hair was slicked back, expensive designer suit but-
toned up tight. His suit was a reflection of him: controlling. I'll
bet the Porsche was waiting for him. He probably masturbated
in that car. Yuck.

Our attorney, Sandra Torelli with the oversized teeth, sat next
to me at the conference table at the hospital. Dr. Baharri was
there again, as was Sydney, and a few hospital administrators
and other doctors who had been involved with Mr. Hassells,
Senior's care.

When Dirk walked in, throwing the door open as if making
an impressive entrance, Sydney whispered soooo unprofession-
ally, "Ta-da! The egomaniacal hero with a short man's complex
on the white horse has charged in!"

Dr. Baharri said, "I will need to meditate extra long tonight."

Sandra said, not quietly, "It's a question of white wine or red
tonight. Maybe both. I shall mix them together."

We had the usual settling-in sorts of conversation, with Dirk
huffing and puffing, the outraged son, I had killed his father,
medical care was poor, what about all that morphine forced
down his father's throat, etc. He kept staring at me, his eyes
wandering down my front, ticked off that I hadn't plopped my

head in his lap when I met him. My blood boiled to the point that I was surprised my skin didn't fall off.

But we had a killer witness, mark my words.

Who?

Beatrice.

Mr. Hassells, Senior's loving, caring daughter and Dirk's sister.

She'd heard about the lawsuit, called me, then Sandra, who had eagerly invited her to come.

Sandra flashed those teeth, the teeth that seem to shine before she goes in for the kill, and said, "Dirk, I'm going to get one more person in here to give us another perspective, if you don't mind." She opened the door to the conference room, and Beatrice walked in.

Beatrice had lost forty pounds since her father died. It was the first time she didn't seem exhausted. Her hair was brushed, she wore makeup. She had greeted me with a hug in the hallway, a kiss on my cheek, and said, "Don't worry, Jaden. Dirk has an asshole for a brain."

Sandra asked Beatrice questions and gave her time to be completely honest, at length. Some of what she said:

"Jaden was at my father's house all the time. She offered my dad, my kids, and me care, comfort, and friendship. In my years of working with medical people, and I had to work with them with my mother's illness, my ex-husband's heart attack, and two friends' bouts with cancer, I found Jaden to be the most competent of all medical personnel." She leaned toward Dr. Baharri. "No offense, Dr. Baharri. You're in second place, but Jaden was with us all the time."

Dr. Baharri smiled and nodded his head. "No offense. It is an honor to be second place to Miss Bruxelle."

Beatrice also detailed how Dirk never did anything to help with his father or his care, and only rarely came to visit his father until he met me. "He started to bring his 'too busy' self on over after he saw Jaden and began pestering her to sleep with him and 'ride him like his Porsche,' that's a direct quote from my brother."

"That's a lie!" Dirk said, flushed and seething.

"Only truths, please," Ralph the attorney intoned.

"My client disputes her claim," Nigel said. He peeked at his cell phone.

"It is not a lie," Beatrice said, chin up. "You accused Jaden of killing Dad, and I will tell the truth to defend her."

"You're going to defend our father's murderer?" Dirk shot me a malevolent glance. It said, *If you had hooked up with me, this wouldn't be happening.*

"Shut up, asshole brain," Beatrice said mildly. "Jaden didn't kill him. The liver cancer killed him."

"Let's be kind, stick to the facts," Nigel the attorney interjected. He seemed bored.

"Beatrice wasn't in there one night, sometimes she was out with her bratty kids, and that's"—Dirk paused—"that's when it happened."

"When what happened?" Sandra asked. Teeth flashed.

"When Jaden poured that morphine into my dad. If she hadn't overdosed him, my father would have had more time."

Sydney said, "False."

"The last time you came to see Dad was a month before he died, Dirk," Beatrice said.

"But I know she used the morphine the same way many more times! Pouring it down him!"

"Again, you are wrong. You are wrong often, aren't you, Mr. Hassells?" Dr. Baharri said, smooth as silk. "Jaden did not overdose your father. Let me tell you once again about liver cancer and your father's medical history." He went off on another medical lecture while Dirk squirmed.

"You have to understand me, Dirk Hassells," Dirk tried again, interrupting Dr. Baharri. "I don't want more trouble."

"What do you want?" Sandra asked.

"I want an apology from her." He stabbed a fat finger at me, then leaned back, arms crossed on his chest. "You, Jaden. A nice apology, too. Where you tell me you did wrong and ask for my forgiveness and tell me you're willing to start over and you mean it. A few tears wouldn't hurt."

Sydney flung her head back, hands in the air, her braids

swinging, as if searching for divine intervention. "Not in my lifetime on this planet."

"I will not allow that," Dr. Baharri said. "As she did nothing wrong."

"You will have to wait forever for that, Dirk," I said. Gall, he was obsessed with me and bringing me down, smashing me, controlling me. "It will not happen."

"And I want a payout for the early death of my father, who was my best friend, and because of poor treatment and poor care and poor bandages and a hospice nurse who would not do as she was told to do to help me, I mean to help my dad, and to tend to my needs as a grieving son, same as she did for Beatrice, which is part of her job to help *all* the members of the family!" He banged his hand again.

Beatrice laughed.

"How come you're not supporting me, Beatrice?" he semi-shouted.

"Because you're a liar."

"I am not. I will never speak to you again after this, Beatrice."

"My relationship with you was over years ago, Dirk. You just didn't know it because you're wrapped up tight in your narcissistic self."

Nigel said, and I knew that he knew there was no case here, but he is a slimy slick lawyer and Dirk was paying him, "We feel our client needs to be compensated for the preventable death of his father, incompetent medical care, medical malpractice."

"Shouldn't have happened," Ralph droned. He needed to earn his outrageous fees. "The father had more time. Payment for lack of companionship is due."

"You're as likely to get that money as I am to grow a lemon tree in Antarctica," Sandra said, smiling.

"And along with the money I want her"—Dirk stabbed a finger at me again; his ego had taken such a hit when I'd turned him down—"to acknowledge that she over-morphined my dad and to say she's sorry to me personally, she and I, in a room alone, sorry, that's what she has to do. A profuse sorry. On her knees, sorry."

"I will not do that," I said. "I especially will never be in a room alone with you on my knees. The image disgusts me. I provided excellent care to your father. I'm sorry that you're pissed off that I didn't want to sleep with you, but you are a vomitous creature with slits for eyes and slobber constantly on your mouth and a forest of hair growing out of your ears and you are egotistical, boring, and have a personality disorder so I wasn't interested at all. My rejection of you doesn't mean you are justified in bringing a false lawsuit against me."

Dirk's mouth gaped open and shut.

Nigel said, "Let's not be brutal, Miss Bruxelle."

Ralph said, "I think that was rather mean."

Dirk stood up, shaking, "I don't have to sit and take this shit anymore. Come on, Nigel, come on, Ralph. Jaden Bruxelle, I will see you and your sorry, tight, thin ass and those weird blue and green eyes of yours in court, and you will regret crossing me, you'll regret being such a snit and a snob and a snit and you will get on your knees and give me a . . . a sorry! On your knees!"

Dirk lumbered out, ran into a chair, and tried to shove it out of the way. It got caught on another chair and he had to push that one out of the way, too, and the first one fell on his foot. I laughed out loud. Beatrice laughed louder than me.

The expensive attorneys stood up and, after saying good-bye to us, have a pleasant day, thanks for your time, no vindictiveness or anger in their voices, they followed Dirk.

They were there for Dirk's money.

What did they care?

The next day was tough, too. Not all deaths are fair, we all know that. When my patients are over seventy, I honestly feel that they had a fair shot at life. Seventy years. That's a long time. Not long enough, but a gift.

And often I have patients in hospice care who have run themselves into the ground. They're smokers, drinkers, obese, addicts or ex-addicts, with sedentary lives, junk food diets, etc. They didn't need to die so young, but they do because of consistent and unbelievably poor lifestyle choices.

But sometimes I am caring for younger people. In their twenties, thirties, forties . . . most are married or have partners. Many have children. They lived healthy yet, for some inexplicable reason, death came knocking.

It was a young one I lost today, and his wife's wailing, the young daughter's sobbing, the son who ran to hide in the closet with a stuffed purple giraffe his dad gave him . . . it was still in my head. Unfair. Not right. It was as if death made a mistake, took the wrong corner and hit the wrong house, the wrong person.

Several days before the young father died, of a disease no one could predict he would have, he held my hand and said, "Thank you, Jaden. You made this easier for me."

I had to eat a dozen red cinnamon Gummi Bears after that and cry in my greenhouse under my Chinese lanterns and hanging lavender.

Some people, emotionally, are ready to die for whatever reason. Maybe they're old and grateful for the time they've had. Maybe they've had it with being critically ill. Maybe they've grieved for the life they're losing but have reached some sort of philosophical, religious, or spiritual peace.

But others are anxious, panicked, depressed, regretful, grieving, angry, and confused. The treatment they received previously has worn them out, physically and emotionally. They are not accepting of their deaths. They will fight for their lives until the last millisecond, usually because of their children. They are "not ready." They're leaving a first grader with an interest in cheetahs or an eighth grader who is headed off the tracks, behaviorally speaking, and nothing can make them ready.

The ending of their life is unfair, and they know it. We all know it.

Death is not always fair or right. I've stopped asking why not.

Sometimes my patients seem to be getting better, a surge of energy, they finally eat a full meal one night, they sit up, even walk around, laugh and talk, and their bodies shut down overnight.

Sometimes patients won't die until they get permission from family to go; other times they seem to wait until everyone is out of the room, as if they can't get their death done with relatives crying over them. Patients have also waited, in semiconscious or unconscious states, for relatives to arrive. I've seen that happen many, many times, with family members saying, "Grandpa, Beth will be here in six hours, can you wait?" Within an hour of Beth being there, Grandpa starts to shut down.

It is different for each person.

As everyone's life is different, too.

Thank you, Jaden. You made this easier for me.

I make the journey easier. That's what I do.

It does not stop the tears, though, shed in my greenhouse or rocking chair, staring out at the fields, the roses and red poppies, the herb and vegetable gardens in summer, the columns of maple trees down the drive, the same scenes that generations of women in my family have stared at, as they rode the joys and sorrows of life, tears coursing down their cheeks, too.

Tate's team won their next game by twenty-two points.

They were on a winning streak, and it revitalized our town.

During the next game, Tate passed the ball off even more than usual. All the players scored. In fact two kids scored who never did so. Both made four points.

Coach called time-out in the fourth quarter and pulled Tate to him. I knew what he was telling him. We all did: Quit passing, let's make some points, we're down by five.

So, Tate shot. And shot. And shot. When we were ahead by eight with one minute to go, Tate started passing the ball off again. In the last seconds, he passed it off to Baron, the one with the problem with dyslexia who thinks he's stupid and who doesn't get to play much.

It was a two-pointer for Baron, top of the key, it was the last basket of the game. The ball swooshed, the whistle blew, and his parents, who had had Baron as a surprise when the mother was forty-five, who were sitting next to me, flew out of their seats, arms raised high in the air, screaming.

They both cried. *Their Baron had made a basket.* To top it off, Tate, dear Tate, hugged the shocked and grateful Baron, and the other kids surrounded Baron, hugging him, slapping him on the back.

We had a winner. His name was Baron. In all the years I've known him, I have never, ever seen a smile like that on that kid's face. Never.

I cried, too. I'm such a baby.

"Tate is the kindest damn kid I know," my mother said to me. She had flown in from Los Angeles and made it in the second quarter. She wore a couture black dress with a Mid Court Mob shirt over it. "Certainly didn't get that from me. I have a mean streak the size of the Mississippi River and you have Witch Mavis, but he has none of our mean and threatening volcanic qualities. *None.*"

She called down to him, fist shaking. "Busted their balls, Tate! You busted their balls!"

"Really, Mother?"

She wiggled her eyebrows at me, then flicked the crystals in my hair. "I say the truth."

"He did bust their balls, he did!" Damini said. "Busted 'em wide open, Aunt Jaden! Wiiiiiide open!"

"Do you think this is proper grandmothering? See what you've done, Mother? Damini's talking about balls!"

She put her hand on Damini's shoulder. "You're a witchly fire breather, Damini."

"Yeah, I know it. I'm a Bruxelle! I've heard all the stories about the royal witch line and Faith and Grace."

"They're all true. Their spells worked. Don't you listen to your aunt Jaden telling you different."

"I won't, Nana," she said solemnly.

Caden led a cheer about Baron and the greatest shot in town.

The rest of the team got in on it, too. The triplets ran onto the court to hug Tate. They were wearing hippie outfits with bandannas and peace signs. Damini threw her hands up in the air and screamed, "He's a pain in my keester, but I still love him!"

TATE'S AWESOME PIGSKIN BLOG

Today I am going to post a photo of myself. See. Here it is. That's General Noggin and I. Here's a photo of my hands around a model of a brain. Remember my hands, Billy and Bob? As in Billy Bob Thornton, the greatest actor ever? Here are profile photos, too, so you can see the famous ears, Bert and Ernie. As you can see, I drew a smiley face on Bert.

Yes, I was born with that thing. Yes, my eyes, Mickey Mouse and Road Runner, are uneven. Here are Mickey Mouse and Road Runner studying neurological anatomy.

I'm done hiding on my own blog because it feels as if I'm insulting myself. This is me. I have a big head.

The thing is, if you're different in America you get a different perspective of life. There are a lot of different people here. Not all of us are blond, thin, with blue or green eyes. We have all colors here, all religions, all shapes. But if you don't fit in with the "norm" of America, then you often feel you're on the outside looking in and you'll never be fully in the club, this silent American club. You're a beat off, a step away, you're off rhythm.

I've been looking in, stuck on the outside of some glass bubble, my whole life, and a whole bunch of people don't want me in the bubble and will hit me to keep me out.

But I've also been able to figure things out. Figure people out. I have had to do a lot of thinking, which is something I think a lot of people don't do, and don't have to do, because they fit in. They are just there. I think some people don't even realize how good they have it.

But lately, I've been wondering. Fitting in perfectly means that you never have to reach outside yourself. You don't have to go through the same kinds of challenges, prejudice, judgment. Is it actually the best thing to fit in with everyone else? It's easiest. But, man, how do you grow? How do you learn to think on your own, or do you simply think what everyone around you thinks? How do you learn to be more compassionate of others, more generous, if you've never had to feel like you've been lost and stuck on the outside with no one being compassionate or generous to you?

I know people who seem to have perfect lives, no problem has ever split their world, but they seem shallow to me. There's nothing of depth on the inside, nothing interesting. It's as if being perfect has taken away their ability to have an intellect. They've never had to reach inside and pull out their strength, or their courage, and see who they are deep down. They seem . . . empty somehow.

Do I like having a big head? Not really. But I don't dislike it, either. This is me. Tate Bruxelle. Oh, and General Noggin, too, Billy and Bob, and Bert and Ernie. Mickey Mouse and Road Runner, practically the bionic eye.

Hello.

From all of us.

How you doing today?

Blog count: 8,000. The comments from people who read his blog? Tate came downstairs grinning. "I'm definitely getting braver about getting out of Tillamina and seeing the world. It seems a lot friendlier now."

"We're gonna win the state title, Boss Mom."

"And I will be there with the Mid Court Mob cheering for you."

"Nuclear fusion and splitting atoms, we're gonna kick some butt." Tate was tinkering in his Experiment Room with wires, a mini-motor, and wood. Now and then small sparks sprinkled around and about. He moved a research article aside that a neurosurgeon had sent him. No sense burning that up.

"Please don't set the house on fire."

"Boss Mom, I ain't gonna be burnin' no house down. I know what I'm doing. I'm a wannabe Einstein, he's da man, but first I'm gonna kick some butt on the court."

"I will enjoy the kick butt show. You don't have fireworks in here anymore, do you?" I ran a hand over his curls, nervous already for the game. *Please don't get hurt.*

"No, I took 'em all out to the garage."

"No mixing chemicals you don't understand."

"You've told me that a million times. I know what will explode when I put them together."

"Then don't mix 'em."

"Back to basketball. We have the best team in the state. We're gonna win the championship."

"I think you'll win, too." The town was going crazy, thrilled to all ends. I hoped down to my toes that we wouldn't play Sunrise. I did not need to see TJ Hooks shoving my son around.

"But I have a question for you, Mom."

"And that question is . . ."

"When is my Other Mother coming up here so I can meet her?"

He saw my expression, it must have reflected the exhaustion, the wariness, the intense trepidation I felt about throwing Brooke back into his life.

"I have to meet her, Boss Mom. I have to." He leaned back in his chair. "I have to. Please. Please, Boss Mom."

Darn it all. "Okay, honey. I'll arrange it. It'll be soon. Remember—"

"I know she's a recovering drug addict. Don't romanticize her. Don't expect anything. Don't get hurt."

"That one is most important, Tate. Don't get hurt."

Don't get hurt, Tate.

I put on my yellow duckie rain boots and plodded through the puddles to my greenhouse on a rainy night. Tate's team had won again, to the delirium of Tillamina. He'd come home and eaten eight pieces of Great Great Grandma Lacy's Cinnamon French toast after using three of the pieces to create a French Toast building.

I checked on the herbs I had in red pots, then moved on to the herbs I had in green pots, then the yellow pots. I get a gardener's thrill watching them grow day by day. I also planted seedlings: impatiens, snapdragons, and petunias.

As usual, I felt compelled to chop up herbs and blend in spices, though my hands trembled like an interior wire was shaking them and what I really wanted to do was run to Siberia. I took a pinch of cilantro, St. John's wort, dill, and sea salt. I kept them in separate piles, then blended them together. I made designs on the crystal plate from Grandma Violet. I used the silver spoons from Faith.

By the third design I was shaking.

Death.

Death again.

Damn.

* * *

I took Tate to play chess with Maggie at her request.

He won. He did not hesitate to checkmate that lady in minutes.

She humphed. "You're a skilled chess player, Bishop Tate."

"And you're a smart woman, Maggie Shoes, even though you're not good at maneuvering your rook and you have to leave your queen protected more."

"I'll remember that."

"Play ya again after I get another slice of that pecan pie in your kitchen?"

"Yes. This time I'm going to whip your young ass."

When Tate won he said, "I whipped your ass, Maggie Shoes. Whipped it back to Wednesday."

Maggie's sticks will bloom with roses again next year. She will not be able to see them.

Tate's team kept winning. There was a possibility that we might, might, *hopefully might* be going to the state play-offs in our league!

The crowds grew and grew. Ethan came to all the games with my family. He videotaped Tate playing so we could all watch it together later.

Tate kept making the most impossible shots.

Another newspaper article ran, this time in the statewide newspaper, about the team, the winning season, and the kid with the big head who kept hitting all those three-pointers.

Tate and I read one of the articles over breakfast one morning. He was eating a five-egg omelet, three pieces of toast, and orange juice.

Here are a few of the reporter's questions:

Q. *This is your first year playing basketball, right, Tate?*

A. First year with real, live, breathing people on a team that is visible to other humans. I've been playing imaginary basketball for years. Even had cute cheerleaders on the side doing high kicks for me. This year I figured I had a lot of points to make up from previous years of not playing, so that's why I keep shooting. It's the revenge of a basketball geek.

Q. *You've made an incredible number of three-point shots. Any advice on how to do that?*

A. I'll tell you what Boss Mom told me: Just throw the damn ball up.

Q. *You've had to endure a lot of taunting and ridicule out on the courts.*

A. Yeah, but General Noggin and I shut it out.

Q. *General Noggin?*

A. That's the name of my head. General Noggin and I keep our brain in the game and I keep shooting. I try to ignore people who call me ugly, freak, gargoyle boy, fire head, 'cause of my hair, you know, Mongloid, asshole, and genetic mistake. But if there's a young woman out there who wants to call me sexy, then that would be a symphony to my ears, Bert and Ernie.

Q. *When did you start playing basketball?*

A. I was playing basketball when I was four days old.

Q. *Seriously.*

A. That would be my serious answer.

Q. *You're an athlete and a 4.0 academic. It's ru-*

mored that you did not miss any answers on your PSAT.

A. Hmmm. Well, on that day, I took my brain out of my head, with General Noggin's permission, and gave my brain the pencil and he took the test. It seems he scored high. Freaked my teacher out, though, to have a brain with a pencil in its hand on my desk.

Q. *What are your plans?*

A. My plan is to get my second lunch. I'm starving.

Q. *I mean, for college, for life after high school ball? Do you think you'll get a basketball scholarship?*

A. I don't think I'll get a scholarship. I am planning on studying brain and cognitive science, molecular neuroscience, biophysics, cell biology, and organic chemistry. I am writing a blog now so that when I get out into the world hopefully people will have seen my face already and won't bust a gut when they see me.

Q. *What are your other interests?*

A. I read all the books and research articles I can about brains, which have a hundred billion neurons each and look like white and gray worms wrapped around each other. I'm also interested in biology and chemicals. I have some skill at catching Skittles in my mouth, eating twelve tacos at a time, standing on my head, even though it's sort of cheating because of the size of it, and I am trying to learn how to dance. Right now I look like a snake that's being slung around by a leopard, but I'm not giving up. I have to learn how to bust a move for the Winter Formal.

Q. *Do you think you'll make the play-offs?*

A. Yes. And we will win all of the games and become the state champions.

Q. *That's pretty confident.*

A. No, it's a fact.

"Boss Mom. Watch this." Tate put one apple and a ceramic elephant on top of his head. "I can eat my omelet and read the article all with an apple and an elephant on top of my head."

"Your talent is mesmerizing. Again, something you can put on your college résumé."

"Yep. Now stand back with a bow and arrow and see if you can shoot it off. I won't move. Film it with your phone, though, I want to post it."

"If I wanted child services to come and take you away from me, I'd shoot that apple off your head."

"Okay, no arrow, but take the picture. I need it for my blog."

I took the photo. He wrote the blog. "There are not many people who can eat an omelet with an apple and an elephant on their head. . . . Hello. It's me, Tate, again."

It was the humor, the humility, the kindness, and his personal story that had people signing up for his blog by the hundreds.

"It's awesome now, Boss Mom. I get to play basketball. People say hi to me in the halls. One girl even yelled at me the other day for tripping over her feet, and I loved it because it meant that she didn't feel sorry for me, didn't feel disgusted or repelled by me, it was me, Tate. She called me a klutz, then she smiled at me. I smiled back. She's pretty, too."

"And you figured out what to do for the Winter Formal, right?"

"Yep. You're going to have a lot of people here, Mom."

"Ethan, Nana, and Caden will come to help." All would be welcome. Tate had friends, and they were coming over to the house. I wanted to click my cowboy heels. "I will try to control whatever outrageous things your Nana Bird wants to say, but there's no telling what the triplets will wear, and if someone ticks Damini off, she'll take off her leg and you know what."

We laughed.

"I couldn't care less," Tate said.

I hugged him. I couldn't be happier.

Tate's team won the next two games.

The Mid Court Mob was rocking out. Each game continued to be standing room only. Now and then I could still hear the catcalls from the opposing fans.

I heard one girl call out, "You're ugly."

I heard another girl call out, "Hey, you! Rectangle head."

And a boy with reddish hair yelled, "Teeter-totter eyes!"

But as I boiled, my son ignored them. The crowd cheered and obliterated most of the mean comments. Ethan came with me to the games and held the camera. He was often overcome watching Tate make baskets, though, and had to sit down, head in his hands, while I patted his back.

"This is one of the most exciting things that has ever happened to me," my mother breathed as we talked on the phone. She was at work in Hollywood wearing a couture gown. Her stylist had added a chignon to the back of her neck. Tiffany had given her jewelry to wear. It didn't matter. "I have never been more thrilled. Tate, our boy Tate, playing basketball!"

"Me, too, Mom. Me, too."

"My insides quiver all the time. I can't wait for the tournament! I think about it every minute! Here, darling, I'm with Dylan, you know I'm blackmailing him, and we're going to have some violence on the set, oooh! It'll be delightful! I'll put you on the speakerphone."

"Hello, Dylan!" He and his wife, Gideon, had been to dinner at my mother's house many times when I was there.

"My love!" Dylan boomed. "Tell me, what are you growing in your greenhouse?"

We talked about that for a while. Dylan was born poor. His mother gave birth, then left with a trucker; his father was in and out of jail for assault, robbery, etc. He now has an expansive greenhouse at his farm in Vermont. When he's not in Los Angeles, he is there because "it brings peace to my soul, the only place, it seems, where that peace is possible."

"What are you two doing in the next scene?" I asked.

"We're in a ballroom, dancing," my mother said, "and I tell Dylan in a hissy voice that he must obey me and my malicious manipulations or his life will end as he knows it. End! He leads me out to the garden, da da da! He's overcome with rage and tries to kill me, but Beck comes running out, hero-like, and defends me. He pummels Dylan with his fists, strangling him against a tree, da da da!"

"Yep. I almost die," Dylan said. "I fight, I sweat and swear, it's useless, I collapse, my head back, mouth open, gag gag gag eyes rolling back, the breath being squeezed out of me, ack ack ack! Hey, Beck! There's the strangler right now, Jaden! Beck! Come on over here! Jaden's on the line!"

"Jaden!" Beck called out. "How are you up in Oregon? You know I'm going to try to kill Dylan here, the old fart. Boom, boom, he's down, his hair all messed up, makeup smudged."

"You're going to smear my makeup?" Dylan said, his voice falsely appalled. "Oh, don't do that! You'll ruin my pretty face!"

"Pretty face." Beck scoffed. "You're Godzilla and King Kong, mixed. Jaden, your mom brought some of your cinnamon rolls with the extra white frosting to the set. They were to die for! I almost cried when I ate one. Tate said I would, and he was right. Tell me about those miniature lemon meringue cakes you made the other night. . . ."

The memory of the night my father, Shel, died, still hurts. It was a lazy summer evening, the first week after my senior year in high school. He told me he would have chocolate mint ice cream waiting for me when I returned home from the movies with my girlfriends and my blond boyfriend, Josh, who made me giddy, as only first loves can do.

Brooke, in withdrawal, nauseous, sweating, and craving drugs, had taken off again two weeks before to hang out with her dealer and other scummy people. My parents were devastated, but it was a controlled devastation as this had happened many times before. My father patted his aching heart, as if comforting it, and wiped the useless tears off his cheeks while he worked on his scripts here in Oregon, while my mother, in Los Angeles, worked on *Foster's Village*. Caden was at a summer wrestling camp.

I had been smelling death in my herbs and spices for months, clinging and foul, and it made abject fear and anxiety a constant companion for me. I thought it was for Brooke. I was wrong.

Several people saw my father's car, driving too fast that night, losing control and disappearing straight over a cliff, arching through the blackness like a flying toy. The police and paramedics were called, but it was too late, his car had exploded on impact. The police called my mother, and she called me.

Amidst our unspeakable grief, we scrambled to locate Brooke before the press did. I called a friend, who had a drug addict friend who might know where she was, and he called his cousin. I told Brooke over the phone about our dad. She was silent for a long time, then let out a shrill, horrified scream that still echoes through my body now and then on lazy summer evenings.

My mother took a private jet to Portland from Hollywood and picked up Brooke, literally right off the streets, in a blighted part of town. She had new tracks up her arm and was stoned and hysterical. My mother drove her straight to the hospital, then to our home in the country, down the lane with the maple trees.

I have never seen my mother that shattered. I'm sure I never will again. Her husband was dead, and her daughter was stoned right out of her mind.

My father's memorial service in Tillamina, on a day filled with tunnels of gold from the sun and blooming red poppies, was packed with hundreds of people and more cameras than I can count outside the church. Two days later, with only family and my parents' best friends, we buried him in a cemetery that held most of our ancestors, under a willow tree that blew in the summer wind.

Brooke was despondent, almost comatose in her grief. "I can't live with this," she whispered. "I can't." Shortly after the funeral, her drug cravings reaching a panting, delirious peak, she took off on a Greyhound bus. Two weeks later she tried to kill herself in a seedy, dirty hotel in west Los Angeles. The manager called an ambulance, then he called the gossip magazines.

It was a neat slit to both wrists. She was forcibly committed for psychiatric help.

To get this picture straight for you: My mother lost my beloved father, her darling Shel, whom she had met and fallen in love with when she was eighteen. Her drug-addicted daughter tried to kill herself. Caden and I were beside ourselves. She whispered later, bereft, as Faith and Grace had said so long ago as they bounced along the sea, "This is the worst shipwreck time of my life."

I missed my deep-thinking, kind father all the way to the core of my being. That hole has never filled. I was depressed and scared about Brooke. My mother was racked with misery and hardly spoke for two weeks, her eyes empty, lost.

She later returned to work, amidst enormous sympathy from the American public. I moved to the Hollywood house with her, as did Caden, for the summer. She would come home at night and we would all cry together. The three of us planted honeysuckle. That's what I remember: honeysuckle. It's huge now, covering two trellises, the only plant that my mother lets grow without any trimming.

Brooke was eventually released from psychiatric/drug addiction care and disappeared. This time my mother didn't search for her. She had given up. There is only so much you can do for a drug addict before you are dragged under the bus with them, the wheels on your chest, breaking your bones, wiping the air out of your lungs. The next time we saw her she was stumbling through our field, pink and white cosmos floating in the wind, pregnant with Tate.

17

~

I rocked in my old rocking chair one night after Tate went to bed, the lights off, pomegranate tea in my hands, facing the windows as the wind howled, pushing snowflakes sideways. I thought of Faith living in this house without central heat, reading one of the fragile books we've saved in the armoires, a cup of tea in her hand. It would have been mighty cold in this house, all fireplaces burning.

I tapped my teacup. How do you introduce your son to his ex-addict mother, whom he has never met? Where's the protocol on that? Where's Emily Post when you need her?

I had decided it would be Brooke, Tate, and me when they met. Not my brother and his family, not my mother.

My mother had bought Brooke a plane ticket and she flew in. When Tate returned from basketball practice, he knew his Other Mother would be at the house.

I thought it would be awkward. It was.

I thought there would be tears. There were.

I thought there would be anger. Anger was around and about, too.

But all in all, with a lemon dill salmon dinner, a tomato salad with white wine, bay leaf, garlic, and olive oil, and hot buttered bread, snowflakes gently falling, the three of us, we did pretty darn well.

Mostly because of Tate's blunt honesty.

* * *

"So, Brooke." Tate helped himself to more salmon.

"Yes." My sister could not stop looking at Tate with those tired green eyes of hers. Not because of his head, but because he was her son. She kept tearing up, kept clasping her charms between her hands. She was also completely sober. That meant she had room in her mind to realize the magnitude of what she'd done all those years ago.

"I'm going to ask you a few questions, okay?"

"Okay. Please do." My sister put her hands in her lap. She was wearing long sleeves, I knew why. She had many scars, but she seemed better. Her face was no longer bruised purple and green, and she had put on some makeup. I think my mother had something done to Brooke's face, too, maybe dermabrasion, because her complexion, which had been rough and pitted, was much clearer. The spa had done a great job on her auburn hair, and it appeared thicker. Brooke wore jeans and boots and a blousy pink shirt. Our styles did not differ that much.

"First is, why did you leave me?"

My sister's eyes flooded again. I did not try to rescue her, or this conversation. I couldn't see their relationship progressing without it. Sometimes you have to walk through the sludge and shattered glass to get to the other side of the marsh.

"Tate," Brooke said. "I . . . I was a screwed-up person. I was on drugs."

"Which ones?" Tate took another hunk of bread. Nothing could keep that kid from his food.

"At that time"—she took a ragged breath—"I was on cocaine, painkillers, heroin, alcohol, and I smoked."

"Whoa!" Tate said. "That's some bad stuff."

"It was."

"Why did you start taking them?"

"I was young, I was stupid, I wanted to fit in. A girl I knew was using them, and I started to, too."

"Yeah. Peer pressure."

"I was lost and became more and more messed up, then became addicted. I had friends, but they weren't true friends."

"Blew your mind, then?"

"Yes. They did."

"And that's why you left me in the hospital?"

I heard Brooke's quick inhale. "Yes. I couldn't think. My mind was a mess. I was coming off of . . . I'm embarrassed to say this. . . ." She made a whimpering sound. "I was coming off being high and I felt ill and desperate and . . . and I left."

"Do you think your drug use is why my head grew so big?"

Whew.

My sister's hands shook. "I don't know."

"I think it probably is."

Whew.

My sister nodded, her guilt so heavy I could almost see it. "You could be right."

"I think I am right." Tate kept eating, but I did not miss the steel glint in his eye. Tate rarely grew angry, but when he did, he focused it to a laser point. I'd seen him in action with other kids, with teachers who weren't treating him fairly, with others who made fun of him. I hadn't expected less. Tate is a kind, compassionate, wise person who gives people a lot of latitude and a lot of forgiveness. But his mother was on drugs when she was pregnant with him, then she took off.

That's a lot to get past. Maybe impossible to get past.

"I'm sorry, Tate." My sister's voice shook, up and down, a verbal roller coaster.

"I'm sorry, too." He had another bite of salmon. "Do you know what it's like to live with a head this size and with crooked eyes?"

"No," she whispered.

"It's hard. People have made fun of me forever. I've been teased and beaten up."

"I'm sorry." The tears were streaming down, onto the tablecloth. "Tate, I am sorry."

"I'm sorry about the teasing, but it's made me a lot better person. And I have to say I'm not sorry you left me at the hospital with Nana Bird and Boss Mom."

"You're not?" She wiped her tears with a napkin.

"No. You were shooting up drugs. Can you imagine the life I

would have had with you? I would have had this huge head, all the medical problems I had when I was younger, and you would have been too drugged out to take care of me. I would have grown up poor, moving around all the time, running into your friends who were doing drugs. It would have been scary, it would have been dangerous, I probably would have been abused or I would have died. So, I'm glad you left."

I took a deep, deep breath. My sister deserved it, but I saw the way her head moved back, as if Tate had slapped her.

"I would have made a lousy mother." Her voice was small.

"Yep. You would have." Tate took an apple and balanced it on his head. "I can eat when I'm balancing things on my head. General Noggin is pretty talented in that way."

I didn't laugh. Neither did Brooke.

"I wanted to meet you, Brooke, and I'm glad I did. I'm glad you're okay."

"I'm glad to meet you, too, Tate. I have been such a bad mom, I hope you can forgive me one day—"

"You haven't been a mom at all."

Oh, whew, again!

No one said anything into that slippery pit for long seconds. All we could hear were Brooke's muffled, squeaking noises as she cried. I didn't think Tate was trying, exactly, to be mean, but he wasn't cutting her any slack, either.

"A mom is Boss Mom here, who is around all the time. She always hugs me and nags at me and feeds me and feeding me takes a long time, too. Five meals a day, that's what I eat. Plus snacks. Last night I ate eight chicken pancakes. That's a pancake that's the size of a chicken. It's a joke. But Boss Mom, she's the one who was up with me all night when something was going wrong and who helped me figure out how to deal with all the mean people out there.

"She's the one who bought me clothes and set up movie nights with popcorn and taught me all about herbs and plants and bought me all the books I wanted, especially ones about brains, and helped me set up my experiment room with all kinds of stuff, which I've only set on fire a few small times and maybe a couple of explosions. Boss Mom gave me all I needed to become me, do you know what I'm saying?"

"Yes, I do." Brooke pulled her arms tight around herself.

"And she was nineteen when she became a mom, too, and she did all that. Nineteen."

Brooke and I locked gazes, and I saw the shattered remains of the last seventeen years in her eyes. She knew what a failure she had been. She knew what she'd missed. She had missed out on being a mother. Can't get that one back, no matter how hard you wish. "You're right. I haven't been a mom to you, Tate. Not at all. And I'm glad you had your mom."

"That's why I have to call you Brooke now that we've met. Are you going to visit now and then, are we going to see you again? Are you going to take drugs again?"

"I would love to stay and visit for a few days and to see you in the tournament, if it's okay. I am not planning on taking drugs again. I would like to get to"—she sobbed, her mouth quivering—"get to know you, Tate, if that's what you want, too."

My sister was tiny. The drugs had wasted her to that sick-skinny appearance addicts get. It was pathetic. But she certainly seemed better than the first time I'd seen her in Hollywood.

Tate thought about that. "Okay. We can get to know each other, but it sort of hurts me in my heart, too. I mean, here you are, my mom, and I'm meeting you after seventeen years. You gave me up at a hospital and I get that you were on drugs, but you still made a choice to stay on drugs. You still chose drugs over me for all these years. You chose drugs over Nana Bird, Boss Mom, and Uncle Caden and his family. I'm not trying to make you feel bad. I'm telling you that it might be awhile before I can say, 'I love you, Mom,' you know what I mean?"

"Yes, I know. I do know, Tate." My sister struggled to stop sobbing.

"You missed out on a lot, Brooke, but, okay, let's shake on it." He offered his hand across the table. "We'll get to know each other."

"I would love that." Her gratefulness went to her core, I knew it. "Thank you."

"Okay dokay. Hey! Do you want to throw Skittles in each other's mouths? I love that. We can have a contest!"

So, when the tears were dried, and many were from Tate as he hugged my sister, the tough guy act had worn him down, we threw Skittles into each other's mouths.

It was fun.

It was a start.

Maybe the start of a new family, new relationships, new people to love.

I had a patient named Nikolai Burlachenko two years ago who saw dead relatives in the days before he died.

Nikolai's parents had brought him to America when he was thirteen. They fled Russia. His father had spoken out against the government, and he'd been jailed and tortured, as had Nikolai's mother. Nikolai remembered both his parents coming home when they were in Russia, beaten up, relatives carrying in their sagging, bloody bodies. He remembered the arrest warrant on his father and how they escaped from their home in the middle of the night.

The Burlachenko family was poverty-stricken. His parents had no money when they arrived in the United States. Both had been college professors. They ended up working as custodians, at first, until they put together their own custodial company and made some money.

"Once you're in poverty, once you go to bed hungry for weeks at a time, you never forget it. Hard work is the only thing that will protect you, that's what I taught my sons," Nikolai told me. "Hard work. Save your money."

He was dying of pancreatic cancer. I had known him for two months.

"Jaden, all I can tell you is that I have a party going on in my bedroom, and all my relatives who have passed are all waiting around until God's ready to take me to heaven. I see people who have already died on one side of me, and on the other side I see my four boys."

People talking to dead relatives is not, I would say, common. But it happens. This was not the first time I'd seen it.

"Who has died that you see?"

"I see my parents." He smiled. "Igor and Nadia. They were tired all the time when I was a boy, scared witless, but now, they are not tired, not frightened for their lives. I see my grandfather who had been executed in Russia, my uncles, one of whom died in prison there, aunts, three cousins, one who disappeared in Siberia, we never saw him again, didn't know what happened. . . . I see my friend, Shane, who died when we were seventeen in Illinois in a car accident. I see a bunch of my buddies . . . Howie, Blake, Peter.

"Most importantly, I see Helga, my wife. She's smilin' at me. Waiting for me. She's waiting. Dying isn't that bad." He cracked a smile.

His sons and their families were there 'round the clock. Nikolai had done something not unusual with his money. When he heard he had less than a year to live, he took his four sons and their families on three vacations: Disney World, Maui, and Russia, to his home in his hometown, so the grandkids would know where they came from. He left each son $100,000, not to be touched until they retired. "I want to know I'm helping to take care of you when you're old like me."

"One more thing I want to tell you, sons," Nicolai said to his sons, the last afternoon I was there. "I love you."

"We love you, too, Dad," they all said, so upset, acutely missing him already.

"All these relatives here, the ones who have passed, they're here for me, waiting, but I have to tell you one thing, sons. I love you. You've been good to me."

"We love you, too, Dad." They held each other, and their father, tenderly.

"I love you, boys. Always have, always will. Your mother loved you, too. Don't forget that we love you. Love your children, the same as we loved you, and I love you."

Nikolai died the next day.

His relatives took him up.

As a hospice nurse, this is what I've noticed: At the end, for the vast majority of people, it's about one thing.

Love.

That's it. That's all.

Love.

The next afternoon, Brooke and I drank Strawberry Berry Tea for Wild Women in my greenhouse, paper whites sprouting nearby, icicles hanging off the gutters. We talked about visiting Grandma Violet and Grandpa Pete during the summer, Grandma's healing business for the townspeople complaining about aches in their heads and aches in their butts, the animals we used to have, the crafts we made, the herbs and spices we used with Grandma Violet for spells, for fun, and for meals.

We even talked about Faith and Grace and the stories Grandma Violet told us about their time on the Oregon Trail.

"Remember where we were when she told us that story the first time, Jaden?" Brooke was pouring potting soil into five red pots for more bulbs.

"No, where?" I studied my colorful Chinese lanterns hanging from the rafters. I had always liked them. I liked my climbing frogs, too, and my collection of birdhouses.

"You and I were sitting next to her at the kitchen table. She had just finished healing Mrs. Hillington, who thought she was possessed by the devil because she had warts on her pinkie finger, and after her was Mr. Akoba, who was having a heart attack. He sat for an hour, drinking one of Grandma Violet's fruit blended drinks, not showing any signs, waiting for her to finish with Mrs. Hillington and her devil possession. Not a word of impatience out of him.

"Mr. Akoba told Grandma Violet later that his mother had taught him never to interrupt women, so he hadn't, even though he was in grave pain. Thankfully, she called the ambulance and he lived. Came back two days later and said it was Grandma's magic drink that fixed his engine and the engine was gunning again, all pistols firing, even the horn worked."

We laughed, then pieced together the Oregon Trail story, which went like this:

Faith, Grace, Russ, and Jack pooled their money and bought a wagon, oxen, and two more horses. They packed hundreds of pounds of flour, sugar, bacon, fat, tea (who could live without tea?), coffee, rice and beans, other food supplies, and whiskey. The women liked it straight-up and in their tea. They brought tools, utensils, clothing, bedding, guns, scissors, ropes, candles, a pot to piss in, and fabrics that the women insisted on.

Most importantly, at least to Faith and Grace, they brought their velvet satchel.

Before they left, Faith and Jack, and Grace and Russ were married in a field on top of a hill with only a preacher and the sun. Simple wedding bands were exchanged, and they had a picnic, the four of them, laughing, delighted, in love, before both couples wandered off to consummate passions that had burst forth the second they'd met over raspberry pie at the town picnic, when the women were desperate to get outta town.

On the trail, they were all soon exhausted and filthy. They traveled for five endless months, through all types of weather. They walked twelve to fifteen miles a day. Food soon became scarce. Though both men were expert shots, clean water was often hard to find. They forded rivers on rickety rafts after helping to stabilize the wagon on top of the raft.

The wagon wheels broke. They guided stubborn oxen and calmed horses when they saw rattlesnakes. Both women became sick. One man in another wagon lost a leg under a wagon wheel. He lived. Barely. Other pioneers died of accidental gunshot wounds, disease, childbirth, one suicide, injury, and sickness, and one pioneer went mad, wandered off, and no one knew where he had gone. The wagon train could not wait around to find him. If they did, they could get stuck in the mountains during winter and everyone would freeze to death.

But there was one fortunate . . . *thing.*

Faith's and Grace's husbands proved they were true men.

They had stuck with the women, protected them, cared for them, and been loyal the whole trip. In return, the cousins had not complained and worked beside their husbands. Faith had pulled Jack out of the river when the raft tilted. Grace had shot a rattlesnake clean out of the ground that was three feet from Russ's feet. They had both nursed the men when they were hurt and sick.

Their bonds could not be tighter. Their laughs, when they came, more pure.

When they arrived in Oregon City, Oregon, the four were fatigued to the bone and half-starved. They settled in for two weeks to rest and rejuvenate.

They decided to move to Portland, a new town on the Willamette River, filled with fir and pine trees, rain, and gray skies. Faith and Grace were dismayed. It was dirty, unsanitary, undeveloped, and somewhat lawless in this Wild West town, but again, they did not complain. It was surely better than being in jail and a hundred times better than being married to the slave torturers, Dwight and John.

Jack and Russ went into the timber business. They bought land in town and built homes. The first homes were small, functional. The next homes, years later, were fancy, on a park in the middle of the city. In both places the cousins planted thyme, sage, rosemary, parsley, oregano, lavender, Canterbury bells, hollyhocks, lilies, irises, sweet peas, cosmos, red poppies, peonies, and rows of roses, out of respect and love of their witchly ancestors.

Faith and Grace started another store, but there were not that many women to cater to at first, so they catered mostly to men and sold food, supplies, tools, etc. They did not think it smart to name it Faith and Grace's, as they knew they might well be hunted down by Dwight and John, therefore they named it The Portland Supply Store.

"And they did well," Brooke said.

"They did. The store was huge. Their kids ran it later."

"Remember how Grandma Violet told us the lesson in the

Oregon Trail story is to keep forging ahead, through the deserts, storms, hardships, near-drownings, illnesses, rattlesnake bites, bad luck, and contaminated water of life? I noted the contaminated water of life part particularly as a kid. I remember I really didn't want to drink messy, dirty water."

"And she told us to keep the hope." I tried to make my voice sound like Grandma Violet's. "Never give up hope, girls, it's what we all cling to to survive." I linked my arm over Brooke's shoulders and handed her a tissue when she teared all up.

"I miss them," she said.

"I miss them, too." I dropped a few tulip bulbs into the pots. "I've missed you, too, Brooke."

She sniffled. I handed her another tissue.

TATE'S AWESOME PIGSKIN BLOG

If we win a couple more games, we'll be in the state tournament, so the basketball pressure is a risin'.

This is what I know:

Yellowstone National Park should be duplicated and dropped in all fifty states. That should be a law. Man, it is awesome. Watching Old Faithful is like watching my mom's temper, Witch Mavis, blow her top except that it's water shooting out of an angry earth and not Boss Mom.

I like Popsicles. I can fit four in my mouth at one time. See the photo below, taken by my buddy Baron, he's the funniest guy you've ever met.

I want the space shuttle to park in my backyard, then I can study it. Here is what is weird: There are billions of people in this world who have no toilet, no running water in their homes, and America has space shuttles. Why is that?

Here is something else weird: We have universities all over the place, and in so many countries of the world people don't even get a basic education. Girls can't even go to school at all. Why is that? Why are some countries so much more advanced than others?

It is possible to overspice chili. I think it's funny when it happens. Last time my friends Milt and Anthony came over, I put extra chili powder in their chili and I thought their faces were gonna fall off. Here's a photo of them. See how there's smoke practically coming out of Milt's elephant ears? Yeah, you have elephant ears, Milt. Didn't your mother ever tell you?

I like orchids. There. I said it. Call me a pansy if you want to, but it's not going to change my orchid love. Speaking of pansies, they have faces and they are watching you. I'm not kidding. Pansies watch people.

I want to meet an alien.

I don't want to meet rabid raccoons.

Notice I didn't write anything about the tournament?

Maybe it's because I'm too nervous.

Maybe it's because I don't want to think about it.

Or maybe it's because I'm excited about it, but I don't want it to take over my whole life. You know how some things can do that. They take over your whole life. Maybe it's something you're worried about. Something you're angry, sad, excited, looking forward to, or freakin' wigged out about, but it's all you can think about and that ain't never right. (Ha! Boss Mom, I used the word ain't. You ain't gonna like that.) Never. You gotta have a lot of things to think about.

That's why I'm thinking about asking Boss Mom to take me to get a dozen doughnuts and then I'll eat them in one sitting and put a photo up.

Here's a picture of Boss Mom and me at the doughnut store along with my uncle Caden, the triplets, who are dressed as sharks, except for Heloise, who says she is a shark-gypsy and that's why she has a scarf with gold coins wrapped around her shark outfit, and my cousin Damini. She took off her leg and put it in the middle of the table when we were eating. See? She put her chocolate doughnut on top of her own leg. She is weird. You are weird, Damini. . . . Keep your leg on!!

Brooke was so frail, I thought she might physically crumble if pushed in the wrong direction. She looked older than her age, her green eyes the recipients of hundreds of memories that scraped the bottom dwellings of human existence.

"I miss Dad," I said one night at the kitchen table as we chopped potatoes for Pacific Ocean Perfect Clam Chowder, using our Grandma Violet's mother's recipe.

"Me too. I can't get him out of my head, ever. I can hardly live with it."

There was an odd tone to her stricken voice. "Brooke—"

"I miss him. I ruined his life." She chopped harder, the knife flying.

"You didn't ruin it—" But I knew that was only part true.

"His daughter was an addict, Jaden. Chasing drugs, drunk, anxious, argumentative, sneaking out, screaming, lying . . . and then I ruined his life."

"He loved you, Brooke. He would be so proud of you now, sober, here, with Tate and me and Mom—"

"And that makes it all the worse for me. He was so good and I was so bad."

She started crying again, and I didn't press further. I put my arm around her shoulders as her tears fell into the potatoes. That's all you can do sometimes, I think, put an arm around someone's shoulders, close your mouth, and let them cry it out.

The clam chowder was delicious that night, though salted with Brooke's misery.

There were sixteen teams in the state play-offs in our league. We would play in the gym of our local university.

The first game we won by twenty-one points. Tate scored twenty-eight points. He was on fire.

Many newspapers and news organizations were there, chronicling the kid with the big head. They called the house, wanted to talk to Tate and me, mostly Tate. They copied parts of his blog, especially where Tate wrote, "Having a big head gives my brain more room to grow," and "My eyes are crooked, but they do have x-ray vision," and, "The size of my head makes me seductive. It's a pheromone scent that attracts women. Yeah, I think it's a chick magnet."

TJ Hooks's team, unfortunately, also won.

The next game, the quarterfinals, we won by eighteen points. Tate scored twenty-four points.

TJ Hooks's team, again unfortunately, also won.

Needless to say, our town was flipping out.

The tournament was one of those turn-off-the-lights-if-you're-the-last-to-leave sort of things. Main Street in Tillamina shut down. The week before the game all the stores had signs up. WE WILL CLOSE EARLY FOR THE STATE BASKETBALL TOURNAMENT DAYS. GO BOBCATS!

The semifinal game was played on a weekday, in the afternoon, and both schools were busing their kids over, including their dance teams, bands, and cheerleaders. It was mobbed.

Caden wore his ripped, muscled Mid Court Mob shirt. Damini wore a gold-sequined skirt, couture from my mother, with her Mid Court Mob shirt, and the triplets dressed as bobcats. Harvey had added goblin claws, Heloise was wearing a gold coin waist chain, and Hazel slung a holster around her waist with a blue toy gun. Ethan came and I hugged him. He kissed me a few times, and it reminded me of the day before under a pile of blankets in my bedroom with a fire in the fireplace. . . .

My mother flew in and wore a svelte black dress with an orange boa. Brooke wore a Mid Court Mob shirt like everyone else. People from our town who had known her years ago did a double take when they saw her, and then embraced her with smiles and laughter.

"I was such a hellion, in endless trouble . . ." she said, and swallowed hard, pushing back her auburn hair. "But they're being nice, as if none of that happened and they're glad to see me."

"They are, but I have to warn you, sister, Martin Hooks may be lurking around spying."

"Yuck. I don't want to see him."

"I don't, either. I'm hoping his team is eliminated today by the team they're playing."

Tate and his teammates and the other team came out to practice to hysterical cheers and yelling. It was so noisy we couldn't hear our own screams so Ethan kissed me. I don't know how the two are linked, they just are.

We were playing North Plateau High School.

The referees blew their whistles, and we were off and running. Tate started and we jumped ahead early. Tate made some incredible shots, including two hook shots, which sent our fans into a tizzy.

The North Plateau students were well-behaved for a while, then a group of maybe twenty kids started chanting, "Martian man, Martian man, Martian man," whenever Tate handled the ball.

For a second Tate was distracted by them and missed a pass. The ball went to the other side. He missed two shots. Another pass he threw was intercepted. His game was off, and the coach pulled him. I could see Coach Boynton psyching him up, yelling some confidence into him, while Tate held his head in his hands, his teammates patting him on the back.

Within minutes Tate was back in again, our crowd went wild,

and the other fans started yelling, "Martian man, Martian man, Martian man."

I turned and started toward the aisle—as did Brooke—but my brother grabbed me around the waist, then he grabbed Damini, who had followed me saying, "Balls and tarnation, I'm gonna punch those assholes."

Turns out I didn't need to do anything.

A kid on the other team, whose name I later learned was Cormac, had the ball. When Cormac heard the chant, he stopped and put his hands in a *T* for time-out. The ref blew the whistle.

Cormac turned to Tate and stuck his hand out to shake it. I could see Tate's hesitation, because he didn't know what was going on and the words "Martian man" were slamming around in his head, but he shook Cormac's hand.

Cormac took it one step further. He ran over to the announcers' table, grabbed a microphone, and jumped on top of it.

His side yelled and cheered for him, but Cormac shouted, "Shut your mouths, home boys."

When the whole gym was quiet, he said, and his voice was particularly deep, "You peoples over there, yeah, yous. The ones who are shoutin' at Tate and saying bad things with you bad mouths. You shut you damn mouths or I'm gonna shut 'em for you, you got that?"

Okay! That settled those kids right down.

"Now you know whose my brothers are, they're right there. Darrell, Michael, Ross, Harold. They came home from college to watch this game. Bros, you come out."

I watched as four huge men stood up right behind Cormac's team on the bleachers. *Huge.*

"You guys don't stop sayin' that smack about my friend, Tate, and my bros are gonna take care of yous, you got that? We gonna play a fair game. A fair game. Don't make me comes after yous, and don't make my brothers move."

Silence.

"You hear me? You shut up and quit yellin' that crap or I'm gonna turn you into crap. Got that?"

The kids were frozen, but a few heads nodded. Cormac

jumped off the announcers' table. Later the whole thing hit YouTube. The girl who downloaded it included a picture of Tate, part of the game they were playing before Cormac jumped onto the announcers' table, the fierce brothers, and Tate's blog site at the end of it. There were 3,900 hits by the next day.

The teams came back out, and Cormac slapped Tate on the back. I saw Tate wipe the tears off his face, touched by what Cormac did, and Cormac slapped him on the back again.

The whistles blew, and we were off and running again.

Cormac's brothers took it upon themselves to stand at the front of the kid section for the rest of the game. Not one more rude thing was said about Tate.

"Class," Caden said, after leading three cheers in a row. "Those men are classy."

"Elegant family," my mother said. "Mark my words, I'll bet the mother wears designer heels."

The game went into double overtime. I could tell that Tate was exhausted. In the last three seconds, when we were down by one point, Baron lobbed Tate the ball. It was a Hail Mary pass and a Hail Mary basket. Tate shot from near to half court, over to the right, his right arm swinging.

The clock wound down, three . . . two . . . the ball was in the air, my mother grabbed my hand, Brooke gasped, the ball arched, spun, spun, spun . . .

Swoosh!

Right through the net.

We descended into chaos.

Our side cheered so hard I thought the roof might cave.

The kids rushed the court.

The team parents cried.

The cameramen and reporters joined the jumping mob in the middle of the court.

Before we could stop them, Damini and the triplets scooted their way down the bleachers, too. The other kids recognized the triplets and pushed them toward Tate, along with Damini. The boys put the triplets on their shoulders and a couple of them held Damini up, too.

There was my son, arms up, smile a mile wide, his teammates cheering, and right by him was Damini with her arm around Tate, her prosthetic leg out, not hidden at all by her gold-sequined skirt because, as she always told me, "why hide what lets me walk?" and the triplets, dressed as strange bobcats, claws in the air.

We were in the finals for the Class 4A state title.

Unfortunately, regrettably, we were playing TJ Hooks's team. I felt a frisson of fear dance up and down my back, leaping from rib to rib.

"I don't feel settled about this," Caden said. "I feel unsettled."

"The air is pierced with Martin's odiousness," my mother said. "I wish he would explode."

The games were usually back-to-back, but we had a week's break because the night of our last game, a whole bunch of pipes burst after being frozen and the mess flooded the gym.

Tate practiced relentlessly, with his team and alone.

As my mother gushed, "I am so thrilled I can hardly stand it! My bones are quivering with glee!"

My bones were quivering with glee, too. And guilt. I wish I'd let him play before this.

Ethan agreed that his bones were also quivering with glee. "Gleeful bones," he said, then kissed me silly. "Let's get our gleeful bones naked together in bed."

Caden's family came over to visit after Brooke arrived.

Caden cried when he saw Brooke, transformed to a shy slip of a woman now, but he was protective, encouraging, and brought her a bouquet of lilies in a long, rectangular glass vase, tulips between them. "So glad you're back, Brooke, so glad you're back. You feeling better now?"

She assured him she was. She took him outside for a walk through our fir trees that first visit. I knew she was apologizing to him, and when they came back in, they'd both been crying.

"Come and work for me in my flower shop, Brooke. We can

make flower arrangements in the shapes of sports cars, dogs, elephants, you name it, we do it."

Brooke hugged him. She hugged Damini, too, who said, "It's great to finally meet you. You've been through a bad time and me, too. Look, I lost a leg because of it."

The triplets bopped around in costumes. This time there was an alligator, a space alien, and a George W. Bush. She hugged them, too.

Tate was getting to know Brooke day by day.

They played chess together, she lost, they walked on the property. She spent hours in his experiment room. She tossed Skittles into his mouth and tried to balance fruit on her head. She baked with him, treats, taco soup, and breads.

At one point Tate said, "I've missed you, Brooke."

Brooke cried.

He patted her back.

"You sure have a lot of tears in you, Brooke. Do you think you're ever gonna run out?"

"No," she whispered. "No."

"Okay. Glad I know. I'll make us popcorn. That daredevil show is on TV again. Do you want to watch it with me?"

They made meatballs while they watched the show, laughing the whole time.

I was beginning to breathe easier. I didn't want to let myself like having Brooke around again, but I did. She was funny and fun. She is the wittiest person I know. She is really deep because she's been through traumatizing experiences that bring on wisdom, perspective, compassion.

I started to dare to hope that maybe this time she could stay clean.

18

On my drive home from work, I stopped my car across the street from the Fischerson house, then climbed out and explored, ignoring the freezing rain.

Later, after a dinner of butternut squash soup, chicken cordon bleu, and vanilla ice cream with chocolate sprinkles, all of which Tate and Brooke helped me make, I grabbed a sketchbook and took it out to the greenhouse. Tate did his homework for his online advanced calculus class next to me, while I drew pages and pages of plans for the interior of my imaginary tea/herb/spice/sandwich/dessert shop.

I thought of the patients I'd had over the years. I still missed some of them.

For example, Mrs. Grosell, who was only fifty, who said that she felt blessed to have had fifty years. "Many people don't even get close to what I've had."

Dale Hu, who taught me how to juggle. Even the day before he died, he was intent on me gaining this skill. I still juggle apples and oranges now and then and think of him.

Sergeant Chen Kim, who had Lou Gehrig's disease and who had loved to cook. I would go to his house and cook in front of him. He loved it.

They all died quietly, no special endings, but I had made them comfortable.

The losses, though, for some reason, have all of a sudden added up to too much for me. Too much.

I grabbed a green colored pencil and added a tree to the outside of my shop, then drew white lights over it. I love white lights in trees.

Death had exhausted me. It was running me down.

I stared at my plans and laughed as a bucket of rain pelted the windows.

The laugh felt freeing.

"What is it, Boss Mom?"

I showed Tate the plans.

He nodded and smiled. "That's sick it's so cool."

I hugged him tight.

TATE'S AWESOME PIGSKIN BLOG

We're in the finals.

Come, my peeps.

Come.

Ethan and I became engaged that Sunday after hiking around our property through a light snow, the snowflakes twirling around, white magic landing on our hats.

He stopped, pulled me into his arms, kissed me silly, and said, "Jaden, will you marry me?"

"Marry you?" A rush of trippy euphoria sped through my body. "But . . . you . . . we . . . it's not been long. . . ."

"It's been years."

"But once you get to know me more, you might not like me. . . ."

"I already like you. I love you."

"I have obsessive rituals. I cut up herbs and mix them with spices. . . ."

"I've seen it. It's creative, thoughtful."

"I also fret and worry about Tate constantly, and I'm overprotective and hover over him."

"I will fret and worry with you when it's something we should fret and worry about, and we'll work on you not hovering too much."

"I have a sarcastic mouth, I'm impatient, and I have some anger issues."

"Your mouth is sexy, you're not impatient with me, and we all have issues."

"I work all the time. I'm way too serious. The fun has been beat out of me."

"Same here. We can change and become more fun together."

"You know my mom thinks she's a witch, from a witch line dating to a queen, and she thinks I'm a witch, too."

"She's a focused, rational woman except for that part, and I find it endearing."

"And I have a temper."

"I've seen it many times. It's an exciting part of your personality, and please notice I didn't blame your red hair."

"Thank you. It's not my hair, though, it's my eyes."

"And I love the blue and the green. I want to be your husband and Tate's father and your witchly mother's son-in-law. I want to be a part of your whole family. I want to live with you forever until I'm old and creaky and you're old and creaky and we'll travel the world and see what else is out there."

"Might as well die having an adventure," I said, overwhelmed at the thought of adventures with Ethan.

"Yes, we might as well."

"I think that sounds nice, Ethan." I sniffled. Nice? Surely I could think of something better to say to his proposal?

"It sounds nice to me, too, Jaden." He dropped to one knee in the snow and took the burgundy-colored box one might expect with a marriage proposal out of his pocket. "Will you marry me, Jaden Bruxelle?"

Would I marry him? "Yes. Oh yes." I dropped to both knees, put my hands on his face, and gave him a long smackeroo. "Yes, oh yes, oh yes, forever yes!" After more smackeroos we decided to run to the house, jump in my four-poster bed and explore the bounce of my mattress. It is a good thing no one was home.

"Wife," Ethan said to me afterward.

"What?"

"Wife." He kissed me. "I love the sound of that word."

"I do, too, husband." My voice wobbled.

"Wife. This is my wife, Jaden. Jaden is my wife. Jaden and Ethan are married. Married couple. Wife. Husband. My wife is the love of my life. I love you, wife."

"I love you and ..." I hesitated, sniffled again.

"And ..."

"And thank you, Ethan. Thank you for asking me." I couldn't believe it. I could hardly understand it. I was going to marry Ethan. Me. Ethan and I would be together forever. I had Ethan. After all those long, sad, lonely years of wanting him, of not being able to have him, to hold him, he was here, in my bed, the snowflakes fluttering down. "Thank you for wanting me to be your wife."

This time it was Ethan whose voice wobbled. "It is I who should thank you, Jaden." He picked up my hand, a chivalrous knight, and kissed it. "Thank you. I think we're going to have a beautiful life together."

"Me too, oh, me too."

"I have wanted this since I met you."

"I have dreamed of you forever."

Oh, pish. We are silly sappy.

We told my family the night before the tournament. I thought the ecstasy was going to kill my mother. She actually spread her arms out wide, closed her eyes, and said, "My spells worked! They took way too long, but they worked. Thank you, and thank you, God." She picked up the charms on her necklace and kissed them.

Caden bawled and said, "I will do all of your flower arrangements! I'll make one arrangement into a raft, because that was your first date. Another will be a greenhouse, and a third will be of Aphrodite, goddess of love."

Damini said, "Whoa, Aunt Jaden. You finally have someone

to make out with. Can I be a bridesmaid?" Yes, absolutely. "I love you, Aunt Jaden." She hugged me. "I'm happy, happy for you. Remember what I said about giving you a leg if you ever needed it."

"I would never forget it." I turned to my sister. "Brooke, would you be a bridesmaid, too?"

She could not answer through all her jumbling emotions, and her face crumpled, but she hugged me with those wispy arms, and I knew that was a yes.

Tate said, "Finally. Now you two can get on with it instead of ogling each other with lusty looks that a person of my age and innocence should never see or be corrupted by. Young gentlemen should not be privy to such unbridled passion. I am easily influenced, and you must be careful with my purity, not fill my imagination with these potent images of uncontrolled love—"

"You're a pain in my keester, Tate," Damini said. He picked her up and threw her over his shoulder.

Tate would walk me down the aisle. "That'll be excellent, Boss Mom. I'll wear your bridal bouquet on my head."

We told the triplets there would be a wedding. I asked Heloise and Hazel to be flower girls and Harvey to be a ring bearer.

"Ya. I do it," Heloise said. "I be bunny!"

"Me, too." Hazel jumped up and down. "I be monster! Roar!"

"I be ring bear!" Harvey said, claws up. "Grrr!"

"This is glorious," my mother said. "I'll have the writers put me in jail for murder for a month before I'm acquitted on a technicality so we can plan the wedding! I'll knock my current husband out, wrap him in ropes, and toss him over the side of a rowboat in the middle of the night. It will be evilly juicy...." She pulled me close, her auburn bob to my locks, tears in her voice. "This is one of the best days of my life, Jaden. Your father would be thrilled. He loved you very much."

I loved him, too.

Ethan hugged my mother and me, then the whole family hugged together.

"Roar!" and "Grrr!" the triplets said.

"I a brown ring bear!" Harvey said.

Maggie Granelli was seeing angels.

In the last few days they were flying in more and more often.

"That one is a beautiful angel, isn't it, Jaden? Came down right off my staircase."

I sat beside Maggie's bed, with the view of her cherished, but dead, rose garden, and held her hand. She was staring, her eyes blank, but wondrous, unblinking, yet fully believing in what she saw.

"She's beautiful," I said.

"Do you see those wings!" Maggie breathed, pointing at her precious, barren rose garden. "White wings, and gold, too. I had no idea! No idea at all! Oh, they're fluttering. But this time they're not flying away. They're ..." She gasped. "They're staying with me now. Oh! Did you hear that?"

Maggie had been declining quickly, almost overnight, her daughters with her always. Things were steep and fast now, as if the disease had realized it was late in killing her and wanted to get things done efficiently.

"Two angels now." Maggie smiled. "I'm pleased! Two!"

"What do they look like, Momma?" one daughter asked, all four crying.

"They look like angels," Maggie said, her voice stunned. "But they're much taller than I expected. Their wings are glowing and full of layers of feathers. ..."

I held her hand, and the daughters sobbed.

I figured Maggie had, at most, a few more days.

She would be going to the rose garden in the sky.

I don't need to write down how many red cinnamon Gummi Bears I ate when I left. It would be embarrassing.

The scent of death was stronger in my herb and spice combinations, almost overpowering.

Who was it? What should I do? Lock everyone up? My mother, Caden, Brooke, and I had talked about it again. We were worried, but what could we do?

Stay at home? That's when your house burns down.

Take Tate out of the tournament in case it was him? He would probably try to get there, by himself, and get hit by a car.

Keep my mother off planes to Los Angeles? She'd take the train and the train would be derailed.

My mother said she was "delving into her spells" twice a day.

I was delving into my worry, and it was a long, black, endless pit. I gripped the cross charm on my necklace.

For the final game I drove Tate to school to ride the school bus with his teammates to the university gym. I tried not to cry as I hugged him. "Good luck, son."

"Boss Mom, I don't need luck." He tapped his head, his ears, and thumped his fists together. "General Noggin, Bert and Ernie, and Billy and Bob are gonna bring down the house. Road Runner is gonna put on his x-ray vision and shoot." He put an apple on his head after he climbed out of the car. His friends ran over to greet him.

Tate put his arms straight out and announced, "Don't touch me! I am Tate Bruxelle, world-famous tightrope walker! Don't make a sound, don't interrupt my deep concentration while I traverse the Grand Canyon on this rope with an apple on my head!"

His friends bent over laughing.

Tate turned slowly back and said to me, not bothering to lower his voice, "By the way, I love you, Boss Mom, even though you don't seem to truly understand quantum physics." The apple wiggled and he froze, eyes rolling up.

"I love you, too, Tate, even though you don't seem to appreciate paprika as much as you should."

He grinned, then placed one foot precisely in front of the other. "I'm going to break the world record for tightrope-walking daredevils! I'm higher than anyone has ever been! I'm crazier than anyone has ever been! No one has ever tried to cross the Grand Canyon before on a rope!"

"Tightrope walker Tate!" Milt yelled.

"Out of his way, one and all," Baron intoned. "Let the record-breaking begin."

"It's a death-defying act!" Anthony said. "He could die and be squished!"

"I am in the middle of the Grand Canyon, on a rope, no net!" Tate said, very dramatic. "The river is rushing below, birds are flying by, the wind is trying to push me off into the canyon, and, oh no, a woman in a helicopter has flashed me her boobies. . . . I must shield my eyes from this depravity!"

He turned one more time and waved at me, then deepened his voice. "I will keep walking! I will not look down! I will do this for America, for America! I've done it! I've crossed the Grand Canyon on a rope despite the distraction of the flashing boobies with an apple on my head!"

His friends cheered his announcement, wrestling, pushing each other as boys do.

"Oh no, I've reached the other side and the women are all over me!" Tate screamed. "They're clutching me, grabbing, trying to kiss me and draw me to their bodies! No one's experienced anything like this ever, the women are in a frenzy, they're going crazy! Someone hold them back, they're all over me, hands going places they shouldn't go, touching things they shouldn't touch!"

His friends bent over cackling.

"Oh no, they're stripping me of my clothes!" Tate shrieked. "I'm totally naked now, but the apple is still balanced on my head, and the women are stripping off their own clothes, too! It's chaos, folks, total chaos! All the women are naked, and me, poor Tate, has women lining up in front of him! Here comes the helicopter boobie flasher again, AHHHHH!"

His friends howled.

"Help me, help me! All these women, what shall I dooooo?"

I blinked real hard. The tightrope walker was a funny, fearless, amazing person.

I sure loved that kid.

The hit came from TJ Hooks.

At the end of the game, Kendrick took the three foul shots for Tate, but it didn't matter anymore.

The university gym was rocking as only a high school basketball tournament can rock. The bands blared, the fans yelled at full throttle, the cheerleaders jumped about.

On the court both teams were running drills, practicing their shots, and trying to shut out the blasting noise of the gym and concentrate before the game officially started.

"Ah, I see we're playing Sunrise with Martin Hooks, he of diarrhea fame," my mother announced, quite loudly, from our seats on the bleachers about ten rows up from our team.

"Yes, we are." I had wished and hoped that the Sunrise team would be eliminated. No such luck. I felt ill and nervous even seeing TJ.

"Ew," Brooke said. "Martin's more repulsive than ever. His face resembles mashed potatoes."

"Did you have to say that, Brooke?" I asked, pinching her elbow. "Now I'll never be able to eat mashed potatoes."

"Me, either," Caden said, wrestling with the triplets on his lap, who were making up a song about hot dogs. "What are we going to do for Thanksgiving now? You ruined it, Brooke."

"I think I feel a loosening-of-the-bowels spell coming on again," my mother said, batting her eyelashes. Today she was wearing an orange wrap dress and black tights, our team colors, in couture. "A release of the gut. A time of reflection and contemplation done while one's bottom is hanging over the toilet, the same spell as last time."

"Toilet!" Hazel shouted. She was dressed as a slice of pizza.

"Poop goes in the toilet, not out!" Heloise said. She was a dolphin.

"I poop, too!" Harvey said. "Poop!" He was a robot.

"Will you teach me that spell, Nana?" Damini asked, bopping up and down, her orange and black ribbons wrapped around her ponytail.

"It will be my pleasure, darling. Tonight."

Martin Hooks, protruding stomach sticking straight out like he'd swallowed the moon, was already on the floor of the gym, telling his hapless son what was what. I saw the opposing coach angrily stalk over to him. Clearly the coach was trying to get him off the floor.

They started to argue and Martin crossed his arms. Two more coaches, both assistants, also came up to Martin, followed by a security officer. They finally managed to get him to lumber up to his seat, three rows from the bench.

"Poor TJ." My mother clucked. "I do have some pity for that obnoxious soul. He didn't have a chance. I am now going to launch a preemptive strike against Martin, the toilet hugger."

"I don't think so."

"I think you should, Nana!" Damini said. "Beep him! Spell him!"

"There is no such thing as spells, Damini." I grabbed my mother's manicured hands as she wiggled them. She wriggled free. I caught them again. We were having a hand-wrestling contest yet again. She laughed, so did I. "I don't believe in your spells anyhow."

"Yes, you do."

"I do," Brooke said. "Spell him."

I held her hands tight, as Martin heaved himself up and started harassing his son again. I loosened my grip. "Gall, Mom. Go for it. If it works, his son will thank you for it."

My mother, with sneaky stealth, tapped her fingers together, then touched the charms on her necklace. Damini did the same thing, touching her charms, too.

I was gobsmacked, that'd be the word, *gobsmacked,* as I watched Martin grab his stomach in the middle of another harangue. He could hardly stand back up and wobbled his loaded body down the aisle, presumably to the toilet.

Honestly, it's not my mother. It's by chance and luck. The

man was the size of an upright rhino. He was screaming. He was stressed because he has only a semi-grip on reality. My mother raised her eyebrows at me, proudly self-satisfied.

"Give me a break, Mother," I said.

"Ha. I gave *him* a break. A gut break. A bowel break."

"Ah. Your witchly skills rise again, Mom," Brooke said. "Nothing surpasses a chant and a spell to get things going."

Caden was soon in front leading cheers, Damini and the pizza, dolphin, and robot beside him. In the midst of the cacophony, Ethan came in. My mother stood up, waved, and yelled, "Over here, handsome!"

Ethan smiled, shook hands with Caden, and hugged the pizza, dolphin, robot, and Damini. He climbed the bleachers and hugged my mother, who said to him, "Aren't you a sight for lusty eyes?" He greeted Brooke, then kissed me, winked, and I felt sexy and protected. Yum.

The whistles blew, the lights dimmed for dramatic effect, the bands played their fight songs, and each player on both teams was introduced to semi-hysterical cheering. The loudest, however, was reserved for Tate.

The ball tipped off, and seconds later Tate shot a three-pointer, first of the game, and made it. Brooke flew out of her seat, arms up in the air. Our side went crazy. We did not sit down the whole game. Brooke's voice was soon raw.

By the half, we were two points ahead. Tate had made four three-pointers, layups, and free throws, and he'd been fouled by TJ Hooks three times, his defender. Martin Hooks wobbled back up the bleachers, his face red and blotchy, and blew out more criticisms at his son and Tate.

I could see TJ's stress. At one point, after Tate had made another three-pointer, I thought TJ was crying. At another point, TJ swore and was called on a technical. I swear he cried then, too, his face crumpling as his father threw a full litany of rage at him. Martin actually thundered down the aisle and had to be restrained by two security guards and taken out at one point when Tate made another shot over TJ.

At the end of the fourth quarter, we were tied. We went into two overtimes. Milt, Anthony, and Baron fouled out. Sunrise lost three players, too. When we had ten seconds left, down by one, Kendrick blasted a pass to Tate from the end of the court and Tate shot outside the three-point line.

That's when it happened.

TJ Hooks, with his father back in the gym and out of control, charged Tate, full speed, almost like a tackle, when Tate was still a foot in the air from the last shot.

I saw it in slow motion, as if the scene was transferred into a speed that I could hold on to.

TJ slammed into Tate. Tate's feet flew out from under him. He sailed up and over, in an arc, as if he'd been sent over an imaginary high jump pole, landing on his head and neck. His head bounced once, twice, three times, hard, on the floor.

I heard my mother scream. I heard Caden yell, "Tate! Oh my God!" I heard Damini say, "Oh no, oh no, oh no."

Ethan was pounding down the bleachers and sprinting across the gym immediately. I followed him, pushing myself into the aisle and shoving people out of the way as I ran to Tate. I pushed his teammates aside, his coach aside, my blood running cold, my body shaking.

I knew. I knew right then.

Tate was not moving, blood pooling beneath his head, a river of blood, streaking here, streaking there. Ethan shouted for an ambulance, then put his hands on Tate's head, holding it tight, the blood spreading through his fingers.

I watched horrified, the noise gone, as I saw my Tate, *my son,* as if I was in a nightmare, the blood flowing out of him, hot and red and sticky . . . all that *blood,* blood that shouldn't be there. This was a basketball game, we were on a court, he shouldn't be bleeding, he shouldn't be still, his eyes shouldn't be closed, he shouldn't be pale and getting more pale by the second. He shouldn't be twitching. The paramedics shouldn't be shouting and putting tubes in and an oxygen mask on as Ethan directed them to do.

Beside me, my mother was making raw screeching noises, Brooke holding her, Caden shouting, "Tate, Tate, my boy, Tate!"

I was too petrified to scream, I could only clutch Tate's cold hand, getting colder and colder it seemed, while I keened, rocking back and forth. "Tate, oh Tate. I love you, honey. It'll all be fine. Oh God. Please. Make everything fine."

I heard my mother praying. I heard Caden swearing, I heard Brooke and Damini crying.

I was in a nightmare of blood, the life draining out of my unconscious, ashen boy.

I thought of the herbs and spices, and a hard chill balled up in my constricted throat, my whole body trembling. I had been smelling death for months.

It was him.

It was for Tate.

I wanted to die, too.

"I don't have comforting news." Ethan sat across the conference room table from me. He was pale white.

My mother made a high-pitched, gasping sound. Caden groaned and pulled me closer.

"No, Ethan, no." I shook my head at him. "No."

Ethan clenched his jaw, his eyes darting to a corner, as if he couldn't bear to meet my eyes until he brought himself under control. There were other doctors and nurses in the room, a number of whom had been with Tate from the second the ambulance rushed to the hospital, siren blaring, and whisked him into the trauma unit.

I had collapsed as soon as I climbed out of the ambulance. Caden picked me up and hauled me to a private waiting room, my mother limping behind, crying, propped up by Brooke, her makeup smeared all over her face. The triplets and Damini had been taken by friends of ours to their home.

"Jaden." Those brown eyes with a touch of cinnamon found mine again. "Tate is not doing well. When he hit the floor the shunt shifted."

"And how is he now? How is he?"

"Hon—" He stopped himself from calling me honey. "I am sorry, I am sorry to tell you this, but he's . . . he's in a coma."

A coma!

A coma! No, he's a boy. A seventeen-year-old boy. He's not in a coma!

"Can't you, Ethan"—I could hardly speak—"can't you get him out of the coma?"

"Yes. But we have to operate. There are complications, there's been bleeding, his vitals are . . . they're struggling. He's struggling."

"Then do something! Do something! Fix it!"

Ethan's eyes filled with tears.

I stood up and pounded the table, the crystals in my hair from Tate swinging forward. "Help him! Help him!"

"Jaden, sit down, let me explain."

"I will not sit down." My voice cracked like broken glass, and I hit the table again, both palms down. "You're going to operate on him. You're going to fix this, Ethan."

He didn't say anything for a few long, hanging seconds. "I don't know if it's fixable."

"What do you mean, you don't know if it's fixable? You'll fix it. You love him." My voice broke as I batted down hysteria. "You love Tate. You know you do."

Ethan leaned back in his chair, his face tight, flushed.

"You love him, you can help him, you can do this, Ethan!"

"Loving Tate has nothing to do with it, Jaden. He's in a critical place, I'm sorry."

I am not stupid. I saw the expression in Ethan's eyes. "He's not going to die."

Ethan would not confirm that. He would not confirm that my son wasn't going to die. I thought I was going to faint. "He's not going to die, he won't. Operate on him!"

"I can't operate on him."

"You can!" I shrieked. "You will."

He wiped the tears from his eyes. "Dr. Raminsky will operate. I will assist."

Dr. Raminsky was sitting next to him. The only thing that registered was that he had black hair. "No, you'll do it. I want you! Tate would want you!"

"I can't operate because you and I are engaged. Tate will soon be, legally, my son. In my heart he is my son already." He ran a hand over his hair. "I can't do it."

"Yes, you can. You can do it." I felt my knees going weak, that weakness spreading to my whole body. "You do it, you'll do it right."

"Dr. Raminsky can—"

"No. No. Not him, *you!*" Tears rolled down my face and onto the table.

Ethan came around the table and tried to pull me to him, but I struggled away. In the background I heard my mother's sobs, Brooke's hiccupping cries, Caden's moan of "God help us."

"It's not right, Jaden," Ethan said, his voice firm, his eyes pleading. "It's not medically sound. I'm involved with you and with Tate. No one operates on his family members or close friends, and there's a reason for it, this is it—"

I yanked off my sparkly engagement ring and banged it onto the table. "We are no longer engaged then! Tate is not your son. He is not your son-to-be. I am not your fiancée. We're done." I was hysterical, I knew I was hysterical, but I had lost all control. "Go operate. Help him, *help him!*"

Ethan grew completely pale.

I grabbed him by the lapels of his white coat. "Listen to me, Ethan." I did not even recognize myself, I did not recognize the wild and rash animal I'd turned into. I had always had Witch Mavis, but this was Witch Mavis multiplied by two, plus raw panic. "I want you to save my son. *Save him.* If I have to give you up, I'll do it. This is my son, don't you get it? Don't you get it?" I screamed. *"Don't you get it?"*

"I get it."

"Good. Then go!" I pushed him in the chest, both hands, hard. I pushed him again, when he didn't move, tears raining down my cheeks. "I am begging you, Ethan. Go! Go! Please, Ethan!"

"Jaden—" he said, his voice soft, comforting, but I knew he was hurting, head to foot.

"Don't Jaden me!" I pushed him again. "Get in there, damn it!"

Dr. Raminsky interjected, "Dr. Robbins, may I see you outside for a minute?"

Ethan pulled me close, hugging me. When he released me, I wobbled, dizziness and despair making me feel ill. Caden leaped up and put me in a chair. I dropped my forehead to the table and banged it. This was *my* fault. I loved Ethan, I had loved him since I met him, but I should never have gotten involved. Never. Tate had seemed healthy the last couple of years, but I knew that anything, medically speaking, could happen, I'd known it all along. Any emergency could come up at any time, and it had! It was my fault.

I had blinded myself to this tragic reality because of what *I* wanted, what was best for *me*, and now I was depriving my son of one of the best pediatric neurosurgeons in the nation. All for love, for lust and passion.

I shouldn't have let him play basketball. I knew it. I'd said yes. And look where we were now! In the emergency room of a hospital arguing about my son getting his head operated on. I left my head on the table, overwhelmed, weakened to nothing.

Dr. Raminsky and Ethan walked outside, already talking. My mother held me as she trembled and sobbed, as did Caden and Brooke. We were a group of horrendously wrecked people.

Within three minutes, Ethan was back in the conference room. He was even whiter than before.

"Jaden," he said, his voice soft, but I heard the steel running through it. "I'll operate on Tate."

I lifted my head, but I could move no other part of my body. "You will?"

"Yes. I will."

"Thank you. Oh, thank you, Ethan." I wanted to get up to hug him, but my knees didn't work; fear had turned them to goo.

Later I was to learn that Ethan had not acquiesced to operate because I'd thrown a fit and whacked his ring on the table. He agreed to it because Dr. Raminsky, who was highly qualified but not as qualified as Ethan, had told Ethan, point-blank, that he wasn't sure he was skilled enough for this operation. Was Dr. Raminsky afraid that Tate might die under his hands? Maybe.

Ethan sat down by me and stared deep into my eyes, so deep that I could see the despair in his, the pessimism, the doubt. "You have to know, as the mother of my patient, that I cannot guarantee you"—he took a deep breath—"I cannot guarantee that I can save him. I am operating because it's our only hope, his only chance. But it is . . ." He paused and his eyes filled, before he blinked and I saw him willfully, with each ounce of strength and professionalism he had, pull himself together. "This is a last-ditch effort, Jaden. You need to know that going in."

I gripped his hands hard. "I know you, Ethan Robbins. I know you, I love you, and I know you'll save my son, and you and I and Tate will go rafting again." My voice became high-pitched and tight. "We'll throw Skittles at each other. We'll hang out in my greenhouse. We'll see Tate graduate. We'll laugh together again. I know it. I know he's going to live. He will, Ethan." I burst into dry heaving. "He *will* live, he will, he will." Mentally, I was gone, lost, devastated. "He will live."

For a brief millisecond, that concrete hard resolve weakened, and I saw the harsh pain on Ethan's face, but he snapped back, his training kicking in. His shoulders straightened and his eyes started to focus elsewhere, as if he was already in the operating room.

"We need to operate immediately."

He whirled around and left, the other doctors and nurses following him.

The sheer hell of waiting began.

The public waiting area of the hospital was jammed. We were hugged and held. People insisted we sit and eat, have something to drink. We couldn't eat, we couldn't drink, we could barely breathe. Over the course of several hours, our neighbors and friends came, along with relatives we hadn't seen in a while. The team was there. Their parents, kids from school. My mother's friends in Hollywood, many from *Foster's Village,* flew up. People prayed, they cried, they held hands.

Three hours into the operation, my crumbling mother, Caden, Brooke, and I were escorted to a private room with a table and chairs. Dr. Raminsky met us. "We're trying," he said, but I saw the defeat in his eyes.

"Try harder!" I yelled. I burst into yet another round of tears as Caden grabbed me. "Damn it, try harder!"

"Some things have gone well, some things have not gone well," Dr. Raminsky said. "It's going to be awhile."

"Then get the things that aren't going well done better!"

He patted my arm. He knew a hysterical mother when he saw one. He did not take it personally. "Jaden, you know that Ethan is the best pediatric neurosurgeon. If anyone can save Tate, it's him."

"I know that, I know! Get in there and do it! Help him, please! Please!"

"It's an extraordinarily complicated operation. Tate received a critical blow to the head." His face was tense, white, stressed. "We'll let you know as soon as we know more. We're doing our best, and we will not quit on your son, Jaden. Please remember that. We will not quit on your son."

"I know you won't!" I told him, my panic turning to anger, Witch Mavis now out and flying. "I'm not quitting on my son, either! I'll never quit on him! Never." I picked up a chair and threw it. I picked up another chair and threw that, too. "I will not quit on Tate! Don't you dare do it, either!"

Caden grabbed me.

I could not throw Caden so we cried together instead, Brooke and my mother wrapped around us.

19

At the end of eleven hours, I felt Tate.

I felt him in my heart. I heard his voice. I had walked outside, by myself, to stand near a fountain that the hospital had designed, undoubtedly, to soothe the rampaging emotions of anyone unfortunate enough to be there. I let myself fall apart and kneeled as near as I could to the water, droplets spraying my face. I held the charms around my neck and prayed for Tate.

It was pitch-black, the stars white and shiny, the air clear and bone-chillingly cold.

"Boss Mom."

I whipped around at Tate's voice, but Tate wasn't there.

Of course he wasn't there.

Tate was in an operating room. His head was cut open. Heads should never be cut open. Never.

People in white coats with sharp instruments, tubes, suctions, computers, and beeping machines were poking into his head, led by Ethan, my Ethan. He was cutting things and shifting things and trying to heal and trying not to kill my son. He was threading in and out of brain mass that should be left alone your whole, whole life.

Ethan was trying to save my son. He was trying. Try, Ethan, try! Please, Ethan. Help me. Help us. Help us.

"Mom."

I heard Tate's voice again. Clearly I was losing my mind. There was no one out here, only the water rushing from the fountain designed to soothe the hearts of the grieving and the petrified.

I felt Tate's arm around me. He put his curly-haired head close to mine. There was no blood. There was no coldness, either; he was warm and I felt his warmth. He held me close and I clung to him. "Oh, Tate!"

This was not the *real* Tate, I knew that. It couldn't be. But I sobbed into his shoulder anyhow, believing I would die from pain. "Oh Tate, hang on, Tate."

"Boss Mom, it's okay. I'm good and everything's okay now."

"Tate, honey." I thought my heart would burst. I thought it would open up and burst.

"I love you, Boss Mom."

I heard those words so clearly, each syllable, the cadence, the lilt of his humor.

"I love you, Tate," I said, rasping. "I love you with my whole heart. You can do this. Stay with me, stay with us. Fight!"

"I'm fighting, Mom. Billy and Bob are up and fighting." I heard him chuckle. "The same way I fought to understand advanced statistics."

"Keep fighting." I clenched my hand around my cross charm. "Don't give up. We're Bruxelles. We don't quit, you know that!"

I smelled Tate, the smell of that musky shampoo he used, Skittles, apples, chicken pancakes. "Oh my God, help me," I cried. "Please help us."

"I'm right here, Boss Mom. Soon I'll be balancing an orange on my head, don't worry."

"I want you right here, with me, with us!" I ran a wobbly hand through my hair, and all the crystals that Tate gave me fell off and into the fountain. "Oh no, oh no . . ." My hands shot into the water and I tried to find them, I tried and tried, the water droplets mixing with my tears, covering my face, my arms, part of my shirt, but the crystals were lost in the bubbles. Lost.

"I'll give you new crystals, don't worry. I'm going for a while, but you'll see me again. You can make me chicken pancakes. They're better when you make them. Bye, Boss Mom."

"Tate? Tate!"

Soaked, defeated, the crystals gone, I knew I was alone again. Completely, utterly alone. It was me and the fountain. That was it.

He was gone.

There was nothing now. There was no Tate.

I felt it as clearly as I had felt his presence earlier.

It was only me now. Only me.

"Tate! Tate!" I screamed, my voice muted by the rush of the fountain. "Come back, Tate, come back, Tate." I pleaded with the heavens, with that blackened sky, "Come back! Please, Tate! Please God!" I curled up, sobbing. I was dying, too, I was dying from the pain, and from the invading, pervasive guilt. All the times I had smelled cloying, rotting death, the scent of it rising from my herbs and spices . . .

I had known the threat was there.

I had smelled death and I had turned away.

I had known that basketball could be dangerous for Tate. *I had known it.*

I had said yes, so he could live the life he wanted.

And now he would not have a life. Because his stupid mother said yes when she should have said no.

It was my fault.

I was responsible.

I would pay for that irresponsibility for the rest of my life.

I would pay for that in the loss of Tate.

I had failed as a mother.

I was alone. I would always be alone. This loss would never leave me. I would never be happy again without Tate.

I had heard of this now and then through my patients' families, the dying, the dead, coming to say good-bye to people who were not present at the death. This was what had happened. He'd come. Tate had said his good-bye.

A stab of pain lanced straight through my heart like a sword had sliced it in half, and I keeled forward, my forehead on the cement, the water from the fountain splashing my hair, but I didn't care. I did not care at all. I had no idea how long I was hunched over; time was gone. Tate was gone.

I heard the door behind me open and I looked up. Two nurses hustled outside, their faces grim, their eyes sad for me. I knew them, but I did not know their names. I pushed the water off my forehead into my hair and rasped, "No, oh no," then put up my hands, to ward them off, to tell them not to come, I didn't want to hear it, didn't want to hear the words, leave me alone, don't say it, go away, please go away . . . not those words.

"Miss Bruxelle—"

My mother, Caden, and Brooke ran out behind them, my mother unstable, leaning on Caden, my brother seeming to have aged in hours, Brooke a pale mess, their faces awash in yet another round of utter despair.

I stayed on my knees and stared at the nurses, at their rigid, stressed expressions.

"No," I whimpered. "Oh God, no."

The nurses bent down so they could be eye-to-eye with me.

"I'm sorry to tell you this," one nurse said, her arms wrapping around me.

My mother stumbled in beside me, her cheek to mine, as Brooke and Caden kneeled with me, a group of people with nothing left.

The nurse looked me right in the eyes. "Miss Bruxelle, Tate's heart has stopped."

Tate's heart has stopped?

What are you talking about?

It was his head that was hurt. His head! Not his heart! They were fixing his head. It was cut open. There was nothing wrong with his heart!

"The doctors are working on him. This sometimes happens during these operations."

They're working on him? How do you work on a heart?

"They're doing all they can."

Doing all they can?

Does that mean he's dying on that table? They're working to prevent his death? They're trying to bring him back? Or that he's dead, his good-bye done? Why do they have to work on his heart?

What is going on?

I heard screaming. I heard wailing. My throat was hoarse, I didn't understand why. Was it me? Was I screaming? People rushed out of the reception room toward us, running, I knew I knew them, but I couldn't figure out who was who. Who were they? Why were they running to me? All I heard were those screams, pitched and high, desperate and petrified, they swirled all around us, then the screams went down my throat, pulsating and harsh and sucking my life out of me in a continuous plunge of pain.

Caden hauled me onto his lap, cradling me, my mother's eyes green pits of agony. Brooke was on all fours and wrapped her arms around me.

Tate was gone, that I knew because I could not feel him anymore.

I could not feel him, but I didn't want them to say it.

I couldn't feel his strong arms, his chicken pancake scent, I couldn't touch his curls. I couldn't hear him say, *I love you, Boss Mom.*

Gone.

Not here.

Not with me.

My son was gone.

I tilted my head back as the excruciating pain ran all the way up my body and out my mouth in a wall of wrenching pain and into that bitter, freezing cold night.

Both Faith and Grace had six children.

Faith's first sweet baby died when she was two of a raging infection. It came on in the morning and four days later she was dead.

Grace lost a darling child when he was three to pneumonia. The doctors were of no help. Nothing the cousins did, with herbs, with their thimble, white lace handkerchief, needle, gold timepiece, charms, their spells and chants, the book with the black cover . . . nothing could save those children.

Faith had a baby with one arm shorter than the other. It wasn't too much of a problem because he was also six foot six inches tall, with a redhead's temper and giant fists. He became the mayor of Portland.

The women never stopped missing their children. They were blessed with many grandchildren and acted as the second mother to their cousin's children, but their grief was never totally gone, and they would often picture the babies they had lost playing outside with their siblings.

Grandma Violet told me it was said that when they died, Faith and Grace uttered their dead children's names, and smiled.

Henrietta Grace.

Russell Philip.

How I have missed you.

I heard about Maggie Granelli's death later from her daughter, which was right after Tate's heart stopped beating.

"There are many angels now. All waiting. They're waiting for me," Maggie said, with awe in her voice, seeing the scene only she could see.

"Her face went from this serene peace to anxious to panicked, Jaden," the daughter told me. "She had been smiling but then she started twitching and jerking. Her eyes didn't move but she said, 'Tate! Oh no, you're not supposed to be here, you're not supposed to be here, go go!' "

The daughter started to cry. "I'm sorry to tell you that, Jaden, I'm so sorry. But I thought you should know. Mom started shaking her head, she was very weak, and said, 'Bishop Tate, not you, not you, honey, not yet.' "

The clay pot went crashing right through the window of my greenhouse, glass shattering into thousands of pointy shards.

The second clay pot took out another window.

The third clay pot took out yet another.

I used both arms and a raving temper to send herbs, flowers, and plants flying off tables and shelves. I sent tools careening through the open glass. The silver watering can from Ethan cracked another window, and I smashed a pot of budding impatiens to the floor, followed by snapdragons and petunias.

"What are you doing?" Brooke yelled, sprinting in, her auburn hair back in a messy ponytail, raindrops on her sweatshirt.

"I'm killing my greenhouse!"

Brooke wrapped her scarred arms around me. "Stop, honey, Jaden, stop it!"

"No, *you* stop it!" I struggled to get free of her. We had both been at the hospital for three straight days. Tate's heart had stopped, they had finally gotten it beating again on its own, but he was now in a coma. I was told that I should think about when I wanted to "let him go."

"I will never let Tate go," I raged at the tiny, pixie-doll doctor who I later found out was an intern and shouldn't have been talking to us at all. "I will not let him go! Never will I let him go, do you have that straight?"

She nodded. "Okay, Miss Bruxelle. I understand. I'll tell Dr. Robbins."

"You tell him that I said never!" I bent over and yelled at her as she walked her irritating pixie self down the corridor. *"Never! Never! Never!"*

Brooke wrapped her arms around me, as did my mother and Caden. My words, "I will never let Tate go!" echoing around the corridor, jagged, raggedy, then I'd fallen to pieces again, sagging against Caden. The whole thing was beyond horrendous.

Caden had brought me home with Brooke so we could take showers, change clothes and, he hoped, rest, because I was a walking emotional zombie who had lost all control and had not slept in forever. "Rest, baby," he'd told me. "Please, you can barely stand up. Rest. I'm going to check on the kids, then I'll be back."

But first, *first* I was going to kill my greenhouse and the spices and herbs that made me smell death. I was going to take it down to its studs. I was going to break all the glass, take an ax to the posts, and rip every living thing apart. Then I was going to burn the herbs and spices. Burn them in a red-hot bonfire, one after another tossed into the flames, until they crinkled and disintegrated, then I would toss in my smiling, dumb red cinnamon Gummi Bears and my teas.

I did not want to see an herb or a spice again in my life. I would not have them anywhere, anytime. The herbs and spices had warned me, I had ignored the warning, now Tate was in a coma because his heart had stopped. There would be another operation today to relieve swelling and pressure in his head. He could die.

Because of me, my son could die. My son! I hurled a wicker chair straight through a broken window. Stupid, stupid chair! Now you can live in the rain!

Tate was essentially dead now. Kept alive artificially. Tubes, machines, blinking lights, doctors and nurses, including Ethan.

I sent the other chair tumbling out into the rain, too. Stupid chair!

"Don't kill your greenhouse, Jaden," Brooke begged. "Please, don't."

She was crying, her skinny body shaking. I finally focused on my sister, my younger sister whom I had adored for years, whom I had lost to a mess of drugs. She had been my friend, my playmate, and she had poisoned our family and hurt Tate. She had hurt Tate! Tate was almost dead and she had hurt him! Where had she been all these years! How dare she hurt my son!

"Please, it's beautiful out here, Jaden. Tate loves it."

"Tate!" I raved, my chest heaving. "What the hell do *you* know about Tate?"

She reached out a hand to support herself on a wood table, now strewn with smashed plants and piles of dirt.

"Do you know how much you've hurt him? Do you have any idea at all, you selfish sister?" I rammed two blue pots into the floor. They broke into a hundred blue pieces. "Do you know what your walking out did to him? He knows I'm not his biological mother. You are! He doesn't even know who his father is because you don't!"

"You're his mother, Jaden, I know that—" She put shaking hands to her face.

"I know that! I am his mother! And he had me, and Caden and Caden's kids and Mom. He knows we love him, but he lived with knowing his mom abandoned him. He would worry about you, and yet—" I hurled two red pots, filled with tulip bulbs, across the greenhouse, getting an odd thrill from the bomb-blast sounds they made. I threw a yellow pot, too. *Boom, boom!* "You didn't deserve his worry. You didn't deserve him caring about you. You didn't care about him."

Brooke leaned more heavily on the table. She knew she deserved my rage.

"He wanted to know that you were okay, he said he worried about you being cold, alone, crying, but you never, not once, stopped enough in your life to check on him, did you?" I took a climbing spotted frog off the post and pitched it through the broken glass, then I grabbed another frog and did the same thing, and a third. Flying frogs! Off they went! Hop hop!

"I asked Mom how he was all the time—"

"You asked Mom," I mocked, panting. "During the infrequent times that you stumbled home, stoned?" I suddenly hated my colorful Chinese lanterns from San Francisco and grabbed a rake and swung at them, bringing them to the floor. So long, happy lanterns! I hate you! I swung at my dried lavender, the dried roses, then crushed them with my shoes.

"Do you know how many hundreds of nights Mom and Dad didn't sleep because they knew you were out in the world somewhere, drugged up and in danger? Do you know Mom's been on sleeping pills for years? She's seen a therapist once a week since you left. Remember when twice during the run of her show she was either put into a coma, how ironic is that now"—I smashed another yellow pot—"or stuck in a mental institution on the show? It was because she had nervous breakdowns. She fell apart because of you, Brooke. Dad did, too. They couldn't take it, couldn't take that any day you could die of a drug overdose, be a victim of a crime . . . it drove them out of their minds."

"I know. I'm sorry. I am sorry. I've never stopped being sorry!"

I brought down the last purple Chinese lantern with a swing of my rake, then started on the hanging wicker baskets. "Sorry isn't good enough. It will never be good enough, never! You ruined years of our lives. Years. And now you're *here*."

"You asked me to come—"

"Yes, I asked an addict to come—"

"I know I'm an addict—"

"And you are a selfish, weak, and thoughtless person. You destroyed part of my childhood because you didn't have the backbone to get yourself cleaned up. You wouldn't do the hard work to get sober." I stomped on the Chinese lanterns. I didn't want any color in my life anymore, anyhow! "You had to relentlessly hurt our family because you were too into yourself, your pleasures, your highs to get it together."

"I know that, I'm trying—"

"Trying? *You're trying?*" My chest was pounding with exertion. I grabbed a pot of zinnias and out it went! I never wanted to grow anything again! Nothing! "You're not *intending* to stay clean? Is that too much to ask? Do you think that you are on this planet all by yourself and you can do anything you want?"

"No, no, I don't—" She used both hands to prop her skinny self up, her eyes huge in that too-thin face.

"My son is in a hospital." I hated my greenhouse now! I hated my herbs and spices and flowers and bulbs. "He may die. And after all this time, you show up."

"But you said Tate wanted to meet me, Jaden," she whispered.

"He did. And now I think it was a mistake. What are your plans, Brooke? To walk away, to stay? What?" I started hacking at the white Christmas lights, bringing the strands to the floor. I would never want to have Christmas without Tate.

"I don't know, I don't know, I don't know—"

"You don't know. You don't know shit because you haven't been around this family enough to know anything." I ignored the hot tears that were falling down my cheeks and hers. "Did you know that Dad died fearing for your life? He was always scared you would die. He lived with your possible death hanging over him."

"I know." She broke into another round of sobs. "I know it. You think that doesn't follow me around? I know that I did that to him. I know it was all my fault."

I checked my rage for a minute, there was something else here. "What do you mean, *you know it was all your fault?* What do you know?"

"Nothing, oh God, nothing—"

"Yes, you know something, Brooke. What is it?" I whipped a strand of lights to the floor.

"Not now, I don't want to tell you now, I don't want to talk about Dad—"

"Tell me, damn you, Brooke, tell me."

She cried, hands to mouth.

I picked up one of my teapots and threw it. It burst three feet from her feet. "Tell me, Brooke! Right now!" I picked up another one, broke it, too, right close to her.

"Oh my God!" She screeched, then turned her shoulders in, huddling into herself. "I know because I called him that night. I called him because I was in Portland and I was tripping and I needed help and I wasn't sure where I was and I thought I was dying."

What? I grabbed a teacup and sent it crashing across the greenhouse. Never would I drink tea again. I wanted to drink it with Tate. Only Tate. "You called him? When?"

"That night."

My air seemed to be stuck, not moving around in my body. "You called him that night he died?"

"Yes, I called him." She started to hyperventilate but I had no pity for her. "I told him the names of signs, street signs, a store in Portland that I could see, I was stoned. . . . And he said he was on his way and he came to help me, to save me. He came to save me. Daddy came to save me. Save Brooke, save me. . . ." Her voice grew small. "To save me . . ."

"Oh my God, oh my God." That was it. He was driving that night to her. To Brooke. That's why he was going too fast, he never drove fast. We thought he'd gone for chocolate mint ice cream for me. . . . He'd told me there would be ice cream when I came home. . . . I picked up a rosemary plant, my rage quivering, and threw it through a window, then thyme, then oregano. "Damn you, Brooke!"

"I called him and he went over . . . over . . . over that cliff."

I envisioned his car, careening out of control, flying into the inky blackness, his face when he realized there was no road under his wheels. He would have thought of my mother, of his children.

I reached for another rosemary plant, but found I had no energy to break it, probably because I couldn't catch my breath, couldn't stand any longer. I sank onto the messy floor of my greenhouse as my legs gave out, my knees weak, the rosemary plant in my lap.

"I've had to live with that since then, Jaden. I killed Dad. I am responsible for Dad dying." She groaned, primal and raw. "I killed him. I killed my own dad. I killed yours and Caden's dad. I killed Mom's husband. He was worried about me dying, he wanted to save me, but I killed him."

"Stop, stop, don't say anymore. I can't take it." I rocked back and forth, filthy with dirt, filthy with black emotions. "Good God, I can't take it. I can't take any more. Not of this, not of you . . ."

"I killed Dad." Brooke tilted her head back, gasping for air, hardly even with me anymore, lost in her own hysterical turbulence. "It was me. It was my fault. All my fault. Forever it's been my fault, all of it. I'm sorry. Mom, I'm sorry, Jaden and Caden, I'm sorry, Dad, I'm sorry. . . . I can never be sorry enough."

I pushed the rosemary plant off my lap and turned over, ripped and exhausted, face down to the ground, to the dirt, and cried a thousand tears while Brooke wailed, the wail escaping out the broken glass of the greenhouse, across the grass and to the country house that Faith and Jack built, where her quilts still hang, her banister my banister, her view of the maple trees my view now. Brooke's soaring wail surrounded the gardens where I grow Canterbury bells, hollyhocks, lilies, irises, sweet peas, cosmos, red poppies, peonies, and rows of roses, the same flowers Faith and Grace grew.

No, Brooke could never be sorry enough.

I sobbed so hard I thought my body would burst.

There was such a heavy load of abject misery in that greenhouse if misery could demolish a building, it would have been demolished, with us in it.

Later, with Brooke shrieking and hyperventilating, I struggled up, dirt dropping off me. I wanted to continue killing my greenhouse, the place where death was stored in my herbs and spices.

I stumbled to my cutting and mixing area and grabbed as many spice jars as I could. I would dump out the spices and the herbs into one pile for my bonfire. I would add all my teas! It would be a bonfire of spices, herbs, and teas! They would all be burned to ash. With shaking hands I started to gather them up to incinerate them and I accidentally knocked over paprika and coriander, which broke on the floor.

I swore up a blue streak.

A jar of parsley fell to the ground, too, and shattered on the floor right on top of it. A box of peppermint herbal tea fell, too, and I smashed it with my boot.

"Hell, double hell! Fine, then! I'll break all of you! You're all going right now! You're dead!" I raised my arms up and with one mighty swoop, spice jars went crashing to the floor and their scents—ginger, sage, chervil, tarragon, nutmeg, dill, oregano, thyme, bay leaves—all floated up, twirling together with the peppermint herbal tea, blending and folding into one another.

When I had finally broken or destroyed anything I could get my hands on, I stopped, panting, in the midst of that total destruction, windows shattered, pots crumbled, dirt scattered, tables overturned, lanterns smashed, my sister trying to breathe while chanting, "It's all my fault, all my fault, it's all my fault."

I closed my eyes and inhaled, deeply, my heart palpitating, racing. I breathed in again, one more time. A third time.

My eyes flew open.

I couldn't believe it.

It couldn't be.

I dropped to my knees and breathed in all those herbs, spices, and teas at one time . . . one breath, two . . .

I didn't smell death.

I inhaled again, exhausted and ruined, utterly crushed . . . but one more time I breathed in . . . then another . . . I couldn't be wrong . . . I couldn't hope if there was no hope, I couldn't believe, if there was nothing to believe in. I could not imagine something that wasn't there, because it would kill me.

But there it was.

It was.

There.

A scent I had longed for, hoped for, prayed for. . . . There was no death wafting up from the herbs, spices, and teas. No blackness, no threat, no rot, no rancid fume. None.

All I smelled was . . . Life.

Life.

I smelled life.

My cell phone rang.

20

⌒

"The doctors are looking for you!" my mother said, sprinting on *bare feet,* toward Caden, Brooke, and me as we burst through the front doors of the hospital, then ran down corridors to the ICU. My mother had never abandoned her high heels, never. Neither had she ever abandoned makeup, but she had given that up, too, and her hair was as messy as mine. Unprecedented. "Come in, come in quick! They want to talk to us right now! Hurry! Hurry!"

With Caden's help, I wobbled and limped down the last corridor, as if my balance was gone, despair mixing with the hope of the impossible, the hope of a wispy scent of life.

We took the elevator up to the fourth floor, Caden tapping his foot and repeating, "Atta boy, Tate, you can do it, my boy." Brooke clung to my mother's hand, my mother whimpering, gripping the cross on her charm necklace. When the doors opened we stumbled toward the nurses' station, as I fought to stay upright, weak from terror. My mother was propped up by Caden, as the doors at the end of the hallway, leading to the ICU, opened. My sister leaned against a wall, sickly, frail, and I reached out a hand to hold hers.

She took it. I leaned over, my other hand on my knees to keep me upright, my charm necklace swinging.

We saw Ethan, Dr. Raminsky, and two other doctors emerge in scrubs. Ethan pulled off his paper mask.

He was ripped with fatigue. He had hardly slept, same with

Dr. Raminsky. They both had lines deeply drawn on their faces. The two other doctors with them were both ghastly looking, too. One of the doctors wiped a hand over her brow, her blond ponytail swinging behind her, the other rolled her shoulders.

They did not see us at first, my mother, Caden, Brooke, and me, a ragtag bunch of desperate people now only half sane. The doctors were not smiling, they were talking back and forth, rapid fire, their tones abrupt, terse.

It was a serious, intense discussion.

Ethan turned and saw me, hardly able to stand, my hand gripped in Brooke's, Tate's Other Mother.

I waited, my eyes begging him, *begging,* as they filled with yet more tears and the tears rushed down my face as if in anticipation of confirmation of an irreplaceable loss. I heard my mother sucking in air, hoarse and raspy, and my brother's continual, "Oh my boy, Tate, oh my boy, save him, Lord," muffled because he could hardly speak through his sobs. Raw sounds of hopelessness tore from Brooke's throat.

"Please, Ethan," I croaked out. "Tell me he's okay. Tell me he's all right."

Oh God, please. For my son, for my son. For Tate. Please, God, anything. Anything. I want my son.

All four of the doctors turned to us, the Bruxelle family, beyond desolate, beyond lost, clinging to their last shred of hope. . . .

They smiled.

Tate was alive.

He was not conscious, but he was alive, his brain scans were normal, his heart was beating, and he was breathing on his own.

He was hooked up to every machine known to man, it seemed. There were medical personnel hovering around talking medical-ese, beeps and hisses, tubes and machines.

"I think he's going to make it, Jaden," Ethan told me, an arm linked over my shoulder, a smile on his worn-out face, bruises under his eyes from fatigue and stress. "I think he's going to make it."

I leaned over and kissed Tate on the forehead, my love for him coming through that kiss, all my love, my eternal, deep, protective love for my child. My tears dropped onto his face and down his cheeks, as if he was crying, too, and I remembered another day that another mother had dropped tears on his cheeks.

My Tate was still with us. *He was alive.* He had improved. There were positive signs. He would wake up. He could, possibly, possibly recover fully and live for a long, long time.

A normal lifespan for a kid who has never been normal.

I was so happy, so relieved. So utterly grateful.

I passed out.

I remember dreaming.

I dreamed of herbs dancing in giant flowered teacups. I dreamed of a singing silver spoon. I dreamed of crystal jars of spices with eyes and smiles chatting back and forth.

I dreamed of my greenhouse. I dreamed of the sun streaking through, then the rain pounding down, a rainbow arching overhead. I dreamed of our white home, the maple trees dancing down the drive, the red poppies swaying, singing in a group, the rows of roses laughing, the Canterbury bells and peonies turning into flower people. . . .

When I woke up, Ethan was leaning over me, his face pinched and worried, his hand on my forehead. "Jaden."

I couldn't form his name with my mouth. I knew I was in a hospital bed. I knew he was Ethan. I knew I was scared, and I knew I wanted to cry again.

My mother held my hand in her trembling one, my brother the other hand. My sister stood in the corner, and I remembered how I'd lashed out at her, a verbal fire-and-brimstone attack.

"Jaden, it's okay, honey. You're fine."

"How . . ." I felt another wave of nausea. "How is Tate?"

Ethan smiled, but this time there was joy in his smile. "He's doing great. He just woke up."

"He's awake?"

"Yes. As soon as you're up to it, I'll take you there."

"Tate's awake?" My son, whose heart had stopped even though they were operating on his head? He was awake? The tears streamed from my eyes like I'd burst two waterfalls in my corneas. "Is he talking?"

Ethan's voice crackled, and he sniffled. "He asked for you. He said, 'Where's Boss Mom?' "

He asked for you. He said, "Where's Boss Mom?"

I was his mother.

I am Boss Mom.

I am here.

I tried to get up, but I couldn't, the nausea swamping me.

"Lie back down, Jaden, hang on to your horses...." Caden said. "I'll carry you on in there if I have to, but get your breath, catch that breath of yours—"

"No. I'm going to Tate." I was limp and weak, dizziness spinning my head. "Get out of my way."

"Lie back, for a moment, honey," Ethan said, but I fought him.

"Breathe, baby," my mother said. "Please breathe. Pretend we're in a bubble of bubble gum."

I blinked at her, still struggling to get up.

"Okay, no. That was silly." She waved her hand, dismissing that idea. "Pretend we're in a box filled with licorice."

What?

"Not that." Another wave of her hand. "Together, we are at the top of a roller coaster and it's going super-sonically fast, and suddenly the car we're in goes off the tracks and we're loose and we're flying through the free blue sky—"

For heaven's sake.

"I'm going," I said, my head swirling. "Right now." I tried to lever myself up through the nausea. I took a deep, deep breath. Deep enough for bubble gum and licorice and roller coaster rides that go haywire and send my mother and me careening into the free blue sky.

"Help me up, please, help me."

Ethan had an arm around my waist, as did Caden.

"We're going to see Tate, honey," Caden said, sniffling. "I can't believe it. We're going to see Tate!"

I started to hobble out and stopped in front of my sister, who seemed to be cowering. "Come with me, Brooke. Please. Our son wants to see us."

"Mom, I saw you."

"I see you, too, honey." It was Tate and me alone in his room for the moment. Mom and son. I pushed what was left of his curly red hair back. I didn't know, exactly, what he was talking about, but I didn't care. He was in his hospital bed. He was alive. He was awake. He was talking. That was all I needed or wanted to see.

His voice was hoarse. "No, Boss Mom, I saw you by the fountain. You were all by yourself."

Oh. My. Goodness. "You . . . you saw me?"

"I saw you when I was being operated on. It was weirdo. Neither physics nor cognitive brain function can explain this one. I was up in the corner watching Dr. Robbins. Another doctor with a blond ponytail had my chest open and it was gross and there was blood and I wasn't moving. I looked dead, and then all of a sudden I was by you at the fountain."

"I . . . Tate—"

"You told me to hang on and I told you that everything was okay."

I collapsed on a chair by his bed.

"I told you that Billy and Bob were up and I was fighting."

I felt faint. I had felt him close to me, his warmth, his arm around my shoulders. . . .

"Mom, you told me you loved me, to stay with you, and your crystals came out of your hair and went into the fountain."

I put a hand to my head. I had not been hallucinating. Tate had had an out-of-body experience. I had talked to him during that experience.

"You're all pale, Mom, are you okay?"

"Am I okay? No, Tate," I squeaked. "I'm not."

"I told you I was fighting the same fight I had when I was learning advanced statistics."

"Statistics." I felt faint again. "Advanced statistics."

"Yeah, and the chicken pancakes? Man, I can't wait to have those. Remember that?"

I nodded, weakly. I remembered.

"Mom, I feel sort of sick and tired, but it's a sick that I know'll take off, shove off, you know? It's the operation and the medicine, the anesthesia, but I'm going to be groovy fine, that is my new sixties word, *groovy,* so I think you need to chill out, you know, take a nap, have a beer or something. Hey! Can I have a beer?"

"No, you may not."

"What about one of Nana Bird's mai tais?"

"No, young man, no."

"I'm kidding about the mai tais. I actually want a strawberry daiquiri." He paused when I didn't smile. "Or whiskey. Whiskey and tea, you know how Faith and Grace the witches drank it in their tea. I love all those stories you and Nana Bird have told me about them."

"They weren't really witches," I said, on automatic. "They thought they were."

"Yeah, okay. Sure. I'm tryin' to make you laugh because you look, you look, uh . . . bad. You know, uh, Mom, you're kind of a green color, a monster green color. And you have a lot of dirt on you, I don't know why, and your hair is all over. Plus, under your blue eye is purplish dark. Your green eye isn't as bad, but it's not . . . uh, normal. But no offense, 'kay? Maybe you should sleep. I think you should sleep. Haven't you slept at all?"

He was a kid. He didn't get it. Parents do not sleep when their children are in critical condition. "I'll be fine, Tate. I'll be fine." I shuddered from relief and sheer exhaustion and wobbled up to kiss his cheek. Yes, I would be fine. Tate was alive, that was all I wanted. "I love you, son."

"Me, too, Boss Mom, me, too. I love you. Hey! Did we win?"

I told him, then watched while he slept, reveling in the miracle that he was here. Reveling in the miracle of a miracle.

I held his hand in both of mine and rested my head on his shoulder.

Thank you.

Many nights later, in my greenhouse, with my white lights twinkling, and my tropical mango tea nearby, I chopped and mixed up bay leaves, cloves, and paprika for Herbal Therapy time. I appreciated the colors and varied textures.

I had, as I told Brooke, killed my greenhouse.

When I came home, my greenhouse was alive again. It was peace with glass.

My mother drawled to me later, her composure securely in place to hide her most recent trauma and upheaval, her lipstick perfect, her auburn bob swinging, her stilettos on, "That was an impressive temper tantrum you threw, daughter. It would have been so entertaining to watch you heave your wicker chairs through the windows. I'm surprised you didn't sprain your boobs."

And, "Did you have to attack the hoppy frogs? How do you think they felt, flying through the windows?"

And, "Why so vengeful against the Chinese lanterns? We'll have to go to San Francisco as a family to buy new ones in China-town. I'll make the reservations."

Finally, "It's the red hair and the blue eye from Faith and the green eye from Grace that blew your mind away."

I asked my mother, "What do my eyes have to do with my wrecking my greenhouse?"

"It's in the family line, this temperamental witchly streak." She hugged me and I hugged her back. While I stayed in the hospital with Tate, my mother, Caden, Caden's kids, Brooke, Ethan, Coach Boynton and Letty, Milt and Anthony's parents, and other friends had completely cleaned up and repaired my greenhouse.

The floors were swept, plants, flowers, and herbs that had died were thrown out, others nurtured back to life and new ones bought. My mother had a painted, wooden sign made for the door by a local artist. It said JADEN'S HERBS AND SPICES.

There was a witch with red hair, one blue eye, and one green eye on a broomstick. She thinks she's so clever. She also bought me two new spice racks.

Caden bought me two new wicker chairs with red and white cushions. "Let's try not to destroy these, Jaden. They're not footballs," he told me, then winked. He also created for me a two foot teapot with wire, ivy, and white and yellow mums.

My sister replanted my bulbs in colorful pots and labeled each one. She also took three glass vases and filled them with the rocks and shells that she and I had collected as kids, which she'd found in the blue cardboard box. She filled the vases with water and placed them on a shelf where the sun hit just right.

She relabeled all the herbs I had. She drew a picture of the herb, then used a calligraphy pen to write its name. She also repaired the frogs with superglue and put them back up on the post. "A frog has to have a place to hop," she told me.

Brooke could make beauty where none existed. It was tragic and sad that she hadn't been able to make beauty in herself for many years.

Ethan ordered new windows, which, I must admit, were fantastic, the light flowed in cleanly in a way that made me feel I was outside. He had two of the busted windows replaced with stained glass, which cast out a myriad of colors. One of the windows had a design of an iris, the other of rosemary, because I had told him the story of Faith and Grace, who used to be, before a torch-wielding mob wanted to flog them for being witches, Iris and Rosemary.

I had a glowing rainbow of color in my greenhouse now. "Colorful windows for a colorful woman," he'd told me, then kissed me silly.

My greenhouse wasn't *my* greenhouse anymore. It was *our* greenhouse.

I bent my head over Grandma Violet's crystal plate, over Faith's silver spoon.

I smelled life.

* * *

The night before Tate was to finally come home from the hospital, Brooke and I sat on his hospital bed together. She still seemed pale and fragile, but my mother and brother had concentrated on feeding her and she was rosier, not completely healthy, but better, her auburn hair thicker, shinier.

She, Tate, and I played Monopoly. She won, her green eyes twinkling.

We had ice cream together. Before she left to go back to my house, she leaned down for an extra-long hug with Tate and kissed his forehead. "I love you, Tate."

"I love you, too, Brooke."

She held him far longer than usual. She hugged me tight, too.

"I love you, Brooke." I had apologized multiple times to her for my fit in the greenhouse, my earth-scorching meanness. She had been gracious and kind, told me that she had deserved all that I'd said. Our conversation had been long and difficult, a minefield, but there was love in it, too.

"Thank you, Tate, for letting me back in your life. You're talented, brilliant, funny, an excellent writer, too. Your blog is amazing."

"Thanks for coming back into my life, Brooke," he said, but his voice wavered. "You're even getting better at catching Skittles in your mouth and balancing an apple on your head."

She kissed his forehead, hugged him again, her tears on his cheek. She hugged me again, then left, closing the door quietly behind her.

Tate and I did not break our gaze from each other for long seconds.

"She's leaving again, isn't she, Boss Mom?"

I stood up and watched the street outside the hospital. We were high enough up so I could see for miles. The trees were beginning to bud again, their bare branches softening. Soon they would be covered in green leaves for spring.

Within a couple of minutes, I saw Brooke's auburn hair whipping back in the wind. She paused in the middle of the street and looked up. I knew she could not see in the windows, and she knew I knew that, but she waved anyhow. I did not bother to wave back.

She headed down the street. A bus pulled up. Who knew where it was going? I didn't. She didn't.

She climbed aboard. I felt her loss immediately.

"Yes, Tate, she's leaving again. I'm sorry."

Why was she leaving? The pull of drugs again? The complications of family life? The cauldron of emotions here? The guilt from our father's death? Was she leaving because of my verbal attack in the greenhouse? Had I blown up at her because I secretly wanted her to leave and felt threatened by her? Or because she'd deserved it and I wanted her to hear my pain? Was I more vengeful than I thought? Maybe I ranted simply because Tate's life-threatening medical condition had been excruciating and she was a convenient target.

Would she have left anyhow?

Did it matter?

Tate silently cried, but this time I didn't feel the same anger I had felt so often with Brooke. I felt an overwhelming sadness for her, my mother, my father, Caden, and for Tate, but the anger was gone.

Tate was here.

Tate had survived.

That was the most important thing. I could deal with losing my sister again, but I could not live without Tate.

I bent to hug him.

One of my tears fell on his cheek.

We did not wipe it away.

On a sunny afternoon, with my pink and white cherry trees blooming, Ethan's truck rumbled up the drive between our column of green-leafed maple trees.

I took a quick breath, as I always do when I see him, and patted my hair in front of a tiny mirror I kept in my greenhouse. My fingers brushed the new crystals Tate had bought me saying, "Keep these out of the fountain, Boss Mom." I tried not to get all mushy-gushy emotional again.

It had been an interesting day at work. One patient, Catalina Goodall, threw a full beer can at me and said to "kiss my fat ass," and another, in her delirium, said she was seeing funny people running out of the TV and thought they might have been sent there by *Star Trek*.

Ethan smiled and waved and I waited for him by the door of my greenhouse, loving the way he moved, shoulders back, smiling, smiling. He wrapped me in his strong arms and held me close.

"Ethan, I know I've told you this a hundred times, but I can't ever thank you enough for saving Tate—" I burst into the sloppy tears I wanted to avoid.

"You already have thanked me." He tilted my head up and kissed me. "You put the ring back on. That's what I wanted."

My nose started to run and I knew I looked awful, red and wet. "I love you, Ethan. I love you so much." I loved that I had him. I loved that I had Ethan in my life.

"I love you, too, Jaden. Have since the first day I met you." He kissed me, held me tight. "I love how you take all the hits life has given you and you come up swinging and hit back. I love the way you do what's right, all the time, no matter how tough. I love how you're open and vulnerable and you cry when you feel like crying and you laugh when you feel like laughing and when you're pissed off you destroy your greenhouse. I even love Witch Mavis. I especially love how you looked in that white lace negligee the other night. Although"—he pretended to ponder—"the purple one was nothing to sneeze at." He pondered again. "The black one with the fishnets and garters was enough to make me stop breathing."

He picked up my left hand and kissed my sparkly engagement ring. "Soon then, Jaden?"

"Anytime, Dr. Robbins." I leaned against him. "Anytime."

"If you had only taken the time to talk to me, Jaden, I think we could have avoided this mess." Dirk leaned across the hospital's conference table and shook his head, as a father might when reprimanding a child. He was decked out in an expensive suit. I knew he'd picked it carefully to be intimidating.

"How so?" Sandra asked, my whip-sharp attorney with the large teeth. She cocked her head to the side as if examining a foreign species. "You're accusing her of killing your father. If Jaden had taken time out to talk to you, why would that have changed your mind?"

Dr. Baharri raised his eyebrows at me. Sydney humphed. My heart rate sped up because I was ticked off.

"I mean that during my father's illness, I asked her out many times, I mean, not on a date. I wanted to talk to Jaden, privately, alone, at my home, for more information about my father, and she declined." Dirk actually wagged a finger at me.

"My employees are not required to go home with the sons of their clients to"—Sydney made quotes in the air—"talk to them."

Dirk's attorneys, Nigel and Ralph, they of the outrageously high hourly rates who knew there was no case, tried to appear appropriately stern and forbidding, but I saw Nigel stifle a yawn. Ralph glanced at his watch. Keep those hours coming!

"Let me wrap my small brain around this," Sandra said. "If she had dated you, you would not now be accusing her of killing your father?"

Dirk's eyes narrowed. He is a weasel and he knew he was being trapped. "Yes. No."

"Dirk means," Nigel said, "that Jaden was remiss in her duties as a hospice nurse, that's why we're here. To talk about. Uh. That."

"My client," Ralph said, coughing, "didn't mean what he said. He meant that if Jaden had talked to him, explained things better, instead of being confusing, evasive, and secretive, about medical issues and concerns, uh, things would have been, uh, more clear, but the result, uh, would be the same."

"I believe Mr. Hassells meant what he said," Sandra chimed in. "We have a court reporter here who tip-tapped it in, too. Dirk, if you think Jaden murdered your father, it seems silly to think you would change your mind about that accusation if you had a romantic dinner date together, but that's what you're suggesting, right, Dirk?"

"My client," Nigel said, "doesn't have to answer that. He's not saying that anyhow—"

"Are you afraid of the question, Dirk?" Sandra said.

Ah, playing to Dirk's ego. He wasn't afraid of anything.

"I'm not afraid of anything." He slapped the table with his open palm.

Ha. I had called it!

"I'm not afraid of nothing! Not anything or anyone! I'm saying if Jaden wasn't standoffish and cold, we could have gotten to know each other . . . personally, the medical part would have been easier to understand. That was bad treatment and it led to a bad outcome for me, I mean, for my dad!"

"She is not required to get to know you"—Sandra paused deliberately—"personally. She was there for the care of your father." She shuffled some papers and addressed Nigel and Ralph. "We believe Mr. Hassells is pressing this lawsuit because Jaden didn't want to date or sleep with him. We can't blame Jaden for feeling that way, plus his behavior makes my skin crawl, it's gross to think of him coming after a woman, but his being pissed off at Jaden for not dating him, or worse, that's no basis for a case, legally or ethically, as you know. We can, and will, countersue."

"We, uh, are filing this lawsuit because, uh, Miss Bruxelle did not follow medical rules and regulations," Nigel said. "Negligence . . ."

"Questionable use of"—Ralph flipped through his paperwork—"morphine."

"For the record, on numerous occasions I told him to stop asking me out," I said. "And Dirk asked me why I wouldn't go home with him. I told him I didn't owe him an explanation."

"You did owe me an explanation." Dirk was red and he clenched a fist. "I figured you had a husband or a boyfriend."

"That's the only reason you can think of that a woman wouldn't want to go out with you?" Sandra said, her shiny teeth shining. "Perhaps there are other reasons?"

"Hey, hey." Dirk chuckled and spread his arms wide. "Nope. Nada. No, I can't think of another reason a woman wouldn't want to date me."

The court reporter continued to tap. . . .

Ralph squirmed. Nigel sighed, then smothered it.

Sydney said, "A snake might."

Dr. Baharri said, quite loudly, "Shameful, unfounded arrogance."

"Jaden didn't want to go out because of the patient, client thing," Dirk said, "but I was trying to convince her it would be fine, that we could get pleasure together out of a hard time—"

Nigel made a gargled sound in his throat, Ralph tried to interrupt.

"I could not get pleasure with you because I find you slimy," I said. "I find you slick, dishonest, and disgusting. I found your lack of care and regard for your father to be appalling and hurtful to him. I thought your disregard of the enormous load your sister worked under to be unfeeling and thoughtless. I thought you treated her as your personal maid. I couldn't stand how you constantly stared at me and tried to encourage me to get in your car with you—"

"It's a Porsche—"

"I don't care. I did not want to go in the living room and lie down, relax, and get a massage as you suggested. I did not want to hug you when I left because all you wanted to do was shove my boobs against your chest, plus you smell like moral rot, which is why the second time I saw you I told you not to hug me again."

Ralph mini-groaned and exchanged a glance with Nigel, who closed his eyes.

Dirk started to sweat.

"It doesn't negate Dirk's concern about the untimely death of his father," Nigel said, but it was a routine comment, thrown out. He was an expensive attorney!

"Not untimely at all," Dr. Baharri said, then he, again, gave a medical lecture about Mr. Hassells's liver cancer.

"What relevance is this?" Ralph asked, but he pulled on his collar. Thank heavens he'd had Dirk pay up-front money!

"The relevance is that Jaden declined Dirk's advances and that pissed him off," Sandra said. "He was rejected, couldn't handle it. She has to pay. In addition, clearly Mr. Hassells is filing this suit because he wants money. That's unethical. This is close to extortion. His father left him five hundred dollars, plus cassette tapes, an old lamp, and his favorite brown belt. He left the rest of his estate to his daughter's children for college. Does the brown belt fit?"

"That's not true," Dirk wheezed.

"It is. You may have to sell the Porsche, Dirk," Sandra said. "Or is it leased? Just because you accuse, falsely, one of our nurses of murder, your words, it doesn't mean the hospital is going to flip over and vomit up some money. But let's have some fun." She flipped her folders shut. "Let's take it to court. Mr. Hassells, you've already spent a ton of money on your two attorneys, who knew from the get-go that you would lose."

"That's not true," Ralph said, his voice almost humorous. He knew what he'd done. "His father could have lived . . . uh . . . a while longer . . . uh."

"False," Dr. Baharri said.

"Impossible," Sydney said.

Nigel coughed. "We think our client has a solid chance of winning! Malpractice! Incompetent medical care. Too much morphine on a dying patient!" It was weak.

"Also false," Dr. Baharri said.

"Wrong," Sydney said.

"Non adherence to medical laws!" Ralph said.

Sandra, Sydney, and Dr. Baharri laughed out loud.

"Go ahead and pay your attorneys some more money," Sandra said. "They're pale. They can use it to go on a cruise to the Bahamas and get tanned up."

Ralph's eye lit up a bit. I think that idea appealed!

"When we take this case to court, a jury will listen to all the testimony, including testimony from Jaden about how Dirk was all riled up because she wouldn't go out with him in his car."

"It's a Porsche—"

"Who the hell cares? This'll be fun. When you lose, the hospital will make sure that you not only pay your legal fees, but ours, too, and court costs. And they'll be significant. Anything else?"

"She did it!" Dirk pointed at me. "She killed my father!"

"Mr. Hassells"—Sandra leaned in, her teeth white and snappy—"if you accuse Jaden Bruxelle of killing your father to anyone in future, I will sue you, on her behalf, for defamation of character. You'll be fried."

He swallowed hard.

"Let's go, Dirk," Ralph said. I think he wanted to plan that Bahamas trip! "We're done."

Sandra called me the next day, when I was sitting in my hundred-year-old rocking chair staring out at the cherry trees and irises, both swaying as puffs of spring wind wandered through.

Ralph and Nigel had dropped the case. They asked the hospital to cover their legal fees. Sandra laughed.

Dirk called me, asked me out on my voice mail, said he wanted to "make amends. You apologize, I apologize, and we can be friends again." He e-mailed me. He stopped his car in front of my home, and my neighbor wrote down his license and called the police. The police came, asked him what he was doing. They called me. I told them I was being stalked by Dirk Hassells.

I have a restraining order against him. One must take revenge when one can.

Last I heard he had decided to move to Florida. Hopefully the alligators will eat him.

21

Part of Tate's head had been shaved where Ethan had cut him open and operated on his brain. There was the expected scar. Tate had named the scar Cleopatra. As in, "General Noggin has a girlfriend, and her name is Cleopatra."

Although his humor was intact, he didn't have his balance back completely, but it was coming. From a devastating blow to his head, a coma, an operation on his brain, his heart stopping, breathing again, to eating chicken pancakes, he was our Tate, and he was recovering rapidly.

Today the basketball team was being honored in a school assembly in the gym for being the Class 4A state champions. Tate's last shot had been a three-pointer. The ball had arched, up up up, Tate had been slammed to the ground, the ball circled the rim, Tate's head had bounced, the ball swooshed through, his head kept bouncing, and the blood had poured out.

We had won the game. The cheers had abruptly stopped, I was told, when Tate didn't move on the floor of the gym.

The community had been invited to attend the celebration, and the gym was packed, the bleachers filled, with rows upon rows of chairs on the gym floor, where my mother, Caden, Ethan, and the kids and I sat. The band played the school fight song, the drumbeat loud and strong. The media had set up cameras all around the gym as Tate's ordeal, his story, his blog had been on the news every night since it happened.

Coach Boynton and the entire team, except for Tate, had been introduced and were on a stage at the end of the gym, below the basketball hoop, in uniform. The principal, Melinda Musfa, who is blond, six feet tall, and former military, had been calling each player's name over a microphone to enthusiastic applause and bleacher pounding. The boys sauntered down the aisle from the back of the gym to the stage, all lights off, a spotlight on each player.

After all the players had been introduced, Melinda said, "We have one more player to honor."

The drums rolled, and we all hooted and hollered.

Tate, Tate, Tate!

The principal held up her hand for silence. "We have a young man who has shown all of us, for years, courage and character. He also has shown us a spectacular three-point shot." She paused, and I knew she was holding her emotions in check. Melinda had been at the hospital almost daily with us, as so many other friends and neighbors had, young and old. Her voice cracked when she spoke again. "A young man who played hard, played to win, but who always gave credit to his teammates. A young man who, I know, we will be hearing about in years to come. He's gonna be a legend."

The band played, and people cheered, the noise so deafening I thought the walls would collapse.

"Ladies and gentleman, please welcome the young man whose last shot won Tillamina High School the 4A state championship!" More pounding. "Taaaatttteeee Bruxxxxelllleeee!!"

If it was any louder in there, my ears would have fallen off my head and run for the doors. Tate high-fived people as he slightly wobbled his way down the aisle in his uniform to the makeshift stage, the spotlight following his path.

I knew that my dear son was crying, tears rolling down his face. He did not wipe them off.

"I have a box load of emotions," he'd told me. "Sometimes in the past I thought I should box them up, lid down, but then I wouldn't be a real person anymore, would I? I'd be a humanoid with a head the size of Kauai and a Bert ear."

I didn't wipe the tears off my face, either.

Caden bellowed, muscled arms up in a V, "That's my boy!" The triplets were dressed as a Life Saver, a lollipop, and a hot dog. It was "Food Day," they'd told me. Damini chanted, "Tate, Tate, Tate!" Ethan was clapping over his head.

"There's my ball breaker!" my mother screamed into my ear. "There's my ball breaker!"

Tate stopped to hug me, Caden, Damini, Ethan, and my mother while the Life Saver, lollipop and hot dog jumped around.

He climbed the steps to the stage, grabbing Coach Boynton's hand for more balance on the way up. We did not realize the triplets were gone until they scampered up on the stage. Caden made a lunge to grab them, but Tate waved him away.

He was hugged by the principal, his teammates, and especially Coach Boynton, who didn't let him out of the hug for a long time. I had seen the man cry a bucket over Tate at the hospital. He had told me, "Jaden, I feel it in my bones, he'll be okay! He'll be okay! He will! *It's in my bones!*"

After the long Boynton/Tate hug, his teammates pushed him toward the microphone.

"Hey, dudes. Dudettes," Tate said.

Tate, Tate, Tate!

He told them to, "Have a seat, fellow galaxy walkers," and they did.

"I got a little banged up at the tournament." Tate tapped his head. "General Noggin is a big target up here to hit. But now General Noggin has a girlfriend, ya see." He pointed at his scar. "I call that scar Cleopatra. The scar looks like an asp, you know, that poisonous snake that bit her? But I didn't want to name the scar asp, that'd be creepy, so it became Cleopatra." He cupped his hands around the microphone and said, conspiratorially, as if he was sharing a secret, "I think General Noggin is in lust with Cleopatra. I think Cleopatra and General Noggin are . . . *getting it on* together behind my back."

Oh, how they laughed. He is darn funny.

"Let's hope they use"—he paused and wiggled his eyebrows—"*pro-tec-tion.*"

Those kids howled. I rolled my eyes, Ethan's laugh booming in my ears.

"Now I'm in trouble with Boss Mom for saying that." Then he lowered his voice and said in a low, deep monotone, "Sex education is part of a solid health education. And using protection is an important lesson for all youngsters to know."

I tried to be mad at him, but oh, his classmates thought he was hilarious.

"But now I wanna talk to you all about my teammates here and our home boy, Coach Boynton. We're friends, all of us here, that's why we won. We went out there believing we would win, and we did. It was a good game, wasn't it?"

Whoo whoo!

And then, Tate, kind Tate, generous Tate, said something special about all of his teammates. "Milt's third quarter steal, man, did you see that? And Baron's baskets. He has magic hands.... Anthony's defense, he's a python, wrapping around his opponent.... Kendrick, if you hadn't pummeled that ball to me on the last shot we'd have had a different game...."

"Tate makes everyone feel special," Ethan said, his voice breaking. "Everyone. That's his gift. An acknowledgment of everyone else."

"The worst part, though"—Tate paused, and I thought he was going to say something serious about his injury, as I think everyone else did, too—"the worst part of the game was that I thought Coach Boynton was going to need a *diaper,* he was so excited that night. A diaper!" Tate pulled out a giant-sized adult diaper from a sack that I'd put on the stage for him, held it up, waved it around, then tossed it to Coach Boynton.

Sooo much laughter and hooting.

"Put it on, man. We don't want any accidents in the gym," Tate said. Coach Boynton did not want to put it on. "Okay, but if you have to head to the toilet, we get it, Coach."

Ha ha ha.

"I'd say it was the coolest game ever until General Noggin was hit." Tate pointed to his head. "And General Noggin shut down for a bit. That would not be classified as a smiley-face day. But see, I had a gift that day, and it wasn't just a gift of winning the state championship, even though that was radical."

He nodded when the drums rolled.

"But see, I died that day in the hospital."

Ah. Now everyone was quiet.

"I died. I died on the table. The ol' ticker stopped. I think most of you know that. A whole bunch of you, I hear, were up at the hospital when I crashed. Thanks for being there, by the way. Good of you to come and visit me when I was such a poor host.

"I want you fellow galaxy walkers to know what happened when I died. No one wants to think about dying, especially us, because we're young and we're gonna rock the world one day, but my mom always says, 'We're all going to die so we all have to love life each day we're still here.' "

The mom who said that was a blubbery mess.

"When I died, all I felt was peace. I saw a friend of mine named Maggie Shoes, too, but I can't talk about her right now. There was that white light that people talk about, too. It was soft. It was safe. It was happy. I felt the happy. I took a visit to heaven. A short one, and I came back." He smiled at everyone, solemnity in a day of celebration. "Live free, galaxy walkers, but take the fear out of death for yourselves 'cause I already went, and dudes and dudettes, there ain't nothin' to fear."

Now those teenagers clapped. They liked the idea of no fear.

"Go out and have fun and laugh, but remember to stick your hand out to help other people. Be a friend. Be kind. Include others so they don't feel left out. Don't be a dick, and don't be scared."

We all clapped.

"I shouldn't have used the word"—he cupped the microphone—"*dick*. Now Boss Mom is going to be upset with me. Okay, I'll rephrase it. Rewind! Everyone"—he spread his arms out—"don't be a *penis!*"

That brought the house down.

I covered my face with my hands in mock embarrassment. I wasn't embarrassed, I was simply, utterly grateful that Tate was even standing up in his basketball uniform again.

"Don't be a penis!" he said again.

The kids about fell over each other with laughter. They started stomping their feet on the bleachers.

"So I hear there's a Winter Formal tonight. . . ."

Tate paused, more stomping, the drums rolled.

"It's gonna be cool!"

The Winter Formal had been moved to accommodate Tate. It had been scheduled for the night after the game but no one wanted to go. The student body voted to move the date for Tate. That date was tonight, and we would be having a whole bunch of kids over to our house beforehand.

"I hope you all go to the dance. If you don't have a date, come anyhow. Once we're all there, no one will know who anybody's date is anyhow, right?" They cheered.

Tate raised his arms up and grinned, that toothy grin stretching across his face. "This is our time, you know what I mean? We're all"—and he paused—"we're all damn sexy! Look at General Noggin with his Cleopatra. Who can resist him? Who?" He pointed at his head as those kids howled. "No, not you, Roderick." He shook his head at a kid in the audience. "General Noggin is not interested in you, sorry, buddy." Roderick laughed so hard he wriggled. "General Noggin is only interested in *the ladies*. The female sort, not you, Roderick. You're a male species. Emphasis on the word *species*. Come to the dance. Let's dance right here. Watch me dance, this is how you do it! Play something, band!"

The band played "Tequila."

Tate performed a dance move. It was awkward, it was unbalanced, it was sweet. He knew it would make people laugh and it did. "There isn't anyone out there who is a worse dancer than I am and I'm going to dance. So, you all coming?"

The kids flew out of their seats, yes, they were! Yes, they were! They were going to the Winter Formal!

"Excellent!" Tate shouted, raising one fist in the air. "Excellent."

He then turned and grabbed Coach Boynton and slow danced with him, cheek to cheek, thigh to thigh. Coach Boynton's head tipped back as he cracked up, as everyone laughed and whistled. Tate dipped Coach Boynton all the way back, that romantic sort of dip that the waltzers do, and *kissed his cheek,* and that brought the house down.

I have never, in my life, seen that many people celebrating with such free-flowing joy, with the exception of Coach Boynton, that Mafia bad-ass tough guy, who cried.

At the end of the song Melinda gave the signal, and orange and black balloons dropped from the ceiling along with confetti. The expected chaos ensued as the kids grabbed the balloons, stuck their tongues out to catch the confetti, danced to a modern song the band struck up, and cut loose as kids do.

Caden stuck both huge fists in the air and yelled, "That's my boy! That's my boy!" My mother sank to her chair and buried her happy head in her hands. The Life Saver, lollipop, and hot dog bee-bopped around the stage with their balloons. Damini said, "He's such a pain in my keester," then ran up and hugged Tate, and he hugged her, then started spinning her around, her short, ruffled pink skirt flying around her legs.

I hugged Ethan and took a moment in the chaos. A moment to *be.* A moment to rejoice, to be grateful, to be loved, to watch my son bring the gift of love and laughter to other people.

Tate was alive.

It was, without a doubt, the most magical moment of my entire life.

Thank you.

Tate's speech was played on the news that night, along with his story. AP picked it up.

His blog site was listed.

42,000.

TATE'S AWESOME PIGSKIN BLOG

Here's a photo of General Noggin and me.

You can see that I don't have much hair on one side of General Noggin. You can see my ear, Bert, now. That's where the ol' doctors, my favorite doctor especially, Dr. Ethan Robbins, shaved my head and cut it open. Good thing Dr. Robbins can wield a knife. It's like being a carpenter, you know, in a way. Except you're cutting and patching up a brain, not a birdhouse or shelves or a house or something.

Here's a photo of Dr. Robbins and me.

My new name for him: Boss Dad.

Yep. My Boss Mom and Dr. Robbins, Boss Dad, are getting married.

Here's a picture of Boss Mom, Boss Dad, and me. Yes, we are balancing bananas and apples on our heads. You can see that I am winning. It's an unfair advantage with General Noggin, but too bad for them.

Yeah, that IS my mom. I know. She's young and you think she's a college girl, but she's not and she's strict and don't mess with her, and especially don't get Witch Mavis going. I love you, Boss Mom!

A lot of people have asked me about the guy who pushed me at the last second of the basketball game and smashed my head open. Here's the thing: That guy hasn't been nice to me. He knows it and so do I. But he came to my house when I came home from the hospital and he apologized, like, 700 times. He knows he shouldn't have done what he did.

But balls and tarnation (that's a saying in our family), I forgive him. He's had a tough life because his dad is an abusive baboon and he and his mom and his mom's husband are moving away from here to Colorado so he can start over. His dad has been diagnosed with some kind of stomach problem.

Here's another picture of Boss Mom and Boss Dad. They're making out in her greenhouse between the rows of herbs. They're making out here, too, in our back field with the red poppies. Yep. And here, too, by the roses, and wait! More making out in the kitchen near the spice racks!

I hope they're using PROTECTION! Actually, I hope they're not. I think a brother or a sister or a whole bunch of brothers and sisters would be a universally sweet idea.

Here's a photo of my cousins and my uncle Caden, pro wrestler turned florist, who can make a Doberman out of flowers. As you can see, the triplets are dressed like normal kids with their blue slacks and skirts and white shirts. That's why they're not smiling and their arms are crossed over their chests. My uncle Caden made them dress normal for one picture, and they were mad and refused to smile. Right after this picture was shot they ran and got in their leprechaun/daisy/scary monster Halloween outfits and my cousin Damini put on the dress she's going to wear to Boss Mom and Boss Dad's wedding. I am a pain in Damini's keester.

Here's a photo of my Nana Bird and me. Yep, she's the evil Elsie Blackton from Foster's Village and yes, we are in Dolly Parton wigs because The Best Little Whorehouse in Texas is our favorite Broadway show.

I love you, family.

> Here's a picture of Boss Mom and me. We are balancing oranges on our heads.
>
> She knows why.
>
> Everybody, send me photos of people you love and I'll put them on my blog.

Tate was deluged with photos. I had to help him get them all up. We're still not done.

At the Emmy awards, my mother and I sat together in the audience at the Nokia Theatre in Los Angeles, Tate next to her, shiny and sparkling pretty people all around.

I had been with my mother all day. We had massages and manicures and pedicures, the sun warm, the wind but a puff. My mother was dressed in a sleek, silver dress. "Get up, boobs!" she told them. "Stand at attention!" She had her smokey makeup done by her stylist, Lacey McAuffy, who did my makeup, too, and I could barely move my face.

My mother had not written a speech. "What the hell. I won't win. I think I'll sneak in a margarita in my purse. . . ."

Helena Schivalli, another long-ranging soap opera star who had had more husbands than my mother on her show and about two more face-lifts, stood in front of the microphone on that glittery stage in a shimmery red thing. She made a speech about the Emmy award for outstanding actress, clips were shown of the five women nominated with people clapping loudest for my mother.

During all that, my mother whispered, without moving her lips hardly at all, her smile tight and unmoving for the cameras, "I *do* hope the winner's vagina falls out."

I smothered a chuckle and whispered, "I hope the winner's boobs jiggle inappropriately and leap from her dress."

She blew a laugh right through her nose. "I think the camera will catch the fact that the winner has three buttocks. Three."

I coughed to cover my noise. "I've heard that one of the women is hiding a fourth buttock."

My mother clenched her teeth together at the vision of that one, but her shoulders were shaking with her giggles.

Funny, oh we thought we were funny!

Finally, Helena in the shimmery red thing came to the point. "And the winner for outstanding lead actress in a drama series is . . ." She started to open the envelope.

My mother rolled her eyes. We found out later that the camera caught the eye roll, then it caught her turning to me and mouthing, "Let's get drunk."

And I mouthed back, "Mai tais on me."

She smiled a fake white smile, knowing the camera was on her now to build the suspense.

"Oh hooray!" Helena called out. "Hooray! It's Rowan Bruxelle! Rowan, it's you, honey!"

My mother froze in her seat, a marble statue wearing couture, and said, "Holy shiiiiit!"

The camera caught that, too.

She said, *Holy shit* again and clapped her hands to her bobbed hair. "I won! Balls and tarnation, I can't believe it! *I won!*"

Then she turned to Tate, who was standing and cheering, and hugged him. I hugged them both, crying. "Mom! Oh Mom! Congratulations!"

"I get to go on stage!" She laughed. "But I don't have a speech!" She kissed Tate then scooted into the aisle, threw her hands up in the air, and yelled, "Yay me! Yay me!"

Her friends from the industry hugged her down the aisle.

She skipped up the steps and Helena wrapped her in a huge hug.

My mom held the statue above her, then yelled, "Finally! Oh, finally! What was wrong with you people? I should have had this years ago! Elsie and I thank you!"

Her standing ovation lasted for several minutes.

"Holy shit!" she said again into the microphone. Those

words were zapped out of the night's broadcast but you could read her lips.

"This is for my family!" she said when people finally settled down. "My family, my heart. I love you!"

Tate stood up, arms spread way out and yelled, right into that cavernous theater, "I love you, too, Nana Bird! You rock!"

The cameras caught that, too.

My mom put the trophy high into the air, head back, her smile, her relief, her delight, a stunning picture.

She had won.

I cried.

"Yeah, Nana Bird!" Tate shouted, "You woooonnnnn!!!!"

TATE'S AWESOME PIGSKIN BLOG

Guess what? My Nana, you know I told you she's Elsie Blackton on the soap opera *Foster's Village*? She won an Emmy award.

Yeah, Nana Bird. You blew it away. You're a house on fire. I sang her a song right before the Emmy's. It's from *The Best Little Whorehouse in Texas,* our favorite Broadway show. I even put on a pink bra stuffed with socks and my Dolly Parton wig. It's about being a woman, surviving, and moving on up!

Nana Bird lost for a lot of years, and yet she kept going. Kept acting. Kept being awesome. So, what I learned from my Nana Bird is to keep trying, keep going, and then when a camera is pointed right at your face you can say, "Holy shit," and, "Let's get drunk," and it'll get bleeped out but everybody knows you said it.

Here's a photo with Boss Mom, Nana Bird, and me at the Emmy's.

Here's a photo of the inside of a brain.

Here's a photo of two lizards mating.

And here's a photo of three doughnuts at one time stuffed in my mouth. Chocolate, strawberry, and sprinkled.

Peace, dudes and dudettes, fellow galaxy walkers.

Peace.

On a sunny, warm Saturday afternoon, Grandma Violet's lavender, irises, cosmos, peonies, red poppies, and rows of roses blooming all over the property, Tate exploded his experiment room.

We heard an enormous, thundering bang. My mother and I dropped our teacups, filled with cinnamon apple tea, and flew up the stairs, my boots pounding. It was hard for her to move fast in her red high heels, but she braved on.

Smoke billowed out from Tate's experiment room and a few flames danced on his worktable. We both scrambled in, grabbed Tate, pulled him out of the room, and clomped down the stairs and out the front door, coughing. I grabbed my cell phone and called the fire department.

The fire department was there pretty quick, they put out the fire, which was actually small, then examined the wall that the explosion had knocked down.

The wall, according to the lieutenant, was actually thin and flimsy . . . and soooo old. Behind that wall was another room. Yes, the secret room that had been rumored to exist since Faith and Jack built the house for a summer retreat and a hideaway.

After the fire department left, we explored the secret room and found a velvet satchel on a small table. Inside was a thimble, white lace handkerchief, needle, gold timepiece, and the three charms I'd heard about my whole life, the cross, heart, and star. A fourth charm was there, too, a clover. For luck. The book with the black leather cover was in there, too, and a knife with a *P* on it. *P* for Platts. Probably the one Faith/Iris Platts used for the killing the first day she arrived in America, the knife from her brother.

"I thought Faith would have been buried with the necklace and charms," I said, awed and humbled.

"Her daughters probably wanted to save it, their mother obviously couldn't take it with her." My mother traced the lettering on the black book, HOLY BIBLE. "This is Faith's. Her name's in it, Iris Platts. She notes here how she had to change her name to Faith Stephenson because people in London had found out she was a witch and her brother wanted her to have a more Christian name and wanted to hide her identity, so they changed it, same with Grace's.

"And here, she wrote how her name became Faith O'Donnell when she married Jack O'Donnell, along with the names of her parents, Henrietta and Oliver Platts, and their parents' and grandparents' names. Her aunt and uncle, Elizabeth and Philip Compton . . . how a mob later burned down parts of both of their mansions outside London, I remember my mother telling me that. She also writes how Grace became Grace McLeary when she married Russ McLeary. Here are all the names of their children and grandchildren and great-grandchildren. Oh my. I feel emotional right down to my Jimmy Choos!"

There were a few journals, written by Faith about her life, which I'd later find were amazingly close to what I'd heard all *my* life about her and Grace. There was even a note in one journal about Dwight and John, the brutal slave owner brothers in South Carolina.

Dwight died when he "fell" on an ax. That he apparently "fell" on the ax at night, far off in the woods, had raised questions, but not convictions, in town. That John had "committed suicide," his wife's assertion, by shooting himself in both knees and then his head, had raised quite a ruckus in Charleston. Still, no convictions, and the police did not dispute that John's wife had come to them for protection many times.

There was also a spell book.

Yes, there was a spell book with spells in it.

There. I said it. There were curses, chants, and notes on how to perform the spells. I knew some of the spells, curses, and chants, my mother and Grandma Violet had taught me. There was information about herbs and spices and how to use them in the spells. Some of the phrases we use today were also written down: a shipwreck time of life, balls and tarnation, and a petticoats-on-fire situation, which was fun to see.

We had found almost 150 years of history.

"I told you we were witches," my mother drawled.

"Mother, we're not witches. We had women relatives who believed they were witches—"

"Family witches."

My mother picked up a bundle of letters tied with pink ribbons.

They were letters from Elizabeth and Henrietta to Rosemary/ Grace and Iris/Faith, letters from their fathers, sisters, brothers, cousins. They loved them, they missed them, family news, family joys and tragedies, a baby born here and there on Faith's side with a problem, which they blamed on The Curse, what they were growing in their herb gardens . . . hints on spells, nothing blatant, one didn't want to be branded as a witch.

"Dear Rosemary . . ." they wrote. "Dear Iris . . ."

I unfolded a piece of paper tucked into the back of the Bible. "Oh my. It's a full family tree."

Tate and my mother leaned over my shoulder.

"Whoa," Tate said. "A queen! Look, right there!" He pointed to the top.

"Yep. I knew it," my mother said, running a hand over her bobbed hair.

"You knew what?"

"We're royalty. Royal witches. That's what I've always told you. My mother told me, her mother told her."

My finger gently touched each name.

"This should be all the proof you'll ever need," my mother said, tapping my shoulder. "Voodoo dolls, thimbles, white lace handkerchiefs, needles, gold timepieces, charms, the book with the black cover, and needles, they've followed us our whole lives."

"Proof of what, Mother?"

She kissed my cheek. "That you're definitely a witch, Jaden. Once a witch, always a witch."

I have a new dream. It involves my love of spices, herbs, tea, and cooking.

I will probably make nothing my first year. I hope not to be in the red, financially. If things go well, I'll make half of what I did as a hospice nurse.

I am going to follow the dream through the next seasons of my life, through the golden sunshine, the blasts of rain, the dainty snowflakes, and whipping windstorms.

I want to play with this dream.

Who said that a dream has to occur when you're in your twenties? Not me.

The old Fischerson house was for sale. I used some of the inheritance money from my dad to buy it. I think he'd be happy with my dream. I have been to the house several times and have never met the reputed Frank the Ghost. I don't believe in ghosts anyhow.

My café is called Jaden's Spells and Scents Café. I will sell tea and coffee, soups and sandwiches, herbs and flowers.

Maybe one day Brooke will come and sit at one of the wooden tables with fresh lilies and hollyhocks in vases on top. I hope so.

But I know my husband, Ethan, will be there, Caden, Damini, and the triplets, my mother and her stilettos, and my son, my precious son, Tate Bruxelle.

I am learning to let go more. It's a hard lesson for me. I am learning to let light into my life, and to dance with my rainbow, as my mother would say. I am learning to love watching Tate dance with his rainbow, to his own beat, and to not hover or interfere with his dance.

Together, Ethan and I are dancing with our own rainbow, sometimes in our red poppy field.

I am changing. I am liking the change. It is not too late at all. I am going to have a new life.

It will be a different kind of normal.

I cannot wait.

TATE'S AWESOME PIGSKIN BLOG

I am going to MIT. This is a photo of Boss Mom, Boss Dad, Nana Bird, Uncle Caden, Damini, and the triplets. That's Hazel in the witch outfit, Heloise in the cowgirl outfit with the red gun, and Harvey is the snowboarder with the helmet on. We're all in front of MIT. Notice I am holding a model of a brain. That's what I'm going to study. Brains. Yes, there is a hamburger with lettuce and pickles on top of my head. We were at a picnic and I wanted to save one.

Here is a photo of Indonesia, which I want to visit one day.

Here is a photo of a brain of a drug addict and a healthy brain. See the difference? Don't do drugs.

If the world has a college for nerds, this is it, and I think I'm going to fit right in. I hope they don't care about my big head. I think they're all smart enough to look past it, and see me.

I hope they will.

I think they will.

What are your plans?

Blog count: 62,000.

Tate's career was most impressive at MIT.

He and his friends built a six-foot-tall spaceship that landed on top of the library. The spaceship was named "General Noggin."

They put motors on their skateboards to get to class quicker. They painted out all the numbers of pi on a strip of white material and wrapped it around a building.

He was only arrested once, with six friends, for a prank. In the pitch blackness of the night, they constructed a volcano in the middle of campus. In the morning, with all the students hurrying here and there, they pushed a button by remote and *boom boom*. The volcano started spewing pink smoke and steam and ketchup poured down the sides. They were charged with disturbing the peace, littering, explosives, etc., but it certainly added humor to the day.

The boys went to court. The judge was most impressed with the pink volcano, which he watched on video, as Tate recorded it. The charges were dropped, although the boys each had to complete twenty hours of community service. They went to local elementary schools, where they did neat exploding experiments to get students excited about science.

All the schools asked them to come back again and again.

At MIT he studies, among other subjects, brain and cognitive science, molecular neuroscience, biophysics, cell biology, and organic chemistry, as he planned. He has also learned that he loves ceramics and baking pastries. He is dating a young woman named Marie Sorenson. They're in the same field, she's a former model, and she is fun and warm and, most importantly, adores Tate. "I want six kids, Jaden, six!" she told me privately. I told her that would be outstanding.

He hopes to continue at MIT for a doctoral degree in neuroscience and have a research lab of his own one day. The name of the lab?

General Noggin's.

"But I'm going to have a photo of you and me, Boss Mom, on my desk, all the time," he told me. "We'll be standing together with apples on our heads in front of your greenhouse. I'll be holding a basketball and you can hold your herbs."

He was born with a big head.

And I have loved him, with all my heart, with all that I have, from that day forward.

Please turn the page for a very special
Q&A with Cathy Lamb!

On one of your blogs you wrote that you "work in images." What images did you piece together to write this story?

My first image was of a teenage boy with a big head. A hospice nurse popped in next. I was thinking of witches and spells at that time (I don't know why). I was also wondering about my ancestors, who have been traced back to England, Ireland, Scotland, and Germany. I started thinking about family lore, slavery, wacky mothers, drug addiction, funny triplets (I have twins), the pathetic state of orphanages in India, red hair, herbs and spices, a greenhouse and, above all, family relationships.

I combined them all together, swirled them around, did a lot of sketching and journaling of plot lines and characters, and pieced together the story...one stitch at a time, only banging my head on the keyboard occasionally.

Why did you make Jaden a hospice nurse?

I made Jaden a hospice nurse because I greatly admire hospice nurses and the work they do. I've been on the receiving end of their gentle kindness and help several times when relatives were dying and I have never forgotten the comfort and outstanding medical care they offered. They're both angelic and highly capable. Talk about a tough job. But what an honorable, courageous, and meaningful way to live your life—caring for people at the end of their lives.

How did you choose the other characters for the book?

I wanted Jaden to have an edgy mother to counteract her intensity, so I invented a glittery Rowan who is outrageous but incessantly sincere.

I invented Caden because I wanted to show what life is like for single fathers. We hear a lot about single mothers; I wanted the other side.

I developed Brooke because drug use is so prevalent in our country, and I wanted to show the impact on family members, not just on the user.

I developed the triplets because the story needed humor, and I developed Damini to show how families are brought together in many beautiful ways.

I developed Grandma Violet, who was a witch/healer, because I wanted to show the impact of grandparents on the next generation and I wanted to continue the ancestral story of Elizabeth and Henrietta, Faith and Grace.

I invented Faith and Grace because I wanted to show how we all come from someone. We did not just magically appear on this planet; our ancestors have struggled, cried, laughed, and had adventures. It's fascinating to find out more about them and their journeys.

What were the themes you were working with?

Sacrifice. Letting go of kids when they need to fly on their own. Seeing parts of life as different seasons that will continually change.

What's the most challenging part about writing a novel?

Sitting down and writing it. I am distracted by the following things, not in any particular order: my kids, my husband, my cat who meows at me and expects me to meow back, coffee, chocolates, silly shows I should not be watching on TV and will not admit to watching, live theater and the symphony, lunch with girlfriends, walking, daydreaming, going to the beach, reading tons of books.

What's next?

More storytelling, more blogging. Visit with me on my website: CathyLamb.net

A DIFFERENT KIND
OF NORMAL

Cathy Lamb

ABOUT THIS GUIDE

The suggested questions are included to enhance
your group's reading of Cathy Lamb's
A Different Kind of Normal.

DISCUSSION QUESTIONS

1. Who was your favorite character? Why? If you could spend the day with one character, who would it be, and what would you do?

2. Jaden says, "I know that my years of free-flowing panic have shaped me into someone I was not before. I am overly serious, and a bit controlling; okay, maybe more than a bit controlling, and I overprotect too much, and I struggle with pervasive worry over Tate, which comes out as anger and a mouth that won't quit when I feel cornered."

    Would you be friends with Jaden? How would you describe her to someone else? What do you have in common? How do you differ?

3. Tate wrote in his blog, "I have been made fun of my entire life. In preschool, the other kids wouldn't play with me. Some of the kids in my class cried when they saw my face, I remember that. I was three. One kid said I was ugly; another kid said I was scary, like a sea monster. A girl with braids told me I had a face like a person on one side, and a face like pigskin on the other. I remember going to sit in a corner and crying almost every day."

    What would it be like to be Tate? To be Tate's parent?

4. Jaden said, "Another reason I became a hospice nurse was because I crave raw, honest relationships and have zero patience for superficiality. When you are working with people who are dying, all pretenses are off. There is no shallowness, no silliness. I don't have the patience for

relationships that float and skim across the top of human existence, relationships that have no depth or that are based on shopping, manicures, gossip, men, clubbing, etc. I want real relationships."

Can you relate to this? Was Jaden a competent hospice nurse? Did it make sense for her to move on to another career by the end of the book?

5. What was your favorite scene in the book and why?

6. Was Jaden right, as a mother, to allow Tate to play basketball? What would you have done?

7. Grandma Violet and Rowan concocted a mixture for Grandpa Pete to swallow so his terminal suffering would end and he would die. Jaden said, "Do I think my mother and Grandma Violet, at that time, with the medicines they didn't have, did the right thing? Yes, I do. Absolutely."

Did they do the right thing? Was it consistent with their characters?

8. Brooke said, "I destroyed a lot of lives to make money. I am up nights wondering how many people I killed who took the drugs I sold them. I am up nights wondering how many pregnant women took my drugs and what that did to their babies. I am up nights wondering how many mothers' sons are now addicted to my drugs, how many fathers' daughters are drugged out and doing scary things with terrible men because they're addicts, like I did."

Do you like Brooke? Was her drug addiction portrayed correctly?

Do you think she will stay clean? Why or why not?

9. Here are a few of Damini's Daminisms.

"Every time you eat, be grateful you're eating. Be nice

to animals. In your next life you might come back as a slug, remember that. Read a lot of books, because they are delicious and if you don't read, how do you learn anything? Watch the seasons. I wear short skirts with ruffles, sequins, and fluff because I love them. I'm not gonna hide my leg. Don't hide anything about yourself. I know what it's like to sit in a dark room in a crib alone and feel as if no one loves you. Love a lot of people for a happy life."

What are your Daminisms?

10. What are the themes of *A Different Kind of Normal*?

11. What did the seasons symbolize? What did the greenhouse symbolize? The herbs and spices? The Canterbury bells, hollyhocks, lilies, irises, sweet peas, cosmos, red poppies, peonies, and rows of roses, which all the women in the family grew?

12. Jaden says, "I'm Earth Momma with an explosive temper meets cowgirl. She's [Rowan] firecracker meets perfume."

How was Rowan as a parent? A grandparent? Using the same type of phraseology, how would you describe yourself?

13. Tate says, "Fitting in perfectly means that you never have to reach outside yourself. You don't have to go through the same kinds of challenges, prejudice, judgment. Is it actually the best thing to fit in with everyone else? It's easiest. But, man, how do you grow? How do you learn to think on your own, or do you simply think what everyone around you thinks? How do you learn to be more compassionate of others, more generous, if you've never had to feel like you've been lost and stuck on the outside with no one being compassionate or generous to you?"

Is Tate right? Was his big head a blessing or a curse for him? What did other people learn from Tate?

14. Jaden says, "I don't believe in witches, or curses, or spells.
No, I don't.
I really don't.
It's a legend. A story. A colorful history to laugh and chuckle about in our family line.
It is a fanciful tale. I am sure of it.
I am, at least, 90 percent sure.
I think."
Does she believe in witches or doesn't she? She smells death in spices and herbs while in her greenhouse. Why? Do the women in her family have special abilities?

15. How have the stories of Faith and Grace impacted Jaden's life? Why did the author include the family history, complete with spells, witches, and a velvet satchel? How did it work for you as a reader?